I0728445

SANTA MUST DIE!
~ THE NOEL KRINGLE CHRONICLES ~

REBECCA M. SENESE

ALSO BY REBECCA M. SENESE

The Noel Kringle Chronicles (in reading order)

Santa Claus: Private Detective

Santa Must Die!

The Claus Connection

The Twelve Deaths of Christmas

Baby, It's Deadly Outside

Do You Fear What I Fear

The Man Who Would Be Santa

Who Killed Santa?

The Elf Who Saved Christmas

Wreck the Halls: 5 Christmas Horror Stories

A Very Zombie Christmas

The Santa Murders

SANTA MUST DIE!

~ THE NOEL KRINGLE CHRONICLES ~

REBECCA M. SENESE

RFAR PUBLISHING
TORONTO, CANADA

Published 2025 by RFAR Publishing
250A Eglinton Avenue East
Suite 147
Toronto, ON M4P 1K2
Canada
https://www.RFARPublishing.com

Trade paperback edition, hardcover edition, and electronic editions designed by Rebecca M. Senese / RFAR Publishing in Vellum Press.

2nd Edition Trade Paperback ISBN: 978-1-927603-89-5

Cover Design copyright © (2018) by
RFAR Publishing
Cover art copyright ©
feedough / DepositPhotos.com;
yankingzhang / DepositPhotos.com;
Wavebreakmedia / DepositPhotos.com
Internal art copyright ©
educester / DepositPhotos.com;
lightsource / DepositPhotos.com
Canva.com

RFAR Publishing Paperback 2nd Edition 2025

Printed and bound by IngramSpark.
Australia: Ingram Content Group AU Pty Ltd, Melbourne, Victoria.
US: Lightning Source LLC, La Vergne, Tennessee / Allentown, Pennsylvania / Jackson, Tennessee, United States.
UK: Lightning Source UK Ltd, Milton Keynes, United Kingdom.
Europe: Lightning Source UK Ltd, with facilities in Germany, France, and Spain.

Authorized Representative in the European Economic Area:
Lightning Source France
1 Av. Johannes Gutenberg, 78310
Maurepas, France.
compliance@lightningsource.fr

DEDICATION

For George C. Chesbro

SANTA MUST DIE!

~ THE NOEL KRINGLE CHRONICLES ~

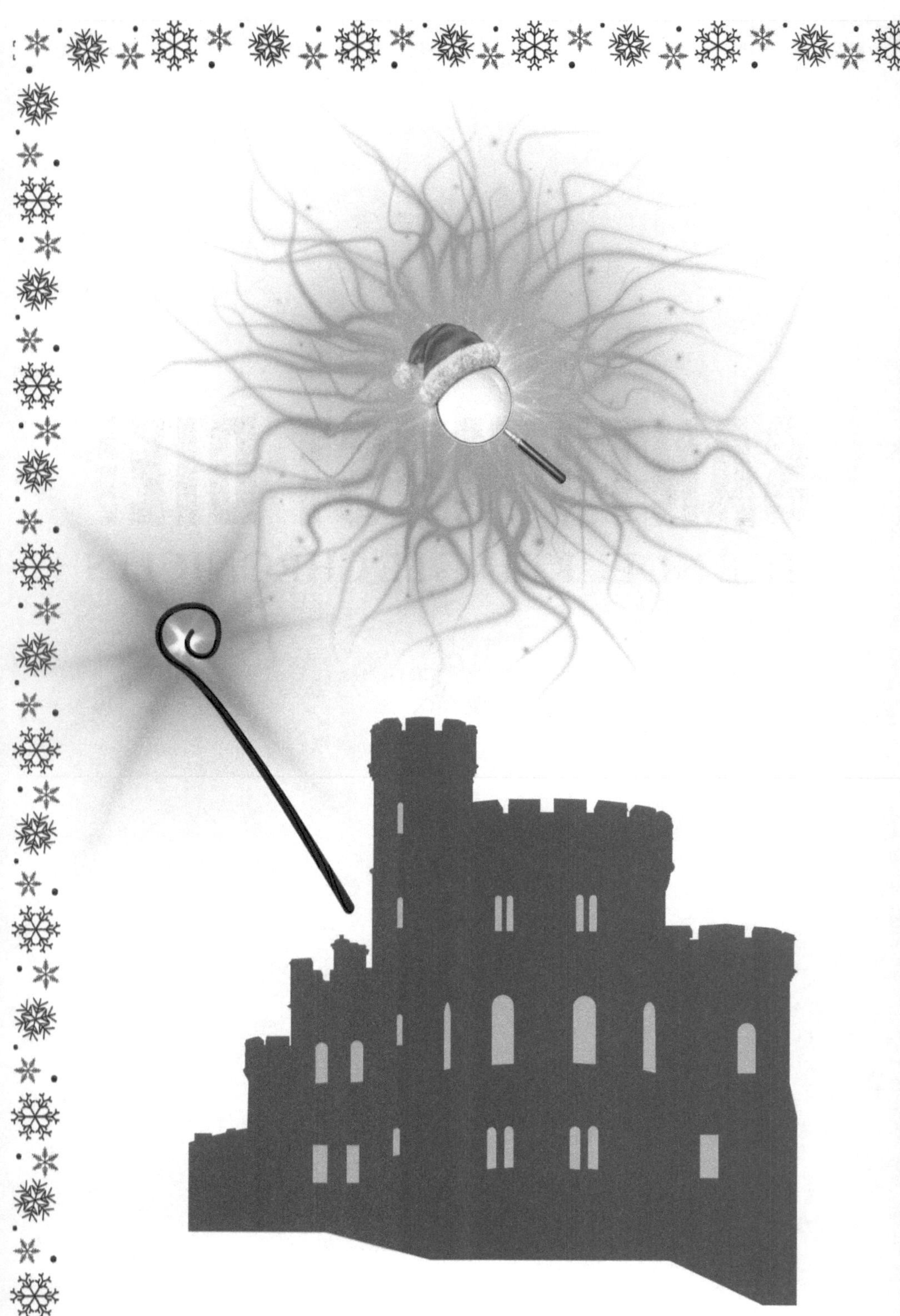

CHAPTER

ONE

When I entered the room, Santa Claus was slumped on the gold throne that sat on the raised stage at the far end. Snow drifts of white cotton fluffed up around the curled feet of the throne and trailed in tendrils across the stage. Two rows of over-sized candy canes stood upright, the curled ends holding the gold rope that lined the path leading straight up the steps to the stage.

The walls behind the stage were painted a bright blue with swirling clouds. Stenciled snowflakes in multiple sizes dotted the wall. I could see a few of them peeling off.

On either side of the stage, evergreens gave off a sickly sweet scent of pine so strong I could almost taste it coating my throat as I breathed. Way too chemically to be real. Not to mention the horrid green colour and the perfect symmetry of the trees, all lined up like green triangles. When I looked closer, I could see the plastic seam on the needles like green pipe cleaners.

Having been raised at the North Pole, I had seen a lot of evergreens in my life and none of them looked that perfect, or smelled that strong.

I glanced back at the night watchman who had come to get me. The man huddled just inside the door, sweating through his beige shirt that strained to contain his belly. The black belt sagged with the weight of his walkie talkie on the left and his flashlight on the right.

"Are you sure you just checked the door ten minutes ago?" I said.

The watchman nodded. His slicked-back, black hair shifted a little on his head. Sweat trickled down the sides of his face.

Poor guy, he probably never figured he'd ever see a Santa like this in the mall.

I never thought he would either.

I had taken this job to head security for the Christmas in July show at the Good View Mall as a favour to a friend. The head of the mall, Paul Guthrey, had liked my name and thought it was perfect for the show.

"Noel Kringle," he said as he leaned forward across the smooth surface of his dark brown desk. "That's perfect for this show."

We had met in the big man's office where he sat and grinned across at me, mouth open wide to show off all his teeth. They were so white they almost reflected in the polished surface of the desk. His brown hair was stylishly cut and parted on the left. A hint of grey at the sides looked like they were supposed to convey age and maturity. He was clean shaven with a hint of fat around his jaw line, giving him a roundish, babyish face. He wore a white shirt under a dark brown sport coat. The tip of a handkerchief poked out from the breast pocket of the coat, as if Guthrey couldn't decide if he wanted to be formal or casual.

I nodded. I sat in the cushioned chair in front of Guthrey's desk. The office had a sort of schizophrenic feel. On the wall behind Guthrey's head was a large cutaway view of the mall, showing all the stores. To the right, hung certificates and photos of Guthrey with various businessmen, posing with a children's softball team, the kids all wearing uniforms sponsored by the mall, Guthrey on the golf course, golf club raised in a ready swing, big grin on his face showing almost as many teeth as he was showing to me.

Against the other wall were two book cases full of books ranging from business to several self help paperbacks with cracks along the spine. For a man who appeared so confident in the photos and listed credentials, those paperbacks hinted at a vulnerability he kept hidden.

I let a smile crack my face. I could tell Guthrey thought my name was just a gimmick.

Little did he know.

Of course who would believe there really was a Kris Kringle, aka Santa Claus, at the North Pole, or that his youngest son would leave to be a private detective? Especially a private detective with a mess of wavy brown hair and a brown, neatly trimmed beard, both with the tendency to grow fast and bushy and turn unnaturally white in the last few months of the year, giving him a suspiciously familiar look to children everywhere if he didn't keep both under control with regular trims and colouring. Who wore black pants, a plain butter yellow shirt and a tan, zippered jacket in the summer instead of his usual long navy coat. His only concession to his famous father was his red scarf.

But July was too hot for both the navy coat and red scarf.

Guthrey would probably also be surprised to learn that I was able to use just a touch of magic to discover that Guthrey's favourite childhood toy had not been any of the cowboy guns or big trucks his father had given him, but his older sister's Easy-Bake Oven.

I crossed my legs. The fake leather of the chair creaked a little at my movement.

"What kind of security are you looking for for your show?" I said.

"I need someone who can oversee the guards. Most of these guys have worked shift work, out of the public eye. I need someone who can project the right image. Someone trustworthy who can talk to the parents."

Sounded like an easy job and I could use the cash.

"Two hundred a day, plus expenses," I said. "That's my usual rate but for you, I'll say one fifty."

"That's a little steep," Guthrey said.

"Sometimes you have to pay a little more for that right image," I said. "Or the right name."

That got a laugh from Guthrey. His white teeth flashed and his jowls jiggled a little.

"Fair enough," he said. "This is our first year with this promotion. July is a slow month traditionally and I'd like to spice that up, get folks thinking Christmas, maybe they can get a jump on the season." He grinned. "They can start their shopping early, then pick up extra stuff later."

He let the grin drop, closing his lips over his white teeth. He folded his hands on the desk in front of him.

"It's important that this first year go off without a hitch. That's why I want extra security. If all goes well, I'd like to continue this going forward, with the stores helping out with future years' expenses. The mall is covering it this year so I'm very anxious it go smoothly."

"I'll do everything I can to see to that, Mr. Guthrey," I said.

Guthrey gave me another toothy grin. "I'm looking forward to it, Mr. Kringle."

So much for that promise.

My loafers were silent as I crossed the room toward the stage. Great tufts of cotton snow rebounded off my shoes as I passed them. They rolled like tumbleweeds across the pebbled black and white tile.

The stairs creaked as I stepped on them. Behind me, the security guard gasped. I stopped and looked back at him.

"What?"

The man pointed with a shaking finger.

"He moved."

I looked back at the slumped Santa. He did look like he was slumped a little more to the right. I stepped onto the stage. The wood under my feet moved a little. The Santa sagged a little lower.

The security guard let out a yelp.

"It's the stage moving him," I said.

I inched a little closer. I didn't want to rock the stage too much and make the body slide onto the floor. The poor security guard might have a heart attack.

I reached the man's side without further incident. This close I could smell the slight mothball odour from the Santa suit. The side of the collar looked a little frayed, stray threads of white showing clear against the red.

My mother would never had stood for that.

I pressed my fingers against the man's neck. Even in the air conditioning, the man's skin felt cool and almost waxy to the touch. For a brief moment, I wondered if maybe the man was just a dummy but who would make a Santa dummy that looked dead?

No, the poor man was no dummy, and he was most certainly dead.

So much for a nice, easy job.

I carefully climbed back down the stairs, careful not to jostle the stage and disturb the body. By the time I reached the security guard, the poor man looked ready to faint.

"I'm going to call a friend of mine," I said. "We'll see if we can keep this quiet. Just tell me, is that the man that was hired to play Santa this year?"

"I think so," said the security guard. "I only met him once."

I dug my phone out of my pocket. The signal was at only one bar.

"I'll take this outside," I said. "Stay inside the door and don't let anyone else in."

The guard froze. After a moment, I wondered if the man had stopped breathing.

"Just stay inside the door. You don't have to go any closer."

The guard nodded and kept nodding as I closed the door on him.

Fortunately Santa's Room had been set up right next to an exit. I pushed through the double glass doors that led to the back parking lot. It was a narrow space with just one lane of cars before the concrete back wall. The blast of air conditioning followed me out but was burned off by the warm, moist July day.

Bright sunlight reflected off the car windows. Heat shimmered off the asphalt. Maple trees poked up above the concrete barrier along the back, waving their bright green leaves, creating speckled shadows on the wall. I cupped my hand over the phone so I could read the screen.

A few taps and I held it ringing to my ear. After a moment, a familiar gruff voice said: "Mallory."

"Hi Stan, it's Noel," I said. "If you're having a slow day, I have some business to throw your way. Any chance we can keep this quiet?"

By the time I checked on the security guard and then returned to the parking lot, Stan Mallory had arrived.

Two police cars pulled into two empty slots along the back concrete wall. The passenger door of the closest car opened and Stan Mallory stepped out.

An average sized man of average weight, Mallory wore a white shirt over black pants that wrinkled just a little. A tan sports coat flicked aside to show the badge on his belt. His dark brown hair, cut short in a crew cut, was sprinkled liberally with white. His wide, weathered face looked calm and still.

He gave me a slight nod as he stepped up.

"Problem?" he said.

"Just a little one," I said. "I'm hoping we can deal with it quietly."

"Let's take a look."

I led the way through the double doors back into the cool hallway of the mall. After the bright sunshine, the dim lighting seemed almost black. I had to blink a few times to get my eyes to adjust.

I moved to the door to the Santa's Room. I grabbed the door knob and turned. The door creaked a little as it opened.

To an empty room.

The throne still sat on the stage. Curled cotton snow still covered the floor. The perfectly spaced and shaped pine trees still stood.

But there was no body.

Mallory poked his head in. "So?"

I felt myself sweating even in the coolness of the air conditioning. The man had been *right there*. I had felt the dry skin under my fingers when I checked for a pulse. I remembered the faint, musty smell of the costume.

And where was the security guard?

Footsteps sounded from the hall. I turned as a shadow appeared on the tile. A moment later, the security guard walked in. His beige shirt was tucked in neatly. No signs of sweat stains. His hair was patted back with the hard look of shellac.

The guard stopped just inside the door. He looked around at Mallory and the two uniformed police officers.

"Can I help you?" he said.

I stepped forward. "I told you to stay just inside the door. Why did you leave?"

The security guard frowned. He tilted his head and

shifted from one foot to the other. His belt, heavy with a walkie talkie, slipped down a little on his waist, making his black pants bulge.

"Sorry?" he said. "What are you talking about?"

One of the police officers made a hrumph sound. My neck felt hot. I hadn't imagined the body, I was sure of it. I had felt the man's cold, waxy flesh when I checked for his pulse. Remembered the overbearing stench of the fake pine trees as I bent over the man.

It *had* happened.

I clenched his fists to stop from grabbing the security guard by the shoulders and shaking him.

"Mind if we take a look around?" Mallory said, in a bland, even tone.

The security guard shrugged.

I turned away from him in time to see Mallory gesturing to the two officers.

"Check around the room and outside. See if there's anything or anyone who saw something."

Both officers nodded, although I could swear I saw the shadow of a smirk on one of them.

As they moved toward the door, I stepped to Mallory's side.

"There was a body here," I said, keeping my voice low. "I swear."

Mallory gave a slight nod. He pointed to the security guard.

"Could you show my officers around?"

"Yes, sir," the guard said. He hitched up his belt and followed the officers through the door.

"There really was," I said.

"I believe you," Mallory said when the guard cleared the doorway. "But where is it?"

I pressed my lips together. I sighed. "I don't know."

Mallory rubbed his chin and turned to survey the room again.

"What is going on here exactly?"

"It's a promotion for the mall," I said. "Christmas in July. I was hired to oversee the security."

"Uh huh," Mallory said. "Why you?"

I looked away at the throne sitting on the raised stage across the room. I hadn't noticed it before but some of the gold was peeling off the curled arms and dotted the puffed cotton snow scattered at the chair's feet.

"They liked my name."

"Pardon? I didn't hear you," Mallory said.

I shoved my hands into my pants pockets to stop from clenching them. I cleared my throat.

"They liked my name." I articulated the words and heard them echo a little around me.

"Ahh," Mallory said. "I see."

I looked up to see a slight smirk on the detective's face.

Oh, so that's how it was going to be.

Great.

"There really was a dead man here, Stan," I said. "Maybe we should concentrate on that."

Mallory spread his hands. "Look, I believe you but there's no body. Unless they come back with one, there isn't anything I can do." The smile faded from his face. "I really am sorry, I."

I looked back at the throne. "Well, can't you do some kind of test on the chair? Find residue or something?" I gestured at the throne. My impatience made my arm lash out like a punch.

"Forensic science isn't magic," Mallory said. "Why can't you do something?"

I winced. Was the detective making fun of me again? Ever since I had left the North Pole, my magic had been at a minimal level. Any exertion drained me like a cheap dollar store battery.

Besides, the Santa had been murdered. Wasn't that Mallory neck of the woods?

The detective was already moving toward the door.

Even if he did believe me, would he ever trust me enough to come when O called again?

How had someone gotten rid of the body? The security guard was supposed to be in here the whole time.

The security guard...

He had looked awfully calm and composed after being so agitated. Even if he had been able to calm down, how had he dried out the sweat stains under his arms?

That seemed almost like... magic?

I turned slowly back toward the throne. The same peeling gold paint, the same curled legs, the same faded looking fabric on the back. I took a couple of steps closer, kicking cotton snow out of the way. When I was within five feet, I reached out my hand and opened my mind.

And felt the tickle of residual magic as it was just fading away.

Oh damn.

This really *was* my kind of case.

CHAPTER

TWO

I caught up to Mallory just outside the exit. The double glass doors hushed shut behind me, sealing off the cool, air conditioned mall. The moist July heat crept up my legs as the coolness dried off. After the dim lighting of the mall, the bright sunlight gave everything a harsh, hyper real look. The chrome of the police cars parked along the concrete barrier. The overly green leaves of the maple trees. The harsh grey of the asphalt.

Mallory had slipped a pair of sunglasses on. They hid his eyes behind mirrored shades. I couldn't tell where he was looking.

"I think I felt..." I said.

The door behind us opened. The two uniformed officers came out.

"Nothing, sir," said the first one, the one who had almost

smirked at me earlier. He'd also slipped on a pair of sunglasses, hiding his eyes, but I could feel his bland gaze as he turned his face toward me.

"We took a look through this whole section of the mall," he said. "No sign of any disturbance."

He tilted his head just enough to make it look like he was looking at me but his bland expression gave nothing away.

"Well, always nice to get out of the office on a day like this," Mallory said.

Trying, but not really succeeding, in softening the blow.

"Sorry to drag you out," I said.

Mallory gave a nod as he headed toward the police cruisers. The two officers trailed behind, glaring back at me before they climbed into the cars. A moment later, the roar of the engines broke the stillness and the cars pulled away.

Leaving me with more questions and no answers.

Back in the coolness and uniformed lighting of the mall, I made sure the Santa's Room was locked before I set off in search of the security guard.

It took me almost five minutes of wandering the wide hallways, passing several high end ladies' clothing stores, a luggage shop, and an electronics store full of people in suits before I spotted the security guard.

He sat at the far edge of the food court at a table for four. The tables were arranged inside the kidney shaped area, following the curve of the walls and the various fast food outlets. Why someone had designed it so the walls curved, I couldn't tell but it somehow seemed to intensify the odours from the various outlets. Spicy curry scent warred with tomato sauce and the thick, greasy smell of deep fried potatoes.

As I made his way through the zig zag of plastic tables with their attached plastic seats, I felt like I was passing through waves of smells. Roasted meat, the yeasty, warm scent of toasted sandwich rolls, and finally the harsh, rich odour of coffee.

The last wafted from the cardboard cup in front of the security guard as he hunched over the table. He seemed to bend over so far, his hair dipped close to his forehead. Another inch and I thought it might slide off, right into his coffee.

I stepped behind the chair opposite the guard.

"Excuse me," I said.

The man lifted his head. His eyes had a gummy look to them as he blinked at me. Had the man been sleeping?

"Whaaa?" he said.

"I just wanted to ask you a couple of questions about the Santa Room." I slid into the plastic seat without asking to sit down. The seat had a curved butt impression but it didn't seem to fit me for some reason. The edges of the chair pinched my thighs. Was my rump that big?

"Santa Room?" the guard said.

"Yes," I said. "Do you remember coming to get me?"

The man shook his head. His head moved but his hair seemed to stay in one place. His face held a vague expression.

Better go farther back in the day.

"What time did you start work?" I said.

"Was scheduled for nine thirty." The man mumbled, barely moving his mouth.

"Do you remember arriving for your shift?" I said.

The guard blinked. His brows pulled together as if thinking was an effort.

"Do you remember getting out of bed this morning?" I said.

The man opened his mouth. No sound came out. He sat with his mouth hanging open as he stared past my shoulder. The vagueness overcame him again.

No use asking any more. Obviously the security guard's memory had been affected, more likely than not by whatever had left the residue of magic behind near the throne in the Santa Room. Without knowing exactly who or what had happened, I might cause harm to the man if I pushed much more.

But I couldn't just leave without trying one more thing.

"Sorry to bother you. Just forget I asked," I said.

The man's mouth closed. The stress line across his brow smoothed out. He leaned a little back in his chair, his body settling down.

I reached out and touched the edge of the man's hand that held the coffee cup.

For a moment, all I felt was the warm skin of his fingers, reflected heat from the cup. The faint brush of whisper-fine hair on the back of the guard's pinkie. The thick bone of a knuckle under skin.

Then the flash blinded me.

I felt the blinding burn of magic scorch my fingers. The smell of thick, earthy vegetation filled his nose. I caught a glimpse of the throne in the Santa Room, the body slumped against the armrest. The form shimmered, then vanished in a black mist, the stench of ozone overpowering the vegetation smell.

It had happened. I hadn't imagined it!

Then the vision jumped. I caught sight of a dark street corner. A figure in red standing in profile against a brown brick building. The tinkle of bells sounded as he shook his hand up and down in front of a hanging clear ball stuffed with money. The figure wore a Santa hat and a white beard. It started to turn. The mouth, pursed in the middle of saying "Ho" stopped and widened into a scream.

A moment later he fell, knocking the ball to the ground.

It rolled and rolled and rolled.

Stopping at the feet of another Santa.

This one standing in the brightly lit hallway of a children's school. He was busy straightening his coat as he stood in front of a pair of double doors. The hum of children's voices excited and anxious drifted out from behind the door. Something caught the Santa's attention and he turned.

To scream.

To die.

Again, and again.

And again.

Too many Santas to count. Too many locations, too many times.

Pounding into my brain, making me want to run and hide.

Hard plastic scraped against my side. Pain flared in my elbow and leg.

I blinked. I was back in the food court, lying on the floor.

I had fallen out of my seat.

The security guard sat across from me, still staring at his coffee cup.

He didn't notice as I grabbed hold of the back of the plastic chair and used it to drag myself to my feet. The people seated at the tables nearby leaned toward each other and whispered as they stared at me like I was a crazy person.

I brushed at my pants and managed to leave the food court with barely a limp.

But I could only stop my hands from shaking by shoving them into my pockets.

I LEFT A MESSAGE FOR PAUL GUTHREY, THE MALL MANAGER, AND headed back to my office.

My office on the top floor of a dingy four storey walk up had an inspiring view of an empty parking lot filled with cracked asphalt and sprouting weeds, backing onto disused railway tracks. The tracks cut past three abandoned factory buildings, all various shades of faded white and slime crawling up the cracked foundations.

Not exactly a swank neighbourhood, but I liked it. Even if the landlord had lied about the lake view.

I pushed open the front door. The frosted glass window held the black letters SC Private Investigations and opened onto the waiting area, a small room with a worn brown leather couch along the left wall and three plastic chairs to the right of the front door. I had added a tiny plastic coffee table from Ikea, some square piece in a bright yellow that I thought might give some colour to the place. Instead it just seemed to be magnetized to dust.

I crossed to the small washroom in the right corner of the waiting room.

The bare bulb showed me a face in the mirror with a few new lines on my forehead. A crinkle of tension between my brows, as if I had been infected with it by the security guard.

Maybe I had been.

Obviously the man had been there when whatever had been there had taken the dead Santa. It had left a strong imprint. Strong enough to show an echo.

Or at least a possible echo.

But was it even real? I knew enough about magic to know that you couldn't always trust everything it showed you. Often times such visions reflected by the own seer's fears as if they were reality. Seeing a Santa die over and over in multiple different ways would definitely qualify as a fear for me.

Every Christmas Eve when Dad left to go on the Run as he called it, I was acutely aware of the amount of magic it took for him to cross the world in one night, dropping off toys to all the girls and boys. The tiniest slip or disruption to that magic could spell disaster. Dad risked death every Christmas.

It wasn't a stretch for my imagination to overwhelm me.

I twisted the taps until the water ran cold and then splashed it on my face. The shock made me hiss. Rivulets of water trickled down my beard as I fumbled for the towel rack just past my right shoulder. I dried my face and found myself looking at the red and white Christmas towel my mother had given me. A red Santa hand with a white puff ball was embroidered on the front.

I clenched the edges of the towel. I couldn't tell her about my vision of seeing Santa dying.

Thank goodness she wasn't due to visit until late August, just before the busy season geared up at the North Pole.

I hung up the towel and turned off the bulb as I left the bathroom.

A few short steps took me to the door of my office. I surveyed the room. The metal desk that I bought at Goodwill. The creaky desk chair behind the desk. The hard-backed chair in front of the desk. On top of the burgundy desk blotter sat the office gifts my mother had given me, the stapler, the clear paperclip holder etched with tiny snowflakes, the silver pen, the bound leather notebook. Beside that was the magnifying glass Dad had given me after my first case. The case where I used up all the magic I had left, only to have Dad rekindle it for me with that magnifying glass.

Everything neat and organized.

The white air conditioner hummed from its spot in the window. It had taken me ages to get the thing correctly positioned at just the right angle, then stuffed with cardboard around it to stem any leaks. But it took the edge off the July heat, and for a North Pole boy that was worth it.

I crossed around the edge of the desk and sat in the desk chair. The seat creaked under me tipping slightly to the left, threatening to spill me onto the floor. Strangely enough, leaning back made the chair more stable, so I leaned, resting my knee against the metal edge of the desk. The cool air from the air conditioner tickled the back of my neck.

How was I going to find out more about those dead Santas? I didn't think I would be able to ask Mallory again, not so soon after the disappearing Santa. I had to find another way to get the information. But who else could I call?

There was a special department at the North Pole that tracked all the Santas around the world, if worst came to worse, I could always contact them to see what they knew, if there was a pattern. But then I wouldn't be able to control who they talked to and sooner or later my investigation would catch my father's attention.

Or worse, my mother's.

I had to find a way to get the information without her learning about it. It would only worry her. I couldn't face that.

The chair wheels squeaked under me as I turned to stare out the window. The glass had a smeary film on it. I had tried to clean it when I was putting in the air conditioner but it seemed to be a flaw inside the glass. Even when I had scrubbed at the glass, it seemed to remove only a single layer of dirt.

But I could still see the deserted parking lot outside over the top of the air conditioner. Heat shimmered above the faded grey asphalt. Even the hardy weeds that sprouted along every crack looked like they were wilting, thin, jagged leaves dipping down to the ground.

Sometimes I heard cats or people outside, their voices drifting up from the parking lot or across the tracks. Somehow the listing factory building created an almost perfect acoustic chamber in my office. But I didn't hear anything moving around today. It was too damned hot.

Weird to be thinking about Santas on a day like this.

Weirder to be thinking about dead Santas.

I turned away from the window and back to my desk. An older laptop sat on the left side. I lifted the lid and turned it on. I tapped a finger on the metal beside the touch screen as it booted up.

Maybe I could do a search on the Internet. I wasn't exactly a wiz on this thing.

Wait a minute. I wasn't. But I knew someone who was.

Shirl Trembley.

An expert hacker who had helped me track down information on a previous job. She was also a big fan of Christmas. Her favourite toy had been a Cinderella doll with a cape she'd added to make the doll a superhero.

Even before the laptop finished booting up, I grabbed my phone and dialled.

"Talk," Shirl's voice announced, loud enough that she could be in the room.

"Hi Shirl," I said. "This is Noel Kringle. You helped me out a while ago."

"Right. Father's name is Kris if I recall." Her laughter boomed in my ear.

"Yes," I said. "You still keeping out of trouble?"

"Best I can."

"I wonder if you can do me a favour," I said. I picked up the silver pen and started doodling on the back of an envelope.

"Favour, huh? What's in it for me?"

"I can put in a good word with my dad."

She laughed. I could almost picture her leaning back in her computer chair, the black braids atop her head shimmering as she laughed, her teeth white against her black skin.

I found myself smiling at the image.

"Okay, Kringle, lay this favour on me," she said.

My smile drained away. Somehow asking this favour didn't seem fun.

"I need you to do a search for as far back as you can on missing or dead Santas. Start in the city and expand to the province if you have to."

"What kinda shit you in?"

How could I explain my vision to her? Even with her faith in Santa it would sound crazy.

"It's a project. I need to verify some things. Can you do it?"

"Corse I can," she said. "Not sure I'm wantin' to is all."

"Please, Shirl."

She huffed in the receiver. I could almost see the frown on her face.

"I do this, I want more 'n a good word."

"What can I give you?" I said.

"Hells, I don't know." She paused. "A hundred bucks. Enough to buy me somethin' to drown my sorrows."

"Deal," I said. "I'll stop by tonight."

"Tomorrow," she said. "After noon. I don't see anybody before then."

"Tomorrow."

The phone clicked in my ear as she hung up.

I replaced the receiver. Okay. One piece of the puzzle being dealt with, now I had to take care of the rest.

While Shirl Tremblay was tracking my vision, I was going to find out more about the current dead, and now missing, Santa.

Before any other Santas turned up dead.

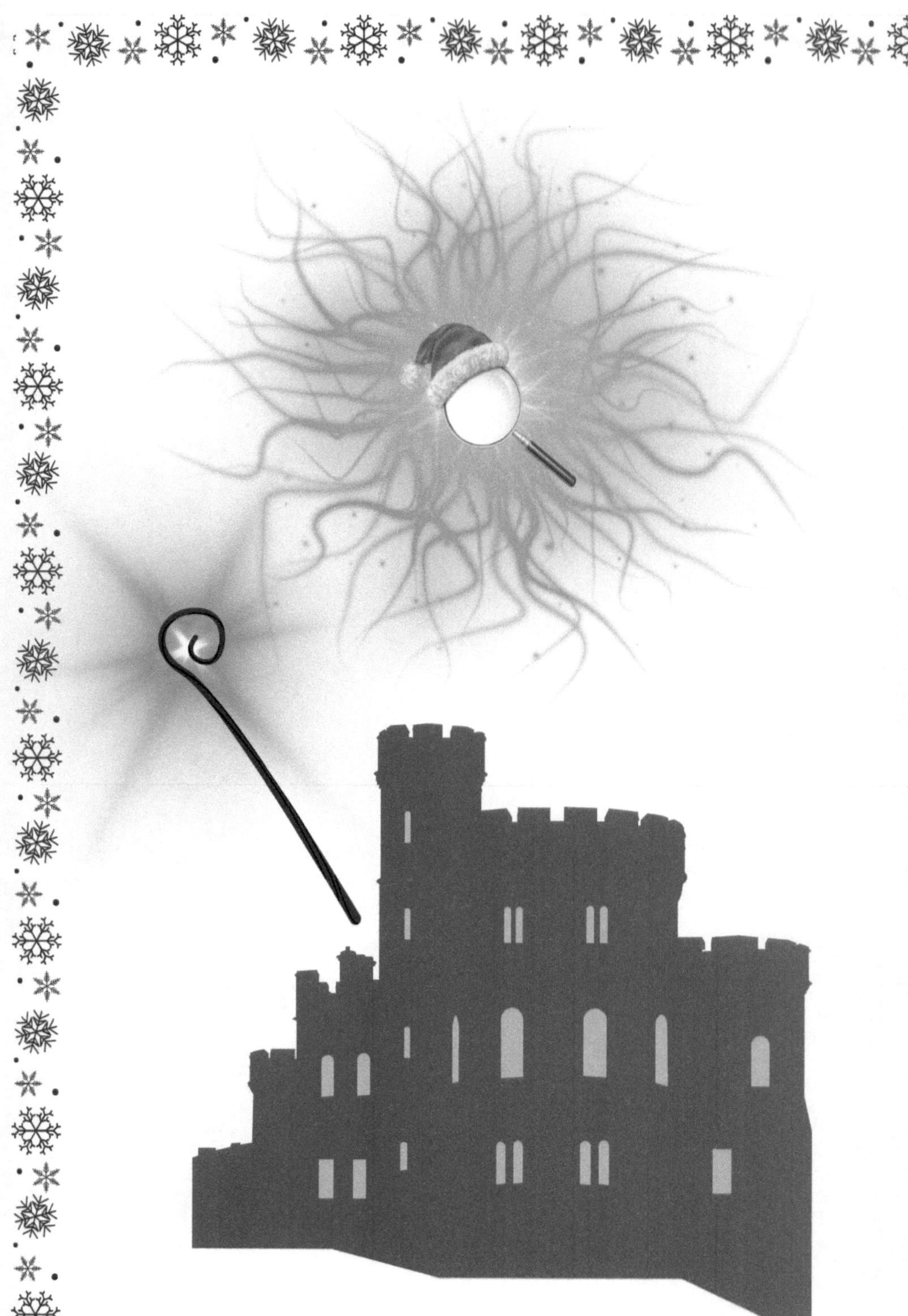

CHAPTER

THREE

From the mall human resources files, I discovered the real name and address of the July Santa.

Christopher Henries, of Mason Park, Scarborough.

The July heat was pressing down like a hot sponge as I walked up from the subway station toward the squat, red-brick walk up. Henries' apartment was on the top floor of the building sandwiched between a dry cleaner and a boarded up restaurant.

My loafers kicked up dust on the cracked sidewalk. As I passed the dry cleaner, I saw a bored looking woman standing behind the white counter lazily flipping through the newspaper. The bagged clothes hanging behind her almost looked like body bags. She wore a white shirt with the sleeves rolled up to her elbows. Brown hair with hints of grey was tied back from her face but wisps curled around her temples, escaping the bobby pins that tried to hold them back.

Just before I passed out of sight, she glanced up. A wave of citrus enveloped me. A shampoo smell. The sound of a girl's high pitched laughter.

A Curly Cue Hair Do Doll.

That was her favourite toy growing up.

I hurried past as the woman's eyes widened and she started to stand up, the paper falling from her hands.

The strong citrus smell faded as I reached the front door of the apartment building. I rubbed at my right temple.

I had to stop instantly flashing on what toys people loved as kids. Dad had trained me to do it and most days I was able to avoid it. Why was it cropping up so much now? The only other time I couldn't stop myself was around Christmas.

Oh that must be it.

This damned Christmas in July thing. It had me tuned in to the Christmas wavelength.

Focus.

As I peered at the smeared glass listing for the apartment building, the inner glass door opened. I caught a glimpse of a black t-shirt and jeans then the outer door flew open. A young man came bouncing out. Voice loud as he chatted on a phone, he left a trail of strong cologne and stale cigarette behind him.

I waited as the man walked down the sidewalk. Just

before the door closed, I grabbed the handle and slipped inside.

The dim cool hallways reminded me of my office building. The same bland beige paint on the walls. The same utilitarian light fixtures: metal grey with a single bare bulb surrounded by a little metal cage.

The stairs were scuffed concrete. Old cigarette butts dotted the landings. By the time I reached the top floor, I had a headache from the moist, rank air.

The air in the hall outside Christopher Henries' apartment was less rank but still stale and humid. I paused outside the brown wood door. I didn't even know if Henries lived alone. I couldn't just barge in there.

I gave a gentle tap and turned to press my left ear to the door.

No sound came from inside.

I glanced up and down the hall. No one around either. No sign of any security cameras.

Okay then.

I reached into the back pocket of my pants and pulled out a key blank. With my magic so limited, I needed all the help I could get to focus it. The silver key blank looked just like a regular key but smooth where the cuts to match the lock would be. All I had to do was slip it into the lock and concentrate...

At least that was my theory.

The blank slid in smoothly enough. I grabbed the door knob with my left hand and focused on the key. Focused on the key fitting the lock. The lock yielding to the key. The lock turning open when I turned the key.

My fingers tingled. I smelled cinnamon, a precursor to any magic for me.

My fingers tightened on the key. I turned it...

The key didn't move.

Frustration quickened my heart beat. I took a deep breath to slow it down. Calm. Getting annoyed would only make it that much more difficult. I had only practiced this in my office before, first time in the real world was bound to be problematic.

Just relax.

Instead of thinking about the lock, I thought about the apartment beyond. What would I find in there? Hopefully hints of who would want to kill Christopher Henries, kill the other Santas. There had to be something in there to give me a starting point.

I pressed the key in and turned...

It resisted. My fingers tightened on the metal. Just a little more.

The lock clicked open.

I pushed open the door and slipped inside. As I pulled the key blank from the lock, I noticed how the edges had changed to conform to the lock. Even as I watched, the edges smoothed out, the magic diminishing until the key blank was smooth again.

I smiled. Worked perfectly.

I slid the key blank back into my pocket and shut the door.

The room beyond was dark. Heavy curtains drawn across the window opposite the door blocked any sunlight from outside. The air was humid and dusty and still.

As my eyesight adjusted to the gloom, I studied the living room. It seemed to be a generous twenty by fifteen feet. A small kitchen was tucked into the left corner, sporting an olive coloured fridge and matching oven with barely two feet of counter space separating them. Several used mugs crowded the space, several with drained teabags still in the bottom.

The main area gave me more hints about Christopher Henries but nothing that shone any light on why someone would kill him.

The narrow sofa turned out to be a futon. A tug on the footboard would flatten the entire thing out, converting it from a seating area to a bed. Ruts on the dark brown area rug exactly how Henries opened the bed.

A metal wheeled coffee table sat in front of the futon sofa. A half full mug of tea made another ring on the cloudy metal surface with an open TV guide covering the rest.

A wall unit of shelves stretched across the opposite wall from the sofa, ending at a door tucked against the right side. A twenty eight inch television, screen black and dusty, took up the centre space, surrounded by shelves full of books. As I stepped forward, I noted most of them were old paperbacks, not in any order I could discern. The cracked spines showed they were well used.

A reading man, was Mr. Henries.

Had been.

Anything to show why he'd taken a job as a July Santa and been killed by magic?

I turned slowly around, opening my mind, scanning around.

Anything? Anything at all?

Nothing. There wasn't anything magical in the place. It was a nice, normal apartment. A real home.

A muffled thump sounded from the doorway. I spun. In the gloom, it looked like a dark shadow filling the space. Large and looming. Then it seemed to shrink into a man's shape.

"What the hell you doin' in my place?" came a gruff voice.

The shape took a step forward, coalescing into a man, shoulders hunched, thinning white hair brushed neatly across his pink scalp. A hooked nose hanging over his thin lips, lips that had been hanging slack and open just a short time ago. He wore dark pants with a butter yellow shirt tucked in. Dark suspenders looped over his shoulders, making it look like his hunch came from trying to keep his pants up.

Even without the red suit and fake hair and beard, I recognized Christopher Henries.

"Mr. Henries," I said.

"Yeah, that's right," Henries said. "I aksed you what you doin' in my home and what you starin' at?"

I snapped his mouth shut. This man had been dead just a few hours ago. I was sure of it. The feel of his waxy flesh still tingled on my fingers.

But if he was dead, how was he standing in his apartment, glaring at me?

"Uh, I'm working with the Grand View Mall, Mr. Henries," I said. "You're portraying Santa in the Christmas in July promotion, isn't that right?"

"Yep, that's right," Henries said.

"Shouldn't you be at the mall for rehearsal?" I said.

Henries tugged at his suspenders. "I is running late. Is that what you're doin' here? Giving me a ride?"

"Well..."

"That's mighty fine of you. Just let me get ma lunch." Henries hurried across the room, brushing past I, wafting a trail of Old Spice behind him. He yanked open the olive-coloured fridge door and came out with a paper bag. He scooped up a paperback book lying on the counter and tucked it under his arm.

"Mickey Spillane, my favourite," Henries said. "You ever read him?"

"Uh, no."

Henries shook his head. "Missing out. Best damn writer. Right up there with Louis."

"Louis?"

"Louis L'Amour. Not much of a reader, are ya?"

"I guess not," I said.

Henries patted his book. "I'm ready. Shall we go?"

"Um, sure."

I stepped back and gestured for Henries to go first. The old man hurried to the door and tugged it open. I followed, slipping by him to wait in the hall while Henries locked the door. The scent of Old Spice nipped at my nostrils. Was there anything underneath it? A scent of death maybe? Decay? I couldn't tell.

How could Henries be alive? Be here? Just this morning he'd been in the Santa room at the mall, slouched in the chair, dead.

Hadn't he?

I remembered the room, the fluffy fake snow, the perspiring security guard, even the way the body shifted on the chair when I touched the neck, feeling for a pulse. Then the feeling of magic making me dizzy and the way the security guard didn't remember anything. The vision of residual magic when I touched the security guard's hand.

It all led to something strange going on.

But as I followed Christopher Henries down the hall, I couldn't detect anything strange about him. No hint of magic, no hint of death.

Was I losing my mind after all? Had it really happened?

When we reached the street, Henries tapped the paper bag against his thigh and glanced up and down the street.

"So where's yer car?" he said.

"I don't have one," I said.

Henries tilted his head. "So how're we gettin' to the mall?"

We ended up taking a taxi. The whole time Henries sat in the back seat behind the driver humming to himself as he read his book.

I sat beside him staring out the window as the houses and shops blurred by, wondering if maybe I really *had* lost my mind.

ALL THROUGH THE RIDE, I COULDN'T DETECT ANYTHING WRONG. Even when we reached the mall and headed into the Santa Room, I sensed nothing. I stood in the doorway as Henries strolled across the tile, brushing past the white cotton tufts. The old man headed around the right side of the raised stage toward the small door that led into the change room.

The door clicked shut behind him.

I waited a moment, testing the air. Old Spice mixed with the cinnamon and candy cane scent. It made me slight nauseous but there wasn't anything magical about it.

There wasn't anything magical here at all.

I knew I was supposed to stay and make sure everything was all right, but I just couldn't stand it.

For the first time in a long time I felt like I really needed a drink.

There was a pub-style restaurant at the other end of the mall but I didn't think that Paul Guthrey would be happy to find his head security for this event in the pub. Didn't exactly look good. But I sure as hell couldn't stay here with the non-dead, non-magical Christopher Henries. Not right now anyway.

I ended up in a coffee shop across from the pub-style restaurant. Instead of mulling about things over a beer as I sat in darkened red leather booth, I sat with a black coffee at a small corner table under harsh fluorescent lights. The over-powering smell of coffee with an undercurrent of burned beans filled the place. I took a sip of the black liquid. Hot and bitter, stinging the roof of my mouth.

Good. Something else to focus on.

What was going on? Had the pressure of dealing with Christmas in July gotten to me? Had the tediousness of the display forced me to imagine the excitement of a murder just to get through it? But surely there would be some other event I could come up with that didn't include death.

If I had imagined it, what did that say about me?

My older brother KJ had kept telling me that it wasn't a good idea to live in the regular world. It would corrupt me. It would ruin me.

Was this what was happening? And if it was, did it mean I had some kind of anger issues with my father?

With KJ, I could understand, we had always had a, what would you call it? A somewhat challenging relationship. But things had always been good with Dad.

Hadn't they?

As I lifted the porcelain mug to my lips I felt the vibration of my phone in my pocket. I set the cup down and dug the phone out.

Shirl's number.

"Hi Shirl," I answered. "What do you have for me?"

"Kringle, you'd better get over here." Her voice sounded more terse than normal over the line.

"What is it?"

"Just come," she said. "You should see this in person."

Before I could say anything else, she hung up.

Okay then. Maybe everything wasn't all in my mind.

I took a final gulp of coffee and grimaced. Definitely needed sugar.

The bitter taste lingered as I left the mall.

CHAPTER

FOUR

Early afternoon sunlight made the brown bricks on Shirl Tremblay's four storey walk up looked washed out and pale. The small patch of grass out in front of the building was yellowed and dry. Obviously the superintendent didn't bother watering between rainy days and it been almost two weeks since the last rain.

July was shaping up to be one hot, humid month.

And it seemed to be specifically trying to torture me.

The bright white of the sidewalk blinded me as I *winked* into place at the side of the building. Not being at the North Pole limited my magic but I could occasionally use it to zip, or as I called it *wink*, around the city, as long as I didn't try to do it too many times in a row. It was a similar kind of magic that Dad used to get around the world in one night. Only I wasn't as good at it.

Now I stood at the front door, trying to remember the code to Shirl's apartment. It wasn't listed under her name and I forgot the name it was under so I couldn't look it up on the apartment listing by the door.

She lived on the top floor, that I remembered but it didn't do me much good. All the codes were four digits. My head pounded as I stared at the faded list. The way the glass reflected my image back didn't help much either. I didn't need to see the way the sweat glistened on my forehead or got caught in the beard that lined my jawline and outlined my mouth.

Finally I yanked out my cell phone and called her.

She answered after one ring. "I tole you ya need to come see it."

"I know," I said. "I'm downstairs but I can't remember your buzzer code."

The door in front of me clicked. I grabbed the metal handle and yanked. The glass door swung open. I felt the tickle of cool air. Heavenly.

"I'm coming up," I said into the phone but she'd already disconnected.

What the superintendent saved on watering the front lawn, he obviously spent on keeping the building cool and I was grateful for it. It even made up for having to walk up four flights of stairs to Shirl's floor.

As I pushed open the beige door onto her floor, I saw her poking her head out of her door at the end of the hall.

She waved me forward. "Hurry up."

The air had a somewhat stale smell to it as I headed toward her. my loafers felt like they were squishing into the carpet and springing back up.

Shirl stepped out into the hall, holding her steel door open with her body. She crossed her arms over her chest. She was wearing a bright yellow t-shirt that seemed to blaze against her black skin. As usual, she kept her mass of black braids piled up on top of her head as if to give herself greater height. Even with them, she barely managed to make it above my shoulders.

She grunted as I came closer and hooked her thumb toward her apartment. Then she turned and headed inside.

I had to dart forward to grab the door before it swung shut. I had the feeling she wasn't going to open it again for me.

I slipped inside and let the door close behind me.

The place didn't look much different from the last time I had seen it. Piles of boxes overflowing with electronic equipment filled every nook and cranny. A large L-shaped desk sat in the middle of the clutter with a worn leather chair in front of it. A row of monitors filled the space on top of the desk. A low electrical hum filled the space, and as usual, there wasn't any sign of dust.

But she'd changed cleaning products. Instead of lemon, I thought I smelled cinnamon apples.

From between two rows of boxes, she slid out a metal chair and opened it. Then gestured at me to sit down. I did so as she moved to her leather chair. She spun away from me toward the monitors, scooping up a wireless keyboard as she turned. A few clicks and the screen savers on the monitors had vanished, leaving screenshots of text on each one.

"I wasn't expecting to hear from you today," I said.

"Wasn't expectin' to be finding all this stuff so easy," she said.

"Easy?" I leaned forward, resting my elbows on my knees. "What did you find?"

She frowned. "Too much. Too many. Don't be askin' me to look up this weird shit, 'kay? I don't like it." She gestured at the screens and wheeled the chair away from them, crossing her arms as if to keep whatever was on them away from herself.

I squinted but couldn't read the text. Finally I stood up and moved toward the desk. The text on the different monitors were readouts of newspaper articles and forensic reports. I didn't want to know how she'd hacked into *those*. As I scanned each one, one item stood out in all of them.

Blugeoned. Santa.

Shot. Santa.

Knife wounds. Santa.

Pistol whipped. Santa.

And the locations. Several in the city. More in the province, then sprinkled around the country.

Around the world.

Someone hunting Santas.

Why?

"How far back did you go?" I asked.

"Five years," she said. "And before you ask, I'm not lookin' for anymore. Now where's my money?"

Her tone was harsh but I could hear the tremble in it. Seeing this list upset her. It upset me too. I fumbled for my wallet in my pocket, counted out bills and handed them back to her.

I didn't want to but I knew I had to ask. "Can I get copies?"

She snatched the money from my hands then shoved me aside as she rolled her chair forward. She grabbed the keyboard. A few keystrokes and the hum of a printer sounded behind him. I turned. Perched on top of a stack of white cardboard boxes, a black laser printer spit out pages.

Shirl hunched in her chair, her arms across her chest again. The keyboard rested on her lap but one knee trembled, jerking the keyboard up and down.

"You got some weird thing for Santa?" she said.

"No," I said. "Of course not. You know I'm a private detective. I know Stan Mallory."

"Yeah, you know him," she said. "Doesn't mean you can't be a loon. Kringle. Who has that name anyhow?"

She frowned at me and I could feel her pulling away. This had been too much for her. Being a fan of Santa Claus had been the exact reason she'd helped me in the first place and now it was going to be the reason she'd stop helping me. All because she thought I was some nutjob.

Could I risk telling her the truth? I knew from the way Mallory talked about her that she was trustworthy but did I have the right to burden her with the knowledge? It wasn't just that I was youngest son of Kris Kringle, aka Santa Claus, but the whole awareness beyond that. She'd learn there were more dangerous things that just bad coding.

Behind him, the printer beeped. Shirl gave a disgusted snort and scooped the keyboard off her lap, dumping it back on the desk as she stood up. She brushed past me, using her shoulder to push me aside.

In that moment I could tell that she didn't like thinking the way she was, didn't want to distrust me but those images had shaken and upset her.

I couldn't just leave her with that.

"You know that cape looked pretty good on her," I said.

"What?" Shirl turned toward me. She held the paper tray in her hand.

"That Cinderella doll. The one you wanted to make into a superhero. The cape looked good on her." I nodded. "I agree. There's no reason she can't have a cape and a pretty dress."

Her eyes widened, the whites blazing against her dark skin. Her mouth dropped open a little.

"What... how...?"

"I told you my dad's name was Kris," I said.

She shook her head. The paper tray dipped in her hand.

"You're crazy."

"It was your favourite present," I said. "The Cinderella doll. Blonde hair and a blue sparkly dress. Almost a foot tall. Right away you thought she needed a cape because she should be a superhero."

Shirl held the paper tray in front of her like a shield. She backed away until she bumped into a box.

"How can you know that?" Her voice rose. Her fingers tightened on the tray until the tips were almost bleached.

Uh oh, she was getting more panicky not less. She probably thought I was some kind of weirdo, that I had been researching her background, stalking her.

It was too late to back off now. I was going to have to really convince her I was the real deal.

And that was why she was so afraid, she was almost convinced and it terrified her.

Damn, I should have thought of that before. Too late now.

I took a step back from her, retreating. Her desk was just behind me now, to my right. I felt the tickle of magic gathering in the air, focusing beyond her desk, behind the monitors. I reached behind there. For a moment, all I felt was the air, empty, a slight movement across my fingers. Then soft fabric, almost flannel, tickled the back of my hand. I closed my fingers, felt the smooth plastic of a doll leg curving against my palm.

I pulled it out.

The Cinderella doll. Blonde hair curled around the cherub cheeks and swept up into a swirl of curls atop the head. The dress billowed out, a deep royal blue with sparkles that shimmered in the light.

And tied around her with a white piece of yarn, was a long stretch of red flannel fabric. It hung past the doll's feet, too long and cut a little too thin, more like a train than a cape, but as I turned it he saw the crude "C" drawn on in marker.

Definitely the mark of a superhero.

I held it out toward Shirl.

Her mouth had dropped open. Her arms hung low near her waist, the paper tray forgotten. Tears shimmered in her eyes, reflecting light from the monitors.

I took a step forward, close enough to grab hold of the paper tray. She released it, her arms flopping to her sides even as I pressed it closer to her.

Closer...

Her hands lifted slowly, gingerly touching the doll, lifting it just under the arms. The sparkly dress crinkled in her fingers.

Shirl sucked in a breath and bit her bottom lip. She blinked her eyes fast to stop the tears from falling.

"Cindy," she said. Her voice was a bare whisper. "Super Cindy, I've missed you."

I smiled. "Not anymore."

She lifted her fingers to trace the doll's face, then crinkled the fabric in her hands. She brought the doll close and sniffed at her hair. A smile broke out on her face as she cradled the doll.

"Still smells of my brother's bottle caps. He kept tryin' to set her hair on fire but I stopped him. She has the scratch on her cheek from my kitty." The far away quality in her voice trailed off. She lifted her head to focus on me. "This is the real Super Cindy. It's really her."

I nodded. "Yes, it is."

"Are you him? Santa Claus?" she said.

"No, that's my dad. Kris Kringle. I'm his youngest son, Noel."

Shirl tilted her head. "Say what? Youngest son?"

"Yes, my older brother is Kris Junior. We call him KJ."

Her arms loosened. She held the doll in her left hand against her side. One hip cocked out under her black jeans.

"Now you're shittin' me."

I held up my hands in surrender and shook my head. "I shit you not."

Shirl laughed. Her peals echoed through the room, breaking the tension. I sighed and smiled. It was okay now. I could feel the relaxation in her. She accepted the doll and had accepted me. It wasn't good for another person to know about me but at least it was someone kindly disposed toward me.

Even if she was laughing at me.

"You shouldn't be talkin' that way," Shirl said. She wagged a finger at me. "Not with your family name and all."

"Now you sound like my mother," I said.

"Does she know what you're doin' here?" she said.

"She knows I'm a detective," I said.

"And she's okay with that."

"She wants me to be happy."

Shirl smiled. "Sounds like a mom."

I nodded. "She's the best."

Shirl's smile faded as she looked past him toward the monitors. Her hand tightened on the doll, pressed it against her thigh.

"So why are you looking for murdered Santas?" she said. She eyed me. "You got some daddy issues or something?"

"No," I said. "It's for a case."

"Really?"

"Yes, really. Honest, Shirl, I don't have any problem with my dad."

Her lips pressed together. I could feel the tension coiling in her as she regarded me. I just had to stay cool. I forced myself to take slow breaths, not react to her sudden tension. Finally the grip on her doll loosened. She nodded at me.

"Okay. Gimme that."

She scooped the paper tray away from me then turned back to the printer. She tucked Super Cindy into the crook of her arm and then fussed with putting the tray back. As she worked, Super Cindy flopped against her upper arm, facing me. The doll eyes seemed to track me, seemed to glare at me.

Better not be lying.

I put my hand on my heart. I swore I wasn't.

With a loud click, Shirl smacked the tray home. The printer hummed and started spitting out paper again. A few moments later it finished.

Shirl scooped up the papers and turned to me. She held them out.

I reached for them but when I grabbed them, she held on.

"Seems like you ain't too good with the research," she said. "Maybe we can come to some sort of arrangement."

The doll's head was tilted to its side, giving me a suggestive look.

"Um, arrangement?" I said.

"Yeah, like consulting," Shirl said. "Maybe a percentage of your fee or something."

"I thought you didn't want anything more to do with this weird stuff," I said.

She shrugged. "That was when I thought you were some creep fixated on Santa." She smiled. "Now I know you're the real thing."

"Oh," I said. "Maybe. I'll think about it."

"Really? You mean it?" she said.

I had a flash of her sitting on the worn beige rug in front of a plastic Christmas tree that tilted too far to the left. A single string of lights zig zagged up the front of the tree, pretending to be more than they were. They blinked in a sporadic pattern. Half a dozen bulbs hung from the plastic branches. Clumps of tinsel gathered on the lower branches, her younger brother's efforts to help with the decorating but he was only five and couldn't reach very high.

Shirl knelt in front of the tree, putting the final finishing touches on her present to her brother. It was Super Cindy with the hair chopped off, the dress removed, and a uniform made from scraps decorating the body. Shirl had coloured a beard on the doll to make it look more like a boy.

Then the flash was gone, leaving her standing in front of me, doll ducked in her arm as if she was being casual.

Maybe that kind of faith was just what I needed.

But did I have the right to expose her to a magical peril?

"I promise, I'll really think about it," I said.

Her smile blossomed on her face. "Great. You'll let me know. Give me a call. We'll figure the arrangements."

"Right." I tugged the papers from her hand and backed away to the door. "I'll let you know."

"When?" she said.

She followed me toward the door.

"I don't know," I said. I fumbled for the door knob. Twisted. Pulled.

"Soon," I said.

And leapt out the door before she could say anything else and persuade me with her thousand watt smile.

"I'll be waitin'!" she yelled down the hall as I escaped.

I knew I should head back to the Grandview Mall to keep an eye on Christopher Henries but I didn't want to review these pages anywhere near the place. If there was some strange business going on and it wasn't just my imagination, I needed somewhere to think clearly.

I headed back to my office.

The air tasted humid as I entered my office. I dumped the papers on my burgundy desk blotter and stuck my shiny black stapler on top of them. Then I turned on the small window air conditioner that was set into the window behind my chair.

I had learned from experience to ground any papers on my desk before turning on the air conditioner. Even on the lowest setting, it seemed to blast out a gale-force wind. At the highest speed, it was almost enough to create icicles in my doorway.

The unit grumbled and began to shimmy and shake in the window frame, as it got up to speed. For a moment, it roared as the air began to stream out, cold enough to tingle on my flesh, then the machine quieted down to a grumbling hum.

I sat down and spread the sheets across my desk blotter, using the stapler and the office phone to hold down the papers. The edges flickered but the papers stayed put.

Good. Now I could take a better look at them.

Shirl had certainly down her job well, I realized as I skimmed through. Not only had she found a list of names but she'd included snippets from any newspaper clippings and even official police reports. How had she gotten those? She couldn't have gotten them through any search engine. She must have hacked into how many departments?

Don't ask.

If I didn't know, I wouldn't have to tell Mallory about it.

As I went through the list, reviewing the names, each one

invoked a tingle of memory from his vision. Each one made my shoulders hitch up just a little higher until I was hunched over the desk like a question mark.

I wasn't losing my mind. Something was going on here. I couldn't pretend it was normal.

Who the hell was Christopher Henries?

Maybe the better question was what was he?

And why was someone killing Santas around the world?

My hands trembled a little as I gathered the papers into a bundle and paper clipped them together. I slid open the top drawer of the desk and stuffed them inside.

They hadn't given me any answers, just more questions.

Time to settle some of them.

I turned off the air conditioner before I left.

The machine shuddered in the window, coughed as it sputtered to a finish, dripping out the last few puffs of cold air as I crossed to my door and let myself out.

Time to check on Christopher Henries, after all I was head security.

And I was damn well going to make sure everyone was safe from whoever - or whatever - Christopher Henries was.

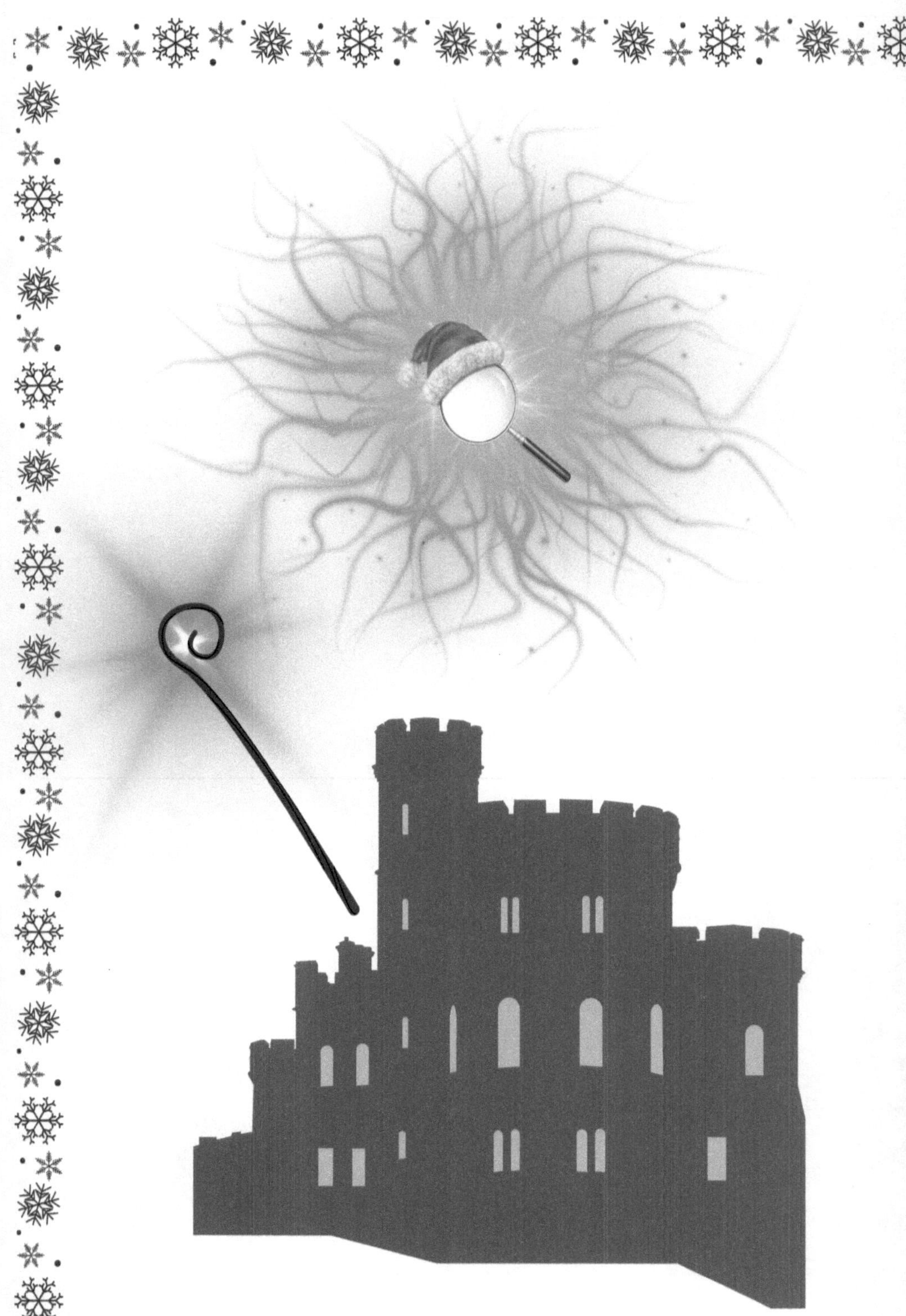

CHAPTER

FIVE

I had a strange feeling of déjà vu as I stepped through the doorway into the Santa Room. The same fluffy cotton snow, the same raised stage, the same gold throne, only this time instead of a dead body, it was the live Christopher Henries that sat on the chair.

He was settling in, brushing wrinkles from his lap, then tugging a little on the beard that covered the bottom half of his face. To me it looked absurdly fake. How could any child not see through that, but I knew that wasn't the point. Their faith and delight made it real.

The thought of children coming anywhere near this Santa made me very nervous.

I couldn't let it happen, not without knowing more.

I pulled the door closed behind me as I stepped into the room.

At the click of the lock, Henries looked up, peering from beneath the flopping Santa hat. The beard wagged as he smiled.

"Oh hey, there you are, Mr. Security Man," he said.

"I came to check on you," I said.

"Sure, sure, check away. Almost ready for 'em. Just have to get everything straight." He tugged on the beard.

"That's exactly what I'm here to do as well," I said. "Get everything straight."

I stepped closer, my shoes tapping on the tile. The sickly sweet pine trees smell thickened with each step. I headed for the stairs. If I was going to confront this man, I wanted the best advantage I could get.

The stairs creaked under my feet. This close I could see how plastic the candy canes were, how faded. With just a little magic, I could fix that...

But I was here for another reason. I couldn't let the promise of Christmas distract me.

"How do I look?" Henries said. He patted the beard down his chest.

"Better," I said. "Much better than this morning."

"Eh?" Henries's brows crinkled under the Santa hat. "What you talkin' about?"

"Early this morning the mall security guard called me," I said. "I found you sitting here in this chair, dead. You've had quite a recovery."

"Wha?" Henries shifted in the chair and shook his head.

His hands gripped the arms of the chair. "That's crazy. You playin' a joke?"

"No joke. I don't think there's a joke here at all. I want to find out what's going on here."

I took a step closer to Henries, loomed over the chair.

Henries leaned away. "Nothing going on. I'm gettin' ready for the kids."

"You aren't getting near any children before I have answers," I said. I grabbed the front of the Santa coat. The red fabric felt scratchy in my palm.

Dad's coat never felt like that.

Just more fakeness.

"Tell me the truth," he said.

Henries shook his head so violently the cap drooped down his forehead. The white fluffy brim covered his brows, pressing against the bridge of his nose.

"You came and got me," he cried. "That's the truth."

"I touched the body," I said. "I felt the last bit of magic leaking away."

The man cringing in the chair froze. He didn't seem to be breathing.

"So?" I said. "What do you say to that?"

Henries's mouth flopped open. His eyes rolled back into his head, exposing the yellowing whites. The acrid smell of his cologne thickened, clogging my nose. I coughed but the stench grew stronger, sharper.

Like something burning.

Oh no!

I jumped off the stage just before the man -- or whatever it was -- in the Santa suit flared and vanished in a flash of white smoke, leaving nothing behind the smoldering Santa hat lying on the seat of the golden throne.

The last tingle of magic prickled along my skin. I could almost seen it flickering in the air, like dust motes.

A phantom, almost life-like, with enough of a presence to allow physical contact.

There was only one way to cast that spell and that was to use the form of the one you wished to copy.

That was why Christopher Henries' body had disappeared, to help create this phantom.

But why?

Behind me, the door rattled as someone tried to open it. Then a knock sounded. After a moment, Paul Guthrey's voice drifted in.

"Hello, we've got some children out here, eager to see Santa."

Oh no, now what was I going to do?

I ran across the room, kicking cotton snow out of the way. At the door, I unlocked it and opened it a crack, blocking the view.

Paul Gunthrey stood on the other side. One jowl and a smatter of grey hair showed through the cracks. He shifted a little and one brown eye peered through, trying to see past me.

"Open up," Guthrey said. "We've got a line up." He stepped back, the blur of his blue suit disappearing. Through the crack, I caught sight of four or five children, hanging on to mother's hands. The line curved away to the right, disappearing from view.

"We just need another five minutes," I said. "Another ten."

Guthrey appeared in the space again, blotting out the children. He frowned.

"Five minutes?"

"Ten," I said.

"You've got five." Guthrey's voice dipped low. "You've better be ready in there, Kringle. This has to go well. We've got a lot of money riding on this."

His hand whitened as he clenched the lapel of his jacket.

I slid the door shut. I locked it again then spun around, pressing my back against it.

Five minutes. Okay. So now what?

I looked around the room. The golden throne sat on the stage. The Santa cap hung over the front. The last of the magic had dissapated. At least it wouldn't be any danger to the children. But they wouldn't like it if there was no Santa.

Should I do it?

I could. I could conjure up a Santa suit and fake my way through the whole thing. It would be as close as I ever got to actually *being* Santa Claus. That honour would fall to my older brother KJ.

But I could do it now.

Couldn't I?

But Gunthrey would recognize me and wonder where the

Santa they'd hired had gone. And I was supposed to be in the room as myself, not as Santa.

I couldn't do it.

I had to get someone else. In five minutes.

No, now four.

I pushed away from the door and crossed the room, heading for the stage. Cotton snow bumped against this legs and rolled away, like puffs of cotton candy. I fumbled in his pants pocket and yanked out my cell phone.

From experience I knew the stage had the best reception.

I dialed.

The phone clicked with the familiar tinkling of bells.

"North Pole operator, may I help you?"

The voice was unfamiliar, a deep melodic tone, not the usual trill of May, the regular operator. She must be on a coffee break.

"This is Noel Kringle. I have a Blitzen priority," I said. "Patch me to KJ immediately."

The operator squeaked. "Right away, Mr. Kringle."

Bells rang as I was connected. Then clicked.

"Kringle." KJ's voice boomed out.

"Blitzen priority," I said. "I need you, KJ."

"Blitzen priority? It's July. This better not be a joke, Noel."

"No joke, please brother."

The phone clicked off in my hand.

Great. That was just like KJ to hang up on me.

Then I caught a whiff of candy cane and cinnamon.

I turned.

KJ stood at the base of the stairs of the stage.

Topping six feet, KJ had the barrel chest and wide stomach of our father. White hair curled around his head just past his chin. His white beard and mustache were trimmed to outline his face but would fill out as Christmas came near. He wore denim jeans and a dark purple shirt with the sleeves rolled to his elbows on arms that now folded across his chest. He peered at me over the top of the round glasses he affected to look more like Dad.

"So what's this Blizten priority?"

I stepped down the stairs and grabbed my brother's arm.

"I need you to be a Santa," I said.

"What?" KJ said.

"The mall is running a Christmas in July promotion," I said. "The man hired to play Santa was killed by magic. I need you to sub in." I tugged on KJ's arm. It was like yanking on a log. "Come on!"

"You have got to be kidding me," KJ said. "*This* is your Blitzen priority? You remember what Blitzen priority is, right? It's just below a Rudolph priority and has to do with protecting the innocent belief of children. What the hell does a mall promotion have to do with that?"

I stuck my face into my brother's. Although I was only an inch or two shorter, I had always felt like it was a foot or more.

"There are at least five children outside that door waiting to see Santa." I hissed the words. "Do you want to disappoint them? I would do it but I can't do that and be security at the same time."

Now a smirk crossed KJ's face. "Security?"

"Are you doing it or not?" I said.

"Okay, okay, hold your reindeer." KJ shook off my hand and stepped onto the stairs. They creaked even louder under his boots. The stage seemed to shake as he crossed to the golden throne. The smirk grew even bigger as he picked up the Santa cap with two fingers. It looked pathetic and forlorn in his hands, an obviously fake cap made of cheap red material.

"You need to get dressed," I said. "I have to let the kids in any minute."

"Just relax." KJ set the cap down on the floor and nudged it under the throne with the toe of his boot. "I'll play Santa for your children and save your job."

I had just started to turn away to head for the door. I stopped at the edge of the stairs and turned back to my brother.

Did KJ really believe that? Did he really think that mattered?

"You know I don't care about that," I said. "Those children are more important to me than any job."

KJ lowered himself into the golden throne. It groaned under his weight. Even dressed in jeans and the purple shirt, he was starting to look like Santa.

More like Santa than I would ever be.

"I was just making sure," KJ said. "You're the one that wanted to be a private detective."

He was still on that. I tried to keep his breath steady.

"You need to dress," he said. "I have to let the children in."

"So let them," KJ said. He waved a hand toward the door. Suddenly the hand was covered with a white fabric glove. White fur curled around his wrist, attached to the vibrant red coat that stretched over KJ's belly. A bright red cap sat on his head, the white ball of fur puffed on the end, quivering in the air. The neatly trimmed beard now curled almost halfway down his chest, matched only by the curls of his white hair on his shoulders.

As he leaned back in the throne, KJ smiled, and his cheeks blossomed with pink cheer.

Perfect. He was a perfect Santa.

I hurried to unlock the door.

"WONDERFUL, JUST WONDERFUL!" GUTHREY GRABBED KJ'S WHITE glove and shook his hand with enthusiasm. "I've never seen a better Santa for the kids. This is the perfect start to Christmas in July."

The last child had just trailed out, all smiles and skipping feet kicking at the cotton snow as he clung to his mother's hand. I closed the door behind them.

KJ stood at the bottom of the stairs with Guthrey. The mall general manager beamed as he shook KJ's hand. Any nervous tension that had gripped him had drained away. He stood straight and tall in his navy suit.

As I stepped up, Guthrey turned, the smile wide on his face.

"Wasn't it perfect?" he said.

"Yes, it was perfect," I said.

Guthrey turned back to KJ. "You are the best Santa we've ever had, that I've ever seen. If you aren't already booked for December, I'd like to hire you. I'll double your rate."

KJ raised his bushy white eyebrows. He peered over the top of his round glasses. His eyes glinted as he looked past Guthrey to Noel.

"I'll have to let you know," he said.

"Of course, of course. Plenty of time." Finally Guthrey released his grip. He smoothed his dark blue tie down over his white shirt. "I'll let you freshen up. Next show is at two and I'm sure it'll be even more popular once word gets around."

He patted KJ's shoulder and headed for the door.

"Good work keeping everything going smoothly, Kringle," he said. As he reached the door, he grabbed the door knob then turned and gave me a thumbs up. I nodded to him. Guthrey yanked the door open and stepped through.

As the door swung shut, I turned back to KJ. The friendly

smile faded from his brother's face. He glared over the top of the round glasses.

"Another show at two?" he said.

"You were great, KJ," I said. "You should have seen the looks on those kids' faces as they left. They were just lit up."

"Another show at two?" KJ said.

"Dad would be so proud of you," I said. "You've really helped me out."

"Another show at two?" KJ's voice deepened into a growl.

"I just need a few hours to figure out what happened to the original Santa," I said. "Shouldn't take that long."

"Another. Show. At. Two." KJ stomped forward with each word until he was an inch from my face. This close, I could see how even the pores between the hairs of KJ's beard were turning red.

Along with the rest of his face.

Any second, smoke would be pouring from his ears.

And his hands would be reaching for my neck.

"Please KJ," I said. "Think about the children. They'll be so disappointed."

It was a cheap shot, and I knew it. KJ would never be able to resist pleasing children.

But first he would have to resist pounding me for manipulating him into it.

But I wouldn't have done it if I didn't need the help.

KJ puffed out a breath. He pushed the glasses up on his face then turned away. He stomped up the stairs, each pounding step making the entire stage shake. The plastic candy canes on either side wobbled. Even the throne shook.

KJ stormed over to it and sat down. The wood groaned, but not too loud, as if it didn't want KJ to notice. One pointing finger jabbed out toward me. I felt tingling on my skin. It reminded me of when we were kids and KJ would threaten to light me up like a Christmas bulb.

"You have one day," KJ said. "That's it. You finish this by tomorrow or else."

"It would be better if I had three days," I said.

KJ's gloved hands gripped the arms of the throne. Wood creaked and groaned.

"One day," KJ said.

"Two?" I said. "The kids would love it. Besides this day is almost half done so really it's only one and a half days."

KJ glared over the top of his glasses.

"You can use my place." I fumbled in my pocket for the keys to my apartment. I pulled them out and extracted the office key from the ring. I tossed the ring toward KJ who didn't make a move to catch them. The keys jangled as they landed at his feet.

"I'll stay in my office. You can have my place all to yourself."

KJ still glared. Finally he let out an explosive breath. He let go of the chair arms. The wood groaned as if in relief. KJ bent and scooped up the keys. He squeezed them, jabbing a finger at me.

"By end of tomorrow, you finish this."

I nodded. "I will."

KJ leaned back. The throne creaked under him.

"You'd better."

I shot a quick glance at the door. If any child accidentally peeked in, seeing this glaring, menacing Santa would traumatize them for life.

As if reading my mind, KJ took a deep breath and let it out. He tucked the keys into his pants pocket. The lines in his face smoothed out. The fiery red of anger faded from his skin. The coiled tension melted from his body.

"End of tomorrow, Noel. Remember that."

"Of course," I said. "That's plenty of time for me. There's a show at two and another one at four and then the final one at six. Then just four more tomorrow and you're done."

"Done," KJ said. "Right."

"I'll come by after that. We could have dinner."

KJ's head tipped. The glasses slipped down his nose. He stared over top of them.

"Or not," I said.

"Tomorrow," KJ said.

"Sure. Tomorrow."

I backed away, managing not to stumble over the cotton snow. My fingers fumbled at the door knob until I finally had to turn to unlock it. I took one last glance back at my glaring brother and then escaped the Santa Room.

A day and a half.

Oh brother.

CHAPTER

SIX

Despite the cool air conditioning in the mall, I found himself sweating as I stood outside the door of the Santa Room. A day and a half. How was I going to solve this in a day and a half?

I had no idea.

But I had to do something fast. KJ wouldn't stay any longer.

I let out a breath as I looked around the mall. Light aqua tile stretched out from the Santa Room. This early only a few people wandered the halls. Mothers pushing strollers. A few older people strolled by, wearing white t-shirts and matching shorts, stepping smartly in their shining white running shoes.

The air still had the tang of ammonia from the cleaning products and a whiff of perfume from the mothers walk-

71

ing by.

A day and a half, and even with Shirl's extensive list of missing Santas, I was no closer to figuring out what was going on.

All I knew was it was something magical.

Christopher Henries' disappearing act laid testament to that.

Maybe his strange reappearance wasn't the only time a Santa had shown up again.

I grinned.

Maybe that was a place to start.

HEAT LEAKED IN FROM THE HALLWAY, LEAVING THE NARROW waiting area in my office humid. Even if I had left my window air conditioner cranked and rattling, it still didn't blast enough cold air out to cool beyond my office.

As I stepped into my office, I could feel the humidity following like an eager puppy. The air still held a chill from the air conditioning but it would be gone as soon as the heat swallowed it up, unless I left the machine running. It didn't seem worth it when I wasn't here. But now, even here for a few minutes, I cranked the machine on.

The rumble started again as it rattled against the window frame. While it got up to speed, I pulled out the list from Shirl again. Pages and pages of Santas, but I only needed another one from here in Toronto.

Then maybe I could enlist Stan Mallory again.

Mallory might be able to search police records and find other instances of Santas reappearing.

It was somewhere to start.

The papers crinkled in my hands. They stuck to my fingers as I tried to flip through them. Even with the cold air now blasting forth, lingering humidity made the papers stick together. My chair creaked as I turned toward the air conditioner.

Maybe if I could dry out the papers...

A hint of gingerbread drifted past my nose. I glanced at the now flapping papers in my hands. Then I sniffed them.

Nothing.

But still another hint of gingerbread, like a warm reminder of home.

I spun around.

A gingerbread cookie shaped like a man stood on my desk beside my phone. Colourful pink and yellow icing outlined his body. Dots of blue for the eyes and a pink smile. Yellow curls for hair. Big white plops of icing traced buttons down the front, reminding me of dad's red coat except it was just the brown of the gingerbread. It teetered on the rounded bottoms of the legs then fell backward.

Landing on a cream coloured envelope.

Was it a gift from my mother? I liked gingerbread well enough but my favourites were her cinnamon short bread.

And of course she knew that.

I shoved the papers back into the top drawer of my desk before reaching for the cookie. I grabbed it with one hand and the envelope with the other before it was blown off my desk by a cold blast from my air conditioner.

The cookie was still warm but losing heat fast under the onslaught of cool air. I touched one of the white buttons. The icing was still a little tacky.

Freshly baked and decorated. Delivered magically.

But not by mom.

I set the cookie down on the desk blotter and turned my attention to the envelope. Thick rich paper with my name scrolled in bold letters on the front. I broke the seal and opened it.

Another whiff of gingerbread drifted out as I pulled out the note. Obviously the letter writer and the baker were the same person. The note had been folded once. I unfolded it. Black swirling letters covered the page.

Noel Kringle, Come to the Centre Island Bridge at midnight. The fate of Christmas rests in your hands.

It was unsigned.

There had to be a way I could find out who wrote it and sent it. Every magical being left behind a signature with their magic, a type of residue. I could easily read it.

No, I *used* to be able to easily read it. Since I had left the North Pole, my magic abilities had been at minimal. Figuring out who was behind this note was probably beyond me.

Or was it? Maybe I had be able to tell something about them, even if I couldn't tell precisely…

My desk phone rang. The sudden clatter made me jump in my chair. The envelope fell to my lap.

I reached for the receiver, fumbled and grabbed it, yanked it to my ear.

"Kringle," I said.

"You got my note," said a gruff voice.

"Who is this?" I said.

"You'll see when you meet me," said Mr. Gruff Voice.

I heard something on the line behind the voice. Something soft and tinkling.

Something like… Christmas bells?

The gingerbread man, the stationary, the warning about Christmas. Now those bells.

And that gruff voice. It sounded so familiar. If I could only put my finger on it. I needed to hear more of the voice.

I tightened my grip on the phone. "Is this some kind of bogus threat about Christmas?"

"Course not. What are you talking about, kid?"

That was it! I had it.

Venir, one of the Christmas Elves.

I leaned back in my chair. I remembered Venir, a tall Elf standing over four feet with white curls poking out from around a bullet-shaped head. Broad shoulders and a barrel chest. I worked in the stables doing upkeep on the sleigh as well as repairs on the tracking station that was used to tracked Santa Claus's progress through the night on Christmas Eve.

Both of those jobs were highly technical, vitally important parts of Christmas and the Elves who worked on them were tough and capable, if not very imaginative.

So where would Venir get the idea to go through this effort to hide his identity?

And why?

The easiest thing would be to ask him outright. If it wasn't for the list of missing Santas in his desk and the strangeness of Christopher Henries' death and reappearance, I might do that. But it couldn't be a coincidence that Venir was contacting me like this, nor was Venir known for pulling any practical jokes.

Maybe it was better to go along with it.

"What is this about then?" I said. "Why should I meet you?"

"It's like I said in the letter," Venir's voice grumbled over the line. "It's about Christmas. If you wanna know more, you gotta meet me tonight on the bridge. I just wanted to make sure you got the note, not give an interview about it."

Before I could reply, a click sounded in my ear then the dial tone.

Hung up.

I reset the receiver and looked at the card in my hand.

The fate of Christmas.

First a dead Santa. Then an entire list of dead or missing Santas, and now an Elf warning me about Christmas.

In July.

What the hell was going on?

I was going to find out if it was the last thing I did.

I stuffed the note back into the envelope and shoved it into my pants pocket. The paper crinkled, releasing another whiff of gingerbread. I pulled out the pages from Shirl and set them on the desk blotter, putting my stapler on top so they wouldn't blow away from the force of the air conditioner.

It had become downright chilly in the room, the gale force cold wind cutting through the July heat. I spun in my chair to face the air conditioner. I could turn it down a little now. The temperature was bearable.

My eyes flicked up and I glanced out the window.

Bright sunlight lit up the pavement outside, highlighting the look of weathered pale grey asphalt bleached by the sun and the surrounding concrete and brick buildings, all colours washed out and faded.

A strong contrast to the bright red Santa suit and fluffy white hair and beard of the man standing in the middle of the parking lot.

I shot to my feet. I yanked the blinds up and stared out the window.

A man in a Santa outfit. In the parking lot. Even from the distance of four storeys, it almost looked like...

Christopher Henries!

I squeezed past the desk and ran out of the office. At the door I hesitated a moment. Elevator or stairs? The elevator was slow but it would be faster if it happened to be here on the floor.

Take a chance.

I took the right toward the elevator. The hallway felt like a wet sponge. The heat slammed me in waves as I ran. The charcoal carpeting seemed to sink under my feet. But even though it was hot, the scent of ammonia lingered in the hall, proof that the landlord at least cleaned the place even if I didn't bother with air conditioner.

Maybe he was hoping for a crop of mushrooms.

I reached the elevator just before I started staggering. The door slid open when I pressed the button.

At least I wouldn't melt walking down the stairs.

The elevator felt like an oven but before I could fully broil, it dinged and released me on the ground floor. Here the regular charcoal carpeting gave way to speckled off-white linoleum and an even stronger scent of ammonia.

The front door of the building was to my left, but my office window faced the back and the parking lot. I headed right, pushing through the beige door leading to the stair-well and the back door.

Maybe now I would get some answers.

The dim light from the single bulb hanging in the stairway above me made me fumble for the door handle. I grabbed it and shoved. The metal door creaked as it opened, splashing me with bright white sunlight.

Blinded, I put my left hand up over my eyes, shielding

them. The door was just to the left of my window. I stepped out, letting it shut. Shuffled to the right.

Sunlight still blinding. I blinked. Just a bright white haze.

Shapes slowly solidified.

The concrete building in the distance, squatting in the sun. Another red brick factory, listing to the side on the right.

Cracked asphalt spreading outward from me, sprouting weeds that wilted in the hot sun.

No Santa. No Christopher Henries.

Maybe it was the sun. It was still so bright.

Maybe I would see better from the shade of my office building.

I stepped back until the cool shade enveloped me. The humidity still sucked at me but it felt at least ten degrees cooler in the shade. But still no sign of Santa, no sign of anyone in the parking lot beyond.

Was I seeing things? Had I lost my mind?

The screeched of metal screamed above me, followed by the tinkling of glass.

What the...?

I caught a glimpse of white metal. Rushing down from above.

I tried to leap to the side. My feet stuck to the gravel.

I felt the tingle of magic.

A rush of hot air pressed down on me.

I screamed...

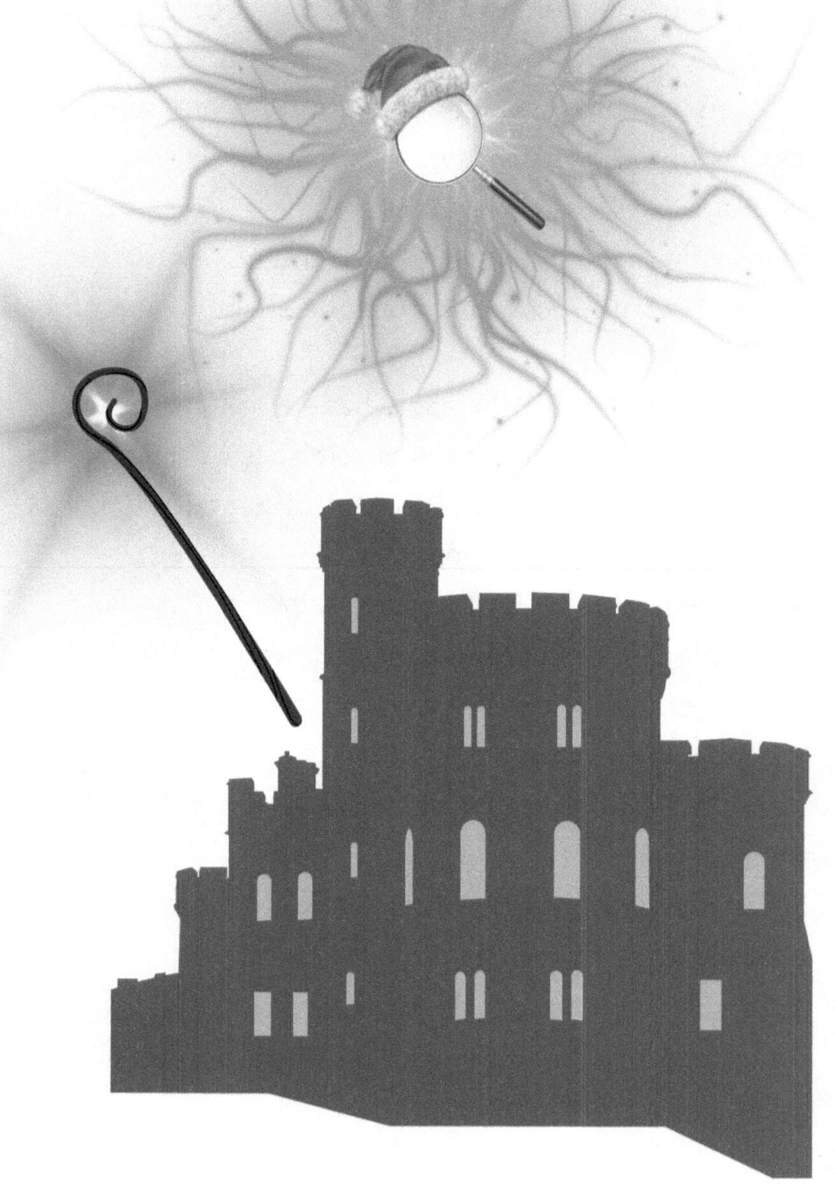

CHAPTER

SEVEN

I winked, wrenching myself aside just before the air conditioner slammed against the ground, followed by a shower of tinkling glass.

I gulped in the hot, humid air then started coughing as I sucked in a mouthful of dust.

The metal remains of the air conditioner lay crumpled before me, the middle collapsed in on itself, the back grill looking like a demented smile. Already dirt was settling onto the exposed white metal.

I got my coughing under control. Holding my hand over my mouth and nose, I took a step forward. Gravel and glass crunched under my feet. Another step and I felt it, the telltale tingle of magic.

Someone had tried to kill me.

I looked up the side of the red brick building. There on

the top floor, my broken window gaped open like a wounded mouth.

The landlord was *not* going to be happy about that.

A chuckle bubbled up from my chest. I pressed my lips closed against it.

No time to lose it. Not when someone was trying to kill me and was willing to wreck my air conditioner to do it.

What if another person had been with me?

That thought flushed any giddy humour from my mind. Time to get back to work.

The dust that had puffed up on the air conditioner's landing settled in a thin layer overtop the ruined metal. I reached for the grill, keeping an eye on the gaping window above me, just in case of the pieces of broken wood from the window frame decided to try and skewer me.

The metal felt cold and hard under my fingers. The residual magic was already draining away, and with it any chance for me to figure out who'd done it. But a whisper of it tingled against his skin, like the flutter of a butterfly wing.

Not that strong to begin with, but then again how much magic was needed to push an air conditioner out of a window? Not nearly as much as manifesting a fake Christopher Henries.

Was the same creature responsible for both or was this attempt something else?

Who did I know that had such limited magic?

Unfortunately one creature came to mind immediately.

A Christmas Elf. Someone like... Venir?

But that made no sense. Why would Venir go to the trouble of contacting me, insisting we meet without saying why or admitting his identity, and then try to kill me?

Distant ringing interrupted me. I glanced back up the building.

The ringing drifted out from my now open window.

My telephone.

I stepped back from the air conditioner. Even the last bit of magic residue could interfere with my efforts to *wink* back to my office. I took a breath and prepared...

The phone stopped ringing.

Damn. Missed it.

Then the left front pocket of my pants started vibrating.

I fumbled for my cell phone and yanked it out. Even as I pressed the button to answer I recognized the number.

"Hello Stan," I said.

"Kringle." Mallory's voice sounded strained and flat. "Meet at Nathan Phillips Square. Now."

"What's going on?" I said.

"I think I've found your missing Santa," Mallory said.

IT TOOK I OVER AN HOUR TO GET THERE. FIRST I HAD TO RETURN TO my office and cover the broken window. The Venetian blinds had been shredded. I managed to drape the dark brown fleece throw from the back of my couch over the rail, blocking the window.

The papers from my list were scattered around the desk. At first I had been afraid they'd be missing but they were just messed up. I gathered them, folded them and stuffed them into a white envelope that bulged with them.

I hesitated. Should I leave them here? With someone magical around, even leaving them in the bottom drawer of my desk, specially infused with magic to stay locked and hidden, might not be strong enough.

Better take them along. I didn't want to lose them.

Just before I left I paused at the door. I looked back through the narrow waiting area to my office, now darkened by the throw covering the window. Should I contact the landlord about the window? They'd probably want me to pay for the damages, something I was happy to do, and stick around, something I couldn't afford to do.

I would deal with it later.

I shut the door and locked it. Maybe no one would notice. It wasn't like anyone hung around the back of the building.

Or really the front for that matter.

By the time I reached Nathan Phillips Square, the heat of noon was beating down, amplified by the concrete blocks that made up the Square. Set at the base of the curved City Hall building, the Square was used to house farmers markets or concerts or Christmas lights in the winter.

As I entered from Queen Street, passing beneath the

arching concrete bridge, I heard the hiss of the fountain. Two rows of spouts ran down the centre of the large, square wading pool, inlaid in the concrete. Water shot out from the sprouts arching into the air and rippling along the surface. The benches surrounding the fountain were full of people enjoying the summer sun. Office workers shed their jackets and stole some fresh air alongside teenagers in ripped shorts and baggy t-shirts. Mothers dressed in sleeveless sun dresses kept an eye on their children as they sat on the edge of the fountain to dip their feet in the water, or splashed in the fountain.

Strange to see the fountain running the way it was, the last time I had been down here had been in the winter when they turned the huge pond into a skating rink. The air had been crisp and cold enough to puff out with each breath. Instead of office workers and mothers enjoying the sun, it had been couples bundled up in jackets with scarves and hats and mittens. Instead of slashing in the fountain, people had skated in graceful circles around the rink, with children laughing and darting in and out around the main skaters. I could always spot the hockey players, the way they stopped their skates with a flare of shaved ice before darting back into the crowd.

Now it was hot enough for a faint rainbow to shimmer in the mist from the fountain's spouts and there wasn't a hint of ice to be seen.

I would have liked to linger longer by the pool but I couldn't see any police officers there. So the body hadn't been found near the front of City Hall, they would have blocked off the fountain area for sure.

I turned away from the fountain. A farmers market stretched across the front doors and back along the aisle toward Queen Street where I had entered. Tables of strawberries, blueberries, peaches, mounds of loose corn on the cob, small plastic pint containers of cucumbers or cherries. I even saw one large table of people selling fresh bread, pies, and tarts.

As I walked past, I caught the scent of cinnamon and apple so warm it reminded me of my mother's special cinnamon Christmas cookies and made my mouth water.

At the very end of the aisle, near the wall, I caught a flash of black and the glint of silver.

A uniform.

I hurried away from the temptation of pie.

As I slipped past a couple contemplating corn at the end of the table, I caught another glimpse of a police uniform. Sure enough, I rounded the corner, slipping down a narrow passage. The concrete wall lined the right. A short brick wall stood to my left before it expanded out, opening the space and revealing a dark blue steel dumpster.

The sickly sweet odour of garbage and compost made I wrinkle my nose. With every step, I was missing that cinnamon and apple pie more and more.

A ribbon of yellow police tape was tied to one end of the dumpster and stretched to an electrical meter hanging against the wall, blocking my progress. Around the dumpster, an officer stepped out. His hand reached for his belt when he spotted me.

"This is police business," he said. "You'll have to go back the way you came."

"I'm here to see Detective Stan Mallory," I said. "Tell him Noel Kringle is here."

The officer gave him a strange look. As he turned away, I caught a glimpse of a G.I. Joe doll, the man's favourite Christmas gift.

A few moments later, Mallory appeared from where the wall curved to the right. Even with the heat, he had the sleeves of his white shirt rolled down and the cuffs buttoned at his wrists. He wore black pants with his detective badge clipped to his belt. A shimmer of sweat glinted on his forehead above the metal framed sunglasses covering his eyes. The dark brown lenses lightened at the bottom. Mallory grabbed the yellow police tape and yanked it up, waving for me to step under it.

I did so.

"You called?" I said.

"Took you long enough," Mallory grumbled.

Before I could reply, Mallory wagged his thumb. "This way."

He turned and led me past the dumpster. Five other dumpsters were lined up behind it, creating a row of fragrant blue steel boxes. At the far end, a group of officers clustered between the last two dumpsters. Sweat glistened on foreheads but they all wore latex gloves. One officer held a camera, crouching to shoot at the space. She straightened as Mallory stepped up.

He waved the group back. Then turned to me.

"Take a look," he said, his voice flat.

I felt the curious gazes of the surrounding officers weighing on me as I edged closer to the far end. Did I really want to see what was between these dumpsters? The tense but bland expression on Mallory's face showed me I didn't have much choice. The sunglasses glinted in the sun, refusing to give me any encouragement.

I tilted my head and looked.

A body was stuffed into the space between the steel boxes, folded like it was some discarded toy. At first glance, I thought it had bled so much that it stained the clothing, then I realized the figure was wearing a red outfit.

And not just any red outfit.

I recognized those fluffy white cuffs, that white collar.

A red Santa suit.

I didn't want to but I had to move closer, had to see better.

The man's back pressed against the side of the left dumpster, shoulders and head curled inward, like some kind of demented fruit rollup. His legs pressed against the right side, black boots pointing upward.

And the face...

I recognized the face.

Christopher Henries.

I backed out of the space, feet scrambling against the

pavement. I only stopped when I bumped into the officer with the camera.

"Watch it," she said.

"Sorry," I mumbled.

"Is it him?" Mallory said.

I nodded. "His name is Christopher Henries. How long…?"

"We got the call at ten," Mallory said. "Body's probably been here since some time last night." He waved to the officers. "Okay, let's get it bagged."

The lull in activity ended. As Mallory stepped toward me, the officers moved toward the space, blocking off my view.

It was a relief.

Mallory took my arm, steering me back to the entrance of the garbage area.

"Are you sure this is the guy you saw?" my voice was low.

"That's him," I said. "And there have been others." I pulled the bulging envelope from my pocket.

Mallory's mouth pursed like he'd tasted something sour. "Not another one of your weird cases."

"Not only this, but when I went to Henries's apartment, I found him there or a doppelganger."

"A what?"

"A copy," I said. "Something was pretending to be him. All the way to the mall. Only when I confronted him did it vanish."

They paused at the yellow tape. Mallory pulled off the sunglasses revealing his dark brown eyes and shook his head. The white hair sprinkled through the brown of his crew cut glinted silver in the sun.

"So what was it?" he said. "What killed this man?"

"I don't know," I said. "I'm hoping to get some answers tonight."

"What's going on tonight?" Mallory said.

"I'm meeting an informant," I said.

Mallory frowned. "I don't like the sound of that. Do you need backup?"

I shook my head. "I'm not in danger from him. Maybe from my brother."

"Your brother?"

"He's filling in at the mall for the next day and a half," I said. "I have to figure this out by then."

The echo of a smirk flittered across Mallory's face. "You like to live dangerous, don't you?"

I sighed. "You don't know the half of it." I yanked a thumb back up the way they came. "Can you let me know how he died?"

"I'll call you," Mallory said. His bushy eyebrows crinkled. "You sure you don't need back up?"

"I'm sure," I said.

Mallory gestured at the papers in my hands.

"I don't suppose you want to tell me how you got that?"

I grinned. "Better you don't know. Officially, anyway. I'll send you a copy. Maybe it'll help."

"Maybe. Just make sure that the person who got you that list is covering her tracks."

"I'm sure she is."

Mallory grunted. He slipped the sunglasses back up his nose. He grabbed the yellow tape and yanked it up. I ducked underneath.

"Tell me there ain't gonna be any more bodies," Mallory said.

I tapped the papers I held. "I wish I could. There've been enough already."

"You can stop it through, right?"

"Sure," I said. "Of course I can."

From behind his sunglasses, Mallory lifted his left eyebrow but he didn't say anything.

Good, I didn't need anymore second guessing. I had my brother for that.

And speaking of, I had better check on KJ to make sure he was keeping his temper around the kids.

That was all I needed, a raging Santa.

EIGHT

I reached the mall just as KJ was finishing up the two o'clock session.

I stood at the door to Santa's Room and peered around the door frame. Three children stood beside their mothers in line at the bottom of the stairs leading to the small stage. A blandly cheerful version of Jingle Bells tinkled through speakers hidden in the ceiling, sounding tinny and slightly off key. But the children didn't notice. They didn't notice the fake cotton snow or the plastic candy canes with paint peeling off them, or even the faded back drop.

All they noticed was the jolly man in the Santa suit sitting on the golden throne.

KJ had his head tipped down so the little girl wearing a green sundress could whisper in his ear. Her mousy brown hair was pulled back in pig tails, the right one slightly lower than the left. When she finished whispering, KJ threw his head back. A jolly laugh bellowed up from his belly and out his chest.

"Ho ho ho, Kimberly, that is a jolly wish for ol' Santa," he said. "I'm sure whatever cookies you leave will be yummy."

Even after the heat from outside, I felt a chill run down my back.

Darned if KJ didn't even *sound* like dad!

"Now you be a good girl and remember to practice your back stroke in camp."

"Thanks Santa," the little girl squeaked. She wrapped her arms around KJ's neck and gave him a big hug then she slid off his lap. She practically levitated down the stairs and raced toward the woman standing at the edge of the stage.

"Momma, momma, did you hear? Santa likes swimming!"

The woman wore a white cotton top with a pink flowered skirt and her mousy brown hair was just like her daughter's. She beamed at the girl. "I heard, honey. And you heard when he told you to pay attention to the rules of the water."

"Yeah, and he likes the back stroke too!"

"Of course, honey."

She took the little girl's hand. The child bounced as they walked toward the door. I stepped back to let them pass. As they moved along, the girl babbled on about Santa and the mother nodded, a smile playing across her thin lips. They didn't even notice me.

That was a good thing for a private detective.

But as a son of Kris Kringle, it did give me a melancholy twinge.

When I glanced back into the room, I gave KJ a nod. KJ dipped his head in acknowledgment. A little boy in an orange t-shirt and blue shorts was loudly describing the surf board he wanted.

After another ten minutes, the contented mother and excited bobbing child excited Santa's Room. I slipped in behind them and closed the door. I locked it to stop anyone else from coming in. When I turned back, KJ had pulled off the hat and was unbuttoning the coat. Underneath, his purple shirt shone out, clashing horribly with the red.

"It's hot in that suit," he said.

"Small crowd," I said.

KJ peered over the top of his round glasses, widening his eyes. "Are you kidding? There was a line up out the door. I had to start at one forty-five or they would have torn the door off its hinges." He tilted his head. "Where were you? Some security you are."

I glanced at my watch. It was just after three and KJ had been seeing children since one forty-five?

"I've been working on the case," I said. "Remember, the dead guy you're replacing? They found his body."

KJ caught his breath. "Where?"

"Between the dumpsters down at City Hall."

KJ frowned.

"How far is that?"

"Pretty far," I said. "More proof that this is magical in

origin. Plus I've got a meeting tonight with an informant. A special informant."

KJ folded his arms over his chest. "Will you stop playing private detective and just spit it up? Who's this informant?"

I frowned. "I'm not playing private detective, I am a private detective."

KJ waved a white gloved hand. "Yeah, yeah, just spit it up."

"You mean spit it out."

"Whatever. Jeez, even the Elves aren't as sensitive as you are."

"Funny you should say that," I said. "The informant is an Elf and he says he's got information about a threat to Christmas."

KJ stiffened. "Which Elf?"

"Venir."

A laugh exploded out of KJ. "Are you kidding me? Venir? What would he know about anything? He's a grumpy, good for nothing disgrace. He's been found drinking on the job more times than I can count. I've told Dad numerous times to can him. You are *not* listening to him."

"Drinking? I've never heard that," I said.

"Of course you didn't, you've always had your head in your books. First your mysteries and then your private detective books..."

I held up my hand to stop my brother. Swirling snow, I did not want to get into it again.

"Tell me more about Venir," I said.

"Just what I told you," KJ said. "He's unreliable and untrustworthy. You shouldn't listen to him."

"Why would he claim to know something about a threat to Christmas?" I said.

"Who knows?" KJ said. "Probably some way to make himself feel more important. Maybe he thinks he can get back into Dad's good graces." KJ frowned. "Or maybe *he's* threatening Christmas. I wouldn't put it past him. Where are you meeting him? I should come with you."

Oh, that didn't sound like a good idea, not with KJ's attitude.

"I can handle him," I said. "Now that you've told me what to expect."

KJ grunted. "Tell him to shove off. You've got a case to solve." KJ pointed a gloved finger at me. "Remember you've got one more day then I'm out of here."

"Sure, sure," I said. "Now that they've found the body, it should be easy to figure it out."

A huge lie but KJ didn't seem to notice. He nodded. "Good."

"You look good in that suit," I said. "It suits you."

For a moment, a genuine smile lit up KJ's face, crinkling his eyes and warming his cheeks. Then it flickered off as fast as it had come.

"Of course it suits me," he said. "I've been training for this for years. I should damn well be good at it."

I pressed my lips together to stop the retort. KJ always had to be snarky, no matter what.

And I always ended up playing peacemaker.

"Want to get a coffee before the four o'clock show?" I said.

KJ glanced at the watch on his wrist. The face was a green present with a glowing red bow. Bright yellow Christmas bulbs marked the numbers.

"It's almost three thirty," KJ said. "Why don't you get me a coffee. I shouldn't leave the room."

Without waiting for a reply, he turned and climbed the stairs back onto the stage. A few quick steps took him back to the golden throne where he sat down, the red coat still hanging open, showing off his purple shirt.

I clenched my teeth as I headed for the door. Sure KJ was doing him a huge favour by covering for Henries but why did he have to be such a prick while doing it?

I yanked open the door and stepped out.

Already a couple of kids with their parents were lined up. At my appearance, they all brightened up, trying to see past me through the doorway as I closed the door.

"Santa will be ready to see you at four," I said.

"Is it four?" said a little girl, her blonde curls bobbing around her head.

I missed the reply as I hurried away.

Not even three thirty and already kids were lining up.

Maybe KJ wasn't being such a prick after all. He seemed to have a real instinct about being Santa and keeping the kids in suspense.

Maybe it was a good thing I had decided to be a private detective after all.

I DROPPED THE LARGE COFFEE (DOUBLE CREAM NO SUGAR) OFF WITH KJ then left before the doors opened. I knew I should stay to help maintain order but KJ seemed to be doing just fine in that department.

Instead, I retreated to my office to consider the list of Santas again.

The dark brown throw was still covering the broken window in my office. I had detoured around the back of the building to see if my ruined air conditioner was still there. It was. As I had suspected, no one had been around to see if or my wrecked window.

Using a smidge of magic, I whisked the air conditioner away, settling it near one of the ruined factories past the empty lot at the back of the building. It nestled in the shade of one of the dull red brick buildings, crushing a smattering of weeds under its metal bulk. Soon they would grow around it, making it look like it had been there for years.

With the air conditioner gone the landlord probably wouldn't ever bother to look up to see the gaping hole where my office window used to be.

Maybe I could repair it on my own. Then I wouldn't risk getting thrown out.

But first, I had to work on the list.

There had to be a pattern. Maybe by location or timing. I spread the sheets across my desk blotter and switched on the desk lamp. Yellowish light brightened the pages.

Unfortunately without the air conditioner, the room felt stuffy. Moist air pressed against my skin, making my shirt stick to my back. As I flipped through the pages, the lingering taste of coffee turned sour in my mouth.

No pattern that I could see. Nothing.

It had to be there. There had to be something.

I started at the beginning again.

With the dark brown throw hiding the window, I couldn't tell what time it was, just an neverending darkness. It reminded me of winter at the North Pole, the deep unending dark. But there it had been refreshing. Stars had twinkled in the liquid black sky above my head. They had always seemed so magical, reminding me of Rudolph's nose, or fairy lights, or the Christmas bulbs winking on the trees, or even the tinsel reflecting silver light.

But the darkness in my office wasn't wide and refreshing. It felt heavy and damp and hot. Sweat trickled down the back of my neck, matted my brown curls to my forehead. Even my beard felt damp.

And still there was no pattern. Just Santas, only Santas. That was the only pattern.

Someone really had a hate on for Santa Claus.

My hands tightened on the paper, crinkling it. Was that it? Was someone after Dad?

Was that what Venir was talking about?

I would find out but not soon enough.

My stomach growled, as if agreeing. Then I felt the hunger pangs. I had had breakfast but then not bothered with lunch. I probably needed to grab something for dinner, maybe see if I could buy KJ dinner. It was the least I could for my brother.

I gathered the papers again and stuffed them back into the envelope. As I stood from my desk, my back creaked and I felt my shirt crinkle. First I was going to mop off in the bathroom.

The overhanging bulb in the small bathroom off the waiting area showed how flat and damp my hair was. I snagged a Christmas washcloth and dumped it in the sink, turning on the cold water. Soon the little Christmas bell embroidered on the end darkened in the water. I squeezed the excess water out, sighing at how good the cool water felt running over my hands.

I wiped my face and neck then splashed some water in my hair. I shook my head, feeling the cool water trickle down my back. My skin felt pleasantly perked up and after sitting for so long, my muscles seemed happy to move.

Now I would see if KJ wanted to meet for dinner…

I pulled my cell phone out of his pocket and hit the button.

Ten forty-seven shone out at me.

Damn the halls!

That couldn't be right. It couldn't possibly be that late.

My stomach growled again, loud and long, as if to say yes, it was that late and it was damned hungry.

So much for dinner with KJ. I would be lucky to get something on the way to the Toronto Island.

I folded the envelope and stuffed it into my other pants pocket as I hurried out the door.

I MANAGED TO FIND A HOT DOG VENDOR OUTSIDE THE FERRY DOCK. The vendor had just been closing up when I emerged from the subway. The bright red umbrella overtop the silver cart was closed. The dense scent of cooking hot dog and the tang of onions still lingered in the air as I hurried down the side-walk toward him.

The man, wearing a white smock over a blue t-shirt, glared at me, his lips pursing around the unlit cigarette in his mouth. He didn't bother to take it out as he spoke.

"What you want?"

"Could I get a hot dog, please?" I said.

"All gone," the man said.

"I'll have whatever you've got," I said. I felt the familiar twinkle in my mind. This man's favourite Christmas toy had been an Etch-a-Sketch because he loved to draw.

I gestured at the decals that decorated the front of the silver cart. Several were permits but the others were decorative decals and the arrangement created an abstract picture of colour and words.

"Nice design," I said. "It almost looks like a cityscape."

The man brightened. "Think so? Hey, I got an extra sausage."

"That would be perfect," I said.

It was just above warm but with ketchup, onions and a smattering of relish, it was perfect. I paid and had half of it wolfed down before I was halfway down the concrete walkway to the ferry docks.

The walkway widened to a round circular space. An office building all glass and grey concrete towered on my left. Rolling grass and a few trees spread out to my right. Ahead, the docks were blocked by the ticket booths that spread across the end of the circular space. Only one booth was open with a stooped, elderly man wearing a pale grey shirt peering through the plexiglass at me. Wisps of white hair poked up from his mottled head hovered about his forehead. Nothing like the look he'd had when he used to wear his favourite charcoal grey fedora, a Christmas present from his best girl when he was fifteen.

The old man frowned when I slid a ten dollar bill through the slot.

"Last ferry across," he said. "There isn't another coming back 'til morning."

"That's okay," I said.

The man shrugged, bony shoulders shifting the grey fabric up and down. He punched at the register then scooped my money away. He slid across a ticket and change.

"Centre Island Ferry is the centre one, leaving in five minutes."

"Thanks." I grabbed the ticket and change then pushed through the turnstile.

The ferry docks spread before me, looking dark and empty. It was a large empty concrete space with a wooden roof soaring to a peak above my head. To my right were the three docks, one for each ferry going to the three islands, Hanlan's Point to the far left, Ward's Island at the far right, and Centre Island in, of course, the centre. A chain link fence separated the boarding spot from the inner holding area. A set of four faded wooden benches were scattered in the now empty space, offering both a spot to get off your feet or a barrier to get past while heading for the ferry.

I heard the gentle lapping of the water as I crossed the concrete pad toward the Centre Island dock. The ferry was already there. The wire fence was pulled open, allowing entrance.

A worn, wooden gang plank led from the concrete dock onto the ferry. A bored looking crew man stood against the right side, chewing something. Probably gum from the way his jaw worked up and down. He wore white shorts and a light grey t-shirt, similar enough to the ticket taker than I wondered if it was a uniform.

He squinted at my ticket, dark hair falling into his eyes.

His jaw worked overtime. Then he nodded and jerked a thumb back behind him.

I took this to mean it was all right to board.

The gang plank rumbled under my feet but the rumbling continued when I reached the deck of the ferry. Must be the engine.

Directly in front of me were dark wooden stairs leading up to the upper deck. I decided just to stay on the bottom deck. Faster getting off from there, not that it seemed like it would be an issue.

From what I could see, I was one of the few passengers for this journey.

I headed right, following the curve of the dark brown deck. Dark brown wood benches lined the exterior hull and the interior walls. Above the benches facing out, I caught glimpses of the lake through the windows. The water was a shimmering pool of blackness with sparkles of light reflecting from the city playing over its rippling surface.

As I reached the far end, I heard the creak of the rising gangplank. A thud sounded and then the rumble of the engines grew louder. I felt the wood deck under my feet shift, just like the way Dad's sleigh would shift as the reindeer leapt into the air.

I found myself grinning. I turned to face the stairs leading to the upper deck.

Why not?

I ran up them two at a time, my shoes slapping on the polished wood steps, my hand sliding up the brass railing.

On the upper deck, I felt the cool rush of air as the ferry gained speed. I turned left to the closest railing. The polished brass was cold under my palms, a welcome respite from the July heat.

Water splashed and sprayed from the front of the ferry. I felt the mist of it sprinkle my skin. I licked the wetness from my lips. Tasteless but not unlike a snowflake at the North Pole.

Ahead, the darkness of the lake spread out like a rippling blanket. I could see suggestions of the islands in the distance, lighter humps that rose from the dark lake. I watched them glide closer for a moment, then turned to look back at the city.

Toronto glistened in the night. Rising above the surrounding sky scrapers, I saw the glowing spear of the CN Tower. Different colours raced up its length and glowed around the top like a Christmas bulb. Red. Green. Blue. The rest of the city glowed golden against the night, a gagged ripple of lower and higher buildings. With every minute, the buildings blurred from distinct shapes to a general fuzz of light.

Miraculous.

Even if all the houses and buildings at the North Pole lit every lantern and every fireplace, then threw open every window and every door, it would never glow with as much splendid majesty.

I watched the city for another few minutes. The wind wiped my hair into my face, misting it. It felt like it was trying to catch my attention. Finally I turned to face forward again.

The island seemed like a dim suggestion in the darkness. After the bright glare of the city, the island lights looked like tiny pin pricks.

The wind smacked me in the face. It carried a chill with it. Now that they were away from the land, the temperature had dropped. After the heavy heat of the day, I found it refreshing.

The wind continued to flick water against my cheeks. It reminded me of the test runs Dad took me on, how the snow would flick my face as the sleigh bounded along onland before the reindeer took to the sky.

The ferry felt like it had even the same lift and drop.

Then the island solidified ahead of them.

Two stretches of wood reached out from the shore, ending in a stack of big black rubber tires floating on the water. It looked like a pair of arms reaching for the ferry to gather it up into its rubbery embrace. The ferry aimed for the space between them.

As I watched, details became clearer. A chain fastened to two concrete posts, hanging across the empty space. Beyond, a concrete patch spread out. To the left I saw fencing that created a holding space. To the right, the path led deeper into the island. I saw the deep shadows of trees but couldn't tell if those hulking shapes were oaks or maples.

The ferry gave a blast of its horn.

The engine rumbled louder. The water frothed higher

against the sides of the ferry. As they passed the stack of rubber tires, I noticed that the ferry was noticeably slowing.

Time to disembark.

As I turned toward the stairs, something near the trees caught my eye. A flicker of something. Light? A shimmer? U peered harder, trying to see farther. A single lamp lit up the concrete path but dimmed farther into the trees.

Maybe I had seen something reflecting light. A trick of the eye.

Or maybe, just maybe, there was something else waiting for me here besides a wayward Elf.

I stopped at the top of the stairs, holding the brass railing in my left hand. It felt smooth and cool against my palm.

I could just stay on the ferry. Ride back to the mainland. Contact Venir and insist on another meeting elsewhere, somewhere closer to home. Somewhere whatever was killing Santas wouldn't be able to take a shot at me.

But I had already burned up hours waiting for this appointment. KJ was only going to cover for one more day.

Besides, something about that this whole case offended me, right down to my toes.

Killing Santas.

No, it wasn't right at all.

I was damned if I was going to let some shimmer scare me off.

I stomped down the stairs to wait for the ferry to dock.

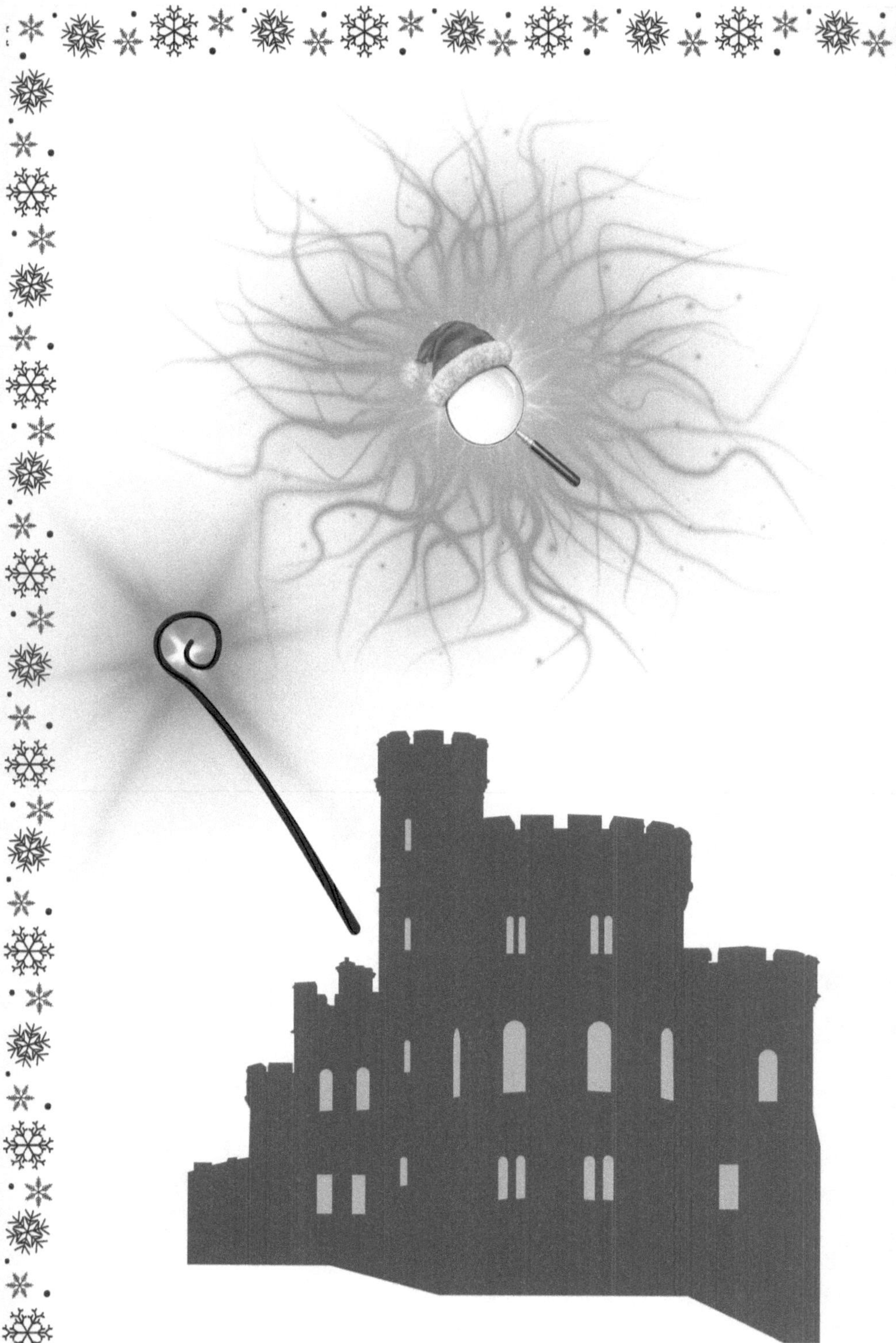

NINE

After disembarking, it took me almost twenty minutes to make it from the ferry dock to the bridge.

Of all the places to meet, why the heck had the Christmas Elf chosen the middle of the Centre Island bridge in the middle of the night?

I leaned against the iron railing and stared down the concrete path that led down across the island toward the ferry dock. In the moonlight, the path shimmered silver and reminded me of the snow at the North Pole. The dark shadows of trees hunched around the path, obscuring it, their dark green leaves almost black in the darkness.

I hunched my shoulders and glanced back at the other end of the bridge. The empty concrete fountain was a vague shape in the dark. A great round concrete pool, like the reindeer paddock.

I shook his head. Why was I thinking like that?

There was no snow anywhere around here, just the lush, dark blossoming trees, sending delicate fragrances through the air. Leaves rustling against each other in the gentle breeze, sounding almost like sleigh runners tracking in the snow.

Even the tall path lights that lined the way toward the ferry docks seemed to take on a reddish glow.

Like Christmas.

Swirling snow, I had Christmas on the brain.

First the mall promotion for Christmas in July, then the whole dead Santas business, and now this damned Elf and his whole Christmas in danger line.

At least when I took a deep breath I wasn't smelling the baked cinnamon scent of my mother's cookies. Instead, I breathed in the earthy scent of the ground with an undercurrent of flowers that lined the entrances to the bridge and heaped in mounds near the fountain.

It was kind of an eerie place for Venir to want to meet. In the day, this wide expanse of concrete would be full of people, families with children giggling and running across to get to the Centreville rides.

But at midnight, it felt like a parking lot. The great empty concrete path stretched across almost ten people wide. The other side of the railing faded into the dimness. But it was probably the same as the curling iron under his hands.

Even the way it swept up in a wave made me think of the rails on the sleigh, how it curled above the front, sparkling silver against the snow.

This railing wasn't silver but a dull dark green that looked muddy and stained, yet it still made me think of home.

The sound of pebbles skidding along the concrete caught my attention. I glanced down the path toward the ferry dock.

Nothing.

Was it from that shimmer I had spotted from the ferry?

Another trickle of pebbles.

Now I could track where it came from.

Behind me.

Toward the fountain.

I turned.

For a moment, the fountain stayed silent and dark and still. Then water burst from the centre and sprayed upward. It rained down in a spray. Coloured light appeared at the bottom, shooting light up through the water. Shimmering, shining. Red and green glowed bright and beautiful.

Oh course it would be red and green.

Perfect for Christmas.

I crossed my arms over my chest.

"Really?" I said. My voice seemed to echo over the distance. "This is your idea of incognito?"

"Hey, it works for me, kid."

The gruff voice came from behind me.

As I turned again, the water in the fountain stopped, as

suddenly as it started. The lights snapped off. The final spray fell in a mass of spattering drops into nothing.

In the ensuing silence, I found myself looking down at an Elf standing in the middle of the concrete path before me.

Venir stood just over four feet, quite tall for an Elf. A whitish fringe of curls poked out from the sides of his bullet shaped head. Even his large pointed ears and the smooth baldness of his dome couldn't distract from the curls. Dark eyebrows accentuated his piercing green eyes. He held the stump of an unlit cigar in the corner of his mouth. He had his thumbs hooked into his black belt. He wore jeans tucked into a set of scuffed, brown cowboy boots and a grey flannel shirt with the top two buttons undone. Beneath the collar, I could see a silver chain with a tiny red stocking on it.

Where was the usual red outfit? The white fluff collar and sleeves? The red hat perched on that bullet head? The black curling boots?

Venir didn't look like any Elf I had ever seen before.

"I am incognito, kid," Venir said.

"You might want to add a hat," I said. I gestured at the Elf's ears.

"These?" Venir shrugged. "Only takes a touch of magic to hide 'em."

One eye blink and I could see the air around Venir's head shimmer. A second blink. The Elf's large pointed ears vanished, replaced by a pair of regular size and shape.

Now he definitely looked like no Elf I had ever seen.

Now he looked like a regular dwarf.

"So," I said. "Care to tell me why you had to meet here in the middle of the night? I have an office in the east end. We could have met there. In the day time."

"Yeah, yeah," Venir said. "I know about your office. So do a lot of others. Easier to cloak things out here in the open air and easy to tell if anyone's listening."

He took the cigar out of his mouth and waved his hand. The dark air around them seemed to shimmer and I smelled a hint of ozone, like a flash of something burning. Then the image of the railing on either side of the bridge seemed to blur, as if in a fog. Even the fountain behind him and the dark trees behind Venir blurred.

Just how much magic could Venir have here away from the North Pole?

"Enough to make sure we aren't overheard," Venir said.

I frowned. "Stop poking in my head."

The Elf shrugged. "Sure. Okay. Fine."

"So are you going to explain your note? How is Christmas in danger?"

The sly look faltered. Venir swung his head left and then right, as if checking to make sure no one was around. When he finally faced me again, the wrinkles on his face had softened. All bravado gone.

"Someone's planning to kill Santa."

Venir's whisper was like the drop of a stone in a pond. The ripples buffeted me as the sound sank into me.

Someone was planning to kill Dad?

A drumming sounded in my ears. My heart beat pounded

away. The cold breeze felt hot and then clammy. The chirping of a cricket startled me. Shoulders jerked. Hands clenched into fists.

Dead Santas. All those dead Santas. Not ends themselves, but a means to an end.

Test runs.

But, no, it was too horrible to think about. I couldn't just accept it.

"You're kidding, right?" I said.

Venir's head jerked up. His lips thinned. His hand clenched the cigar, crushing it between his thin fingers.

"You think I trudge all the way down to this sweatbox as a joke, boy?"

Oh. Wrong thing to say.

"You think I'd waste my time with some... some idiot like you for no reason?"

Very wrong thing to say.

Half of the cigar fell to the concrete in a shower of crushed tobacco. The frayed end was still clamped in the Elf's clenched hand.

The clenched hand that shook so much that I knew the Elf wanted to swing.

The only thing holding him back was the Kringle name.

My shoulders drooped. So much for hoping the Elf was wrong. I wiped a hand across my forehead.

"You're right. I know you are," I said. "Sorry."

Venir's head hitched back. His eyes widened in surprised. He stuck the remains of the cigar into his mouth.

"Yeah, okay," he mumbled around the end.

"What else do you know? Do you know who or why?" I said.

"If I knew that I wouldn't need you, would I?" The Elf shook his head. "Are you sure you're a detective?"

Now I wanted to clench his hands into fists. Who did this Elf think he was? Steady, be steady. The Elf was talking about Dad. Keep that in mind. That was the important thing, not the opinion of some wayward Elf, even one with as bad a reputation as Venir.

"How did you hear about it? It didn't just occur to you."

"Well no," Venir said.

"So," I said. "Where did you hear it?"

Venir gave another covert glance around at their surroundings. I did the same thing. The shimmering blur remained intact.

Venir edged another step closer. He stuck his head forward and yanked the cigar from his mouth.

"The faerie told me," he said.

The faerie.

Now I knew the Elf was making it up.

Sure, there were a number of creatures in the Magical Realm that interacted in the regular world. Some even made a life here. Some, like Dad, drew their magic from the Realm and used it for the betterment of all.

But there were no fairies.

I crossed his arms. "The faerie told you."

Venir nodded. "Yeah, he said it was a bid for power."

"A bid for power," I said. "By who?"

Venir fiddled with the cigar and mumbled.

"What?" I said.

"I said he didn't tell me that."

I sighed. Of course he hadn't told him, because he didn't exist. As a joke this wasn't even funny.

"Did someone put you up to this?" I said.

"What?" the Elf said. "What are you talking about?"

"I'm talking about you and this crazy story."

"Story! I'm not telling a story. I'm telling you what I heard."

"Right," I said. "Sure you are. There are no such thing as fairies."

"Just cuz you ain't met them doesn't mean they don't exist, kiddo." Venir stabbed the cigar in his direction. His cheeks reddened with anger, puffing out round. The normal human ears vanished and his regular large, pointed ones appeared.

He'd lost all concentration to hold onto the illusion to cover them.

Maybe it wasn't a joke. Or at least he wasn't lying.

Maybe he believed what he was saying.

That didn't make it any more plausible.

I held up my hands in surrender. "Okay, okay. Let's start again. Did you get any other details about who wants to kill Santa?"

The Elf still glared but his cheeks were a little less ruddy. "Details like what?"

"Like when this might happen? Or where?"

Venir ducked his head. "He didn't say anything about that. But you're the..."

"Yes, I know," I said. "I'm the detective but I need more information. This might tie into another case I'm working but I can't know that with what you've given me."

"Look, I'm tellin' you all I know. The faerie said somebody was planning to kill Santa. I figered I should tell somebody. Excuse me for makin' the wrong choice."

"Now wait just a minute," I said.

"Forget it. Sorry to bother you."

Venir started to turn away. Around us, the shimmer faded. Night sounds intruded again. The breeze rustling the leaves in the trees, the hum of the crickets.

And the Elf's pudgy form was already growing faint.

"You got a hell of a nerve!"

The pointed ears solidified back. Venir jerked around.

"What?"

"You heard me. You show up here with some lame story and get all pissy when I don't jump high enough for you. If you're going to leave, fine, but first you're going to take me to this so called faerie so I can get more details. Then you can bugger off to the North Pole for all I care."

Even in the coolish air, I could feel the heat of my own face.

Venir grinned and nodded.

"Got a little fight in ya after all. Good to see, kid. You

might just be up for this. I had my doubts but he seemed to think you did."

I frowned. "What? Who?"

"You'll see."

Venir held up his hand. He dropped the cigar from his fingers. It fell toward the concrete in a weird, slow motion way. The air around us sparkled.

Oh no.

Venir snapped his fingers.

And the bridge disappeared.

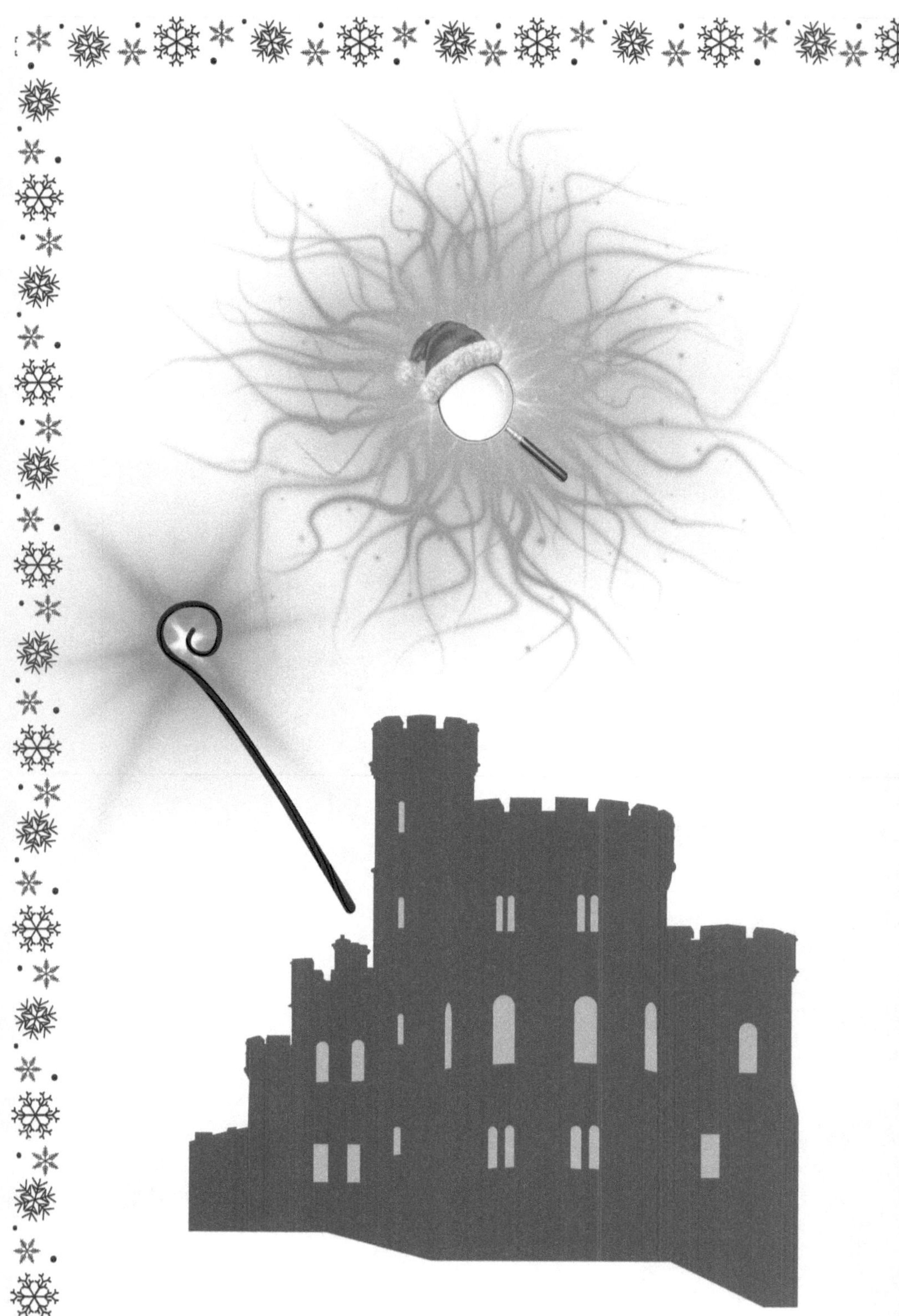

CHAPTER

TEN

The air had a mossy, damp feel, the flavour of old carpeting. I gagged. It felt like it was coating the roof my mouth. My tongue felt slimy. The muscles in my body trembled. After effects of sudden, magical transportation. I hadn't had any time to prepare.

Now I suffered for it.

My head ached from the transition. My skin felt like it was stretched tight over my scalp. Fortunately, the dim lighting didn't hurt my now-sensitive eyes. Unfortunately, it made it difficult to see where I was.

Vague hulking shapes surrounded me. With a few eye blinks, they coalesced into some kind of vegetation, large thin leaves with sharp purplish edges, sprouting from branches almost as thick as my wrist. The branches twisted and turned in on themselves like people crossing their arms over their chests, giving the bushes an almost petulant attitude.

Trees with thin, greyish trunks hunched over them, as if to get a closer look. Through the dense thatch of leaves, I could see darkness above.

Still night then. Wherever this was.

Venir stood about ten feet away on a small mossy mound. He still wore the jeans and the grey flannel shirt. The heels of his cowboy boots sank into the moss.

He grinned.

"Glad you're having a good time," I said. "Could you maybe give me a heads up next time?" I touched my pounding temple.

"Whatsa matter, kid? Getting all sensitive? Sorry for the bum's rush but I didn't want us followed."

He turned and pushed through a set of branches, disappearing behind a thick pack of bushes.

"Hey, wait a minute." I hurried to follow. My shoes sank into the squishy ground. I had to pull hard to release his feet. The ground gave them up reluctantly with a loud plop and a puff of putrid air.

I covered my mouth and nose with my hand but it didn't help much. The stench even made my eyes water.

After a couple of steps, I got the hang of walking. With an exaggerated side to side motion, I managed to cross the patch to where the Elf had disappeared. As I struggled up to the small mound, the ground gained a firmer feel. Soon I didn't have to yank to release my shoes.

I removed my hand from my mouth and nose. The air still had a damp, musky scent, heavy with the odour of vegetation. But I could almost smell something else, something light and delicate.

Then I realized I wasn't smelling it. It was something magical I was sensing.

I reached for the spot where Venir had pushed through. The bushes clustered close together, the branches twisted back in on each other. The edges of the leaves were jagged and scratched at my hands as I tried to reach through. As I pushed, the leaves resisted. The edges snapped away from me, locked together until there was almost a wall of leaves.

Definitely something magical going on.

How was I supposed to follow Venir if I couldn't even manage to push through a thatch of leaves? Physical strength wasn't doing it.

Maybe I needed to try something else.

But I didn't have a lot of magic in me. Most of it had leaked away when I left the North Pole. I managed to keep a little for myself, enough to enchant the lower drawer in my desk, enough to *wink* myself to places when I needed to get there fast. Anything else drained my magical batteries almost to nothing.

So if I tried, it would only result in not much happening.

Wouldn't it?

This was a different place, a different realm. Maybe my magic would work differently here.

Yeah, maybe it would make things worse.

But I would never know if I didn't try.

I took a breath. I lifted my right hand, pressed my palm against the leaves and splayed my fingers.

"Move!"

I focused on my hand, sending a blast of my magic through to my palm.

The leaves blasted apart. Branches yanked up. Bushes bent away, almost perpendicular to the ground, leaving a five foot wide path. Through the gash, I spotted Venir peering from behind a dark trunk almost ten feet beyond. His face looked pale in the gloom.

"What the heck are you doing, kiddo?" he said. "Tryin' to announce us to the entire flippin' place?"

I lowered my hand. I wasn't even breathing hard. My heart thumped a little faster in my chest but slowed down quick enough.

That had taken hardly any effort and I had almost blown those bushes away.

I was going to have to be more careful. This place definitely had a different magical level then the normal human realm.

I slipped through the empty patch and hurried over to Venir.

"Sorry," I said. "I didn't realize I had that much magic here."

"Whada you talkin' about?" Venir said. "You got magic."

"Here yes," I said. "Not so much back in the human realm."

Venir chewed on his cigar. "Really? But at the North Pole, youse always…"

"That was at the North Pole," I said. "When I left there, I left most of my magic behind." I frowned. "Actually I was surprised you could do as much as you could, hiding your ears, your little fountain display, and getting us here." I waved a hand to take in the surrounding area.

Venir grinned. "Ain't no mystery in that. I ain't human like you, kiddo. I'm an Elf. My magic ain't linked to the North Pole. It's in me." He took the unlit cigar out of his mouth and jabbed it at his chest.

Interesting. I hadn't realized there would be a difference. I hadn't thought magic would work so well in the Human Realm but then again when the goblin had come through it had been able to use its magic.

Maybe it was only me who was handicapped in that area.

Great.

"So what now?" I said to the Elf.

Venir stuck the unlit cigar into his left side of his mouth. "Le' me just check." He stuck a hand into the jeans and pulled out a silver pocket watch. A silver chain telescoped out with it, hanging down. When he flicked the watch open, I saw sparkles of light flicker up and hover over the white face. They arranged themselves in little patterns that flashed in different colours. Red, blue, then green.

Venir gave a snort and snapped it shut. He stuffed it back into his pocket, the chain hung down, glinting in the dimness.

"He'll be here any minute now," he said. "We just gotta wait by the fountain. Come on."

Without waiting for my reply, the Elf ducked back behind the black truck. I heard his cowboy boots shuffling on the hard ground.

"Wait up," I said.

Damn Elves, always darting all over the place. At least in that respect Venir was typical, even if his look and vernacular wasn't.

I headed after him.

Past the black trunk, I found myself facing more dark trunks. Thin, maybe a foot or two in diameter, they seemed to be planted in rows. The ground was covered with a soft, moss-like ground cover that gave off a dim purple glow.

With the glow, it wasn't too hard to see where Venir had gone. The impression from his cowboy boots pressed into the purple vegetation but the closest prints to me were already starting to spring back.

If I didn't follow, I would lose the trail.

And maybe until I knew exactly where I was and what Venir was up to, I should stick very close to the Elf's trail.

I started to hop from one imprint to the next. With his shorter legs, Venir's stride was much shorter than mine and strangely enough, it made me move slower to make sure I didn't miss a step.

One of the impressions was near one of the dark trunks. Tottering, I put a hand to steady myself. The truck was smooth, almost silky under my hand and cool to the touch. As my palm rested on it, I noticed the trunk began to glow. A deeper purple hue spread from where my hand rested and raced upward.

I looked up.

About five feet above my head, branches appeared to uncoil from the trunk. Thick, leathery-looking leaves, bigger than my hands, spread out. Bright purple light began to glow from them.

"Stop that!"

Venir's sharp retort caught my attention. I jerked my hand from the trunk. Slowly the purple faded. Above my head, the leaves curled back up, the branches almost folded up.

Venir's white face appeared in the gloom. He glared at me.

"Don't touch anything," he said. "It'll suck yer magic out of ya and they'll know we're here."

"Who will know?" I said. "Where the hell are we?"

The Elf shook his head. "Come on. We got to go. Then I'll tell ya."

"Tell me now."

I crossed my arms over my chest. It probably made me look like a petulant child but I didn't care. Enough was enough. The Elf was going to give me some answers and now.

"We'll miss him!"

"We will for sure if you keep arguing," I said. I nodded toward the Elf's pocket watch. "Time is ticking."

Venir shook his head.

"Kiddo, you take the cake. Gettin' all uppity cuz you're having to wait a few minutes. It's like you don't care about Santa at all."

I stomped forward, not even looking at the moss under my feet. I jabbed a finger into Venir's chest.

"Don't you dare," I said. "You think you're the first to find out about this? There've been dead Santas all over the place for years, including one at a mall promotion I'm working and that KJ is covering for. Don't you tell me I don't care."

I yanked the envelope out of my pocket and pulled out the papers. Then I shoved them under the Elf's nose.

"What?" Venir said. "What's this?"

"This is what I've been investigating," I said. "Now are you going to help me or not?"

Venir's chubby fingers grabbed the papers. They shook as he flipped through them. His eyes widened and the pallor on his skin grew even whiter. Finally he left the papers droop in his hands. His mouth hung open. The unlit cigar balanced on the left side of his mouth.

"I didn't know," he said.

The obvious distress on his face made me feel ashamed. What was I doing, letting myself get riled because Venir was teasing me about being a private detective? Was I that petty? Was I that insecure about my own choices?

And with all the wisecracking from Venir, I had forgotten one other dependable trait in Elves. No matter what, they were driven to do good.

My face felt warm. I slipped the papers out of Venir's hands and refolded them. I stuffed them back into the envelope.

"Well," I said. "I just wanted to make sure we both knew how serious this was."

God, even to me that sounded like a lame excuse but Venir nodded.

"Yeah, I got it, kiddo. I didn't know it had gone so far." Venir shifted the unlit cigar from one corner of his mouth to the other. "We're in the Neutral Lands, the divide between the Seelie and Unseelie Court. You know Summer and Winter." I nodded at him to go on.

"Okay, so here the unbound fairies reside and they got a few lords overseein' 'em. They're like reserves for the main courts when they're needed. My contact is an officer in the army of the faerie lord Flaktar Dramal. He passed me information about this plot to kill Santa but that's all he told me. He said he'll only give details to someone higher up." Venir pointed at Noel. "Someone like you."

"Okay," I said, "but I've never heard of any Neutral Lands in any of the faerie lore. Are you sure this officer knows what he's talking about?"

Venir straightened his shoulders like a goose ruffling its feathers. "A' course he does. How can you not a heard about it? It's stopped the Great Fae War hundreds a years ago."

"And how did that get stopped?" I said.

Venir smirked. "Your dad did it."

I stiffened in shock. "What?"

"Oh yeah, the faeries here really respect your dad. He brokered the peace, set up the Neutral Lands, got it all organized."

"Okay," I nodded. Now I felt like an even bigger idiot. "Let's get that information then."

A grin lightened Venir's face, crinkling all the lines in his skin. "Right."

We started forward again, moving down a row between the trees. The air felt crisp and cool, carrying a sweet scent that reminded me of jasmine. Their feet make soft crunching sounds in the moss that covered the ground.

After they passed about a dozen trees, I spotted a stone wall just ahead. It was made of squarish bricks of a deep blue seemed to shimmer in the dark. As we moved closer, I saw that it towered above our heads, maybe twenty feet high. Soon the rows of dark trunks ended, leaving an empty space of about ten feet before the wall.

I glanced left and right. The wall extended into the gloom, as far as I could see in both directions.

Right where the tree line ended, I also noticed that the mossy ground cover stopped abruptly. Not in any natural fashion, a straight line cut across, extending to our right and left, the same way as the wall. In the space between them and the wall, the ground was bare, flat. Not even any pebbles or stones, not an indentation or curve to the ground, just empty space.

But not really empty. I could feel the quiver of magic.

I glanced down at Venir. The Elf had a frown on his face. He pulled out his pocket watch and stared at it.

"He's late," he mumbled.

"Do we wait?" I said.

Venir snapped the pocket watch closed and shoved it back in his pocket. "I can get us through there." He gestured at the wall. "But he was supposed to meet us on this side. It's the changing of the guard and he coulda slipped away."

"If he's running late will he have time?" I said.

Venir shrugged. "I don't know."

I looked back at the wall. From this distance, the bricks had a rough texture. The blue sparkled with inlaid facets that reminded me of quartz. With those indentations, they would be able to climb the wall easily. But that magic would give them away.

Even though the Elf wasn't looking at me, I sensed he was waiting for me to make the decision. But without all the information, how could I? Venir hadn't been exactly forthcoming.

And I hadn't been all that patient if I had to tell the truth.

Okay, if I was supposed to make the decision, I would make it.

"Take us through," I said.

Venir glanced up. "You sure?"

I nodded. "We can't wait forever. We have to know what's going on. Take us through."

"Whatever you say, kiddo." Venir closed his eyes and lifted his hands. He murmured too low for me to make out any words but already I could feel something shift in the air before them. A wedge in the magic encasing the wall.

Even in the dimness, I could see sweat glisten on Venir's forehead, dampening the tufts of hair on the sides of his head, darkening the back of his shirt.

The wedge seemed to widen.

And then I could see it.

Directly in front of them a path filled with glistening blue stones, laid out like stepping stones. As I moved closer, I saw they were a richer, deeper blue than the wall and almost reflective. They seemed to glow in the dimness.

"Go," Venir said.

I looked back.

The Elf was sagging, shoulders drooping, arms hanging slack at his sides. His hair dripped with perspiration. Even his ears looked like they were drooping. He drew in a ragged breath and waved a flopping hand at me.

"Go. I just need a minute."

I remembered KJ's warning about Venir. Unreliable. Disgraceful.

But that was KJ's opinion. I could just imagine what my brother would say about me.

Elves basically wanted to do good.

I turned back to the path and stepped onto the first stone.

It darkened, like the glow had snuffed out. Turned off. Disappeared.

Invisible.

Of course! The path the Elf had created would be invisible to the magic I felt swirling around him.

Next step. The glow vanished again. The next step and the next. Each one felt solid, strong beneath my feet even as the glow winked out. But if I walking on them extinguished the light, how would Venir get across.

I glanced back. Behind me, the dark blue stones glowed softly, the light a little less strong but there never the less. As I watched, Venir stepped on the first stone. The light flashed off.

Venir waved his hands at me in a shooing motion. He mouthed the words 'Get going.'

I faced the wall again and moved on. Each stone winked off. Each step brought me closer.

I could feel the magic in the air around me almost like an electrical current. Patterns of light darted just at the edge of my vision. I could feel it almost trying to catch my attention and I knew if I looked at it, it would catch me. My awareness would bring me to its awareness, and then this early warning system would trigger.

The wall. Focus on the wall.

Each step I drew closer. The blue of the bricks now

looked mottled, darkening as I got near. One final stone and I would reach it.

Then what?

But just as I stepped. The bricks in front of me faded and I was facing a door made from deep, dark brown wood. Made from the trees behind them, I suspected. Brass inlaid in a pattern, crossing the door, splitting it into quarters. Swirling script curled in the top sections.

But there was no handle.

How was I going to get through?

Behind me, he heard Venir's breath puffing. The Elf was close, would be right behind me. I stole a quick glance over my shoulder. Past Venir, the stones stayed stubbornly dark.

Only one way. Through the door.

When I had touched the trunk, it had responded to me. Maybe it would again.

I had no other choice.

I pressed my right palm against the side of the door, near where a handle would be. The wood felt smooth and cool under my skin. Then it began to get warmer. A light, whitish glow started. The sweet, heady scent that reminded me of jasmine deepened.

Behind me, I could feel the magical field stir. It was becoming aware of them.

Open door. Come on!

The wood moved. The door swung inward.

I jumped through.

The ground on the other side was a few inches below. I

staggered. My right ankle twisted and I fell, rolling over a carpet of soft grass. My shoulder bumped something, stopping my roll.

Good thing it had. I didn't want to be rolling into the middle of some courtyard, immediately obvious to some guards.

I sat up and brushed some loose grass from my knees. My right ankle ached a little but I didn't think I had sprained it. I put my left hand down. Felt silky fabric. An arm.

I twisted around to look.

And came face to face with a corpse.

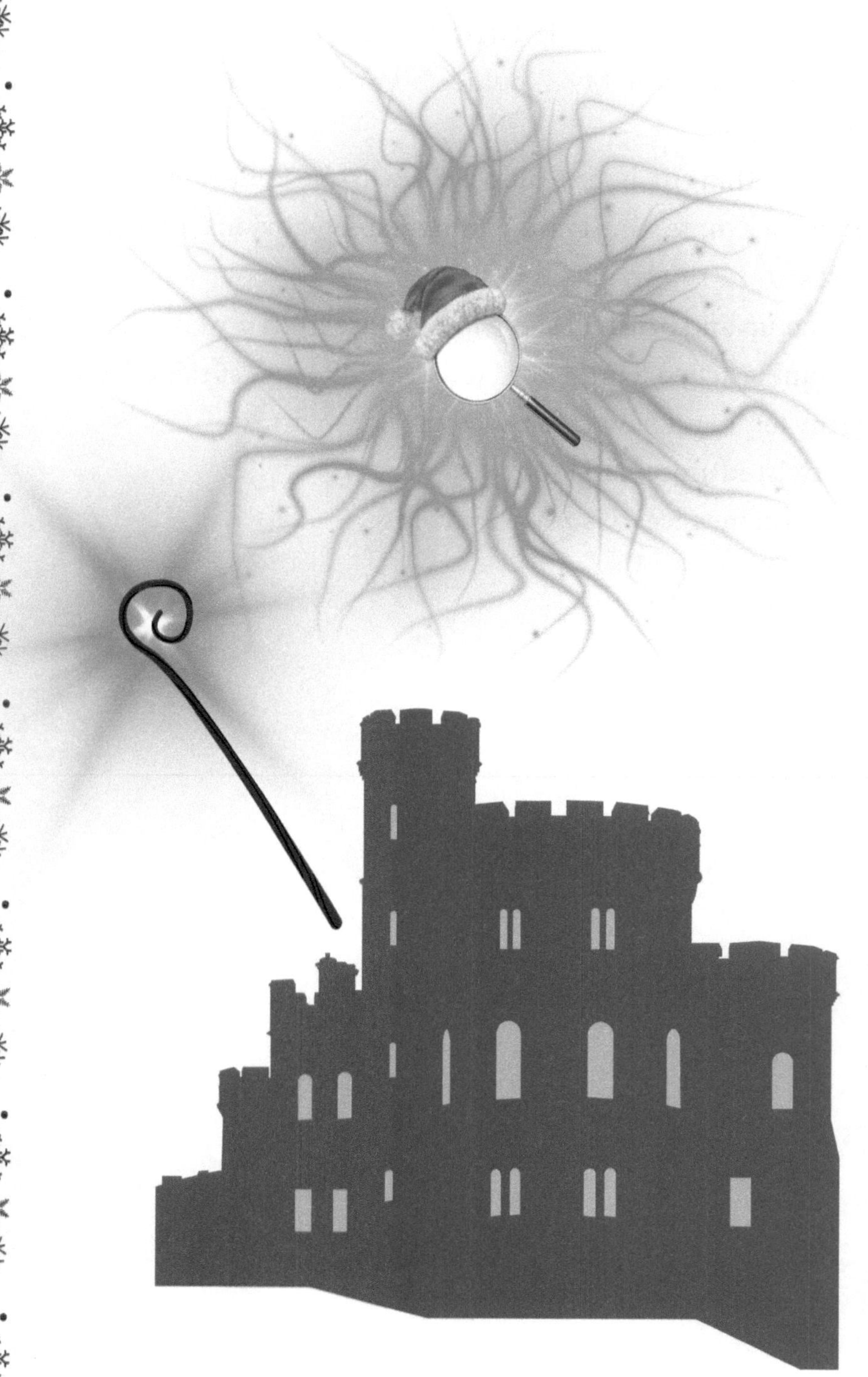

CHAPTER

ELEVEN

I stifled a yell. My heart hammered in my chest.

Now I knew what I had bumped into.

The corpse was lying face up. It was a young man with pale, ethereal features: slim, straight nose, delicate lips, long eyelashes that framed the pale green eyes that stared up at me, lifeless. He wore dark purple trousers and a matching dark purple shirt in a silken material. No, the shirt wasn't dark purple, it was the blood that stained his chest that made it look that dark. Leather-like straps hung from his shoulders, frayed at the ends. I saw a breast plate shoved down on the other side of the dead man's body.

It must have been a two or more person job. Someone to cut the straps to the breast plate and someone else to stab him in the chest.

How else would there be so much blood?

Just over the man's shoulders, I spotted two translucent ovals. They looked dull, lifeless, like shapeless plastic wrap instead of what they were. And oh yes, I realized what they were.

Faeirie wings.

A soft thump sounded behind me. I glanced over my shoulder.

Venir had landed on his rump. He jumped to his feet and brushed off the seat of his pants.

"Right," he said. "Let's find…"

As he looked up, he shut up.

Then his mouth dropped open.

"No! Lekzar!"

Venir shoved past me and knelt beside the fallen faerie. He shook the man, then pressed his fingers to the man's neck and felt his chest. Finally, Venir's shoulders sagged. He shook his head.

"No, I can't believe it. No."

The Elf mumbled the words over and over.

I glanced around. This close to the wall, the ground was sparsely decorated by short, spiny bushes set in decorative clumps in a somewhat uneven zig-zag pattern. Past them, I couldn't see much, the darkness was too thick. There might be something rising up in the distance but I couldn't tell.

And I really didn't want to know.

I touched Venir's shoulder. "I'm sorry for your friend."

"He wasn't just my friend, he was our contact," Venir said. "He was the one who knew everything."

I felt a chill trickle down my spine that had nothing to do with the evening air. "You don't know anything other than what you told me."

I didn't even bother to make it a question. It was obvious from the way Venir's shoulders drooped.

"We have to get back," I said. "I'll work on it from the human realm."

"You will be going nowhere, killer."

The deep voice rang out from the darkness in front of us. The clump of heavy footfalls echoed around us. I squinted but I could only make out shadows.

I pushed up from the ground. "Wait, we didn't..."

A creak sounded from my left. I jumped back.

A whoosh of air. The arrow thudded into the ground two inches from my feet. The silver end vibrated.

"Halt! Do not move," the voice commanded.

I froze, as much as I could freeze with my heart pounding so hard I felt like I was swaying back and forth like a metronome.

Footsteps moved closer. From the gloom, a tall, pale man emerged. He wore dark purple pants similar to the dead man's. His chest plate was securely fastened. It was decorated with an image of the black trees, a single dark trunk rising in the centre with the branches spilling at the top, unfolding with a multitude of crystals inlaid into the surface. They glittered in the dimness.

As he moved closer, I noticed the slender face, the slim nose, and the high cheekbones. A beard of light brown hair framed his mouth. Waves of brown hair flowed to his shoulders, tucked back behind sharply pointed ears. Pale green eyes glared across the space that separated them and made me realize that, boy, they sure looked similar to the dead man at his feet.

Oh, this was not good. This was so not good.

"Fiends, I arrest you in the name of Lord Flaktar Dramal, for the murder of my brother officer Lekzar Trayborn!"

So not good at all.

BEFORE I COULD SQUEAK OUT A DENIAL, THE FAERIE GUARDS HAD seized both me and Venir, dragging us off to what had to be the dungeon.

The guards on either side of me held my arms in a vise-like grip as they raced forward, dragging me along. After a moment, I realized they weren't just running, they were flying. The backs of the guards ahead of him blurred. Wings beating so fast I couldn't see them.

At this speed, I only got vague impressions of our surroundings. The soft moss-like grass spreading out around us. The intricate shadows of trees and bushes forming odds shapes, the edges blurring against the black sky.

But one final shape grew in solidity and height as we raced forward.

A looming fortress. It soon drew high enough to blot out the dark sky from my sight.

The wall looked like it was made of matte black glass, smooth, hard, perfectly formed and fitted together with a barely centimeter of space. Ahead of us, the first officer lifted his hand. The black bricks shimmered in front of him then vanished, revealing a doorway.

I felt myself thrust through then the hands let go. My feet hit the ground, but my velocity wouldn't be stopped. My left foot folded over the right one. I tried to stagger but couldn't pull my left leg out fast enough.

I hit my right hip and shoulder hard against a rock floor that felt like solid cement. I tried to roll to lessen the damage, but as I smacked against the far wall, it felt like I had only managed to spread bruises across my body.

A yelp sounded behind me.

Venir came flying through the air, his ears flapping at the sides of his head as though they were trying to help him stay in the air. Before I could roll aside, the Elf smashed into me, a tangle of arms, elbows, and knees.

A few more aches to add to the bruises.

As I disentangled myself from Venir, the opening on the opposite wall vanished, leaving only a tingling sensation on my skin. Now only the matte black bricks faced me.

Venir groaned as he got to his feet. Somewhere he'd lost his unlit cigar and he looked naked without it. His white hair stuck out at the sides of his head. His ears drooped. Dirt smeared across his shirt.

I figured I probably didn't look much better.

In fact, it was surprising I could manage to see anything at all.

I turned my head to look around. Pain shot down my neck, through my body, making me wince. Everywhere I felt bruised. I held onto the wall as I pushed myself up to my feet.

In the ceiling corners, pale white light flickered, casting a soft glow through the room. Whatever it was, I couldn't see any fixture. Probably magical.

I turned back to the Elf.

"I'm sorry about your friend."

Venir shook his head. "He musta been discovered," he said. "Damn fool. I told him to be careful. Not to try anything stupid. I told him I was bringing help." He shook his head again.

"He didn't tell you anything else?" I asked.

"Just that someone was planning to kill Santa." Venir bowed his head. "I thought we had more time. Didn't know they was getting so close to doing it." He gestured toward my pocket and the stash of papers.

The Elf looked forlorn. Without the unlit cigar and his usual swagger, he looked thinner, more fragile.

Hopeless.

I felt the stirrings of anger inside. Dammit, I had been reacting too long to this. First a missing Santa, then a dead one, and now this, Venir's contact dead and a credible threat to the real Santa – to Dad – was still out there!

No more. I wasn't going to put up with this any more.

I wasn't a Kringle for nothing.

I meant to leap to my feet but the bruises and aches made it more of a creeping stagger. Finally, I got my feet under me and pushed myself up to my full height. While my anger flamed, my body was reminding me to take it easy. My shoulder and hip still ached from when I had landed.

Okay, so I wouldn't win any marathons. I didn't need to in order to use my magic.

And here it appeared I had full use of it.

I straightened, feeling my back crack, and put a hand on Venir's shoulder.

"We're not going to let them do it," I said. "I've got access to all my magic now and we're getting out of here."

"Um," Venir said. "Kiddo."

I stepped past him, moving to the centre of the cell. It was about a twenty by ten foot space. I focused on where the door had disappeared, at the same smooth, black bricks that now glinted in the dim light. A tug on my shirt from Venir distracted me, but I shrugged the Elf off.

Focus. Concentrate.

I felt the telltale tingle in my mind. My blood felt warm, rushing out to my extremities. The hairs on the back of my neck shot up, followed by the hairs on my arm. I caught a whiff of cinnamon, clean and pure. I felt my magic crackle in the air. Felt it swirl around me. Felt it ready, ready...

Ready to blast out.

I thrust my hands toward the wall, toward the opening, focusing.

My magic rushed out, blanketing the wall.

And bounced back.

I felt the shock of the ricochet before it hit me. The blast of my returning magic seared my nose hairs. I threw my arms out.

"*Velitas,*" I chanted. A gathering spell.

Like I meant to do this. Sure.

The blast of power swirled around me. The stench of burning cinnamon clogged my lungs. I felt it scorching my skin then the burning reduced to an itching and then finally to a tingling.

Then to nothing.

I staggered back, felt Venir's hand tighten on my elbow, keeping me upright. My whole body felt even more bruised, if that was possible.

"I tried to tell you," Venir said. "The wall is bewitched against magic."

"Thanks the warning," I said.

"You wouldn't listen," Venir said.

"Okay." I straightened. My back creaked. My knees cracked. I could still smell the lingering scent of cinnamon, rank and sour. It burned the back of my throat. I coughed and spat it out. My saliva glistened on the mud grey floor then vanished, absorbed into the surface.

Interesting. The cell was warded against magic but had its own.

Fat lot of good that knowledge would do me.

"We have to get out of here," I said to the Elf. Venir nodded.

"Yeah," he said. "And how are we gonna manage that? They got us bound up tight."

Bound and jailed on suspicion of murder of a faerie officer. The Lord here, Flaktar Dramal, would not take kindly to the crime. If they were lucky, they would just face imprisonment. If they were unlucky...

I had heard rumours about faerie torments. It wasn't something I wanted to experience.

I limped across to the wall and placed my hand on it. The black bricks felt smooth and cool against my palm. I could still a residual tingle on my skin. Bits of my own magic still locked up in the wall.

Interesting. It wasn't a perfect ricochet. A little of my magic had been absorbed into the spell that encased the bricks.

Now why would that be?

I stared at the bricks. The slim lines shimmered. For a brief moment I caught a glimpse of the door out of the corner of my eye. I blinked. It vanished.

My palm pressing against the brick tingled.

Maybe...

I took a deep breath and let it out slowly. At the same time, I fed a bit of magic down to my hand. It rolled off my shoulders and trickled down my arm, drip-dripping into my hand. After a moment, I felt the build-up in the wall, the beginning of resistance, of ricochet. I pulled it back. Slower. It had to be even slower.

Patience. Something I was never that good at.

Another deep breath. A little more magic doled out. Drip by drip.

At this slow pace, the wall didn't react.

But it should have. It shouldn't matter how fast or slow my application of magic, if it was a true ricochet spell, it should still rebound back to me.

But they had made a mistake with the spell. In order to strengthen the rebound effect, they had restricted the type matching. Every creature that did magic did it in its own way, had its own blend. Affecting other types of magic demanded a certain relaxing of power in order to broaden the effect. With sufficient power or the desired effect, it didn't matter but when you wanted to be precise...

They had infused the wall with faerie magic. The spell was strong enough to ricochet any massive blast from me, but my magic was sufficiently different that a little got through. The wall absorbed a small portion of it.

And a little was all I needed to create a wedge and crack the opening.

I kept breathing, slow and steady. Letting the smallest bit of my magic trickled down into the wall. With every moment, I could feel it resonating up my arm. The outline of the door shimmered in and out, still more faded than not, but now it seemed to linger long enough for me to get a good look at it.

Triangular locks showed on three sides of the door handle, above, below, and to the left.

Even if I managed to stabilize the door, I didn't know if I could get through three locks like that.

A low grunt sounded at my elbow.

Venir stood peering at the door, rubbing his chin. He glanced up at me.

"Yer a little more useful than I expected, kiddo," he said.

I wanted to make some crack back at the Elf but I didn't have the energy. Holding back my magic was difficult work. The slow drip-drip took constant focus and concentration. If I even let a small blast through, it could undo all of my work.

Sweat trickled down my forehead and stung my eyes. Effort dried my mouth and gummed the stale cinnamon taste on my lips.

"Just a little more," Venir said.

He reached his stubby fingers toward the door handle, aiming for the locks. They still looked like shadows but every moment brought them into sharper focus.

Just a little bit more.

My head pounded in pace with my heart. My breath was getting ragged. It was harder and harder to keep an even pace. I felt the power of my magic building around me. It hadn't felt this strong since I left the North Pole. I had forgotten how easy it was to let go of it, how much of a challenge it was to keep it under a tight rein.

Back in Toronto, it was a bare shadow of itself, hardly

any trouble at all. I barely had enough to *wink* myself across town a couple of times a week.

But now it was like a tidal wave.

And it wanted to flow.

"Open the door." My voice came out in a low croak.

Venir tilted his head up. "Huh?"

"Open. The. Door." I clenched my teeth, barely holding on.

"Oh right." Venir bent to the door handle. The triangular locks shimmered. Venir's fingers twisted and turned, forming magical shapes and images in the air. The after images felt like they shimmered in my eyes but when I blinked they vanished. Still I felt the tug of them reverberate through me.

For some reason the Elf's magic was resonating with my own. Why would that be? He was human, well, mostly. My magic came from being the son of Kris Kringle who was emboldened as Santa Claus, a figure riff with magic. Although I was basically human, the magic of Santa Claus and the North Pole infused me even when I wasn't there. The only way to get rid of it would be to fully renounce it forever and even though I wanted to be a private detective, I wasn't going to completely give up my birthright.

Of course. That was why the Elf's magic resonated with me, it came from the North Pole as well. So it only made sense that it would magnify mine.

Uh oh.

I felt the build-up in the wall. All the hairs on my body

quivered. My skin felt parched. Magic swirled in my head, raced down my arms.

Venir reached for the door.

"No!" I grabbed the Elf's elbow, yanking his arm up.

Venir's fingers missed the handle. But still pointed at the door.

My magic flared out. I tried to yank it back, but I was out of practice. It had been so long since I had had any real power.

It mingled with the Elf's and exploded out of Venir's fingertips.

I shut my eyes.

The flash blazed white against the insides of my eyelids. A scorching flare.

But where was the ricochet? Why wasn't it hurling them back against the opposite wall? Why wasn't it frying their bones?

Cautiously, I opened my eyes a sliver.

The door was gone, leaving a smoking hole in the middle of the brick wall. Ragged edges shimmered with residual energy. I could almost feel it sparking where the faerie magic hit the last bits of my magic.

Just enough of it had infiltrated and wrecked the integrity of the spell to short circuit the ricochet. Just enough to blast open the door.

Venir let out a whoop. He yanked his arm out of my hand and scurried forward. He poked his head out of the whole and looked right then left.

When he turned back, a big grin lit up his face.

"Great job, kiddo," he said. "The coast is clear."

The Elf took a big step over the ragged threshold of the ruined door frame. His cowboy boots clicked on the hard stone floor.

He started to turn back, motioning to me.

I swayed a little on my feet. My muscles felt sore and put-out. First being yanked into another realm, then being tossed around the room, both physically and magically, and finally enduring the effects of such a large focus of magic. My body wanted to just curl up in a ball.

Later. After they got the heck out of here.

"C'mon." Venir stuck his hand through the hole.

I grabbed it and used it to leverage myself out of the cell.

My feet hit the solid floor. The air felt cool on my skin. Refreshing. I took a deep breath.

In front of me, Venir grinned. Then the grin slowly faded as he looked past me.

No. Oh no.

I did not want to turn around. No, I didn't.

I turned.

And the flare of faerie magic blinded me.

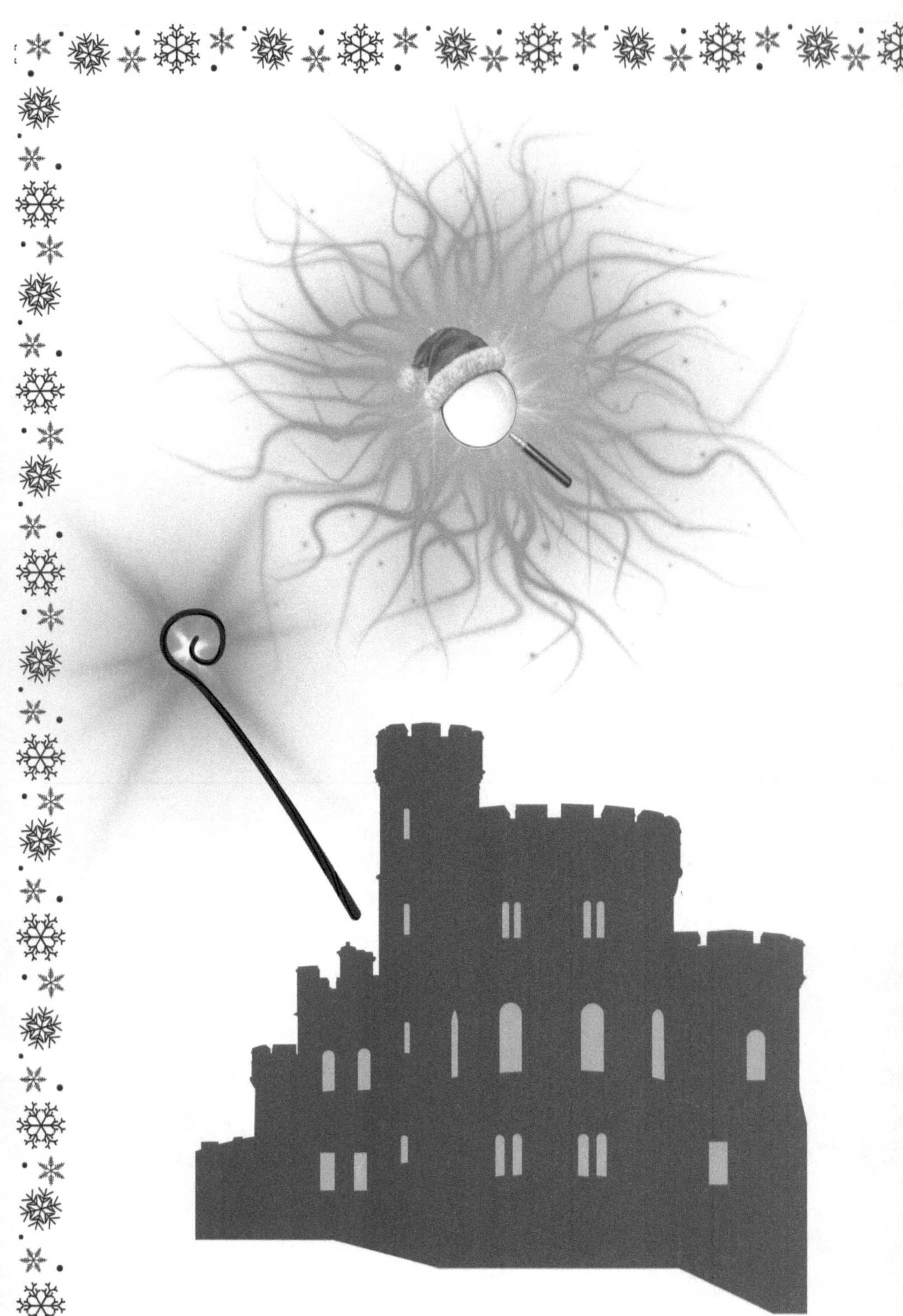

CHAPTER
TWELVE

"Do not move, monsters!"

The voice snarled from behind the glare.

I put my hands up, spreading the fingers to show they were empty. Venir did the same.

"I said do not move."

"Okay," I said. "Can you turn down the light? It's rather bright."

The light dimmed, retreating to a soft yellowish glow coming from a small orb. I blinked several times until my eyes adjusted.

A young female fae stood before us, holding the orb in her hand. She stood just over five feet tall. She wore dark purple trousers stuffed into worn black boots. Her shirt was a light grey with black piping down the arms. Faint black wings rose above her shoulders, the membrane looking as thin as plastic wrap. Black hair pulled back from her face and fastened into a bun that poked just above the top of her head. Her pale features were fine but the grim set of her mouth took away some of the prettiness. She glared at me with sharp green eyes that seemed to glow in the light from the orb.

"You will pay for what you have done to my cousin," she said. She lifted the orb higher. The glow shifted from yellow to a fiery orange.

"Hey, are you Darya?" Venir asked.

The woman stopped. The angry orange glow in the orb lessened. She frowned at Venir.

"How do you know my name?"

"Right, of course you are," Venir said. He wagged a finger at her. "I thought so. You're just like Lekzar said you were. Though he didn't mention how pretty you were."

The woman stiffened. A scowl darkened her face.

"You lie. You did not know my cousin. He would never consort with your kind."

"He would if he knew someone was trying to kill Santa Claus."

This time she lowered the orb until it was almost to her side. "How would he know that?"

"Good question," I said. "We came here to ask him for more details. It isn't just a threat anymore. Someone is trying to make it happen. They've been practicing." I reached into my pocket.

At my movement, her hand jerked up, lifting the orb again.

"Easy," I said. I moved more slowly, gently peeling the paper out of my pocket before offering it to her.

She eyed it warily. "What is that?"

"A list of missing or dead Santas from my realm," I said. "Someone has been practicing, gathering strength and knowledge. They'll be ready for the real thing soon."

Darya tilted her head. "Why do you care?"

I glanced down at Venir. I hadn't planned to reveal my identity like this. It was one thing to reveal it to Venir's contact but with him dead, I didn't want it to be used against me, or against Dad.

Venir shrugged. His lips twisted in a frown, as if he still had the unlit cigar in his mouth.

Great, no help there.

And no real choice. Not really.

Not if they wanted to get out of here.

"I'm Noel Kringle," he said. "Youngest son of Kris Kringle, Santa Claus."

Her fingers tightened on the orb. The light flared fiery orange again, deep and angry.

"You lie!"

"I am not," I said.

She lifted her chin as if to look taller. "Prove it."

Prove it? How could he prove it? I threw another glance at Venir. The Elf looked almost as shocked as I felt.

Great, still no help.

How could I prove my identity to this faerie? I had a wallet full of identification but that meant nothing here in the Faerie Realm. If she had been human I could probably tap into her Christmas memories and pull out her favourite gift. But faeries didn't have Christmas.

Did they?

She'd certainly reacted to the name 'Santa Claus.' Back in my realm, I knew there were other names for Christmas, other traditions. Dad had used to joke about how many different names he had. Was it possible that he didn't just mean in that realm?

Did this realm have its own version of a night of gift-giving?

How did she know the name 'Santa Claus'?

I focused on her green eyes and allowed my attention to narrow. With my full magic, it took only a moment to connect into her memory, to find the celebration of Fae-Thaal, Holy Sun, the darkest night before the coming of spring.

A night of gift-giving. Of celebration.

A night of Santa Claus.

I caught my breath.

Santa Claus here in the Faerie Realm.

And if here, why not in all the realms?

I knew Dad worked hard but I had no idea.

I shook that thought away. Focus. I had to find her favourite present from Santa.

And there it was. Her first magic orb when she was four

years old. As tiny as a single pea. Clear with one thread of white swirl through it, off centre, creating a beautiful flaw. Darya had learned her first castings with that orb.

I felt a slight pressure in the front pocket of my pants. Slowly he transferred the papers into my left hand.

"I have something for you in my pocket," I said. "Can I take it out?"

Her green eyes narrowed. Finally she gave a nod. "Yes."

It took me a moment for my fingers to close on the tiny round bead at the bottom of my pocket. Soft lint stuck to my nails as I pulled it out. I blew it away, careful to make sure the tiny prize remained.

Then I held it out to her.

The tiny clear orb was almost invisible in my palm but Darya sucked in a breath in surprise. She leaned forward as if to get a better look but wouldn't step forward. I tried to stretch my hand closer to her. It made my muscles ache.

Finally she took a step closer. Then another. Her hand trembled a little as she reached out toward the tiny orb.

"How?" she said.

"It was your favourite gift for Fae-Thaal from Santa," I said.

She jerked her hand back. The orb in her other hand started to glow fiery orange again.

"How can you know this? How?"

"I told you," I said. "I'm the youngest son of Kris Kringle. I know all about people's favourite gifts." I held up the papers. "Someone's trying to kill Santa. Your cousin was trying to stop it and I believe it got him killed. Will you help us?"

A line appeared between her brows as she frowned. That look wasn't too promising but as her hand lowered, the orb in her palm began to dim. After a moment, all light faded, leaving behind a polished light blue glow.

"Lekzar spoke with you?" she said.

I started to turn but Venir popped forward.

"Yeah, that's right. He contacted me through some friends of mine."

"Friends?" she said.

"We gotta game going. It's no big deal." Venir shrugged and spread his hands.

Darya started to frown again. Her fingers tightened on the orb.

Better reassure her before she changed her mind.

"Obviously Lekzar wanted to help stop this atrocity," I said. "Venir and I came here to talk to him. You wouldn't know what else he could have told us?"

Darya shook her head. Her shoulders seemed to stiffen then slump a little. She slipped the orb back into a small pouch at her waist.

"We were no longer so close, Lekzar and I," she said. "He did not take his oaths seriously. He preferred to spend his time on luxuries."

"But wasn't he an officer?" I said.

Darya seemed to stiffen. Her chin lifted high again. The tips of her black wings quivered.

"Our family name affords us the title," she said. "Lekzar thought it was fun."

"You wanted to earn it," I said.

The hand that hovered over the small pouch tightened into a fist.

Oh, she didn't like that I had figured *that* out.

"We really need to know more about what Lekzar knew," I said. "Can you help us? Preferably somewhere away from here?"

I gestured at the black brick walls around us.

Darya hesitated a moment and then nodded. She turned and waved us on. "Follow."

We hurried after her. Although she was much shorter than me, I had to run to just barely keep up with her. Her boots seemed to glide over the hard stone floor but then I noticed how her wings vibrated.

Sure, flying. No wonder I could barely keep up.

I glanced over my shoulder to see Venir chugged along behind me. The Elf's face was red from exertion. His ears flapped at the sides of his head. But still he made a go on motion to me.

The hall dead-ended against another wall of the same matte, black bricks. Darya lifted her orb toward it. The bricks shimmered and a dark wood door appeared. The same three triangle locks showed surrounding the handle. This time this handle shone with a coppery glow instead of looking dull.

Probably because she was accessing it properly while I had been trying to break out.

She turned back to us, her face serious. Her right hand clenched the pouch at her waist.

"When you cross the threshold of this door, an alarm will sound. I can not deactivate it. I do not have the authority. We will have only moments to escape the compound. You must follow me and keep up. Do you understand?"

"Ah, yes," I said. I glanced back at Venir who stood just behind me, hands resting on his knees as he bent over panting. With his short legs, would the Elf be able to keep up?

Venir waved away the concern in my face. "I'm fine. I can do it. Let's stop with the yakkin' already."

"Then we'll do it." I turned back to Darya.

"Before we go, I wish to see your documents." She held out her hand.

After a moment, I passed her the papers. I knew magic allowed them all to talk to each other, to understand each other, that was one of the effects. I remembered Dad teaching us when me and KJ were kids about how magic facilitated communication across all realms. I hadn't thought it would apply to written communication.

But apparently it did.

Darya flipped through the pages. Her face became even paler until she let the pages hang limp from her fingers.

"All of these were Santa Claus?" she said. "We believed it was only one."

"It is only one," I said. "These men were actors portraying Santa Claus."

"Portraying?"

"Pretending to be."

"We only told stories," she said. "We did not do this pretending." She held out the papers. I took them back, folded them, and stuffed them back into my pocket.

"They still don't deserve to die," I said.

"No, they do not." She nodded to the door. "Are you ready?"

I glanced at Venir. The Elf was standing upright again, his breath easy. He gave a nod and a thumbs up.

"Ready," I said.

Darya gave a final nod. She turned back to the door. She passed her hands over it and it dissolved away. Beyond, I saw the lilting curve of the mossy grounds. Cool night air, tinged with a citris scent, drifted in.

Then light exploded around us.

It bathed the hall in brilliant yellow. Through the doorway, I saw how it lit up the ground halfway to the outer walls.

There was no sound but still, this was some alarm.

Darya raced out. I followed right behind. My feet hit the ground hard. The moss felt almost like a carpet, giving me a bit of a bounce. But each step reverberated up my body, reminding me of every ache.

A soft buzzing sounded behind me. I glanced over my shoulder.

At first, all I saw was Venir running, puffing to keep up. The Elf was pumping with his arms, knees lifting high as he ran. Then I caught movement behind him.

Figures rose up from the top of the building behind us. Arms stretched out, reached behind them, then drew forward.

They let go.

Arrows hissed through the air. They thudded into the ground around them. Sparks flashed up in different colours. Flares of red, blue, purple, orange.

The air tingled around me. Magic. Faerie magic. I felt it reaching for me, trying to grab on.

An arrow smacked right in front of me. Without thinking, I jumped high over it. Golden light flared from the arrow, tried to grab me.

My feet hit the ground. Don't look back, keep going.

I ran. The cold tendrils of magic slipped away even as they tried to hold on.

The air tasted of ash. Flares of light burst all around, blinding me. My eyes never had a chance to adjust. I just kept running, running blind. My lungs ached from the exertion and cold air. My feet kept pounding on the ground.

Then Venir's wordless shout stopped me.

I spun, squinted behind me. The colourful flares of light made everything hazy. Smoke drifted across my vision, making it even harder to see. Orange flickered on the left, a tongue tasting the air, find it good.

Flames.

Shadows moved through the smoke. Lights flicker. Near the ground, I caught sight of a flopping ear, white hair frazzled around it.

Venir!

I took a step forward then felt a hand grab my arm, stopping me. Darya yanked me back.

"Let go," I said. "Venir..."

"Too late," she said. "They have already got him."

"No!"

"Come on." She pulled harder. Her faerie strength overpowered me, but I managed to dig in my heels, make it harder for her to drag me away.

The smoke thickened. Flashes of light dissolved into soft glows. Figures swarmed out of the smoke, cut off Venir from my sight.

Then a taller figure stepped in front of the flames, lifting its arms. Aiming at me.

I turned and ran into the darkness.

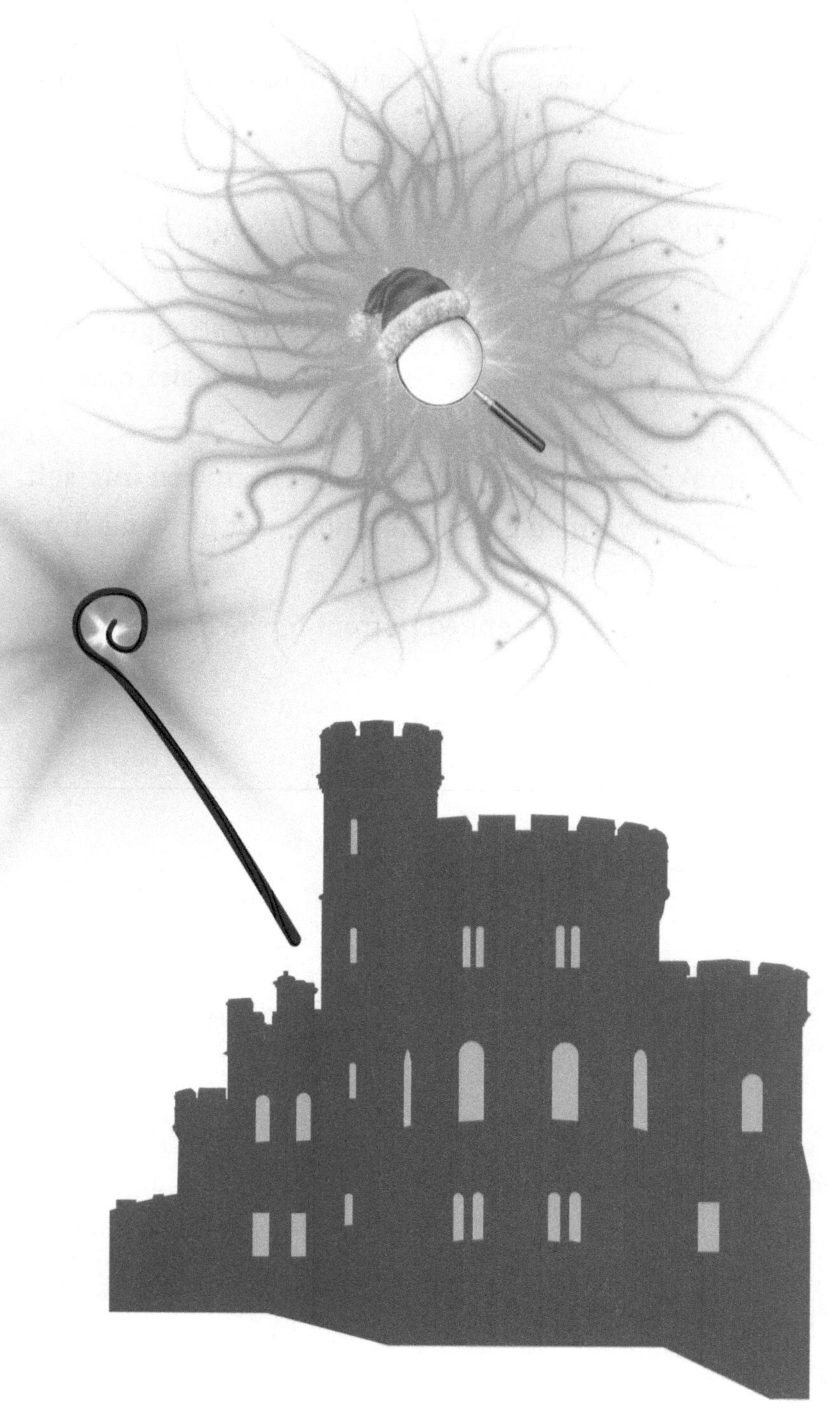

THIRTEEN

By the time my eyes adjusted to the darkness, I found myself under the thick canopy of the black trees. Their silky trunks glimmered in the starlight. My feet sank into the mossy carpet that covered the ground.

I stopped beside one of the trees and gulped in air. Ahead of me, Darya slipped beyond one of the trunks. Her black hair almost gleamed blue in the dark.

"Why are you stopping?" she said. "They are right behind us."

My entire body ached. Muscles unused to running were screaming at me, on top of the bruises from being thrown across a room. But none of that mattered as much as the ache I felt inside.

I had left a man behind. I had never done that.

"Venir," I said.

Darya moved closer. Her pale face appeared in the darkness, like a shimmering wraith.

"Will being captured help him? I think not. And you are in no condition to best them."

"I can't just leave him," I said.

"And you cannot help him like this." Darya tilted her head. "Would he wish you to abandon your mission to stop this plot?"

"No," I said. Damn the halls.

"Then come."

She stepped away. I had no choice but to follow her.

But I didn't have to like it.

I fell into the same side to side walking pattern, letting the mossy buoyancy do some of the work of pushing me forward. I noticed Darya walked in similar fashion, with a more gliding smooth stroke, like she was skating across the top of the moss. She moved quickly in and out of the deep shadows, skirting close to the inky blackness of the trees.

As we moved deeper and deeper into the forest, the orderly rows of the trees broke down. The moss deepened until it was almost up to my ankles. Squat, thick-leafed bushes appeared, growing near the trees and then starting to fill in the spaces. The leaves were heavily veined and looked darker than any green would ever look.

"Stop," I finally called out to Darya as the bushes pressed against my legs. I could almost feel them tingle with every touch.

Like the trees, they would suck out my magic if they could.

From about ten metres ahead, Darya paused to look back. Her pale face was the only part of her I could see clearly in the darkness. She hesitated and then returned to me, moving faster than I could through the moss and bushes.

"They will not stop looking for us," she said.

"Because they believe I killed your cousin?" I said.

She nodded. "And they will think I conspired with you."

She kept her face turned away but I could tell how much it hurt her to admit that. Just by helping them she'd put herself in the line of fire. To be thought of as a betrayer of your lord and a murderer of your kin... I shook my head.

"I'm sorry," I said.

"Lekzar would have done the same," she said. A bitter smile twisted her lips. "Of course, he was a damn fool."

"Or an honourable man," I said.

That thought made me wince. How honourable was I being leaving Venir behind? But the Elf had known what we were getting in to. Maybe if I could find the information Lekzar had gathered, it might be enough to bargain for Venir's freedom.

Or point to the real killer.

Two birds, one very large stone, assuming Lekzar's killer was the same one plotting to kill Santa Claus. Unless Lekzar had other enemies, the odds were pretty high they were one and the same.

"What else can you tell me about your cousin?" I said to Darya.

"He was the youngest of us and he acted the part," she said. "Always casting prank spells. Always pushing the boundaries. He would jump into the Between but not cross directly into other Realms. We are forbidden by the King to cross out of our Realm but there is no such restriction to the Between. Lekzar used this to stretch the spirit of the law. He never crossed into other Realms but he could see into them. Sometimes he could wield influence with his fae power." She shook her head. "He was always doing nonsense like that."

"Could that be how he learned about this plot?" I said.

Darya bowed her head. She seemed intensely interested in her footsteps. I struggled to keep pace even as her steps quickened.

"He did not tell me," she said. "He did not talk to me very often."

Pain tinged her voice, hinting at words unspoken. Normally I wouldn't want to pry but this was not ordinary circumstances. One person in this Realm was already dead, not to mention Venir's fate, and all the others already dead in the Human Realm.

There was no time for niceties.

But that didn't mean I wouldn't try to spare her feelings.

"Maybe he didn't want to worry you," I said.

Darya shook her head. "He knew I disapproved of his activities. I told him often enough and finally told him it would reflect badly on me if he continued. He took it to mean

I wished distance between us. I did not." She lifted her face and glared at me. Her eyes flashed with defiance. I met her gaze calmly. A flush darkened her pale cheeks. She dropped her gaze.

"Perhaps I did," she said quietly. "But I only wished him to mature, to stop playing childish games. I had no idea it would come to this. If I had been willing to listen, if I had still been a confidante to him..."

"You might be dead too," I said. "Make no mistake, Lekzar stumbled onto something he wasn't supposed to and it killed him. But he was trying to do the right thing, trying to stop it. I say we shouldn't let his sacrifice be in vain."

Darya lifted her head. Her green eyes seemed even more luminous. "Yes, I agree."

"Great," I said. "Now where would he have cast the spell to cross into the Between? I don't suppose he'd do it anywhere in the castle." I jerked a thumb back the way we had come.

"No, such magic would be detected immediately there," Darya said. "He would probably have done it some ways from here. There are a set of old ruins where we used to play as children. No one goes there. It is probably the only place where Lekzar could cast his spells without inter-ruption."

I nodded. "That sounds like the place. Can you get us there fast?"

"As fast as necessary."

She clamped her hand around my left bicep. It felt like

being gripped by a vice. Before I could ask her to loosen her grip, she leapt into the air.

And dragged me with her.

Her black wings blurred. My arm tingled where her hand grasped me. The effect of magic. She wasn't just carrying me with her wings but with her fae magic as well.

Cold air whipped my face. Wide leaves scratched at me as they ascended through the trees, then they were gone. Dark sky soared above them. The sparkle of strange stars dotted the sky in odd configurations. In the distance, dark clouds obscured the sky, blurring the edges of the trees.

It wasn't quite the same as flying in the sleigh. I had often taken the reindeer out for practice runs. Eight reindeer pulling together created a stable flight that being dragged by one faerie couldn't match.

High wind whipped my face and made me feel wobbly in her grip. I glanced down at the canopy passing only a few feet below me. The leaves seemed to move and sway like an ocean but I knew it wouldn't catch me the same way if I fell. There would be no cushioning that blow.

My heart pounded. My armpits felt moist but if there was any other sweat on me, the wind wicked it away. My mouth felt dry. My nose throbbed with the cold air.

The canopy below me dropped away, leaving a deep darkness to the ground below. I caught sight of suggestions of buildings, humps that rose up below us, but they were gone so fast I couldn't tell. I couldn't tell how fast we were moving although the wings on Darya's back were almost invisible.

Dad had never let me run the reindeers *this* fast.

The tingling on my left arm started to weaken. Darya's grip was lessening. I glanced over at her. Even in the darkness, her pale skin shone with a strange luminance. Now I could see her lips pressed tight together, her forehead crinkled in concentration.

We started to loose altitude. I caught more details of the ground they were passing. Short, bristly-looking grass sprouted in tuffs on rough dirt. I couldn't see any paths or roads, just the ground. Hard, uneven.

And coming up fast!

I felt her fingers slip on my arm. The ground soared closer. I pulled my legs up. Closer.

Her hand let go. I fell. The ground rushed up.

My right foot hit first. Stayed straight then twisted. My leg buckled.

I turned it into a roll.

I tucked my head, let the brunt hit my shoulder and back as my body turned. I did one full somersault and half of a second one before I ended up lying on his back, face up to the dark sky. My shoulders ached and my back felt scraped, but I was alive.

After a moment, I moved my limbs, testing, climbing to my feet. My right ankle ached a little but not enough for a sprain. Just a hard twist. Nothing broken. I took a deep breath and let it out in relief.

Darya landed in front of me. Her head bowed.

"I am sorry I could not hold you up," she said.

"That's okay," I said. "You brought me close enough to the ground that I landed safe. At least you didn't drop me over the trees."

When she glanced up, I could see the weariness in her face. Her black wings even seemed to droop over her shoulders.

"Are we close?" I said.

She nodded. "Just over that rise."

She pointed back behind herself. The ground sloped upward. Hard packed earth, jagged and interspersed with the squat, prickly looking vegetation. Even the narrow leaves looked like they had spikes on them.

"Let's go."

She led the way, darting up the slope with the surefootedness of a reindeer leaping through snow. I trudged after her. Each step felt uneven or brushed too close to the spindling thorns that tore at my pants. My right ankle twinged.

The air held a sharp tinge of something that reminded me of furniture polish, harsh and coated with lemon. As I passed one of the shorter bushes, the thin leaves shifted, facing their faces toward me. Their edges uncurled as they tried to press closer.

Coveting my magic, like the trees. I would have to be careful of the vegetation in this Realm.

I scrambled up a jutting slope to land where Darya crouched, waiting. In the dark, her clothes blended in, leaving only her pale face showing. She was frowning. As I crouched at her side and peered over the lip of the rise, I could see why.

Piles of rubble formed an uneven circle on a flat empty space below us. I could still smell the dust hanging in the air. But it could just be from the light breeze that brushed my hair across my forehead. It didn't have to mean anything else.

I was always such the optimist.

"Is that how it looked before?" I said.

Darya shook her head.

So much for optimism.

"They were ruins," she said, "but still enough left to see the pillars and part of a wall there." She pointed to the left, at a large pile of crumbled dirt.

There wasn't even a single brick left.

Someone wanted to make damn sure that any residual energy held in the ruins was destroyed.

Or at least they'd tried to. Maybe a trace remained.

I just couldn't give up on that optimism crap.

"Let's go down there," I said.

"Why? It is destroyed. There will be nothing remaining."

Her head stayed bowed. Her hair obscured her face.

"Maybe there'll be something," I said. "We won't know if we don't look. It might help point us in a further direction to look to find your cousin's killer. We need to to get Venir back." I touched her shoulder. "Please."

She lifted her head. "But it has been destroyed. Whatever magic that was there is gone."

"Maybe not all of it," he said. "You used to be close to your cousin. Maybe you'll feel something."

Damn my optimism.

But she listened. Her shoulders straightened. She gave a nod.

"All right."

Darya started down toward the rubble. I slid after her. Where her feet were quick and light, darting over the ground, I stumbled, my heels catching, my toes kicking up dust in clouds that clogged my nose. Grit made my eyes sting and water. My right ankle throbbed.

Maybe it wasn't just twisted.

I leaned back trying to keep my balance, then leaned too far and fell on my rump. Great, another bruise. He struggled to my feet again and continued down, flailing after the faerie.

Finally the ground levelled out under my feet. I finished in a cloud of dust by Darya.

The piles around them topped out at about four feet high. From this close, I could see how completely any ruins had been obliterated. They were little more than big piles of dirt with stones and pebbles mixed in. They reminded me of the dirty snow piles in parking lots left over after ploughing.

Worse yet, I couldn't feel any residual trace of magic at all. But I had never been here before. Maybe Darya would feel something.

"Anything?" I asked.

She shook her head. Her brow crinkled with effort. Her hands tightened into fists. She took a small step forward and then another.

"I do not... I think..." She stopped and tilted her head. A light breeze rose up, ruffling her hair. It brought with it an underlying scent of musk, slight, not enough to be from an animal.

More like a perfume.

In the stillness, I couldn't sense anything else out there, just Darya. So who was wearing the perfume?

Or maybe the question was who *had* been wearing it?

I opened my mouth to ask but then Darya opened up the pouch at her waist and pulled out her orb. It gave off a soft golden glow, bright enough to shimmer in her eyes. Then I realized they were tears.

"There is something here," she said. Her voice was a soft whisper that carried in the quiet.

My heart began to pound. "Lekzar?"

"It is so faint, I can't be sure," she said. "I need help to be able to draw it in." She turned to me. "Will you help me?"

"Uh..." I hesitated. Even with my magic at full strength, I wasn't up to par with a faerie. Not to mention I was more than a little out of practice. I had even gotten use to taking the subway around.

But her eyes were glistening in the orb's light. How could I say no to that?

"Okay," I said. "I don't really know what to do."

"We need to create the circle again, that will draw in what remains."

"Circle," I said. "Right. How do we do that?"

Darya pointed at the piles of rubble. "They used to be in a circle. That is what gave this place its power."

I looked around at the mounds of dirt and stone. I counted eight of them and of the eight, three had been pushed out far enough to break any circle unless it was drawn by a drunken child.

"You're not suggesting we move those piles?" I pointed at the two to their left.

She tilted her head at him. "Not the entire thing."

"Oh right."

Not the entire thing. I got it. Just enough to help create the circle.

She placed the glowing orb down on the ground then moved to the first pile and started digging out handfuls. She carried it forward then checked her distance from the closer pile to her right. Then she dumped the dirt and stones onto the ground.

I moved to the second pile of rubble. My knees cracked as I bent down. I scooped up two handfuls of dirts. It felt cool in my palms and tingled on my skin. I retreated to a spot that looked about halfway between two mounds.

I let the dirt pour from my hands. Grains seemed to sparkle in the darkness. I glanced up. The same sparkle appeared around the other mounds as we filled in the circle. Was this enough to complete it and hold it? Probably not for long.

I needed more dirt.

I hurried back to the mound and scooped up more. Stones and pebbles dug into my skin. I felt the grit under my nails. Instead of the dusty smell I expected, it smelled of deep, rich earth. What had this ruin been before it had been a ruin? I had the sudden image of a huge stone cathedral with arching doorways and jagged walls of gleaming white brick. The heavy smoke of cooking fires tinged my nose. The sun glared in my eyes. I heard the cry of warrior faeries as they hurled themselves forward...

"Let go!"

Darya yanked my arm. My hands opened. Dirt splayed through my fingers, scattering on the ground and across my shoes.

Darkness. Night. No cathedral. No army. No cooking fire.

I shook myself. The vision had been so real.

I was going to have to be careful. Faerie magic could be overpowering. If I didn't watch out I could get lost in a vision and never find my way out.

"Are you all right?" Darya asked. "You are pale."

"Yeah, I'm fine." I wiped the back of my hand across my forehead. It came away damp. "Is this enough?" I gestured at the small pile at my feet.

Darya frowned. "No but I will finish it. You step inside."

I did as she suggested and kept my gaze down at my feet.

I heard the soft trickle of dirt from her hands, then silence, then another soft trickle. If not for the sound of the falling dirt, I wouldn't hear her at all.

But I could feel her and I could feel the circle growing in strength. It tingled on my skin like static electricity.

"Ready." Her voice sounded near my elbow. I started a little. I hadn't heard her come up.

"Yeah, okay," I said.

The energy in the air made me dizzy. Was this such a great idea? I glanced over at her. Her pale face looked luminescent. Her black hair seemed to flow around her head like tendrils. Even her wings now looked pump and quivering.

Venir, I remembered. The dead Santas and KJ, holding down the fort, waiting for me to come back. Was he also in the line of fire now? Quite possibly.

Mother would *kill* me if I let anything happen to KJ.

Darya held out her hands to me. I took them. Her skin felt cool and dry.

She moved a few paces to the left and spread her arms, using mine to create a circle. In the centre at their feet sat her glowing orb. The golden glow deepened into a rich purple. Energy crackled against my skin, making my hair stand on end.

This was just residual? I sure didn't want to feel fae magic when it was at full strength.

The glow around the orb expanded until the light touched our feet. For a moment, it stayed inside the circle of our arms, then it began to expand again, like a fog. It flowed out toward the mounds of rubble that encircled them.

Darya stood with her eyes closed. Her lips moved but I couldn't hear her words. Some kind of enchantment or spell. Drawing in the energy, trying to get the last traces that Lekzar may have left to manifest.

The deep purple glow reached the outer circle. In the light, I could see the rough surface of the ground, potted and scraped from scores of boots over how long. There was no vegetation, not even the rough scrub bushes with the dark veins. Just empty space.

Then to my left, a figure appeared.

It was vaguely man-shaped and as I watched, it solidified enough that I couldn't quite see through it. Pale, ethereal features. Large green eyes that stared at me unseeing.

The last time I had seen them they had been unseeing then too. On a corpse.

Lekzar.

Darya was still chanting with her eyes closed. Should I catch her attention? Would Lekzar vanish? I couldn't take the chance.

I was going to have to talk to the figure myself.

But before I could even open my mouth, Lekzar's eyes widened in fear. He raised his hands to defend himself then staggered back as if from a hit. Something snapped the shoulder strap on his breast plate. The plate swung away from his body. Lekzar's back arched. He grabbed for the plate.

Blood sprouted from his chest, darkening the purple fabric to black. Lekzar's mouth opened in a silent scream. He dropped to his knees.

A shadow crossed in front of him. Then it turned its attention.

Toward me.

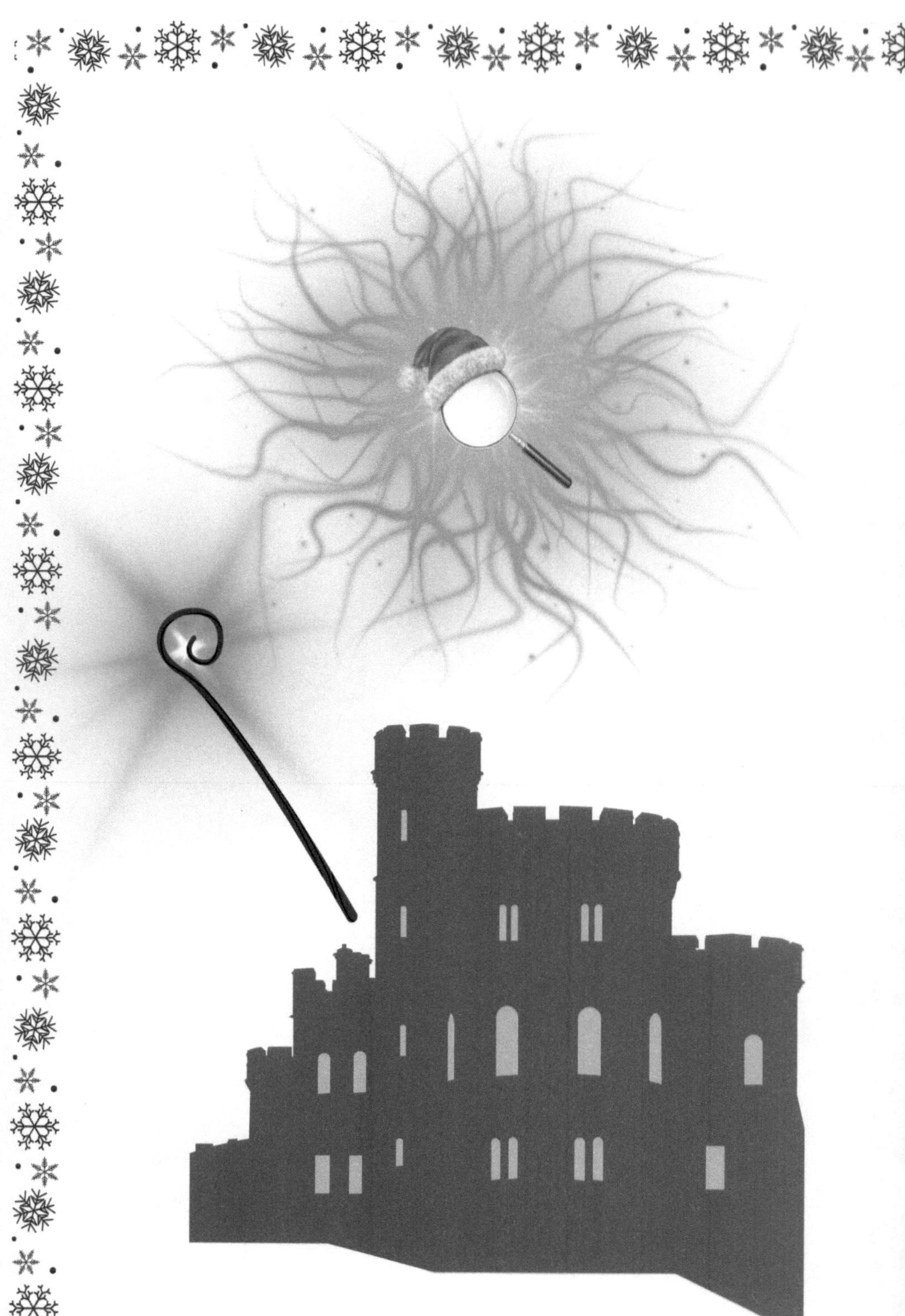

A flash of freezing cold, colder than anything I had ever felt, washed over me. The rotting stench of putrid iron clogged my nose.

And from the depths of the shadow reached out a hand so thin the flesh was stretched over the skeletal fingers.

Reaching for me.

The cold hardened, deepened, freezing me. Holding me as the hand reached closer.

I felt my heart rate slowing. My body felt so cold I couldn't even shiver.

And that hand crept closer.

Big mistake using cold on me.

I sucked in a breath through my lips that felt frozen shut. The cold air made my teeth ache and burned the roof of my mouth with the cold. But even as it froze me, I felt the change in it. Growing up at the North Pole had made cold my natural habitat.

And my own magic rallied to it.

I felt it swirl around me, rising like a wind. The edges of the shadow started to ripple. A moan issued from within, long and drawn out. The skeletal hand jerked closer.

The cold locked around me but I was already focusing on the North Pole. The way the snow drifted fluffy and white. How it blazed in whiteness in the sunlight and dimmed to comforting puffs in the darkness. The friendly warmth of the village homes all nested together, single-storey red brick homes with black pointed roofs covered with mounds of snow, drip-dripping off because of the warmth. Chimneys sending up puffs of smoke from numerous hearths, all blazing with fires stoked and cared for by the Elves and families that lived there. They made sugar and cinnamon cookies and heated hot chocolate in steel pots that steamed over the fire.

This was the cold of the North Pole. This was the cold I knew.

I gathered it up within myself, lips cracking with cold as I sucked in the air, fingers creaking as I tightened them into fists.

Then I lifted them and *shoved* at the shadow.

My own cold blasted forth. The shadow edges whipped back. The skeletal hand shook, fingers still grasping, trying to clench. They shuddered and shook...

Then snapped back.

The shadow flew out of the circle, breaking it.

The cold swirled away. The humid warmth of the night rushed in. I felt it almost stinging my cheeks. Water dripped from my eyelashes as they thawed out. My body started to shiver as the frigid cold dropped away. I lowered my hands.

Darya's eyes snapped open. She sucked in a breath. Her head jerked as she looked around. A shudder ran up her body.

"What was it?" she said. "Was it Lekzar?"

"At first," I managed to blurt out. My teeth chattered but with each moment, my shivering diminished. Soon they slowed to brief spasms that shook him occasionally.

"First, I saw Lekzar," he said. "Then he reacted to something or someone. Then I felt cold. Horrible cold." He shuddered.

"An echo," she said. "That was all that was left. Just an echo from Lekzar." She frowned. "Did you see what caused this cold?"

I shook my head. "Just a shadow."

"Veiled. That would take some magic here in the Fae Realm." Darya bent to retrieve the orb. "Come. We will retreat to my father's house. He has a sorcerer who will be able to assist us."

"What about Venir?" I asked.

"One step at a time, northern man," she said. "We will retrieve your..."

"Halt in the lord's name!"

Figures appeared from behind the piles of rubble. Arrows

and swords pointed inward at me and Darya. In the dim light, I caught a glint of armour.

One of the guards stepped forward. A silver helmet covered the top half of his face, slitted eye sockets deepened in shadow. He reached out a metal gloved hand and plucked the orb from Darya's palm.

"Will you come quietly, child, or shall we meet in battle?"

Darya lifted her chin, glaring at the man in front of her. He lifted a finger. Around them, the guards flashed into readiness. Swords lifted. Arrows aimed.

Darya pressed her lips tightly together. Then bowed her head. Her shoulders sagged.

Several guards surrounded me, swords at the ready. I held up my hands in surrender and tried to look as unthreatening as possible. That wasn't hard.

The lead guard didn't even look at me, just waved his hand.

"Bring him."

So much for our brilliant escape.

THE GUARDS ESCORTED US BACK IN SILENCE. ALMOST AS ONE, THE wings on their backs began to blur and the entire squad rose into the air. Two guards clenched my arms, holding me suspended between them. As they lifted above the tree line, any thought of trying to escape vanished.

It would be super easy for them to just drop me.

The cool night air stung my face as they flew. The ground below us was still shrouded in darkness but I saw the first glimmer of light along the horizon. Did that match up at all with my Realm? Time moved differently between different realms, I knew, but there was no way for me to know how quickly it was moving back home.

How much longer did I have to find the killer? How much longer before they struck again?

How much longer before KJ said to hell with it and returned to the North Pole?

Maybe it would be better if he did that, but he had given his word and I knew KJ would never go back on it. It might be safer for him if he did.

Just what I needed, having my brother in the line of fire and all because I asked. If anything happened to KJ...

No. Nothing would happen because I was going to figure it out and then I was going to stop it.

Just as soon as these faeries put me down.

Below my feet, I spotted the band of wall then the smooth, rolling lawn and finally the black stone of the castle. Then suddenly it was rushing forward as we dropped out of the sky. Cold wind whipped at my hair, my beard, and teared my eyes. I tried to blink the tears away although I didn't really want to watch them falling.

I wasn't falling, I knew it, it was a controlled landing. I

could still feel the faeries' hands gripping my arms. But the wind, and the land was rushing up. Way too fast.

From the look of a doll's house to full-sized walls rushing past me in a few eye blinks. A smooth black stone courtyard raced to meet me. Any moment, my feet would slam into it, sending the vibration up my legs. Would my leg bones snap under the impact? Would my hip bones be driven up through my torso?

Would I smash flat on the ground?

I wanted to close my eyes but I couldn't. I had to see every crack, every line, every pebble of the black surface that would going to squish me.

Then the speeding rush pulled up as the faeries skimmed the surface. They lifted me up about five metres, losing speed as they went, then slowly brought ,e back down.

They placed me on the stone floor. First the toes of my shoes touched, then settled down to my heels.

All nice and gentle.

Proving a point.

And boy, I got it.

A moment later, Darya appeared beside me. The flutter of her wings blurred then slowed as she touched down. I glanced over at her but she was looking at the ground, frowning.

Just how much trouble was she in for trying to help me? It didn't seem fair that she should be punished when it was her cousin who was killed.

But fair didn't seem to have much to do with everything that was going on.

The heavy sound of thick boots stomping on the courtyard stones made me look up. A row of guards in silver and black armour stood in front of me, effectively hemming me in with the others arranged behind me.

I glanced up.

A few remaining guards hovered above me, cutting off that escape as well.

They weren't taking any chances this time.

The guard in the centre stepped forward. A black helmet covered the top half of his face. Slits covered his eyes, the shadows inside deep and dark.

"The lord will see you and pass judgment," he said.

Before I could reply, someone pushed me from behind. I stumbled forward.

"Hey," I said.

"Silence!" snapped the lead guard in front of me. "Step forward or we will drag you."

Well at least they were giving me an option.

I followed the helmeted guard through the courtyard. The rest of the guards fell in line, one on either side of the leader, then along either side of me. Darya followed behind me and behind her, I saw the other guards closing up ranks.

Their boots clomped in a single fashion across the stones. Just as they reached the black stone of the wall it shimmered and vanished. Without missing a beat, the guards moved through and into a wide hall.

I had no choice but to follow.

The hall expanded out around them, faster than the pace of their walking. I could feel the magical energy in the place, pressing against my skin, making the hairs on my arm stand up with goose pimples.

The tile under our feet was a swirling grey marble, polished and shining. A domed ceiling stretched high above my head. Ten gigantic chandeliers of glistening crystals arranged in six tiers hung suspended in the air with no visible support. They crisscrossed through the space. Each crystal glowed with a soft golden light and with each placement, filled the hall with a warm glow.

The sweet scent of blossoms drifted in the air, mingling with something that reminded me of cinnamon and candy canes. Was that the true scent or was it just picking up the scents in my memory that comforted me? Faeries had such complex magic, I couldn't tell the difference.

Before I realized it, they had crossed the wide expanse and approached a raised platform with several chairs on it. It reminded me of the stage at the Grand View Mall without the Christmas decorations. But instead of a dead Santa sitting on a golden throne, this platform held a tall, powerfully built faerie sitting on a plain black chair. He wore an armoured breastplate and a black velvet cloak that draped over his shoulders. Long black hair streaked with grey flowed almost to his waist. Black pants were tucked into shining black boots. Silver gauntlets gleamed on his forearms. His left hand rested casually on the armrest of the chair. His right hand grasped a tall staff made of gleaming, black wood. A swirl of twinkling colour twined upward around the shaft until it reached a golden crystal that pulsed with a soft glow. I felt the glow deepen and almost pull me toward it.

The faerie lord leaned forward to peer at me.

The guards around me bowed low as they reached the front of the platform. Besides me, even Darya bowed.

I stayed upright.

Lord Flaktar Dramal narrowed his eyes as he studied me. I felt the tingle of faerie magic running along my skin, tingling on my scalp. Trying to get into my head, to get a read on me. The crystal glowed even deeper.

I shook my head and mouthed a spell under my breath. The magic snapped back.

Lord Dramal looked startled. His hands tightened on the armrest and the staff, the pale skin on his knuckles turning white.

I kept my face bland, resisting the urge to smirk. If the faerie lord wanted information from me he was going to have to speak aloud. I wasn't going to submit to any spell work.

"You have entered my land without permission and killed one of my guards," Lord Dramal said.

"That's not true," I said. "I came with my companion to meet with Lekzar Trayborn but we found him dead. I didn't kill him."

Lord Dramal tilted his head. "How can I know that when you refuse to submit to my vision?"

"You could try asking," I said. "Just like I'm asking you what happened to my friend Venir?"

"He is here," Lord Dramal said.

I let out a slow breath. The faerie lord hadn't killed the Elf yet. At least that was something. Since I was now talking to the man, maybe I could get some information out of him. Like maybe what Lekzar had known.

"I'm glad," I said. I spread my hands out, holding them away from my body. "I am Noel Kringle and the Elf you have is named Venir. We came here to meet with Lekzar who had information about a plot to kill Santa Claus."

Lord Dramal frowned. "Kringle? What plot is this?"

"Someone has been killing Santa Clauses in the Human Realm," I said. From the startled looks around me, I realized they didn't understand how there could be multiple Santas.

Better back up.

"In the Human Realm, before our festival of Christmas, when Santa Claus delivers gifts, people dress up in costume as Santa and children tell him what presents they want."

"This is allowed?" Lord Dramal said.

I nodded. "Humans believe Santa Claus is just a story."

Around him, I could hear murmurs of disquiet. Lord Dramal held up his hand and the entire hall fell silent.

"How can Santa Claus allows this?" he asked.

I smiled. "He doesn't mind."

The faerie lord looked troubled but he gestured for me to continue.

"Magic doesn't work that well in the Human Realm," I said. "So things that are magic are thought to just be stories. But the men who are pretending to be Santa are being killed. That's no story. I came here to learn more so I can stop it."

The faerie lord's slim fingers rested back on the armrest, tapping a slow rhythm. He tilted his head at me.

"How do I know you are who you claim?" Lord Dramal said. "This could be your own story and you could be pretending to be Noel Kringle. Perhaps that is how you duped Lekzar so you could kill him."

Was no one ever going to believe me? I sighed. I hated being called a liar but there was only one way to convince the faerie lord.

I took a deep breath and relaxed.

Questing outward. What had been his favourite gift?

It was even easier than with Darya.

The image of the bow flooded my mind. A shining black shaft with a barely visible draw string that hummed as the slim, younger version of Lord Dramal pulled it back. He wasn't the lord then, just the second in line for the title behind his elder brother, Xasmier.

This bow had been Xasmier's favourite, handed down to Flaktar on his fifteenth Fae-Thaal.

Though it wasn't technically from Santa, it was the faerie lord's favourite gift. That along with the... yes, there it was.

The set of perfectly balanced arrows for use with the bow. That had been Santa's contribution.

I focused back on Lord Dramal. The slim fingers resting on the armrests looked soft.

"How long has it been since you've used that black bow?" I asked quietly.

The faerie's grim countenance faltered. His eyes widened and his lips parted in wonder. For a brief moment, years fell off his thin face, lines around his mouth vanished as his face seemed to fill out, his forehead smoothed over. For a brief moment, he was that boy again, delighting in the gift of a secondhand bow and brand new arrows.

Then his mouth snapped shut. A curtain of age seemed to drop over his face. Lines deepened as his cheeks narrowed. Muscles along his jaw jumped.

"That is an interesting trick," he said. "But it is not proof of who you are."

"I would vouch for him, my lord."

Darya's voice rang out through the hall. I glanced over as she stepped up to my side.

"You don't have to do this," I whispered.

"Quiet," she said. She lifted her chin. "I vouch for his identify."

Lord Dramal's eyes narrowed. He leaned forward in his chair.

"You understand what you say," he said. "His words and deeds would be upon you, my lady. Your station would be no protection for his misbehaviour. You would pay the price."

Darya nodded. "I understand, Lord."

Lord Dramal pressed his lips tight together. His gaze flicked from her to me. I could feel the burning weight of it pressing against me. The pressure felt like a wave of heat, searing against my skin, poking at my mind. The faerie lord was trying to worm past my defenses but I wouldn't let him. Who did this guy think he was trying to invade my mind? It was one thing to not believe I was Noel Kringle, it was quite another to be so... so... *rude!*

If there was one thing I hated, it was that. My mother had drilled it into me and I wouldn't put up with it.

I breathed in, drawing up the cool currents of air in the room, mustering forth all thoughts of frost and ice. Then I slammed it into a wall of deepest cold in my mind. When it was strong and thick, I blasted it toward the faerie lord.

Lord Dramal jerked back. His eyes widened. His hands gripped the arms of the chair, fingers whitening with pressure. Then his fingernails turned blue. His lips paled.

And a tinge of frost appeared on the tip of his nose.

Uh oh, maybe that was a little too far.

The sound of ice cracked as the faerie lord yanked his right hand off his chair. He pointed at me.

"Seize him!"

So much for diplomacy.

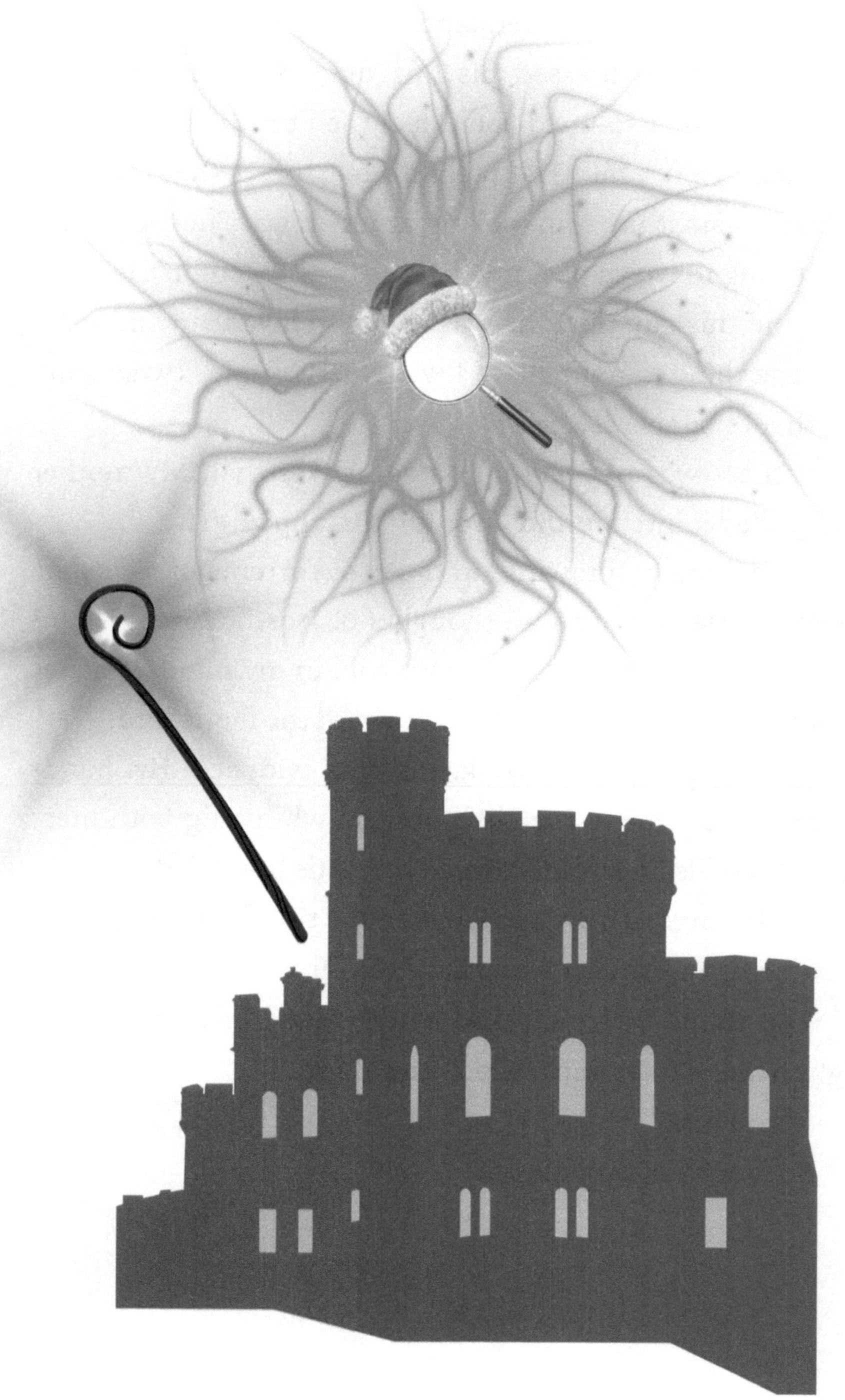

CHAPTER

FIFTEEN

This time the cell they tossed me in to was even smaller than the first. Just before the door slammed shut, I managed to catch a glimpse of Darya as the set of four guards marched her past, presumably to her own cell. She frowned, a look of deep disappointment etched on her face.

Just another person I'd let down. Add it to the list.

Venir, my brother waiting for me to come back, Lekzar, even poor Christopher Hitchens whose body had been stuffed behind a dumpster. I'd let them all down.

This private detective business wasn't going the way I thought it would.

Enough. Enough wallowing. I stared around the tiny cell. It was maybe seven feet across, barely five or six steps wide. The walls were the same black, matte brick. Cool to the

199

touch and tingling against the tips of my fingers, hinting at magic within. If I tried anything with my own magic it would just boomerang back at me.

Somehow having access to more of my magic wasn't any better than having none of it.

A short bench made of some dark wood were set along the right side of the wall. Probably carved from the wood of those black trees in the forest. Even without a cushion, it felt moderately comfortable as I sat down. If there was one thing faeries knew, it was comfort.

Light glowed from a sparkle up at the top of the ceiling, almost fifteen feet above my head. I could feel the hum of the magic from it. A single purpose to light the cell.

At least I didn't have to sit in the dark.

I sighed and ran a hand through my hair. The waves were tangled, resisting my fingers. Even my beard felt unruly on my cheeks. How long had I been in the Faerie Realm? Long enough that I needed to neaten my beard and I usually only had to do that once a week. I hadn't done it for several days before I met up with Venir.

Had I been here that long? How long was it to the Human Realm?

Would KJ keep covering for me? Was my brother even now in danger?

I had to get out of here. Maybe Lord Dramal would listen to me in the morning but maybe he wouldn't. Either way, I couldn't wait around any longer.

Someone was willing to kill in this realm to keep their

secret. Who else might be in the line of fire if I didn't do something? Venir? Maybe even Darya?

My own magic crackled along my skin in response to my anxiety. It was comforting to feel it so strong again but useless in this cell. They'd obviously set up charms against any magic other than faerie magic and they probably had special cells for their own kind that nullified even their magic. Darya would have been put there.

So I couldn't use magic. What could I use?

The only thing in the cell with me was the bench. I stood and ran my hands over the smooth surface. It seemed to flow right out of the wall. I grabbed hold of one end and tried to lift. My fingers dug into the wood edge. I felt it pressing on my fingernails, pushing them back. My arms strained but the bench didn't budge. I let go.

It was definitely solid in its place.

No help there.

So what else did I have?

I patted down my shirt and pants. My keys, cell phone, and wallet. I stuffed the wallet back into my pocket. Then I pressed the on button on my cell phone.

And waited.

After a few moments I had to admit it wasn't going to turn on. Crossing into this realm and the magics swirling around had probably damaged the phone, maybe beyond repair.

Oh well, it had been worth a try.

I stuffed that into my other pocket.

That left me with the keys. They certainly wouldn't be able to open the door but maybe I could use them to jimmie the lock.

I hurried to the door. In the dim light, the surface appeared unbroken. Smooth. No sign of any kind of keyhole or even a handle. Just a smooth, flat expanse. It could have been the same as the walls if it wasn't for the slim doorframe that traced around the outside.

Damn the halls, how was I going to get out of here now?

I clenched the keys in my fist. The steel edges pinched my skin. The pain was the only thing I could do.

I was Noel Kringle, Santa's youngest son. There was no way I could be imprisoned by faeries so easily.

Another quick glance around the cell showed me nothing new. The bench. The glowing light at the ceiling. Emptiness. My frustration rose, made me tightened my fists even more. The key bit deeper into my palm.

Any deeper and I'd start bleeding.

Of course!

Blood magic.

Even the dampening effects in the cell wouldn't be able to resist blood magic. At least I hoped it wouldn't.

All I had was the key and my intention, no other ingredients to perform a proper spell. I couldn't even move the bench closer to help me.

I glanced up at the light.

Maybe?

The sparkle was nestled in the far corner of the cell so its light bounced off the matte walls. It wasn't electrical. As far as I knew, the Faerie Realm didn't have electricity. So it had to be magic.

And magic I could use.

I grinned. All I had to do was draw it near.

This key was going to be useful afterall.

I opened my fist. The key lay in my palm. The teeth of it had made deep indentations in my skin but not broken it. I ran my thumb over the edges. Mostly smooth but a tiny piece of metal jutted out near the tiny, sharp and jagged. A flaw.

I pressed it against the fleshy part of my left palm. The scratch caused a twinge of pain, a slight mark, but didn't break the skin.

I was going to have to try harder.

Gritting my teeth, I pressed the key against my skin. The dull pain sharpened. I pressed harder.

Harder.

A fierce pang and the key bit into my flesh. A tiny drop of blood welled up. Perfect and round.

I squeezed the skin, pushing more blood through the tiny puncture. The drop grew from a pin prick to a quarter of an inch.

It would have to do.

I dabbed my right index finger into the blood, then wiped it in a vertical line down the centre of my lips. I turned my palm toward the light, holding it up in the air.

I focused on the sparkle, focused on the light. The golden glow that seemed to pulse near the ceiling.

Slowly I breathed the incantation through my lips, through the blood. Focusing on the sparkle. Drawing it closer.

Come closer.

The image of sparkle filled my vision, nestled in the corner at the ceiling. A bright gold centre fading to a golden yellow at the edges. Pulsing and glowing. The pulsing seemed to quicken, thumping in a matching rhythm to my heart. Flash contract, flash contract, flash contract.

My awareness focused even tighter on it. The outer edges fell away. I no longer saw the black matte walls that reflected the glow. All I saw was the centre. Glowing. Golden. Pulsing, matching my heart.

Flash contract, flash contract, flash contract.

In the very centre, I thought I saw the glow change from a warm golden to a fierce white. White like freshly fallen snow at the North Pole, so white that the reflected sunlight could burn your eyes. I felt my eyes watering. Tears on my cheeks. The glow blurred. My eyes wanted to close, to squint, but I couldn't let them. Couldn't lose the focus now.

Flash contract, flash contract, flash contract.

The burning white centre expanded, crowding out the golden glow. I felt the pulsing thudding in my head, my temples. My scalp felt tight and hot. My eyes, still tearing madly, felt like they were drying out like husks. Like every tear was evaporating under this white, burning, light.

It filled my vision.

Then I felt the warmth of it on the tip of my nose.

I blinked. The sparkle hovered in front of my face, a scant two inches away.

Faerie magic! I'd called it and it had come to me!

My heart hammered in my chest. The sparkle flashed in sympathy, pulse pulse pulse. It started to drift away.

No, I had to hold onto it! I focused again and the drift slowed.

It was going to take all my effort to keep hold of it.

Keeping my focus on the sparkle, I turned to the left and reached out, palm first. Questing.

My fingers touched a cool surface. Smooth. No ridges from bricks.

The door.

Perfect.

I pressed my palm against the door. The puncture gave a flash of pain, almost enough to distract me. I winced at it, kept my gaze locked on the sparkle.

It quivered but stayed in place.

Slowly I traced a circle on the door, starting at the top. Then when I reached the end, I drew my initial, N, focusing on my name. Owning it. My name in my blood.

Owning the door.

I held my hand out to the sparkle. My palm ached. Blood dribbled down my wrist.

I breathed out my wish.

Open.

The sparkle hovered in front of me, pulsing, then whipped toward the door. Brilliant golden light flashed. The centre was icy white. It engulfed the black surface of the door. My initial N glowed in the middle, looking a little lopsided.

Then the door vanished.

The golden glow died. The sparkle extinguished. The magic in it had been burned up by the effort.

I stood shaking in the doorway. My heart hammered in my chest. Sweat prickled all over my skin, dampened my pants, stuck my shirt to my back.

My hand shook as I reached for the doorframe.

I leaned forward to look out into the hall.

Empty. But I could feel the magical energies drifting through the air.

I didn't have much time. As soon as I stepped out it would be like setting off an alarm.

Okay, before I did it, I had to be smart. Which way to go? Where was Venir and Darya? I had to use whatever precious seconds I had to find them.

I steadied myself in the doorway and closed my eyes. I had been around both of them long enough to recognize their energies. I tested my senses through the hallway.

Darya's was the strongest which made sense because she'd passed by here recently. Her trail led off to the left, then stopped halfway down.

Next I had to find Venir.

The Elf's trail was much fainter but easy to see. Like a

trail of black pepper through white snow. His also led off to the left, but farther, all the way to the end of the hall.

And beyond.

I opened my eyes. Tilting my head, I tried to peer around the door frame without sticking my head out. I couldn't see any farther. No way to know how far Venir's trail led. Was he even on this floor? Maybe the faeries had moved him to another floor.

That was going to complicate things.

Okay, first things first. Get Darya and then with her help, Venir. Assuming I would be able to open the door to Darya's cell. But it should be easier to open from the outside.

Right?

Yeah, sure. That's what I told myself.

Big breath, I wouldn't have a lot of time. I focused on Darya's trail again.

And stepped through the doorway.

Silence and stillness filled the corridor. Plain black walls led forward. Golden light from glowing sparkles placed at intervals near the ceiling lit the hall in an even yellow light. Nothing seemed to pulse in alarm. No warning shouts. No pounding of racing footsteps to cut me off.

Silence.

I could stand here and admire the calm or I could move.

I moved.

My footsteps seemed to echo through the corridor even as I tried to walk softly. The air seemed cool and dry.

Or maybe that was just my mouth.

The black walls were featureless, just the same matte brick pattern. I passed beneath one glowing sparkle and then another, moving farther down the corridor. Still no sign of a doorway.

Had they used magic to hide them? If so, how would I know when I reached Darya's spell?

And how would I get the door open?

One problem at a time. First I had to find her cell.

I had to hope I would be able to see the door.

The stillness made me feel jumpy. My shoulder blades itched and I kept glancing back behind me, expecting to see a fae guard come rushing forward, trungent raised.

Nothing.

I was so sure an alarm would sound.

What were they waiting for? Were they waiting for me to bust Darya out? To get Venir? Maybe then they would take care of all of us at once.

Charming thought.

I pushed it away. I didn't have time for that.

Ahead of me, the hallway curved to the left. I crept forward, my shoes tapping on the hard stone floor. I reached the corner and peered around.

I wouldn't need to worry about seeing the door after all.

A pair of fae guards stood halfway down the hall. The breast plates gleamed in the light from the glowing flickers hanging near the ceiling above them. Gossemer black wings folded and still against their backs. Dark purple trousers were tucked into gleaming black boots. They both had long, dark hair, pulled back from their face, secured at the base of the neck. The one closest to me wore a face plate of etched silver that jutted out in a triangle from his face. Swirls were carved into the metal. I watched sparkling colours race along the swirls. He gripped a tall staff of wood in his right hand.

I think it was a safe bet to assume that Darya was right behind where they guarded.

Now I had to just get past them.

Sure, that was going to be easy.

I clenched my fist. The nails of my left hand dug into my palm. Sharp pain flared from the wound. I winced and caught my breath.

Pain.

I slowly opened my hand. Fresh blood smeared over my skin.

It had worked once.

Sure, when I'd had time to concentrate and had been alone to do it. There were two fae guards right there who weren't going to just stand around, waiting for me to slip by them or knock them out. I wasn't going to have the luxury of being in full control of my blood magic.

Okay, so quick and dirty it was going to have to be.

I just had to hope I could be faster with my magic than they were with theirs.

I pulled my keys from my pocket and dug them into my left palm. The wound opened wider. Blood pooled in my palm. My hand ached.

Even my pain would help fuel the magic, I kept telling myself that. Didn't make it hurt any less though.

I dipped my fingers into the blood. It glistened on my fingertips as I raised them in the air. I began to whisper the chant as I drew the circle before me. The air seemed to thicken, to darkened, or maybe my eyes were dimming from the loss of blood.

Right, a few ounces would do that.

I pressed my fingers to my lips, smearing the blood as I traced out the N for my name, sealing the magic to me, to my breath.

Then I focused on the glowing sphere above the two fae guards.

Mine. It was mine. I claimed it and I would control it.

I would.

I peered around the corner.

The sphere seemed to sputter then the glow steadied. It was tucked up near the ceiling just opposite the two guards. A perfect spot to light up the entire hallway. A perfect spot to ambush them.

I took a breath.

"Now," I hissed.

And clenched my left fist.

Pain shot up my arm. Blood seeped between my fingers.

The glowing sphere flared. Then flashed toward the guards.

One of them yelled but they both dove out of the way, heading to either side. Metal clanged as they landed on the stone floor. The hand of the guard closest to me spasmed open as his knuckles smashed down. The wooden staff clattered and rolled toward me.

But the sphere kept going. It hit the wall. Light flared out, blinding.

My vision went white. I blinked, felt tears on my cheeks from my madly tearing eyes.

But everything stayed white.

Oh swirling snow, what had I done? I hadn't been close enough to finesse the door opening, instead I'd gone for brute force.

Had I destroyed the door? The wall?

Had I killed Darya inside the cell?

A few more eye blinks and the white faded. Fuzzy images appeared before me. Two figures lay on the floor. The fae guards. Both were struggling to rise, shaking their heads in disorientation.

At least I wasn't the only one blinded by the light.

Just like I'd planned.

Yeah, that was right.

Shadows filled the hall but dim light shone from where the glowing sphere had impacted the wall. A greyish haze seemed to drift from the impact site.

Almost like smoke.

I blinked again. My vision cleared.

It was smoke.

How would a glowing sphere make smoke?

Crunching sounded from inside the smoke. The grinding of pebbles against stone.

A black boot emerged. Then another.

Smoke billowed as Darya stepped out.

She held her hand to her nose and mouth. Her eyes squinted. Grey dust coated her black hair and her shoulders. Her wings shuddered on her back. She glanced at the two fallen guards.

The one closest to me stirred. He turned his head toward Darya and gave a yell.

Darya darted forward. The guard swung his leg, trying to trip her, but she jumped over him. She landed by his side, close to the staff.

With a sweep of her hand, she grabbed it. As the guard started to sit up, Darya flipped the staff up and smacked him across the head.

The guard fell back.

Through the haze of smoke, I saw the other one start to rise. He had something in his hand.

"Darya!" I called.

She turned and started toward me.

The second guard called out. I could feel the rustle of magic in the air, like static on my arms, raising the hairs on my skin.

If he managed to finish his spell all my efforts could be for naught.

Not if I could help it.

I tightened my left fist, felt the blood pulse between my fingers.

It echoed a faint pulse from the remnants of the glowing sphere in Darya's cell.

I *yanked* on it.

A pinprick of light flashed out of the smoke and slammed into the second guard, hitting him hard in the chest. He fell back, splayed on the stone floor. He didn't move.

A smirk crossed Darya's face. She nodded to me.

"Very good."

She stepped over the guard, moved to my side and planted the staff beside her.

"Now what?" she said.

"Venir," I said. "We have to find him."

She nodded and tapped the staff. "We will. With this."

"Can that help us stay under the radar?" I said.

Her smirk faded, replaced by a slight frown of puzzlement. "Radar?"

"Never mind." I waved that away. "Can it help us stay hidden from the guards?"

"Ah," she said. "Somewhat. It will mask us but not completely."

"Good enough," I said. "Let's get Venir."

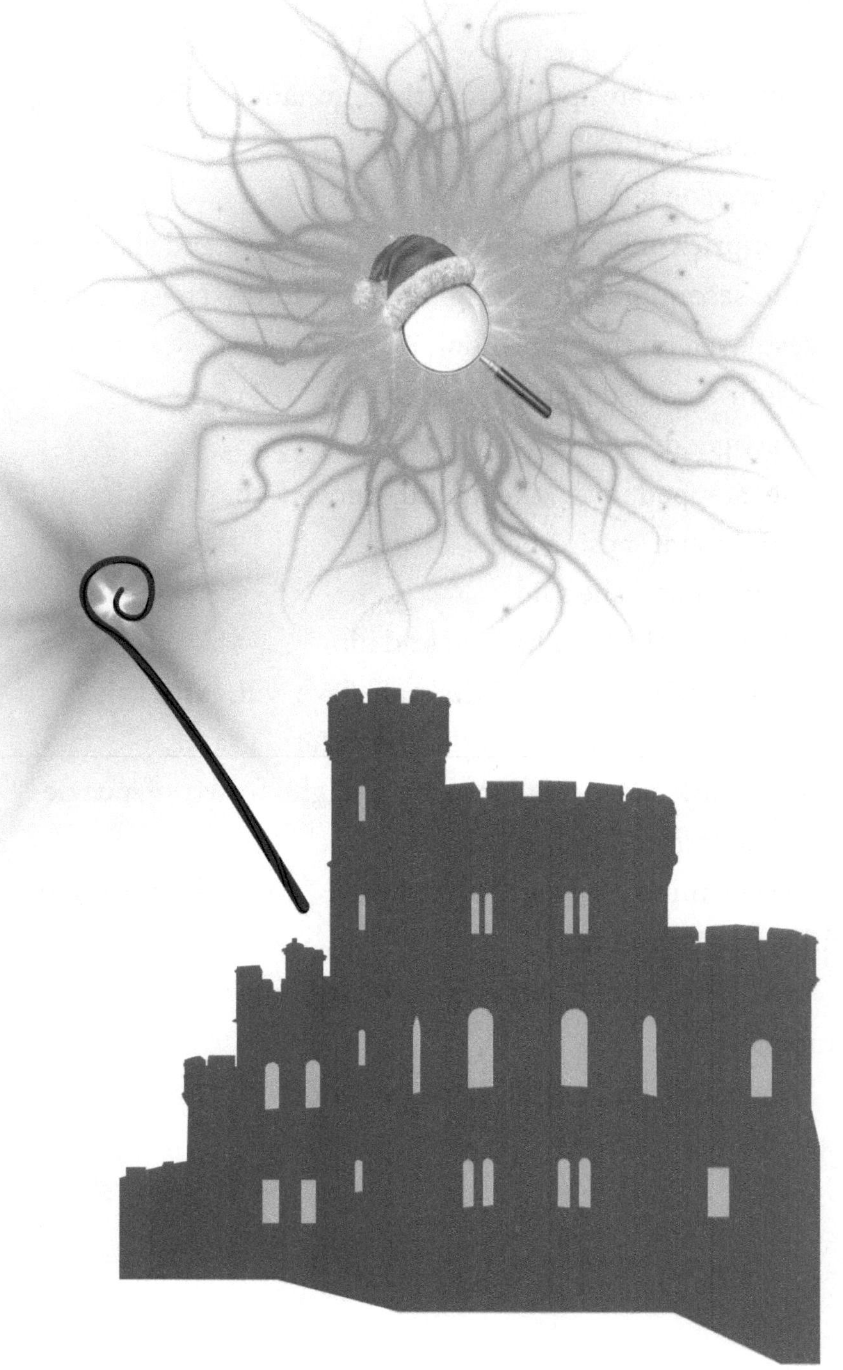

CHAPTER

SIXTEEN

I thought we would immediately head out to find the Elf, but Darya had other ideas.

"If they are found like this it will not matter how masked we are," she said. "They will hunt us down."

She was making sense but every moment felt like it was closer to something happening to Venir.

Or my brother back in the Human Realm.

I couldn't waste any time.

So I didn't argue.

I tore a strip of cloth from the bottom of my shirt and wound it around my wounded hand. Then I crossed to help Darya grab the first guard. She grabbed his black booted feet while I lifted beneath his arms. Sharp pain pierced my left palm, almost making me drop him. I clenched my teeth against the pain and lifted a couple of inches.

We fast shuffled across the stone tiles and through the open door of Darya's cell. It was only slightly bigger than mine with the same black, matte stone walls. Two of the wooden benches sat across from each other, attached to the wall like mine. Darya started shuffling toward the one on the right.

I had just assumed we'd leave them on the floor but she obviously had other ideas.

She stopped in front of the first bench and lifted the guard's feet to rest on the wood. Although I would have liked to I couldn't very well leave his upper body lying on the floor. I lifted higher. One of his hands brushed the wood, getting tangled beneath his body.

My hand throbbed in pain. I breath hissed out between my clenched teeth.

"Get his arm," I managed.

"Of course." Darya reached across and slowly extracted his arm out from beneath him. She seemed to be moving in slow motion.

"Hurry," I said.

My arms trembled from holding him up. I wasn't used to dead weight like this but it was more the piercing pain in my left palm, reminding me that it was very unhappy with my current position and it intended to let me know its thoughts for some time to come.

"Let him down," Darya said.

I released him, just fast enough that his head didn't bounce off the wood. I backed away, cradling my left hand.

We still had one more guard to bring in.

"I will retrieve the other one," Darya said.

She stepped past me and, grabbing the second one under the arms, dragged him along the floor into the cell. The wings on her back fluttered in a blur. As she reached the bench, she had her lips pressed tight together with the effort.

I stepped forward and together we got him onto the bench. As I let go of his arms, I could feel the wetness of my blood seeping through the scrap of shirt.

So much for that makeshift bandage. But at least it wasn't dripping. As long as I didn't leave any blood behind no one could use it in their own magic to track me down.

As I followed her back into the hallway, the lingering smoke tickled my nose. It smelled of ash and burnt stone.

"What about the door?" I said. I pointed at the gaping hole.

"I will take care of that."

Darya knelt on the floor. She scooped up some stray pebbles and rubbed them in the palms of her hands. Her wings on her back vibrated as she began to murmur. I couldn't make out the words she spoke.

For a moment, the smell of the smoke sharpened, almost enough to make me gag then it vanished as the cell door appeared in front of us, sealing off the hole.

Darya dropped the pebbles to the floor and climbed to her feet. Her wings drooped on her back. Moisture beaded on her forehead.

"That should hold long enough for us to find the Elf," she said.

"How did you shut it?" I asked.

She tilted her head. "Shut it? It is not shut. That is a veil."

She turned. "Come, we must go now."

I looked back at the wall. It appeared completely real. The flat, matte blackness of it. The thin seal around the doorframe. I just had to know.

I reached out and touched it.

The stone felt cool against my finger tips. Hard. Real.

That was some veil.

And it made me think of something.

Christopher Hitchens. That had been some veil as well.

Like the veil of the skeletal figure who had killed Lekzar.

"Kringle," Darya called.

I hurried to catch up.

I HADN'T BEEN ABLE TO TRACE THE ELF'S FAINT PATH BUT DARYA knew where to go.

I followed her along the dimly lit hallways. Glowing spheres appeared at regular intervals, hovering near the ceiling. The black matte of the walls seemed to absorb most of the light, leaving the hall in an almost twilight.

The air tingled with magic, enough that it was giving me

a bit of a headache. My mouth tasted sour and dry. How long since I'd had water or food? My morning coffee seemed so long ago.

That led me to wondering about KJ. How long had passed back home? Was he even now in danger?

Thinking about it made my head ache even more.

At a corner, Darya paused, holding her hand up. I stopped right behind her.

"What is it?" I whispered.

"Guards," she whispered back.

Great.

"That is probably where your friend is kept," she said. "His trail leads right toward them."

Of course it did.

I peered around her.

A pair of guards stood against the left side of the hall, an almost mirror image of the ones that had been in front of Darya's cell. Unfortunately they were between two glowing spheres, both far enough away that the guards would probably notice immediately if either started toward them. That would give them time to counter my magic.

But Darya seemed to have another idea.

She turned to me. "You stay here and wait for my signal."

Before I could say anything, she turned back and headed around the corner.

My mouth dropped open and I gagged on a yell. Swirling snow, what was she doing?

As Darya moved forward, she shoved her hand into the

pocket of her pants. When she pulled it out, I saw the glint of her orb between her fingers. Hadn't they taken that from her? They must have. I couldn't imagine them leaving it with her.

Unless they only *imagined* they'd taken it from her.

Veils. How many layers were there?

I glanced at the matte brick wall beside me. Was this even the actual appearance of the wall? Did Darya look how I thought she did?

How would I know? The authenticity of it was staggering.

Just another reason to get Venir and get out of here as fast as possible. If there really was a plot to kill Dad, I was going to have to stop it another way. I wasn't going to be able to do it stuck in this castle.

Except Venir's contact Lekznar had served here. Could there be something in his quarters to give us a clue as to who would have killed him? As to who was plotting against Dad?

My stomach tightened. I felt a tingling on the back of my neck, a sure sign that I was on to something. At home at the North Pole, I'd always gotten a tingle on the back of my neck when I'd had a great idea. Mother had always said it made the hair on my neck curlier from all the ideas I had.

I definitely had one now.

I peeked around the corner again.

Darya stood in the hallway in front of the two guards. The orb glowed with a soft, purplish light as it hovered above her out-stretched left palm. Her mouth was moving but I couldn't hear her words. The light from the glowing spheres above her reflected a glistening sheen of perspiration on her forehead. Her black wings vibrated as she concentrated.

As I watched, the head of the guard closest to me starting to sag forward. Soon his chin rested on his chest. His eyes closed. Even his wings seemed to droop. His body wavered then tilted back until his shoulders hit the wall. Just past him, I could see the second guard slumped against the wall too.

Darya continued chanting as she turned her face toward me. She nodded and then tilted her chin toward the door.

I slipped around the corner. Even as I tried to walk quietly, my shoes tapping on the stone sounded loud in my ears. I winced. I didn't want to do anything to either break Darya's concentration or startle the guards awake.

But I needn't have worried. As I drew closer I could see how deeply they were entranced.

Sweat glistened on Darya's forehead. Her left hand shook with a slight tremor under the floating orb. Her voice, still a bare whisper, sounded strained. Her wide eyes glared at me then flickered toward the door.

Right. This was my job.

I stepped between the two sleeping guards. The expanse of brick wall between them looked as smooth and unbroken as the rest of the wall but I was getting used to seeing the thin seam that delineated the door. Was it actually easier for me to see or was I just getting used to seeing through the veil covering it?

Here in the Fae Realm, that almost seemed like a philosophical question.

Forget it. Just get the thing open.

I lifted my hands and moved them toward the surface of the door. From a couple of inches away, I could feel the hum of magic holding the door closed. It felt like a high frequency vibration, almost enough to rattle my teeth.

I took a deep breath. The air tasted cooler. Crisper. It reminded me of peppermint. Candy canes. I breathed out and could almost see my breath frosting in the dim light.

How?

The door slid open.

Venir stood on the other side. His large ears quivered over the top of his head. A grin spread over his face. Even without his cigar, he looked pleased with himself.

"Took yer sweet time, didn't you, boy?" he said.

"Come on," I said. "We have to get out of here."

"Right." Venir followed as I stepped out of the doorway and back into the hall. We moved past Darya who said a final few words of chanting before capturing her orb and moving behind us.

We headed around the next corner, out of sight of the guards. Another pair of glowing spheres lit the way, extending down the corridor.

"So we head home, right?" Venir said.

"Not just yet," I said.

Darya tucked the orb into her fabric pouch before slipping it into her pocket.

"You must leave," she said. Fatigue made her voice rasp. "They will not imprison you the next time they catch you. Next time they will just kill you."

"That's motivatin' to me, boy," Venir said. "Let's boot it."

"Not yet," I said. "I've got an idea of where to look for a clue."

"Oh yeah?" Venir said. "Where's that, Mr. Private Detective?"

"Lekznar's quarters," I said. "We might find out what he wanted to tell you, Venir. And maybe it will vindicate Darya."

A frown deepened the wrinkles in Venir's face.

"Just one look," I said. "I don't want to leave until I know I've done all I can to find out about this plot against Dad."

At that, Venir bowed his head. The frown still creased his face. His lips thinned. "I don't know, kiddo."

Darya sighed. "If I can get you into my cousin's room, will you then leave?"

I nodded.

"Very well," she said. "Follow."

She pushed past me and headed down the corridor. Although Venir still kept frowning, we didn't have any other option but to follow her.

Darya led us through a maze of corridors, all matte black brick, illuminated by the glowing spheres near the ceiling. Finally, after what felt like the millionth left turn, we reached a door that looked significantly different from all the others. Instead of black, it was a deep, rich brown, carved into intricate shapes. A golden handle curved down.

Before reaching for it, Darya pulled out her small pouch and unwrapped her orb. It twinkled in the light and levitated above her hand.

"Stay back," she cautioned.

I took a couple of steps back, tugging on Venir's sleeve until he stumbled back with me. We retreated about halfway down the corridor.

That seemed far enough for Darya. She turned back to the door. The orb began to glow with a deeper purplish hue. It followed her hand as she reached for the door handle.

I felt the tingle of telltale magic just before she touched it.

"Darya, wait!"

I darted forward.

My feet slammed on the stone tiles. Each step jarred my body. My teeth rattled in my mouth.

Something pulling at me, trying to stop me from reaching her.

I sucked in a breath, tasted ashes.

No. It wasn't going to stop me.

I breathed out. Cold, crisp air.

The ashes taste twisted. Changed. To peppermint.

My steps raced.

I reached her side, grabbed her hand before she touched the handle.

"It's enchanted," I said.

"Of course it is," she said. "That's why I'm using my orb to belay it."

I shook my head. "It's expecting that. It's faerie magic and it knows your magic. We have to find another way to open it."

Her fingers tightened around the orb. The purplish light from it faded. Her lips pressed tight together.

"So how are we going to do that?" she said.

How indeed?

I could feel the magic reflecting off the door like a tingle in my mind. Irritating, like a musical instrument off key. I breathed in and tried to harmonize with it, but it skittered away, staying just enough off key that I couldn't match it. If I couldn't match it, I couldn't disable it.

Somehow this faerie spell had been designed to resist all kinds of magic, not just other faerie magic.

Darya tilted her head. She was expecting an answer. Here I was, the big private detective with the idea to search her cousin's room and we couldn't even get into it.

This wasn't doing much for my credibility.

The soft tap of shoes sounded behind me. Venir appeared at my elbow. He sniffed, lifting his chin. His big ears quivered.

"Yep, that's strong magic, that is," he said. "Gonna be tougher 'n a reindeer's hoof to get in there."

"Thanks for the commentary," I said.

The Elf grinned. "Just sayin' it how I sees it, boy."

Darya stuffed her orb back into her pocket and crossed her arms over her chest.

"So have you figured out how we are to get inside the room?" she said. "This was your idea instead of fleeing the castle. Even now the guards are hunting us, getting ever closer. Shall we stand around waiting for them?"

"You guys are such a big help," I said. "No pressure here."

Darya's frown deepened. Even Venir looked annoyed.

Like everything was my fault.

And the faerie magic pouring off the door continued to irritate me, picking at me like worrying a scab.

Irritating...

Of course!

That was the effect of that magic, to irritate, to cause disruption. Both Darya and Venir had been affected and turned that irritation on me. I was turning it on myself.

So how could I turn it on the door?

"So, we gonna keep standing around here, boy? I'm not keen for that cell again," Venir said.

I ignored him and turned to face the door. Yes, the magic that tingled against my mind was irritating but the more I focused on it, focused on the door, the more I could feel how thin it was.

Fragile.

Darya huffed out a breath. Her boot tapped on the stone floor. The scrape of it sounded loud. Harsh. Echoey.

Irritating.

Nice try, really nice try. But I'd grown up at the North Pole surrounded by cheerful Elves, prancing reindeer, and an insufferable older brother, I knew how to put up with irritation.

I took a step closer to the door. The air tingled around me. The temperature seemed to drop. The little hairs on my arm stood up and almost tried to huddle together as I reached toward the door.

"Hey kid, don't do that," Venir said. "You gonna blow us up or something."

I ignored him and kept reaching for the door.

Darya took a stomping step toward me. Her hands now clenched into fists at her side.

"What are you doing?" she asked. "If you trigger the magic, the guards will find us immediately. Stop it!"

I felt Venir grab my pant leg.

"Stop, kiddo!"

Darya grabbed my right arm. "Stop!"

I took a deep, calming breath and shoved my left hand toward the door.

The curved wood felt cool under my skin but as I pressed against it, I felt it begin to warm up. Cold magic swirled and tingled up and down my arm. It felt like little ants, irritating but not lethal. I let the thought of them pass through me as I breathed. Still. Calm.

As the warmth began to spread in rhythm to my breathing, the magic began to dissipate. The tingling faded.

One breath, two, and it melted away, leaving my nose itchy and a shiver up my spine.

Venir let go of my leg.

Darya released my arm.

They both had frowns of puzzlement on their faces.

I grinned. "Shall we go inside?"

I pushed on the door. It swung open.

The room beyond was dark. Faint rays from the glowing spheres in the hall illuminated a couple of feet of turquoise tile until it darkened into blackness.

I couldn't see anything in that inky stillness.

Darya stepped forward to stand beside me. She lifted her hand and opened it. Her orb floated upward. Purplish light spilled forth. For a moment, it twinkled in the darkness, then light filled the room, bursting out as if someone had thrown up a window shade.

I blinked at the blinding light. After a moment, my eyes adjusted and I could see into the room.

Turquoise tiles led the way in but were soon covered by thick throw rugs of deep burgundy or shimmering gold. What wasn't covered by rugs was piled with mounds of clothing. Sleeves and pants legs stuck out, making the mounds almost look like strange octopi.

Against the left wall, a large oval sat on the floor. From the swirl of blankets on it, I guessed it was the bed. Across from it, sat a table with a chair angled toward it. A stack of bronze boxes sat on the table top, perched close to the edge.

There was no window in the room, but colourful tapestries hung on the black matte walls. Across from the doorway, a rectangular one hung with the long side horizontal. A landscape shimmered on it, the view of the forest outside but in daytime, with golden sunlight shimmering against the deep purple leaves. For a moment, it almost looked like those leaves were swaying in a breeze but when I blinked it was static again. The illusion shattered.

Darya cocked an eyebrow in my direction.

"You wanted to see if my cousin had anything of use in his room." She gestured at it. "Take a look."

How would I know if there was anything in this room that could help us? I'd never even met him. Almost landing on his corpse didn't count.

"You knew him best. Can you see if there's anything unusual in here?" I said.

She snorted and shook her head. "You see this room. How would I ever know? Lekzar was meticulous as a guard but kept his room in a mess. He did not believe he had to pick up after himself. I would not visit him here unless absolutely necessary which means I never did so how would I know either?" She crossed her arms over her chest again. "You are wasting time. The guards will be here momentarily. We should get out now."

After getting the door open, could I really leave without at least taking a cursory look? I stepped through the doorway. Just then, Venir pushed past Darya and tumbled into the room. He landed feet first, braced on either side of a small pile of clothes in the centre of the gold throw rug. He gave a great sniff and looked around.

"I visited Lekzar here," he said. "I'll look."

I glanced at Darya. Her brow crinkled in worry as she shot a glance back over her shoulder down the hall.

"Hurry up about it," I said.

Instead of starting to rummage through the mounds of clothes and clutter, Venir held out his hands palms facing out. He took even breaths and began to turn in a circle. The tops of his ears quivered. Sweat beaded on his forehead. His mouth worked as if he was chewing on his cigar. I could almost smell the smoke drift toward me.

But it wasn't smoke I was smelling, it was something else. Something familiar.

I breathed in as I stepped deeper into the room. I felt something pulling me toward the far corner, where a bed was tucked close to the wall. In the centre of the room, Venir stopped spinning. His ears quivered faster.

He faced the same direction I moved in.

I sniffed the air. Definitely something with a hint of smoke. But a richer, deeper scent.

I reached the end of the bed. An ornate headboard of carved black, edged with gold was pushed almost against the wall. A long shirt was draped over the corner, hanging almost to the floor. I lifted it aside.

The scent deepened.

The head of the bed was a good three inches from the wall. I dropped the shirt on the bed and crouched. The shadow of the wood headboard darkened along the wall, turning almost black in the far corner.

The warm smell made my head swim.

I fumbled along the wall. It felt cool against the back of my hand. Dust smeared on my fingers. Then I touched a smooth, roundish edge.

I fumbled for it. Tightened my hand as I felt it nestle into my palm. I rose to my feet as I pulled it out.

"What is it?" Venir said.

A greyish layer of dust covered my fingers. I opened my hand.

A roasted chestnut lay in my palm.

Just like the kind my mother would roast around Christmas time.

How had a roasted chestnut ended up here?

And why did it fill me with dread?

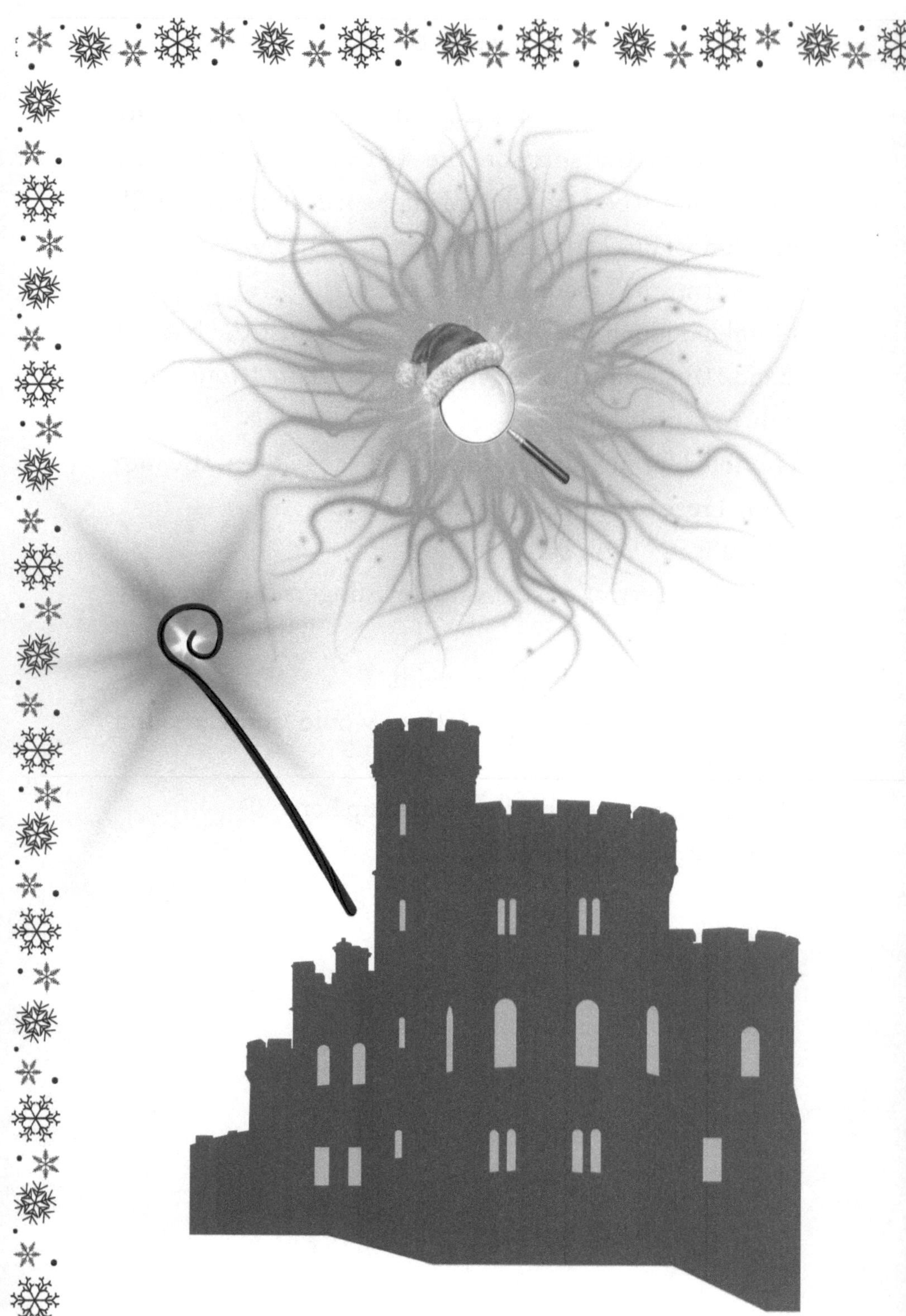

CHAPTER

SEVENTEEN

"So?" Venir said. "C'on kid, tell me what it is."

I opened my mouth to reply when Darya darted into the room. With a wave of her hand, the heavy wood door slid shut.

"Guards," she said. "I felt their wings flutter."

Venir, distracted by her entrance, turned back to me. Both of them stared at me.

Like I would know what to do.

I tightened my fist over the roasted chestnut. My mouth tasted as dry as the dust that coated my knuckles. I had no time to ponder how a roasted chestnut had ended up in Lekzar's quarters, in the Magical Realm. Guards were coming to get us.

And I had no idea what to do.

The orb above Darya's hand seemed to dim. Deep shadows emphasized the lines around her mouth, the creases in Venir's forehead. Even deeper shadows seemed to pool around us. The piles of clothing darkened into mounds of black.

Just how thorough would those guards look in this room?

I shoved the roasted chestnut into my pants pocket.

"Quick, get under one of the piles of clothes," I said.

I dropped to the floor. Where exposed, the turquoise tiles were cool under my skin. I shimmied to the nearest pile at the foot of the bed. My knee bumped into the edge of the one of the thick rugs.

I heard Venir's gruff mumble as he scrambled in another direction.

Darya was silent but still kept her orb glowing a low, dim purple.

Just enough for me to see the pile in front of me.

I seized the pile and dragged it over me. Soft silken fabric slipped against my arm and my bandaged hand, making my palm ache. Heavy, coarse fabric pooled around my ankles. Thick, stiff, leather-like material pressed against my back.

I breathed in the different scents of them. A muddy, earthen smell from the stiff, leathery material. A bright, almost lemon-citris aroma from the silken fabric. A spicy headiness from the coarse fabric that covered my legs.

I ducked my head under a final drooping top. Through

the weave, I saw Darya's orb descend to her palm, then wink out just as her arm disappeared into a pile in the middle of the floor.

Inky blackness filled my vision.

My breathing sounded like a rumble in the silence. I pursed my lips, breathing slowing in and out. I held my breath for a count of eight and breathed it out. My jack-hammering heart slowed.

Just a little.

I was a pile of clothing, that was all. I had to keep repeating that to myself. Nothing in here but a messy room.

And the roasted chestnut that was now digging into my hip because I was lying on it.

How had the thing ended up in here? I couldn't believe it was a coincidence, not with Lekzar dead, along with the multiple Santas in my realm. But it didn't make sense.

A creak sounded from across the room.

I held my breath. Was it Venir?

The door swung open, banging against the wall.

I flinched.

Had the pile of clothing around me moved? Ah swirling snow!

Booted steps stomped into the room. The tile seemed to creak in protest.

Clothes. I was a pile of clothes.

More steps, getting closer. Still clomping on the tile, then softened as they hit the rugs.

What if they tried to kick the clothing piles? Would they do that?

"Did you see them come this way?" a deep voice said.

"I cannot be sure, sir," another voice said. "The aura around the man is strange. Difficult to keep a reading on."

"Not of our realm," a third voice murmured.

"And the reason why we must capture him. He cannot be allowed to taint us," said the first voice.

I heard more shuffling in the room, more boots against the tiles. Would they start poking around, looking for my strange aura? My mouth dried up as my heart sped faster. It seemed to pound in my ears. The press of clothes against my face felt almost suffocating. The pile above me felt heavier and heavier, as if gravity had increased, pulling it down on top of me. I had a crazy urge to throw the clothing off, sending shirts and pants flying around the room.

Steady, just be steady. I breathed through my mouth, pursing my lips again, but my breath came in stuttering pulses. I tried to think calm but my body was having none of it. My muscles coiled. Sweated beaded my head and made the soft fabric stick to my skin. It felt even clammier, more claustrophobic.

I could feel my panic rising...

I closed my eyes and thought of the North Pole.

My brother and I had played hide and seek when we were boys. We were limited to the house and the stables. Mother forbade us from using the village in the game. One time I hid in a pile of wood chips in the back corner of the barn. The pile had felt soft at first, cushioning my five-year-old body as I wiggled into the centre. Before I knew it, the small chips had flowed all around me, cutting me off from the view of the bare ground which in the frozen north, was harder than stone.

The barn, a monolith of gleaming white wood that soared over my young head, was cool enough that I needed my trusty woollen coat, but under the wood chips I soon found myself getting warm.

The chips had a rich, thick scent of fresh wood that seemed to settle just a little deeper into my throat with every breath. The soft pile beneath me soon compressed and I felt a few sharp edges pinching my legs. The chips covering the top of me didn't feel too heavy, but I could feel grit from them scratching my eyes and making my nose itchy.

But even as the smell thickened and my eyes blurred, I could hear KJ yelling as he searched. It had been a whole five minutes, a record for me of hiding from KJ who seemed to have a knack for finding me in less than a minute no matter how well I hid.

But not this time.

I wanted to stay in the wood pile, but the pinch of the chips, the thick stench, the dust, were all making it difficult to stay still.

Then I heard a clomp on the hard dirt floor.

Several more followed. They stopped in front of the wood pile.

I froze, barely breathing. Tasting the thick coating of wood pulp in my throat.

Then a heavy snort sounded. A few chips in front of my face trickled away as a soft velvet nose pushed through.

KJ hadn't found me, but Blizten had.

Her snort puffed warm air over my face, momentarily clearing away the thick smell of the wood. Her nose pressed against my cheek. I felt the soft warmth of her tongue as she licked my face.

I had wanted to push her away because KJ would see her and find me, but the soothing reindeer musk and her velvet nose stopped me. Her strong, calm presence calmed me under the wood chips. The smell no longer seemed to choke me. The sharp edges no longer seemed to pinch.

After a moment, she had withdrawn her nose but I could still hear her deep breathing as she stood beside the wood chip pile. I hear the occasional crunching as she nibbled on a stray chip.

KJ never did find me under that wood chip pile.

Just like these guards wouldn't find me.

Remembering Blitzen's soothing, calming presence relaxed me. Even if one of the guards kicked at this pile, I would flop around like the clothes. They would wander away again.

Just like KJ.

The clothes cushioned me although I still felt the edge of the roasted chestnut digging into my hip. But that wasn't of any consequence now. Now I focused on just being part of the piles of clothes.

Boot stomps sounded again, still muffled by the rugs, then the sound strengthened as they reached the tile.

Heading for the door.

Leaving?

I kept my breathing steady but my heart sped up.

More boot sounds near the door.

"Report," said a new voice, gruffer, deeper.

"I thought there was something here," said the first voice. "But it is as you see, captain."

"Hmm, Lekzar was not known for tidiness in his home," said the second voice.

"But the aura trace led you here," said the captain.

"Yes, sir, but now there is nothing."

Shuffling sounded near the door. I held my breath. My mouth tasted like dry socks. Were there even socks in this pile of clothing?

My heart pounded so loud and hard, I was sure it was starting to make the pile pulse in rhythm. I tried more to be the clothing. Just be soft silken fabric. Be thicker leather.

Ignore the fierce poke of the roasted chestnut digging into my hip bone.

Finally the boot steps moved off the sharp click of the tile. I heard them thump on the harder stone floor in the corridor.

"We will start again from the last known location," the captain said.

More boot steps followed then the creek of the wood door as it swung shut. A soft click filled the room.

I stayed frozen.

Would they have left someone behind to guard just in case?

I opened my eyes but the clothing around me shrouded me in darkness. The only way to know if there was any guard would be to throw the pile off.

Did I want to take that risk?

As I pondered, I noticed that I could see the edges of the top in front of me. The collar of the purple shirt almost poked me in the nose.

A light source was shining somewhere in the room.

They *had* left someone behind!

I could feel my muscles clench. I had to assume the guard would be near the door. That made sense. Perhaps if I leapt up fast enough, tossing clothing in his face, I would be able to take him by surprise.

Would a punch take down a fae guard? I couldn't risk that it wouldn't. I took a deep breath, gathering my magic...

"Kringle, are you coming out?" Darya said.

I shoved the top out of my face. The soft purplish glow from the orb in her hand greeted me. I peered out.

Darya crouched in front of my pile of clothing. Venir stood just over her right shoulder. His arms were crossed over his chest and his lips were pursed. They quivered as they held in laughter.

"They are gone," Darya said.

"So I gathered," I said. My voice sounded raspy and dry.

The heavy leather-like fabric seemed to try to hang on as I pushed myself out of the pile. Finally, my limbs came free and I flopped onto the turquoise tiles.

A silken top was curled around my left ankle.

Darya gave a disgusted snort as I peeled it off and dropped it to the floor.

"Your cousin had some interesting clothing choices," I said.

"Not all of these clothes are his," she said.

Her frown deepened as she glanced back at the door.

"That was a close one," Venir said. "They gotta be all over the place. So how we gonna get out, kiddo?"

Again looking at me like I had the answer.

Maybe this private detective business wasn't all it was cracked up to be. At least not in the Faerie Realm.

I shoved my hands into my pockets and felt the smooth surface of the chestnut. I pulled it out and held it in my palm.

"What do you know about this?" I said to Darya.

She turned back and peered at the chestnut in my hand.

"I have never seen that before," she said. "What is it?"

Venir stood on his tiptoes, wavering from side to side to catch a glimpse. I lowered my hand.

"Is that a roasted chestnut?" he said.

I nodded. "I found it on the floor."

"What would Lekzar be doin' with a roasted chestnut?" Venir said.

"Good question," I said. "And how would he have gotten

it if they don't exist in this realm?" I held it closer to Darya. "Are you sure you've never seen this before? You don't have these here?"

She shook her head. "Our seedlings are much small. Many are soft. Even the great darbo trees come from tiny black seedlings. None so large or hard as this."

I closed my fingers on the chestnut, feeling the smooth surface against my palm, the sharp edges press against my skin.

So that was it then.

Proof that Lekzar at the very least had been to the Human Realm.

Was that what got him killed?

At some point, he had travelled to the Human Realm. Alone? I didn't think so. If he had, there would have been no reason to kill him. It seemed clear that his murder was related to the Human Realm if only because Venir and I had crossed over from it. We'd made convenient and easy patsies, except it also told me that whoever had killed Lekzar had a hand with the chaos going on back home.

Chaos that was going to engulf my brother sooner rather than later.

It was time to stop running and start investigating.

"We gotta go," Venir said.

"Not so fast," I said. "I want to look around some more."

Venir shook his head. In the dim light from Darya's orb, the tips of his ears quivered.

"Are you crazy, boy? They'll be comin' back any minute."

"No, they will not," Darya said. "Even if they trace Kringle's aura back here, they will not come back right away." She gave a slow blink. For a moment, her eyes glittered yellow, then another blink and they were back to their normal smokey blue.

My skin tingled from the feel of magic in the air, like static discharge. Just another hint that what I was seeing wasn't all there was to the Faerie Realm. Were they cloaking it or was I just unable to look beyond their veils?

Was I even going to be able to find anything here? Would I recognize a clue if I did?

I had to believe I could or there would be no point in looking. I had to look everywhere. I couldn't just leave with nothing. Even the roasted chestnut wasn't enough.

I stepped around a pile of clothes and crossed to the table set beside the wall near the door. The wood surface was covered a stack of leather-bound books. The top one showed the stylized emblem of a dragon, half covered by a sheaf of papers. I picked up the top one. It was off white and so light I could barely feel it in my fingers. The surface was blank. I tilted it toward the dim light from Darya's orb. A shimmer ran across the surface, then text appeared, in a script I couldn't read.

"Darya, what does this say?" I asked.

Her brow crinkled in puzzlement. "What does what say? The paper is blank."

My mouth went dry. She couldn't see the text? Was I even seeing it?

I looked back at the paper, tilting it again in the light. The text was now clearly visible, a deep rich black against the soft white. Hand lettered, I could tell from the variations in the print. I tilted it toward Venir.

If he didn't see it, I might have to question my own mind...

The Elf nodded. "Yep, there's writing there all right. I can't read it either."

Darya's gaze shifted from me to Venir and back.

"You see writing on the page?"

"Sure do," he said.

"And you?"

I nodded.

She reached for the sheet. As her fingers got close, the paper crinkled and curled in my hand as if trying to get away. A wisp of grey smoke came from the top. I caught a whiff of burning paper.

"No, stop," I said. "The paper is self-destructing."

Darya yanked her hand back.

"A spell," Venir said, "to keep that paper outta Fae hands." He chuckled. "That's just like Lekzar to write it all down but make it so no one could read it."

Darya nodded. "He would have enchanted the text to ensure it could not be casually deciphered. Obviously he did not wish one of his compatriots to get hold of it. It was meant for you."

Great, but how was I supposed to figure out what it said?

I stared at the shimmering print. The text seemed to be

made up of letters and symbols. I could almost tell how they were arranged into sentences and then into paragraphs.

Until the final sentence trailed off the page.

Looking unfinished.

"There's more," I said. The paper seemed to quiver in my hand, as if to let me know I was right, there was more.

I rifled through the rest of the desk. Like the floor behind me covered in clothing, the desktop was covered with books and papers but somehow I could tell most of these didn't have anything to do with my off white page of goobly gook.

Still, several of them felt tinged with magic. A thick book bound with a deep brown hide that felt velvety smooth practically hummed when I picked it up. The vibration up my arm was so strong I almost tossed it away. Instead, I set it down on the far right of the desk, moving other papers over it to mask its effects.

Another stack of papers released a strong musky odour. Despite myself, my lungs seemed to drag the scent in. I felt a lethargy pull me down. My eyelids drooped. My limbs felt heavy. Even as I released the pages, I felt my legs begin to buckle. I barely managed to grab hold of the edge of the desk.

Darya stepped up, grabbing my arm. I felt Venir on my other side, steadying me at the waist.

"You all right, Noel?" he asked. "You're as shaky as the Elves after a few cups of our celebratory cider."

Darya peeled the papers from my fingers and dropped them on the stack on the right side.

"More enchantments," she said. "Lekzar practiced often."

The musky stench faded. Energy flowed back into my muscles. My limbs felt stronger. I straightened.

"Powerful stuff," I said.

Darya cocked an eyebrow as if to say *to you*.

Now a faerie was making fun of me. But she still couldn't read the paper. Technically, I couldn't either but at least I could *see* the text. Reading could come after.

I was a little more careful with the rest of the items on the desk. Any strange sensation or smell, I dropped them immediately but nothing had the same pungent odour as the musky pages.

Finally, as I reached the scratched wooden surface, I found another two pages with similar writing on it. I tilted it toward the light from Darya's orb. Definitely the same hand had scripted these pages. I recognized the tilt of the printing, the way the ink blotted the page.

"Do you see that?" I asked her.

She shook her head.

Good enough for me.

Now I just had to figure out a way to read them.

And I had a suspicion about that.

But first, we had to get out of here.

"Venir, is the place we came through the only way to get back to our realm?" I said.

"It's the closest portal," he said. "I might be able to open another but it'd take way more energy. I just not feeling it, kiddo."

"Okay, so we have to get there. Darya, can you get us out of the castle? We have to get back through the woods."

"The guards are already on high alert," she said. "It will be almost impossible." A sly smile stole across her lips. "It is a good thing I trained with them."

I grinned back at her.

"Just get us out of the castle," I said. "I can take care of the rest."

CHAPTER
EIGHTEEN

Instead of leading us to the outer walls, Darya led us down into the depths of the castle. As the air drew damper and the stone walls more ragged looking, I wanted to ask her if she knew where she was going but the look of concentration on her face stopped me. Lines deepened around her mouth and her green eyes seemed to glow in the dimness.

I glanced back at Venir. The Elf was hurrying along behind me, his short legs double timing as he rushed along. His breath puffed out and his cheeks were red.

"Maybe cut down on the cigars," I whispered to him.

He gave me the finger but a smile creased his mouth, erasing the worry that dug into his face.

At least that made one of us.

Darya reached a corner and stopped. She pushed her

small glowing orb out in front of her, like a magical sensor. Orangish light brightened. It drifted away from her palm, moving toward the corner. She stayed frozen in place, barely breathing.

I stopped behind her and waited. I could feel the press of Lekzar's paper in my pocket. I'd folded them into my list and stuffed them down but it didn't diminish the feel of them. They felt like a cold itch in the back of my head, like a whisper I couldn't quite make out. Irritating and annoying. Like the chestnut I had in my other pocket.

Where had Lekzar gotten it if he hadn't crossed over into the other Realms? He couldn't have drawn it to himself while remaining in the Between and if he'd crossed over, the other fae would have known.

Wouldn't they?

If I assumed that Lekzar had stayed in the Between, only causing minor mischief, how would he had gotten the chestnut?

Had someone else crossed over? Someone that Lekzar had seen? Had he taken the chestnut as proof?

Too many questions. I only hoped some answers would be in these pages and that my plan to read them would work.

It had to. I was running out of ideas.

Ahead of me, the grey piping on Darya's shoulders straightened as she relaxed. She beckoned with her left hand and her orb flowed back to her from around the corner.

She nodded her head to us and pointed at the corner.

All clear.

Venir gave a grunt and stepped around me. Darya turned to lead.

I started to follow. My foot caught on an edge of tile, making me stumble. I reached out with my right hand. My palm hit the wall. Pain bit into it as the wound opened again.

And I felt the reverberation of fae energy humming from around the corner.

We were being followed!

I yanked my hand from the stone wall, scraping my palm against the rough brick. I gasped as I left a few flakes of skin behind.

"Be still," Darya said.

"Too late for that," I said. "They're right behind us."

"Huh?" Venir said.

"I could feel them in the wall," I said. "Just a few minutes away."

Darya's frown deepened. "Run!"

She spun away from us and sprinted down the corridor.

Venir gave a yelp and raced after her.

I brought up the rear.

My feet pounded on the hard tile floor. It dipped lower, leading down. I gulped in air. Did it taste a little cooler?

Were we closer to the exterior of the castle?

I heard a shout from behind me. Pounding footsteps sounded. I felt a crackle like static in the air. Fae magic.

I knew I shouldn't but I had to know.

I shot a quick glance behind me.

Rounding the corner, a pair of guards raced forward,

heads bent, arms pumping. Their black wings blurred behind them. Air sparkled around them as they got more and more distant from me.

No, that wasn't right.

They weren't getting distant.

They were shrinking.

Another moment and they shrank to a quarter of their regular size. They leapt into the air and flew toward me.

Zooming like miniature missiles.

Swirling snow!

I poured on the speed. My feet blurred. Air grabbed at my hair. I spotted Venir just ahead. Sparkles shimmered around him. He was also using magic to run but I would soon overtake him.

Then the fae guards would be on him. I couldn't just leave him for them.

What kind of Kringle would that make me?

But I could feel the guards gaining. Their magic was a scorching heat against my back. Yet with every step, cool air wafted from the wall to my left. The exterior wall.

I could use that.

I breathed it in, focusing. My skin prickled as my own magic shimmered. It swirled outward to combine with Venir's.

Another resident from the North Pole.

My magic fed on his, absorbing it.

I breathed out and my breath came out in a fog.

Close. Just a few more steps.

I sucked in another breath. The hairs in my nose froze. My eyelashes crinkled with frost.

I spun and *shoved*.

Freezing wind slammed into the heat from the fae guards. The air steamed with a loud hiss. Billowing clouds of fog filled the corridor, blocking my view of the guards.

A good start but it wouldn't be enough to stop them.

I focused on the foggy air, pumping more cold into it. My skin goose-pimped. As the air swirled, I felt the first telltale specks of frozen liquid alit on my cheeks and melt.

Almost. Just a little bit more...

I breathed out again, drawing more of the cold from the exterior wall. It was only the cold of late night but that didn't matter. I could still use it. I could still focus it. I could still amplify it, until it became...

Winter!

The swirling air crystalized. I felt the sting of ice. The fog thickened and turned white as snow spun.

And lashed at the advancing guards.

Suddenly, in the middle of the corridor, they were facing a blizzard.

Snow and ice crusted on the walls. I backed away, still facing the guards. Snow crunched under my feet. It was already almost covering the toes of my shoes. Ice crystals hung from the ceiling, growing downward like sharp teeth. Eddies of snow swirled, thickening on the walls, narrowing the corridor with every pass moment.

The fae poured on the heat, melting the snow. The ice

shards hanging from the ceiling began to drip, then dribble, then pour water. Soon the snow lining the corridor walls began to recede.

Good, that was good.

I inched away. The remaining snow still crunched under my feet. I felt the heat of the faerie guards as they drew closer.

Ten feet.

Five.

I *shoved* again.

Frigid air blasted them. The dribbling icicles froze, looking almost like jail cell bars. The water on the tile floor flash froze. Suddenly the guards running from behind were sliding along.

And the faerie guards flying toward me dropped to the floor, surrounded by frozen blocks of water.

I stumbled backward. My legs felt like jelly. My breath wheezed in my chest. Energy seeped from my limbs, making me feel heavy. The cold from the mini snow storm, normally so comforting and familiar, now made my bones ache and my teeth chatter. I blinked and felt my eye lashes crusting with cold.

Even here in the Magical Realm where I could access my North Pole magic, I could go too far.

And I certainly had.

My fingertips ached and then began to burn with cold. My lungs wheezed as I tried to pull in air. My vision began to cloud as if a film was creeping from the sides. No, not film. Ice. Crusting over my face, over my eyes.

Creeping over my nostrils.

I tried to open my mouth but my jaw felt locked into place. Heavy. My entire head felt heavy. My entire body. But I couldn't even bend my legs or move my arms. Everything was locked into place.

Frozen.

I wheezed in the last tiny trickle of air through my nostrils. My throat ached. My lungs began to burn. My head felt light, as if the heavy ice coating my hair had suddenly been removed, but even as I thought it I knew it was the lack of oxygen in my brain.

I knew I should feel panicked but somehow that idea seemed very far away. And I was so, so tired.

The film over my eyes thickened. At first I could still see light, but as it deepened, the light faded, leaving me in darkness.

Frozen, and running out of air.

CHAPTER
NINETEEN

I felt myself freefalling in darkness. The black had a thick, inky quality that reminded me of the night sky at the North Pole. Except there were no twinkling stars breaking the smothering dark.

My body was a distant memory. The images of the faerie guards faded.

Everything was blackness. Just inky blackness. Like the deepest part of the deepest river. Something like movement flowed over me, but it was so far above me, I couldn't tell if it was real.

I was just drifting. Drifting...

Something pressed against me. A distant signal from my distant body. Pressure against my back. Had I fallen over as I froze? It occurred to me that I should try to move my limbs but I couldn't feel them. Were they still frozen or was I still too far down in the darkness?

And if I was so far down, how did I even know it?

Something like concern stirred me out of the heavy lethargy I felt.

Was I dead? I didn't feel dead. Maybe instead I was frozen and the faerie lord had placed me on a pedestal in his court. Both as a warning and a boast to all. What would have happened to Venir and Darya? Were they imprisoned? And my brother, was he even now being stalked by the monster that had killed the other Santas? Would KJ just be the warm up for killing Dad?

A heavy thumping surrounded me, growing faster and faster in rhythm. Someone pounding on me?

My heart! I could feel my heart pounding.

Maybe I wasn't so frozen after all.

Wouldn't that be a shock when I fell off my pedestal. It would have been nice to leap off but I had no illusions about my current state. If I was able to rise to my knees without help it would be a miracle.

So what would happen when I finally moved? Would I be imprisoned like Venir and Darya? Or maybe they'd decide to just execute me instead.

Staying frozen didn't sound so bad anymore.

But as I felt the sensation of my limbs come tingling back, I knew I didn't have much choice in the matter.

Aches began to ripple through me. I felt like an old rug being shaken out. Soon the aches dissolved into pinpricks of pain, radiating across my back and through my limbs. I felt something hard against my back. Was that the feel of the stone floor?

With effort, I willed my right hand to move. Even with the tingling pain, it felt like a distant part of me. Just feel the floor, that's all I wanted, to trace the line of the tiles.

I grunted with effort. My mouth felt dry, tasted of dried out pine needles. Moisture dotted my forehead, sweat from my effort.

Finally I felt my fingers move, scratch at the floor beneath me.

Strange, it didn't feel like tile. The surface was too rough.

A piece of it rolled under my pinkie.

The inky blackness seemed to thin out. I saw dim light creating a thin line. My eyelids flickered.

The light expanded.

My eyes watered as I opened them.

A shadow dimmed the light. A puff of cigar-tinged breath blew in my face.

"Kid, can ya hear me? Are you all right?"

Another blast of cigar stench bathed my nose and coated the inside of my throat, making me gag. I started coughing. My body spasmed. I rolled onto my left side.

Venir pounded me on the back. "That's it, kiddo, get it all out?"

I felt cool fingers brush against my forehead. "Is he all right?"

Darya.

I blinked the residual tears from my eyes. My hands shook as I pressed them against the floor to push myself up. I didn't get very far before I fell back down but I soon felt Darya and Venir pull/push me into a sitting position.

Outside. In darkness.

No, not quite.

I blinked and focused around me.

The rough stone was asphalt. The dim glow from a yellow street light about twenty feet away. As Venir pulled away, taking his cigar breath with him, I caught a whiff of fresh air, laidened with a hint of moisture and the earthy smell of trees.

Silence surrounded us. No yells of guards, no stomping feet.

Just the whisper of wind and the rustle of leaves against branches.

My whole body ached but I still rolled over to push myself up on my feet. I swayed a little until Darya took my elbow, steadying me.

She looked even paler in the soft light. Her green eyes had a dim glow. Lines of fatigue deepened across her forehead and around her mouth. Even as she steadied me, her shoulders drooped.

She seemed to be missing something there but I couldn't tell what.

I took another glance at our surroundings. It felt familiar, like I should know the place. A wide expanse of asphalt. Outside of the ring of yellow light, hulking shadows of trees.

As I turned around, I caught a glimpse of a large tiered object, building upward in a triangle shape.

A fountain.

Wait a minute...

I spun back toward Venir so fast I would have fallen if not for Darya's steadying grip.

"Venir, where are we?"

The Elf grinned. "We got home, kiddo. Darya opened a portal and we jumped through after you froze the guards." He pounded me on the arm, trying to reach up to my shoulder but his arm wasn't long enough. "That was a beautiful thing, kid, the way you took 'em out. Perfect."

Took them out. My mouth dropped open.

"I didn't kill anyone, did I?"

"What?" Venir said. "Of course not, you just froze 'em is all. They should be fine."

"Once we passed through to this Realm, your magic would have been nullified," Darya said.

"Nullified. You mean unfrozen?"

She nodded. Her head bowed and her shoulders hunched up.

"I should not be here," she said.

She was disobeying her lord's command. Not even Lekzar had done that. Or hadn't he? How else would he have obtained a roasted chestnut?

I dug into my pants pocket. My nails scraped up some lint before closing on the nut. I pulled it out. Good, it had made the transition.

Maybe we could find out where it came from. Hopefully with Darya's help.

"Maybe not," I said. "But you are so we should make the best of it. If you help me, I'm sure we can smooth things over for you at home."

She frowned at me. "How can you be so sure?"

I couldn't, not really. But eager hope flickered in her eyes. I just couldn't douse it.

"Don't worry," I said. "Once we've figured out what's going on and stopped the attempt on Santa Claus's life, we'll take care of it."

A slight smile curved her lips. She gave me a nod.

"Venir, do you know what day it is?" I said, turning back to the Elf.

He was just waving a match in the air. The tiny flame flicked out and a thin stream of smoke died on it. He had a cigar clamped in his mouth. A few puffs made the end glow red. He took the cigar from his lips and blew smoke out, pursing his lips to the right and aiming the smoke away.

"It's the same night, kid," he said. "Pro'lly..." He pulled a silver pocket watch from his left jeans pocket. His finger flicked the lid. It popped open, the first strand of Jingle Bells tinkled.

"Ha, only been ten minutes." He snapped the lid shut and stuffed the watch into his pocket.

"Ten minutes," I said. "That's not possible."

"It is very possible," Darya said. "I aimed the portal to return you to your realm. It brought you as close to it as possible. Including the time." She bowed her head. "I regret I could not get sooner than ten minutes."

"Ten minutes is fine," I said.

Swirling snow, it wasn't only fine, it was perfect. I straightened even more and felt my back crack. My heart pounded even harder, stronger, like it was finally get back up to speed after being frozen. As well, I felt a flicker of hope myself.

If we'd only been away for ten minutes in our realm, there was still time. I would still be able to save KJ.

I would still be able to save Dad.

My hand tightened on the chestnut.

Now I just had to figure out how to do it.

And even with crossing into a different realm, I didn't feel any closer to figuring that out.

Along with the thudding of my heart came the prickle of sweat starting on the back of my neck.

Both Venir and Darya were looking at me with expectation, like I would know what to do next. I was the private detective. This was what I was supposed to be good at. But this whole case had been screwy from the beginning. Christopher Hitchens dead in the middle of July just because he was dressed in a Santa suit. But his corpse disappearing and then reappearing. The other dead Santas.

Now the threat to KJ.

Wait a minute...

The phantom that had pretended to be Hitchens.

It had to have been some kind of spell, some magic. But

to wield it, the magic user would have had to have been in this realm.

And if Lekzar had known who it was...

He had been with the magic user. The proof was in my hand.

I grinned at the Elf and the Faerie standing in front of me.

"I've got an idea of where to investigate next," I said. "Let's get the ferry back to the mainland."

"How will I get you back to the mainland?" Darya said. She seemed to droop with fatigue.

Venir chuckled. "He didn't mean you. He meant a ferry, like a boat. We're on an island here."

"Come on," I said. I led them back down the paved path. Soft yellow light from the widely spaced streetlights glowed, illuminating our way. The trees were deep shadows around us, reminding me of the forest in the Faerie Realm. Sinister and full of dread.

It wasn't just the cool air that was making my skin tighten.

Was it possible that something had followed us through the portal?

I turned to my left where Darya walked and opened my mouth to ask.

Just as a foul wind rose up from the right.

Hot, dry air with the smell of charred bones reached my nose. I heard the crackle of something like leather snap and click above my head. The yellow lights along the path flickered and sputtered, reacting.

"Great bells!" Venir yelled.

I yanked my gaze up.

A dark shadow hovered over us. Another leather snap and the shadow expanded, stretching out on either side. Swirling snow, wings! They flapped, sending down another gust of dry, charred air. I heard a rumbling roar.

"Dragon," Darya breathed. Her shoulders hunched.

"Run!" I shouted.

I darted forward, dragging Darya by her hand and Venir by the scruff of his collar. My feet pounded the pavement.

The rumbling increased in volume. Hot air turned from a breeze to a billowing wind.

I shoved Darya and Venir off the path and into the trees to my right.

"Venir, get her to the ferry," I said.

"Right kid." Venir's voice floated back to me as I skidded to a stop. I spun and started running again.

Back the way I'd come.

Above me, the dragon's leathery wings crackled and snapped as it beat at the air, trying to gain altitude. Maybe there was something different about the atmosphere in the Human Realm, just enough to throw the dragon off balance.

Enough to let me gain a few steps.

I pumped my arms as my legs drove me forward.

The pavement curved to the left. I caught sight of the bridge stretching wide.

The river it crossed could help but the dragon might be expecting it. I wanted to make sure it couldn't anticipate my move.

My heart pounded as I sucked in air. The warmth felt like it was crisping my nose hairs. I could almost feel my beard curling against my skin.

I glanced back over my shoulder.

The shadow hovered behind me, smaller as the dragon gained altitude. Probably trying to keep all of us in sight.

Smart of it, bad for me.

I didn't want it to go after Venir and Darya. I couldn't let its tiny pea brain make the decision to go after the greater number of prey. Time to catch its attention again.

I reached the mouth of the bridge and stopped, grabbing hold of the railing. My heart was still pounding, reminding me that with my insistence on using my sparse magic to *wink* all over the city I wasn't getting enough cardio to be running at this pace.

I sucked in two deep breaths before I turned to face the hovering shadow.

"Hey bad breath, you need some major mints to cover that stink!"

Not the wittiest of repartee but I yelled it at the top of my lungs, hoping the dragon would connect to my voice and maybe even get the gist of the insult.

A bellowing roar answered me. It sent a blast of wind down, shaking the trees until the leaves seemed to hiss in protest. I glanced back at the winking lights of the city across the water. How long would they last if the dragon headed there? Even if the city had some kind of air defense (which it didn't), I couldn't be sure anything here would have an impact on such a magical beast.

It would have to be me.

And although my yell had caught its attention, I couldn't be sure of holding it.

I unwrapped the remnants of my torn shirt from my hand. It still stuck to my palm. I clenched my teeth and yanked it off. It tore and through the sharp sting of pain I felt a fresh welling of blood on my skin.

I lifted my hand and waved it in the hot, dry air.

The next bellow was even louder. The tiny dot darkening the sky began to grow larger.

It was diving.

Straight for me.

I turned and ran back over the bridge. It sloped upward to the centre before gently angling back down.

The hard concrete jarred my feet with each pounding step. Pain throbbed in my hand. My lungs burned. My heart galloped. The angle felt impossibly sharp.

Was I running up a mountain?

The crack and snap of leathery wings sounded again. Getting closer.

Closer.

I reached the middle. The pavement curved down. Now my feet began to race faster, as if they were trying to outrun the rest of my body. My run became more of a barely controlled stumble as I lurched onward.

Hot air pushed at my back, propelling me. Another roar blasted out. I felt the hair on the back of my neck shrivelling as if singed.

I didn't dare glance back. The foul, charred stench made it seem like the dragon was right behind me.

I didn't want confirmation.

Just another few steps.

The ground began to level out. I poured on the speed, pumping my arms. Drops of blood flew from my hand.

I heard the dragon's mouth snap. Teeth crashed together like clattering bones.

Any minute it would be my body between those teeth, being pulverized in that jaw like a vice.

Just another few steps.

Out of the gloom, the concrete fountain rose above me. Three tiers of flat, concrete platters, now silent and still, rose from the bottom well. Under the hot, dry stench, I could detect the faintest hint of moisture in the air.

All I had to do was get to that fountain.

Something hit me on the right shoulder. Razor sharp claws shredded my shirt. I ducked, stumbling forward, but I'd been knocked off my stride. My left ankle twisted, my leg followed, and buckled.

I spilled onto the concrete. Felt myself rolling. Leathery snaps crackled inches from my face. I caught a glimpse of a clawed foot. It stretched huge, filling my vision.

Reaching...

I rolled again.

The dragon shrieked as it missed me. I felt my shirt tear again, the lightest scrape of the claws against my arm. Tightening. Trying to grab but missing.

I kept rolling.

My vision blurred.

White asphalt. Black sky. Grey concrete. All of it swirling as I rolled.

I was getting dizzy. My breath came in gasps. My hand throbbed. My body felt like a large bruise.

The dragon's roar blasted me. Its hot breath seared my skin as I rolled into it.

It was waiting for me to come to it.

Swirling snow!

Thick, brownish legs slammed into the asphalt in front of my face. A jagged claw sliced the air an inch from my nose. I felt the dragon curling above me, drawing in a breath to a wave of fire blasting over me.

I closed my eyes. Clenched my fists.

Rolled harder.

My shoulder and hip struck the legs just below the knee. I felt the dragon shudder, unbalance. The leather wings billowed out, flapping madly to regain its equilibrium.

And it would have made it too.

If it hadn't been standing right in front of the fountain.

I opened my eyes to see the dragon just starting to

topple. Its head lifted high and opened its mouth to shriek, spraying fire upward into the sky. A moment earlier, I would have been burned to a cinder.

I lunged upward. I could only reach just above the dragon's knees. Its skin felt thick and dry under my fingers, like heavy parchment.

I let out my own roar as I shoved.

Its feet came up off the asphalt. One claw racked across my cheek as it flipped upward. I jerked my head back. It barely missed my eye.

For a moment, the dragon seemed to hang in the air on its back, like it was going to the do the back stroke. Wings extended far out to each side. Mouth open in a shrieking wail.

Then gravity grabbed the creature and slammed it down.

Right into the fountain.

Water splashed up in a hissing rise of steam. Clouds of it billowed out, coating my skin in charred slime. The dragon's roar turned to a shrill shriek of agony. Frantic splashing sent waves of water churning over the sides of the fountain. Through the grey fog of steam I saw a single clawed foot rise up, reaching out, clawed toes clenching before it slammed down against the concrete edge of the fountain.

The concrete clattered. A hunk fell out and splashed in the water. The foot appeared again but this time the thick, leathery skin looked like it was flaking off, running like black sludge.

Another moment and the splashing stopped. The shrieks died.

Leaving only the hissing of the water as it continued to billow up in great clouds.

With a groan, I lurched to my feet. My body felt like I had been pummelled. The throbbing in my hand had dimmed to a dull ache.

The grey fog stank of charred flesh. I wanted to back away from it before it settled into the pores of my skin, into the very foundations of my body where I would never be able to scrub it out. But I couldn't. I had to wait for the clouds to dissipate. I had to see.

I had to make sure the dragon was gone.

Its tenuous hold in this realm should not have been able to survive the full dousing of water in the fountain. In its own realm, the water would have just slowed it down a little. Dragons didn't much like water. I had gambled that the magic holding the dragon here wasn't strong enough to resist submersion.

But I couldn't be sure.

If the dragon had somehow survived...

I swallowed. My throat felt raw. The charred stench seemed to permeate my mouth. My eyes watered from the stinging steam. I inched closer, trying to peer through the grey clouds. They seemed a little thinner. Any minute now I should be able to see the fountain.

Any minute now, I should know if the dragon was truly gone.

I readied myself, tried to draw in the tiny bit of magic I had.

A scraping sound split the air behind me.

CHAPTER

TWENTY

I lurched around, swaying like an overburdened, snow-covered pine tree.

Billowing steam filled the air around me, smudging the night from black to grey. The distant park lights looked like dollops of yellow. I widened my stance, trying to stay up right as I swayed on the hard concrete.

Through the thinning steam, I glimpsed Venir and Darya standing a few yards away.

"I told you to run." My voice came out in a croak. I tasted the charred slime that tried to slither down my throat. I coughed and hacked, finally spitting out the worst of it.

A hand patted my back. Darya stood at my side.

"Spit all of it out," she said. "It is best to avoid swallowing it. Dragon remains can cause sickness and even death if too much is inhaled."

Sickness and death. Great. Just what I needed.

I bent over, hands on my knees, and spit out as much as I could. When the saliva dried up from my mouth, I could still taste the charred residue. I stood, wiping my hand across my mouth.

"So that running thing I told you to do," I said. "Why didn't you do it?"

"I couldn't just leave you to face it yourself, kid," Venir said. "If I cut and run like that, whadya think your dad woulda said? How could I ever show my face at the North Pole?"

I raised an eyebrow at him then winced. Even my forehead felt bruised.

But Venir caught the look. He spread his hands. "Hey, I had your back, kid."

Sure he had.

I turned away from the Elf.

"Darya, could anything else have followed us through the portal you opened?"

The Faerie shook her head. "It should not have been able to follow us at all. I opened a portal for only a moment and it was tuned to only us. I do not understand how it could have followed us at all."

Interesting. I patted my pants pocket with the chestnut. The inkling of an idea was starting to scratch at my mind but I felt too sore to be able to focus on it.

"Let's get out of here," I said. "Ferry or no, I have to get back to my office."

Venir pulled the cigar from between his lips. Ash trickled down to the asphalt, making me think of the dragon.

"You don't care if we take the ferry?" he said. "Why didn't you say that first thing, kid? I can get us there."

"What?" I said.

But the Elf grabbed my wrist and Darya's hand. For a moment all I could feel were his little fingers wrapped around my skin. His hands were so small he could barely reach around my wrist. Then I felt the pop of air pressure. My vision dimmed. My head swirled with vertigo. I felt empty space under my shoes then a hard surface smacked up against them, making my knees bend. I stumbled. Venir released my wrist.

My vision returned.

Darkness. Vague shadows around me. As I turned, I spotted an open rectangle that let in anaemic, yellowish light.

And the warm breeze tinged with the familiar scent of dust.

I moved forward, fumbling at waist level. My knees bumped into a large piece of furniture. My left hand felt the familiar cool knob of a desk lamp.

I turned it on.

Light sprang from my fifty watt bulb revealing my scuffed Goodwill desk, my leather chair, and the remains of my damaged window.

I had never been so happy to see my office.

Suddenly my entire body started to ache, like it had

waited until it felt safe to let me know exactly how injured it was and how upset it was about it. I dragged myself around the edge of the desk and flopped into the leather chair. It squeaked in protest under me.

Darya stood just inside the doorway looking around. Venir had crossed to the single wooden chair and sat down, resting his boots on the corner of my desk. He puffed on his cigar.

"I figered you'd wanna come here," he said.

"Is this your home?" Darya said.

"No, it's my office," I said. "Where I work."

Puzzlement creased her brow. "This is not a place I would have believed Santa Claus would work in."

Venir chuckled as I shook my head.

"No, my dad doesn't work here," I said. "I work here. As a private detective. I investigate from here."

"How will you discover who is killing the Santa Claus's?" she asked.

Good question. Too bad I had no clue how to answer.

"You got coffee here, kid?" Venir said.

"I'm out."

He huffed as he lifted his feet from the desk. Ash from his cigar trickled onto the floor as he stood.

"We'll get some," he said. He gave me a nod as he took Darya's arm to steer her toward the outer door.

"What is coffee?" Darya asked.

"Elixir of the gods," Venir said. "Or so some say."

Their voices faded to murmurs as the door clicked shut, leaving me to my thoughts.

Which seemed to be just as Venir had planned.

I gave a thin smile. He probably figured not having to answer a litany of questions from Darya might help me organize my thoughts and come up with some ideas.

I hoped he was right. But sitting in my chair in slime-covered clothes wasn't helping my concentration.

My groan filled the office as I got up. I shuffled past the desk and out to the small waiting area. In front of me across the room was the door to the hall. Against the right wall, just outside my office door, was my faithful, brown couch. I could almost hear it whispering to me to just lie down for a few minutes, until they came back with the coffee. Surely a lie down would help me think.

Not likely. Sleep was more likely to happen and I couldn't afford to do that right now.

I shuffled left, heading into the small bathroom. It held only a small, porcelain sink and a toilet.

The white bulbs blazed forth as I hit the switch. The guy in the mirror looked ghastly. Grime smeared across my cheeks and forehead. My brown curls were matted in some places and sticking out in others. A scrape on my right cheek disappeared under the beard that framed my jawline.

Great halls, I would hate to be him.

I closed the door and slowly peeled off my shirt and pants. Both pieces of clothing had more rips and stains than clean, cohesive cloth. I dropped them into the waste basket under the sink.

From the medicine cabinet hiding behind the mirror, I found some extra strength Aspirin. I shook out two and swallowed them, sticking my mouth under the tap to gulp down some water. It tasted cool and clean, washing the slime taste from my mouth.

After I drank my fill, I let the water run in the sink, finally managing to coax some warmth into it before I used a wash-cloth to wipe myself off.

I really had to see if there was a way to install a shower in here considering how often I had to find a way to clean up. It was a familiar complaint of mine and a sure sign that I was feeling a little better as I wiped the dirt away and the Aspirin took effect.

Finally, I ducked my head under the tap and used soap to wash the worst of the dirt out of my hair. As the last of the suds drained away, I grabbed the white hand towel and used to it towel dry my hair. The fabric had a layer of light brown when I pulled it away. Not completely clean but it would do.

I shut off the water and wiped the last drops from my beard. That guy in the mirror looked a little more human if still worn around the edges.

Maybe he would survive this. I gave him a nod and a slight smile.

I turned away from the mirror and toward the door. A suit bag hung there with a extra set of clothes. I unzipped it to find a pair of heavy wool pants and a flannel shirt. Not exactly the best wear for July but it would have to do.

By the time I finished dressing and stepped out of the bathroom I was starting to feel almost good again. Aspirin and movement had taken care of the worst of my body's aches. I breathed in the night air and headed back to my office.

A breeze from the shattered remains of my window tugged at my hair. As I saw down in my chair, smiling at the comforting creaking, I noticed the papers and chestnut I had placed on my blotter.

The chestnut and papers from Lekzar's room. The chestnut proof that he had not only watched our Realm but been here, in contradiction to all Faerie laws.

The papers proof of...what? Had Lekzar written a confession of his deeds?

Had some other agent from the Faerie Realm also been here? From what I'd learned of Lekzar, he didn't sound like the kind of person with the initiative to do this on his own. Had he been commanded? Had he stowed away?

I spread the three sheets papers out on my burgundy desk blotter and angled the desk lamp over them. They were all still thin, like onion skin, but pure white, except for one of the sheets with the bottom right edge curled and burned looking.

That had been when Darya had reached for it.

It took a few moment of finagling but I finally got the angle of the lamp right. Faint, printed writing appeared on the white paper, darkening to black with every passing second.

It still looked like gibberish to me. I was still no closer to reading it.

I sighed. My fingers brushed against the chestnut. A moment later I was rolling it on the desk. Back and forth. Toward the tips of my fingers, then back toward my wrist.

Back and forth.

Did some of the lettering on the papers look like English? If I tilted my head, a few of the higher marks almost looked like 'T'.

Back and forth.

Back and forth.

I felt a tingle running from my wrist to my fingers.

Was I pressing the chestnut too hard?

I glanced over. The chestnut rested against the edge of my wrist, easily balanced on the top edge of the desk blotter. It was almost touching my paper clip holder. I rolled the chestnut back. The tingling vanished.

I wasn't getting some kind of carpel tunnel in my wrist, was I?

I moved my fingers and pressed my wrist down on the chestnut. Nothing. Just the smooth, cool surface of the nut.

No tingling.

Strange.

I rolled it again, away from me, watching it as if it was going to do something.

It got close to the paper clip holder. The tingle started. I rolled it back.

And the tingling stopped.

Not a muscular tingle, not something from a compressed nerve. But I knew that already, didn't I?

The paper clip holder was a gift from my mother. It seemed ordinary to me but there was probably some magic residue on it.

Residue that might be reacting to a different type of magic residue on the chestnut?

Maybe. Only one way to be sure.

I rolled the chestnut toward the paper clip holder again. This time as the tingling started, I pushed it even closer until the chestnut was almost touching the plastic side.

The tingling turned to a slight burning on my fingers, like I was holding my hand too close to a fire. I could feel a vibration start in the chestnut, thrumming through my finger tips at a deep level.

The chestnut was from this realm but had been exposed to something with enough magic to leave an imprint. That didn't sound like Lekzar. Yet more proof that he hadn't come through here on his own.

So who had he come through with? And what were they doing?

Creating portals to other realms wasn't an easy thing. It required a lot of magic and expertise. Darya had been drooping with fatigue. Sure, Venir didn't look any different but who could tell with Elves?

Whoever it was had tremendous power, enough to leave an imprint on this chestnut.

That list wouldn't be very long.

Sure, there were a lot of creatures with magical abilities, sharing magical realms just beyond the Human Realm. According to treaties and traditions, they stayed within their boundaries even though their influence still mirrored in stories here. Spells and rituals could draw them across, like the goblin Red Hat I had defeated some time ago. But the creatures who could step between realms like crossing a street, the ones who used magic as easily as breathing, they were even mythical to the magic users.

Had it been one of those that slipped into our world, stalking and killing Santa Claus figures in preparation for the real thing?

If it was and Lekzar had been pulled along, it would explain the residue on the chestnut. It could even explain the avatar of Christopher Henries, left behind to continue the charade until an appropriate time.

And when would that time have been if I hadn't exposed it?

Maybe this creature was no longer content with just killing images of Santa Claus. That avatar could have done any number of things to the children coming to see him, including stealing or tainting their life essence.

That would be something a magical creature would be very interested in. Nothing boosted magic like life essence. It was an even stronger magic than blood magic.

My mouth tasted as dry and sour as my thoughts. Venir and Darya couldn't get back here fast enough with the coffee.

I rolled the chestnut around on the desk blotter. It bumped and shifted as its uneven shape tottered along.

Had Lekzar had an inkling of what awaited him when he returned to the Faerie Realm? Was that why he'd picked up the chestnut? Had he suspected that shadowed figure with the skeletal hand would reach out and cut him down? Was that what he'd written about on these pages?

Had he even written these pages?

If only there had been a little more information from the vision of Lekzar's death at the ruins.

My hand stopped at the edge of the blotter. The rounded edge of the chestnut fit snugly in my palm.

Lekzar had used the ruins as a place of power to enter into the Between and then cross into our Realm. But where had he come out?

Where *had* Lekzar picked up this chestnut?

It could have been any place and considering the list I had from Shirl, the creature had come out in various spots around the world. But I had an idea that Lekzar had only traveled to one location.

My fingers tightened on the chestnut.

And I had an idea of how to find it.

And just who might be able to read these pages.

CHAPTER

TWENTY-ONE

I was opening the magically protected drawer at the bottom of my desk when the outside door swung open.

"Got yer coffee black, kid," Venir's voice called through the office. "I didn't know how you liked it."

"Black is good enough," I called.

Venir entered, carrying a cardboard tray stuffed with three large cups. The cardboard tray looked huge in his hands, almost wider than he was and reminding me just how short he was.

I was reaching for it even before he set one of them down in front of me. A strong, bitter aroma drifted toward me as I grabbed the cup. It burned my hand but I didn't care. I had enough aches and bruises, what was one more?

Still I took a careful sip of the hot liquid. Black and a little too bitter, I swallowed a gulp and another. I felt energy flow through my limbs. Probably psychosomatic. Caffeine couldn't work that fast. But the strong taste and rich aroma was as good as a night's sleep.

Well, almost.

I gathered the pages and set them on the left side of my burgundy desk blotter. It wouldn't do to spill coffee all over them.

"We brought baked food." Darya stood behind Venir. She held up a paper bag.

"Donuts," Venir said.

I smiled. "Just what I need. Caffeine and sugar."

I took a cruller and devoured it in three bites. I was just finishing chewing as Darya took her first bite. She smiled as she chewed.

"This doo nut is as good as the black ilixir," she said.

She looked more relaxed that I'd ever seen her even as she curled over the donut she held in both hands. Her face looked a little less pale. A lively light glowed in her green eyes. Even without her wings showing behind her, she looked almost fairy-like, a gossamer hue seeming to infuse her.

"She's already had a coffee?" I asked Venir.

"She needed one," Venir said. The Elf perched on one of my hard wood chairs. From the way he was balanced I knew his feet weren't even touching the floor.

I took a second donut, a plain glazed this time, and ate it as I finished my coffee. My stomach felt pleasantly full, as if it suddenly realized it was hungry just as I fed it. I finished the final swallow of coffee, even with the residual bitterness, and dropped the paper cup in my metal waste basket beside my desk.

"I discovered something," I said.

Both Darya and Venir froze in mid bite.

I held up the chestnut. "Lekzar had this. It's been exposed to something magical. It still has some residual magic on it."

"Is that a talisman of some kind?" Darya asked.

"It's a nut," Venir said. "A chestnut. Are you sure it's got magic?"

I nodded. "It reacts to the gifts my mother gave me. I was just going to try to figure out where Lekzar got it when you came in." I tapped the papers beside me. "I also had an idea of who might be able to read these pages. Or might find a way these pages could be read."

Darya sat up so straight I thought her back might snap. I could almost hear the quiver of her wings like a subliminal current in the air.

"You know of a magic user here that could read them?" she asked.

"Well, not a magic user," I said. "I've got a friend, an associate who's good with computers. She could probably find some linguistic program that could read it."

At least I hoped Shirl could.

"She said she could?" Venir said.

"I haven't asked her yet," I said. "I will first thing in the morning."

"Why not now?" Darya said. "We must be quick."

I jerked my thumb back at the empty spot where my window had been. I could still feel the warm night breeze bringing the smell of exhaust and dust from outside.

"It's too late now. It's almost midnight."

Both of them looked grim and disappointed at the same time. But it was probably too late to call on Shirl.

Wasn't it?

I glanced at my computer and realized I was just assuming. I didn't really know her well enough to know her schedule for sure. At least I could try.

And email seemed the way to go.

I turned on the computer and in a few moments was typing up an email. I gave a quick mention of the pages and the translation I was looking for then hit send. Even before I sat back, a message pinged in my in-box.

Bring them over.

I grinned. Great. One idea down but that still left the chestnut.

"She'll look at them," I said. "But I want to try something first."

I finished opening the magically protected drawer and rummaged inside. I knew I had it there somewhere. At the back, my fingers brushed against the brittle edge and I'll pulled out the old world map.

The paper it was printed on was old and yellowing. The

lines of the continents were blurring. Colours that had denoted topographical features on the land masses had faded and mingled into a muddy brown. The dark blue of the oceans had lightened to a soft pale blue, more like a highlight than a colour. The creases were so deep in the paper I had to unfold it with care. The paper crackled with every movement. It felt like it might start to tear or disintegrate in my hands if I wasn't careful.

Slowly, I unfolded each section, laying it across the desk as I went. First it covered the desk blotter then expanded over the each side. The map was so large it covered the surface of my desk and spilled over the edges. I had to stand in order to unfold it all.

Although it was impossible to read and the continents looked like blotches on the page, I could never throw this map away. It had been Dad's.

The first map he ever used for plotting his course on Christmas Eve.

Now the sleigh was equipped with satellite GPS and the Elves had a special tracking station at the North Pole, but in the very beginning of his tenure as Santa Claus, Dad had been old fashioned enough to use a paper map.

And he'd given it to me when I was ten.

I never understood why. It was kind of gift he should have given his eldest son, the one who would succeed him as Santa Claus. I was the youngest. I would never be Santa Claus. Even at ten, I'd known that.

But my protests had fallen on deaf ears. Dad had only

smiled his jolly smile and pushed the map back into my hands.

Now I might actually have a use for it.

Both Darya and Venir stood, peering over the edge of the map. Venir had an almost wistful look on his face. Did he recognize it? Of course he must have. He would have seen this map over the years with Dad. Darya had a look of wonder. She must be able to feel the magic in it.

I pulled the chestnut from my pocket as I leaned over. Clenching it in my palm, I held it over the map. Slowly I lowered my hand. Five inches from the surface of the paper, I felt the nut tingling in my hand. Three inches and the burning began. Another inch and the chestnut was vibrating.

An inch from the paper, I dropped it.

The chestnut landed in the middle of the map, in the centre of the Atlantic Ocean. It rolled in a tight circle, almost like it had landed on its edge and would stop.

But it didn't.

The circle became tighter and faster.

I heard Venir's sharp intake of breath. He peered over the top of the map, fittingly his chair was seated near the blur of the North Pole. His eyes were wide, his mouth curled into an 'o'. With all the smart alec artifice dropped away, he reminded me so much of an Elf from home that it made my heart ache.

Darya bent closer as well. Her brow was crinkled as she watched the chestnut.

I shifted my attention back to it.

The circle had widened. The chestnut was hitting the edge of North America and Africa. Then the chestnut wobbled. Its circle shifted. It darted across the paper, making it crackle. Was it going to tear the map? I could barely hold myself back from grabbing the chestnut to stop it from damaging the old paper.

Then the chestnut stopped. It quivered in place.

With all the markings so blurry, I had to bend closer to see where it rested. Soft smears of blue denoted the Great Lakes. I recognized the St. Lawrence Seaway. There at the bottom end was Niagara Falls. But the chestnut quivered a little north east of there.

Over where Toronto would be.

Was that possible?

Then I smelled the harsh crinkle of old paper burning.

I snatched up the chestnut. The heat of it scalded my palm but I didn't care. It had burned the map!

A red blotch desecrated the yellow paper.

I wanted to throw the damn chestnut out the window. I wanted to howl my despair. My Dad's gift, ruined. The first time I'd thought to use it and I'd destroyed it.

I sank back into my chair. It groaned under me, giving voice to my disappointment and shame. I'd always known it had been a mistake for Dad to give me the map when it should have gone to KJ instead.

"Hey," Venir said. He bent half over the map, his nose just a few inches from the paper. "Isn't that Scarborough?"

"What?" I said.

He pointed at the red splotch.

It had shrunk from the anger red blotch to a precise pinprick mark. And where the rest of the blotch had been...

The map showed through clear and bright.

Solid lines denoted streets, marked in print that was easily readable.

Not ruined after all. Activated!

I sagged with relief and then remembered what Venir had said.

Scarborough. Of course!

Christopher Henries had lived in Scarborough. That must have been where Lekzar had come across with whoever was killing Santas. I had to get there.

But I had to take the papers to Shirl for deciphering.

I couldn't do both at once but both needed to be done immediately.

I looked across the desk at Darya and Venir. They looked back, both with eager, ready expressions.

But could I really send them out alone?

Venir at least had some sense of the world but he was still an Elf, and his knowledge probably didn't extend much farther than weather patterns, cigars, and coffee.

For Darya, everything would be completely foreign even though she looked more regular than Venir. But there was still something about her, something otherworldly, that might call unwanted attention. Even with Venir along, would she be able to handle it?

Or maybe the better question was, would she be able to hold back?

"C'mon kid, what do we do?" Venir said.

I didn't have any choice, not if I wanted to solve this as soon as possible. KJ had only one day left and any minute there could be something – or someone – trying to kill him.

I couldn't wait.

"Okay," I said. "I'll take the papers to my contact. You guys head to the location on the map. Take the chestnut." I dropped it into Venir's outstretched hand. "But don't do anything. Just scope out the place. See what's around."

Venir nodded. "Reconnaissance."

"Right," I said. "Just look. Nothing else."

"We will look," Darya said. "We will find where this chestnut came from and what remains there."

"Just not too close," I said.

"Hey, we'll be fine," Venir said. "We did great with the coffee and donuts, didn't we?"

Right. That was exactly a measure of how they would do out in the field.

But Venir was already edging toward the door. Darya was sliding along after him. She nodded to me.

"We will report," she said.

"Not just a report," I said. "Meet me back here." I pointed at my desk.

Darya hand raised almost in a salute. For a moment, the two of them stood silhouetted in the doorframe then they were gone.

Vanished between one blink and the next.

Taking the chestnut with them.

I looked back down at the map. The red dot looked like the tiniest drop of blood, glistening on the faded yellow paper. Would it smear if I folded the map? I didn't want to take the chance.

I lifted the edge and pulled out the pages I had to take to Shirl. She would be waiting, curled into the leather of her armchair, lit by the surrounding computer monitors. Would her computers help her figure out what was on these pages? Was this a complete dead end? Was I making a fool of myself?

I had to believe it would help.

KJ's life, and Dad's, might very well depend on it.

CHAPTER

TWENTY-TWO

The street outside Shirl's apartment building was well lit but empty. I emerged from the shadows near the wall where I had *winked*. My body felt a little shaky, like I'd been using too much magic.

Was I being affected by what I'd done in the Magical Realm?

Maybe.

Good thing the sidewalk and street were clear. I could sag against the lamp post without any questions or weird looks.

The warm night air had finally started to cool a little. The breeze along Bathurst carried a hint of dust, humidity, and freshly cut grass. Pools of yellowish light lit up the asphalt, giving it a worn grey appearance.

For a brief moment, I could imagine it in winter, just

waiting for Dad. Snow piled high alongside the buildings. The sidewalks cleared but still showing a thin layer of snow. Grooves on the street showing where the cars ran. The snow a sloppy, sodden brown on the road but a soft white blanket covering the grass and bushes.

I blinked and the image vanished.

Strange. I didn't usually get caught up in memories of winter like that.

Maybe it was part of the magic use. Being away from the North Pole, I was both out of practice and not use to it. There might be any kind of side effect.

Along this stretch of street, most of the buildings were low rises. All of them stood quiet and dark, everyone tucked in their beds. Even Shirl's building looked still and quiet. All the windows drawn with curtains or blinds. No sign of anyone awake.

But Shirl lived in the back.

I climbed the few concrete steps and hit the buzzer. Even before I could speak, the door clicked open.

Inside the air tasted closed in and stale. The steel box of the elevator hummed to itself as it took me up then clanked a little when it reached her floor. Even brightly lit, the beige hallway felt deserted and hushed. I crept along to her door.

Shirl opened it before I reached it. She peered out, her braids falling along her shoulder.

I held up the pages. "Here they are."

"Keep it down," she whispered. "Get in here."

She waved me forward. I slipped past her into her apartment.

The lighting looked a little more subdued than usual. Only two lamps were turned on, both with old style beige shades with fringe along the bottom. The stem of the lamps were carved crystal, reflecting the light in an almost kaleidoscope fashion. But even that did little to brighten the room.

Shadows darkened the walls behind her row of three monitors, making it look like her chocolate-brown leather chair was the only thing in a pool of light. The leather looked worn and faded, the perfect softness of comfort. Looking at it made me want to crawl into it and just sink into the padded depths. I could already feel my muscles and joints loosen in anticipation.

But I couldn't sit down and rest, not now, not even though it felt so much later than... whatever time it was. I peered closer at the right monitor. Time numbers spelled out one oh three.

"Sorry it's so late," I said to Shirl.

She finished snapping the last lock shut. As she moved past me, her left hand flipped out in a casual wave.

"Whatever," she said. "I'm up all hours. So what's doin'?"

She hauled herself into her chair and crossed her legs. Tonight she wore black jeans tucked into scuffed brown cowboy boots. A black t-shirt with white scrolled writing was mostly hidden by a tan vest with fringes. Her usual braids were piled on her head, several falling loose around her face. With the shadows, her skin looked like polished ebony. She rested her right arm on the chair arm and her chin on her fist, regarding me with her dark eyes.

I held out the papers to her.

"I need these translated," I said.

Shirl reared back with a frown. "Do I look like a rosetta stone?"

"I thought you might be able to do something." I wagged the pages in the general direction of her monitor set up.

She barked a laugh. "What? You think computers are like magic or somethin'? I wave these pages and poof, you can read 'em? Ain't that your domain?"

I shrugged helplessly and tried to look pathetic.

It wasn't hard.

She sighed and held out her hand. "Give 'em here."

I handed them over.

The waver-thin pages crinkled as she flipped through them. With relief, I could tell she could see the text like I could. Further proof that Lekzar had enchanted the script to hide it from his kinsmen. But if he'd wanted me, or someone like me, to read it why had he made it so difficult to decipher?

Unless he hadn't had any choice.

Shirl's frown deepened.

"What's this writing?" she said. "Ain't never seen it before."

I shrugged. Would it do any good to tell her where I'd gotten them? She would probably toss them back in my face. I had to get her to at least try to decipher them.

"What do you think?" I said.

She hmphed as a response. The chair creaked a little as she turned back to her desk. She pushed the wireless keyboard to one side and laid one of the sheets of paper down on the desktop. She grabbed something that looked like a fat, metal wand and began running it overtop the page. A bluish light appeared on the bottom of the wand, running over the paper.

A scanner.

Shirl scanned each page then stacked them in a pile on the corner of her desk. She pulled the keyboard into her lap. Her fingers began to blur over the keys. In front of her, the monitors lit up. The centre monitor showed the image of one of the pages. The monitor on the left was opened to a web browser. Links and articles began to scroll by. On the right monitor, a program opened and the spinning time keeper whirled.

"I'm running the OCR but I don't except it'll get far," she said. "It ain't so good with hand writing. Woulda been better if it were printed."

"OCR?" I asked.

"Optical character recognition, means translating from a picture to digital." She shook her head. "Never mind. Don't matter. Like I said, probably won't get much outta it."

She finished scanning the pages. The blue light clicked off from the scanner which still reminded me way too much of a wand. I shook my head; I had magic on the brain. It wasn't doing me any good. I was no closer to being able to decipher those pages.

I could only hope Shirl's technological wizardry could help.

She straightened the pages and handed them back to me.

"Just so ya know, it's gonna be a while," she said. "I'm searching for anything that resembles any of the features of the words."

"You have a database?" I asked.

She smirked. "Sure. It's called the internet." She gestured at the left monitor and the unending scroll flashing by. "Like I said, it's gonna take a while."

"Um, how long is a while?"

"I'll know better by morning. Give me 'til seven, then I'll have a better idea."

That was almost six hours away.

"You'll know what it says by then?"

She shook her head. "I'll have a better idea of how long it'll take by then."

My hope plummeted. So much for using the power of technology to help me find answers. Lekzar might as well have not left anything behind.

But what if Shirl could find a way to crack it? I had to believe that was a possibility.

It was that Kringle optimism, my mother would have said, although I thought she had even more of it than any of us.

"Do what you can," I said. "I'll check back with you."

"I'll call if I get somethin' sooner," she said. "You gonna be in your office?"

"No, I'll be out." I scribbled my cell phone number on a pad of paper on her desk.

"So, where'd you get this stuff?" she said. "Don't feel like any paper I've ever felt. Almost soft and creamy, but light like that old onion skin paper."

Would it be a good idea to tell her? Shirl was willing to work with me. She knew about me now and keeping her in the dark about my cases probably won't help her assist me. But I didn't want to possibly put her in any danger. Was there danger from those pages? Since we'd returned to the Human Realm, I hadn't felt anything magical from them. But that didn't mean whoever we were hunting couldn't feel them.

But if I didn't tell Shirl I could be leaving her completely unprepared. Not there was much preparation she could do.

"C'mon Kringle, cough it up already," she said. "That writing is weird enough. You gonna pretend it ain't from one of your strange cases?"

"Okay," I said. "It was written by a faerie and I brought it back from the Magical Realm."

"Faerie? Realm?" She held up her hands. "Don't tell me any more. I don't wanna know." She scooped up the pages from the side of her desk and thrust them at me. "Now get gone. I'll call you when I got something."

I grabbed the pages. "Thanks, Shirl."

She waved me away. "I'll bill you."

I escaped before she could quote me her rate. I had a feeling I might find it more terrifying that anything on those pages.

Maybe.

I WINKED BACK TO MY OFFICE. A BREEZE FROM THE BROKEN window behind my chair had pushed the old map half off my desk. The northern end hung over the side, resting on the seat of the hard backed chair.

I set the papers down on the seat of my desk chair before I returned the front of my desk to pick up the map. The yellowed paper was so fragile I didn't want to grab it and yank it back onto the desk. The thought of tearing it was too horrible to contemplate.

When I touched the top edge, my fingers brushed the white expanse of the Arctic. It began to glow with a golden light. I could feel comforting warmth spread through my hands. How many years had Dad carried this map with him on his whirlwind journey around the planet? I could almost feel his joy, his dedication, the excitement of the Elves, of the reindeer, the hope poured in to all the toys, it felt like all of it had infused the map.

It was a powerful talisman.

One that I was going to keep safe.

And it was time to put it back where it belonged.

Even though it still had the bright red spot, marking where the chestnut had been taken from, I didn't want the map just lying on my desk anymore. Seeing it blown around by the destroyed window decided me.

I gingerly folded each end inward. The paper crackled as it moved, almost like it didn't want to be folded up, didn't want to be put away.

Too bad. I didn't want it getting wrecked.

The bright red spot disappeared as I closed it into the large accordion shape. I flipped over the top.

Then a gust of wind blasted through the window behind me.

The force of the wind slammed against my desk. I crumpled over the top. The stapler dug into my chest. My shoulder knocked over the paper clip holder.

My hands jerked open. The map fell over the end of my desk.

I lunged to grab it.

The wind blasted my hair into my eyes. I heard paper rustling behind me.

Lekzar's papers!

I'd been so worried about the map I'd completely forgotten about them.

I rolled onto my back. My stapler jabbed me between my shoulder blades. I felt my upper arm knock over the desk lamp. The light shifted, spotlighting the back wall.

The blinds from my ruined window flapped like tissue

paper, exposing the shattered hole. But instead of the view of the empty parking lot and darkened warehouses beneath the night sky, a dark shadow filled the space.

It looked huge, filling the hole. Edges and folds rippled as if it was made of some kind of fabric. Cold air blasted forth, colder than anything my pathetic, destroyed air conditioner could summon. And beneath that, I smelled the clotted stench of cheap cologne.

Like the kind the fake Christopher Henries had worn.

Proof that what had killed Lekzar had killed Henries as well!

And it still hadn't learned its lesson about cold. Although this time, I wasn't in the Magical Realm with access to my North Pole magic.

But that didn't mean I wasn't going to put up a fight.

I grabbed the edge of the desk and used it to pull myself up to a sitting position. The wind was like a powerful force, pushing at me. I had to squint against it. Tears flowed from my eyes. My hair was slicked back against my head. I felt my clothes plastered to my body.

I tried to gather the cold to me, the way I had in the Magical Realm, but it felt like trying to gather water in a sieve. My magical energy was low and scattered. I'd used everything up by *winking* back and forth to Shirl's apartment.

The shadow fabric rippled around the edges of the window. From within something that looked like folds, I thought I saw spindly protrusions sticking out. Skeletal fingers. Skin stretched so thin it looked mottled and grey, tips reddened where the flesh was tearing apart.

It reached out. Stretching forth from the centre of the shadow.

Reaching...

Reaching... for me!

Even with the wind shoving me backward, I felt the pull of that skeletal hand, like a magnet. I fought against it, pulling back.

Couldn't let it touch me.

Couldn't let it get close.

I tried to push myself over the top of my desk. I felt the desk blotter sliding under my back. Over the roar of the wind I heard the tinkling of items falling off the front edge of the desk.

My coffee cup hit the floor and shattered.

My feet lifted off the floor. I kicked out, scrambling to get away.

My right foot hit my desk chair.

It flew back toward the wall. The papers on it slid , spilling over the edge.

Then the skeletal hand snapped out.

And snatched them up!

"No!"

My shout was lost in the roar of the wind. I heard a throaty laughter inside it as the skeletal fingers tightened around the pages, crinkling them. Then the hand yanked out the window. The grey shadow flew back, disappearing into the night.

The wind stopped. The blinds fell back against the shattered hole of the window with a clatter.

I lay almost halfway over my desk, panting with exertion. The shadow had left a sour, burning stench hanging in the air so thick I could taste it in the back of my throat.

It tasted like failure and disappointment.

Damn the halls, it had tricked me. Pretended to try for me again like it had during the vision in the Magical Realm but it had been after the papers all along.

And I'd fallen for it.

Maybe I wasn't as good a private detective as I thought.

How could I expect to beat this thing when I couldn't even keep a hold of some papers? How could I expect to beat it when I didn't even know what it was?

I slid off the desk to my feet. My legs wobbled a little as I stumbled around. My shattered coffee mug lay near the doorway. I picked up the pieces and dumped them into my waste basket.

Thankfully my Dad's map lay on the seat of the chair in front of my desk. It didn't look any worse for the blistering wind that had blasted through the room.

That was a relief. At least one thing hadn't been destroyed.

I picked up the map. It felt warm and soothing in my hand. Holding it made me feel like losing the papers was just a minor setback. All I had to do was keep going.

Okay, I could do that. If there was anything I knew how to do it was to keep going. I was stubborn that way.

At least I'd gotten the papers to Shirl for scanning. There was still a chance she could find something out about them. Meanwhile, it was time to check in on Venir and Darya. If that shadow creature had come for the papers, maybe it would make a try for the chestnut. Or maybe it would retreat to one place I knew it had been.

Christopher Henries' apartment.

It almost felt like things to coming full circle.

If only I knew what any of it meant.

I stepped back from my desk. The desk blotter was now near the front. Almost everything had been pushed onto the floor. No time to clean up now. I'd deal with it later.

I still had Dad's old map in my hand. I should put it back into the bottom drawer where it would be protected but it felt comforting to have it with me.

Somehow I felt like I needed all the comfort I could get.

I folded it over and slipped it into the pocket of my jeans, tucked behind my cell phone.

And I *winked* out of the office.

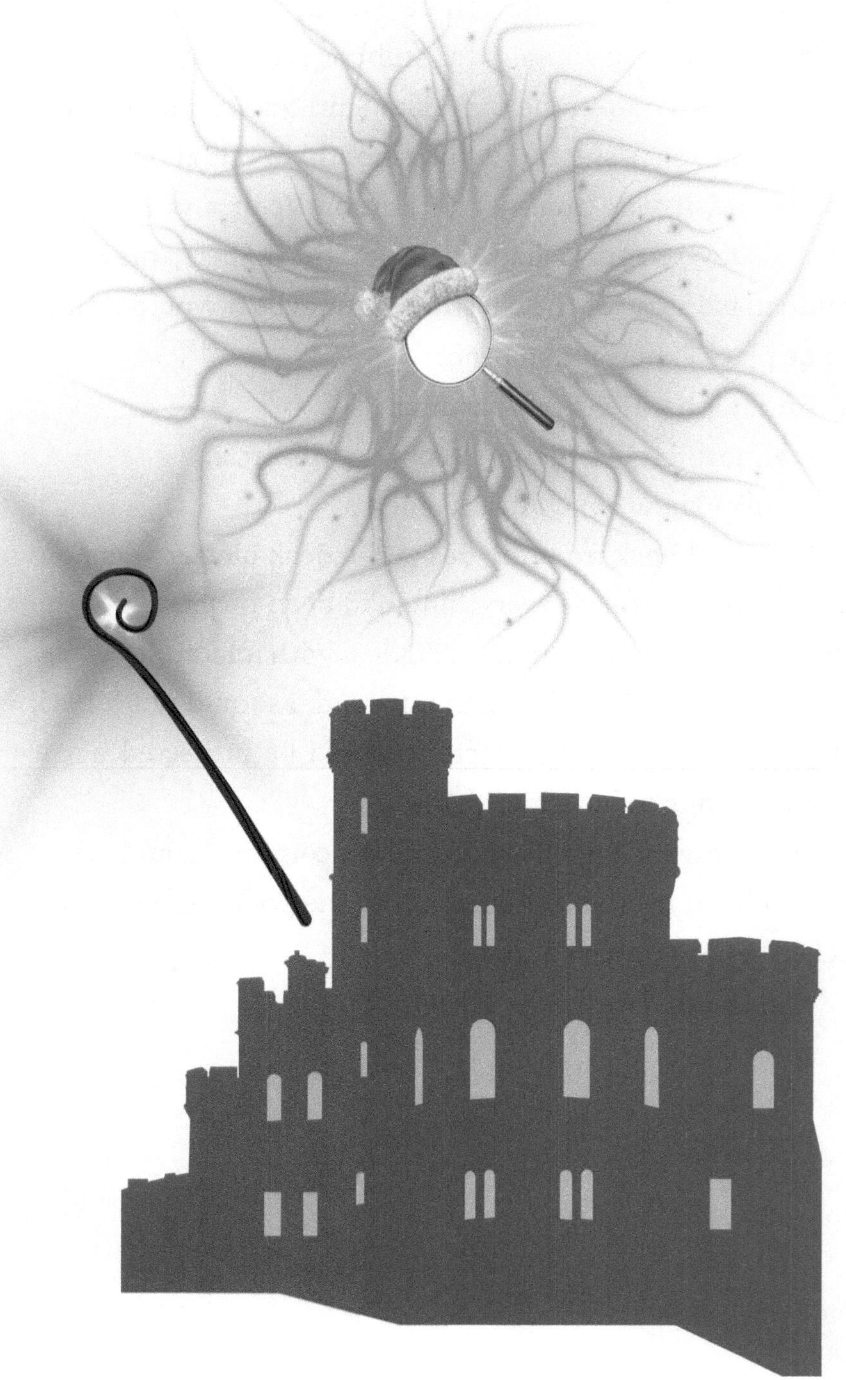

CHAPTER

TWENTY-THREE

Fatigue made me stumble when I appeared on the cracked sidewalk. I stuck out my hand to catch myself and felt the cool glass of a storefront. The convenience store was closed. Through the smeared window I could see the front counter shrouded in gloom. The plastic white cash register squatted on the counter. Opposite it, rows of metal shelves retreated into the darkness. Boxes and bags of food and other items reminded me of wrapped presents.

I'd landed about a block from Henries' apartment. The July heat was finally relinquishing its grip, allowing cooler air to descend. It brought with it the sooty tang of stale car exhaust and dust hanging in the air.

My legs trembled a little as I pushed away from the convenience store. I could feel a headache start to pound at my temples, tension tightening my neck. I've over exerted myself with my meagre magic. Being in the Magical Realm and having access to my full magic again had spoiled me. I had to remember that I couldn't use up all my resources without resting to replenish myself.

I'd done one too many *winks* and I was feeling the results.

But it was almost two and the subway had stopped running. Sure, it probably would have been pretty quick to grab a taxi and get out here. The traffic at this time wouldn't have posed much problem.

But I hadn't heard from Venir and Darya. They should have come back after they checked out the location. They should have contacted me after they investigated the tree where Lekzar found the chestnut.

But not a word. Not a message. Nothing.

That couldn't be good.

Venir might be a smoking, mischievous, sarcastic, sorry excuse for an Elf but I didn't think he'd forget to return. Certainly Darya wouldn't.

As I headed down the cracked sidewalk toward Henries' red brick apartment building, the cold shiver I felt running up my back had nothing to do with the air temperature.

Something had happened.

I could feel it.

Had the same shadow creature that had come for the papers attacked them?

Even as my head pounded, I hurried forward. I spotted Henries' building sandwiched between the dry cleaners and the empty restaurant. Both now were dark. The entire street looked deserted. The mix of storefronts squat walk-ups looked dark and devoid of life. Every window was shuttered, all curtains closed, drapes drawn, blinds pulled down. Only a few cars were parked along the street and most of them were a block or two down.

The pale white light from the streetlights gave the asphalt and the sidewalk a washed out look, mixing the black of the asphalt and the white of the sidewalk into a muddy grey.

But nowhere along this street could I spot a chestnut tree.

No trees at all.

Had that been why Venir and Darya hadn't returned? Because they hadn't found the tree here and so they kept looking?

I had to hope so.

As I moved past the door to Henries' building, I felt the temperature drop even more. My breath came out in a fog that vanished almost instantly. I caught a whiff of sweet candy cane.

Venir's signature scent. He'd been here!

I spun around. Gravel crunched under my feet. Dust rose in the air, clogged my nose. Cut off the candy cane smell.

The damp heat flooded back.

I retraced my steps.

Nothing. The trace Venir had left was gone.

Damn the halls.

Where was he?

I took a deep breath. The dust choked me. I coughed it out and wiped my mouth.

Okay, I had to think like they would have. They'd come here to find where the chestnut had come from. Obviously it wasn't on this street. But it had to be somewhere near here, somewhere near Henries' building.

So if not in front.

Maybe in back.

Both the dry cleaner's and the restaurant butted right up against the red brick of Henries' apartment building. No way to get around back that way. I glanced up and down the block. Another two buildings stretched on the other side of the dry cleaners. Nothing beside the restaurant.

I headed that way.

As I passed the restaurant, I glanced inside. It looked like an old diner. Yellowing newsprint had been taped to the inside of the windows but several of the sections had loosened and were peeling down. Inside, the light from the street lights penetrated maybe a few inches, revealing dusty black and white checkered flooring before the darkness hid everything else.

I felt that shiver up my back again. It felt like something was in that restaurant. Watching. Waiting.

I hurried around the corner, my shoes scuffing up the dust from the sidewalk.

A narrow alley cut between the restaurant and the next building. A line of battered blue recycling bins sagged against the restaurant wall like tired wooden soldiers. I thought I saw a glimmer of something metallic at the far end.

The street lights barely penetrated past the third recycling bin. And of course I hadn't brought a flashlight.

The air smelled humid, with an undercurrent of sickly sweet, like garbage. My nose crinkled at the stench. I didn't really want to wander down there, but looking for another way around the buildings would take time.

And I'd already spent what felt like enough precious moments.

If that shadow thing had come for them…

I hurried forward.

A few steps in, I closed my eyes briefly then opened them. The gloom didn't seem quite so deep. The row of sagging recycling bins stood on my left, as if trying to stand to attention. I kicked discarded food wrappers and tin cans. They clattered in front of me like eager puppies.

The sickly sweet stench thickened. I pinched my nose, breathing through my mouth but the stench seemed to even coat my tongue.

A few more steps and the glimmer of metal I'd spotted relieved itself. A dark blue dumpster tucked up against the right side of the wall near the end of the alley. Even empty, it retained the stench of garbage like a rotted memory. I heard the lazy buzz of flies puttering around the closed lid.

It jutted halfway into the alley. I had to jog closer to the recycling bins to get past. As I cleared them, I spotted a left turn to the wall. I hurried forward and peered around it.

It opened to a large space behind the buildings. Gravel mingled with crabgrass. A wire fence cut across the opposite end to me. Even in the dim light, the fence had the darkened look of rust. Tall weeds grew along the bottom. The fence went straight back from the building, carving out a lot until it reached the back of another building on the opposite side. And tucked up against that other building…

I saw the spreading shadow of a tree.

My heart began to pound. That tree, it had to be the one!

I took a step forward.

And if it was, where was Venir and Darya?

Had something happened to them? Had I sent them to their death? Had the shadow thing attacked them before it came for the papers?

The guilt of it clenched my stomach. My feet kicked at the gravel as I hurried toward the tree. If only there was some hint, some clue as to what had happened, maybe I could help them. Save them.

The bark on the tree trunk looked black and corroded, like it had been scorched. The edges peeled away from the trunk, leaving the inside looking pulpy and a sick-looking grey. The branch above my head seemed to sag with sickness, bowing almost to breaking. All the leaves were curled in on themselves, dead or dying.

I could feel the rot in the tree, strong enough to stop me five feet away.

But it wasn't any regular infestation.

"The life was drained," a soft voice whispered behind me.

I jumped and spun around.

Darya stepped out of the shadows from the building to my right. Dust covered her uniform. Her dark hair hung in disarray around her head.

Venir peered out from behind her legs. His eyes were widened in barely restrained panic.

"What happened?" I asked.

Darya glanced back at Venir then squared her shoulders.

"We travelled here and discovered the tree," she said. "It was still alive when we reached it. I could feel the echo of the chestnut from the tree. Lekzar had been here. He had waited beneath the branches while the being he travelled with went inside that place." She pointed toward Henries' apartment building.

"Then it came," Venir blurted out. "We was standin' right there." He nodded just past me. "This shadow thing came blasting outta the sky. Damn near killed us. Woulda too if Darya hadn't reacted so fast." The Elf hung his head. "I just froze."

"You are not a warrior," Darya said. "I have been trained to fight. There is no shame in your reaction."

Venir shook his head. Whatever bravado he'd had was gone. Now he just looked tired and worn, the lines in his face deepened around his eyes and mouth. Even his large, pointed ears drooped over his greying curls.

"Go on," I said.

"I managed to evade it, make it think we had fled," Darya said. "Instead I blended us into the shadows. It seemed enraged and it attacked the tree."

"You said you could tell it was the tree that Lekzar had gotten the chestnut from, that he'd been under that tree," I said. "Could it be that the shadow was after the tree all along?"

"It came right at us," Darya said.

"Yeah, but we was standing right there," Venir said. "It coulda been after the tree."

"Do you still have the chestnut?" I asked.

Venir dug into his pants pocket and pulled out the chestnut. It seemed to gleam in the dim lighting.

"Let's check it out," I said.

The three of us moved closer to the tree. Darya took a quick breath. Her face paled against her dark hair. Venir grimaced but stomped forward in determination. He clenched his hand into a fist around the chestnut.

I felt myself having to push forward as well, as if through a dense fog of foulness. The image of Christopher Henries sprawled on the Christmas throne flashed into my mind, followed by all the images I'd imagined when I first read the list of dead Santas. I shuddered under the assault of murder and mayhem.

Whatever had infested that tree poured off it like a psychic poison and it was trying to keep us away.

But if there was nothing left here, if the shadow thing

had completely destroyed the tree, there would be no feeling left.

I felt a flicker of hope under the despair dredged up by all the dead Santas. Whatever the shadow creature was it hadn't been able to completely destroy the tree. Its power was finite. Just like it hadn't destroyed the papers it had to be satisfied with snatching them away.

And if it wasn't all powerful, we could beat it, no matter how unbeatable it tried to appear.

I grabbed Venir's wrist.

"Show me the chestnut," I said.

Venir grit his teeth. His lips pulled back from his teeth in a sneer. Sweat popped up like beads on his forehead. His wispy hair hung limp around his ears.

Slowly his fingers unpeeled from his fist.

The chestnut lay on his palm. I picked it up and ran my thumb over the smooth surface. Although before I hadn't felt the residual magic in it, I could feel it now like a warm glow in reaction to the foulness before us.

Warmth? That was strange. If the magic adhering to the chestnut came from the shadow creature...

But what if it hadn't? What it Lekzar had imbued it as a message, like the papers?

My heart quickened in excitement. I clenched the chestnut in my fist. I was on to something. I could feel it.

I took another step closer to the tree. And another.

The ground crunched beneath my feet like ash. A foul thickness pressed against my face, tried to invade my nose. I coughed it back. I was still about five feet from the trunk, too far. I needed to touch it even though the curling bark looked sharp enough to slice my palm.

The branches over my head creaked in sodden heat. They could come crashing down at any moment. I could feel the pressure of them above me, ready to fall. My knees bent as my legs tried to buckle.

A hand grabbed my arm. I looked up into Darya's pale face. Her green eyes were wide but she nodded me on. I took a step and she kept pace. Behind me I could hear Venir huff as he followed.

The three of us moved toward the tree.

Three feet now. Two feet. Another step closer. The air was thick with heat. My fresh shirt stuck like plastic wrap to my skin. I felt like a present someone had wrapped using too much tape. Constrained. Trapped. My muscles twitched to run.

Another step.

I lunged toward to the tree. My left hand grabbed at the trunk. Brittle bark crumbled under my palm, scratched my skin.

A frigid, freezing force raced up my arm like a jolt of electricity. I heard Darya cry out but her voice was distant. Far away.

Gone.

The air pressed humid and hot against my face. Darkness shrouded the lot around me but light from the full moon gave it an eerie glow. I smelled the fresh earth smell of the tree, full of life, of purpose. It was the only thing in this strange place that made sense.

I closed my eyes but could still see the red brick of the building across the lot.

Not real, not now. I wasn't seeing this with my eyes. But someone else's.

Lekzar.

I could feel him now, shaken, as he held on to the tree for support. His little prying spell had given him more than he had anticipated. A glimpse of something he couldn't unsee but not enough to know what to do. What he had done and seen had been so far beyond what he'd meant to do. All he wanted was to look around, see the other Realms.

But his gift with the spell had pulled him along.

Or had it made it easier for something else to slip through?

It was difficult to discern Lekzar's true memories from his emotions.

I could feel his anxiety and turmoil churning inside like a stomach ache. I tried to ignore it, to concentrate on the building before me, but it was difficult. Lekzar's focus kept pulling me back.

A light flickered in one of the windows on the third floor. A voice cried out. A brief wail of fear, then cut off.

Lekzar pressed against the tree. I could feel his lips moving but couldn't discern any sound. His fingers tapped along the trunk like morse code, following the curve down the bark toward the ground until he splayed his fingers against the earth.

His right pinkie brushed a chestnut.

He grabbed it. I felt the pressure of it against Lekzar's palm, the familiar shape. He was still moving his lips, still chanting, and I still couldn't hear it.

Was it a spell? What was he trying to do?

Was he trying to find a way to stop the shadow creature?

The light in the window went off. Lekzar froze. A moment later the door to the building burst open.

A dark shadow spread out like a stain. From within it, I could see a figure moving forward, getting closer. With each step, it became clearer, coalescing into the form of... Lord Flaktar Dramal!

The faerie lord moved with liquid smoothness over the ground. He wore plain black pants and shirt with no insignia. A black cloak flowed around him, seeming to mingle with his long greying, black hair. His face was pale white, looking almost translucent against the shadow fog around him.

I felt Lekzar's fear and dismay ripple through me like a tremor.

"Come." Dramal's command pierced my skull, compelling with a magical force behind the word.

Lekzar bowed, his hands pressed against his pants.

He slipped the chestnut into his pocket.

The shadow fog billowed forth to swallow me as Dramal reached his side.

Hard earth scratched my right cheek. I blinked. I was lying on the ground. A groan sounded beside me. I lifted my head.

Venir was on his back, arms splayed out. He rubbed his forehead and gave another groan before he pushed himself up on his elbows.

"What was that, kid?" he asked.

"A vision," Darya said. She was the only one of us still on her feet but even she was sagging. She had grabbed onto the desiccated tree trunk for support.

My mouth tasted like gravel. I spit and got my hands under me to push myself up.

"The chestnut," I said.

She nodded. "Set to trigger when it was brought back to the place of its origin."

"Okay," Venir said. As I got to my feet, he held out his hand and wiggled his fingers at me. I grabbed his wrist and hauled him up.

He stomped his feet to get the dirt off his boots and brushed the seat of his pants. "So how come it didn't trigger when we got here?" he said.

Darya frowned. "I do not know."

"It must have been set to trigger when there were enough people around," I said.

Darya shook her head. "These types of spells do not work that way." She tilted her head. "It was focused on a particular person. On you."

"Me? That can't be, I've never even heard of Lekzar before

this never mind met him."

She spread her hands out. Confusion crinkled her brow. "I do not understand either."

"He knew me though," Venir said. "Are ya sure it weren't aimed at me?"

"It should then have triggered when we first arrived," Darya said.

I glanced back at the building and felt an idea prickle the back of my neck. "Maybe it wasn't specifically me he was thinking of," I said.

"What do you mean?" Darya said.

I pointed at the second floor window. "Christopher Henries lived there," I said. "He was hired to play Santa Claus. The shadow creature came here to kill him. Lekzar either got caught up in it or followed. He had moments to set up this vision in the chestnut. He was trying to warn someone. Who else would he set it up for but for Santa Claus?"

"Why would it then trigger for you?" Darya said.

"I'm his son," I said. "Must be close enough. And that's a good thing because Dad doesn't come down here during the summer."

"Why wouldn't he be carryin' it when we found him?" Venir said.

I shrugged. "Maybe he knew they were tracking his magic and he had to hide it."

Venir nodded. "Makes sense since it was Lord Dramal. The faerie lord would have the power to cross realms."

"I do not know." Darya bent her head. Her hair curled

around her face. "He is a terse task master but I cannot believe this."

"I'm not sure I do either," I said.

"Whadare ya talkin' about?" Venir said. "We all saw him. He was right there." He pointed back toward the red brick building. I followed the line of his finger toward the back door. I *had* seen Dramal sweep out of that door, but it had been a vision. Could I trust it?

"We know what we were shown," I said. "We don't know if it's really what happened. Even if it's what Lekzar saw, can we be sure he wasn't fooled as well?"

Venir frowned. Elves weren't known for their imagination but Venir had proved himself somewhat different from the usual Christmas Elf. And that difference might make him more argumentative. Something I didn't need right now.

Before I could say anything else I felt my cell phone vibrate in my left pants pocket. I dug it out.

A text from Shirl. It read: *Cracked it. Come now.*

I texted back: *On my way*. Then shoved the phone back in my pocket.

"Come on," I said. "I've had the papers deciphered. We're taking this debate on the road."

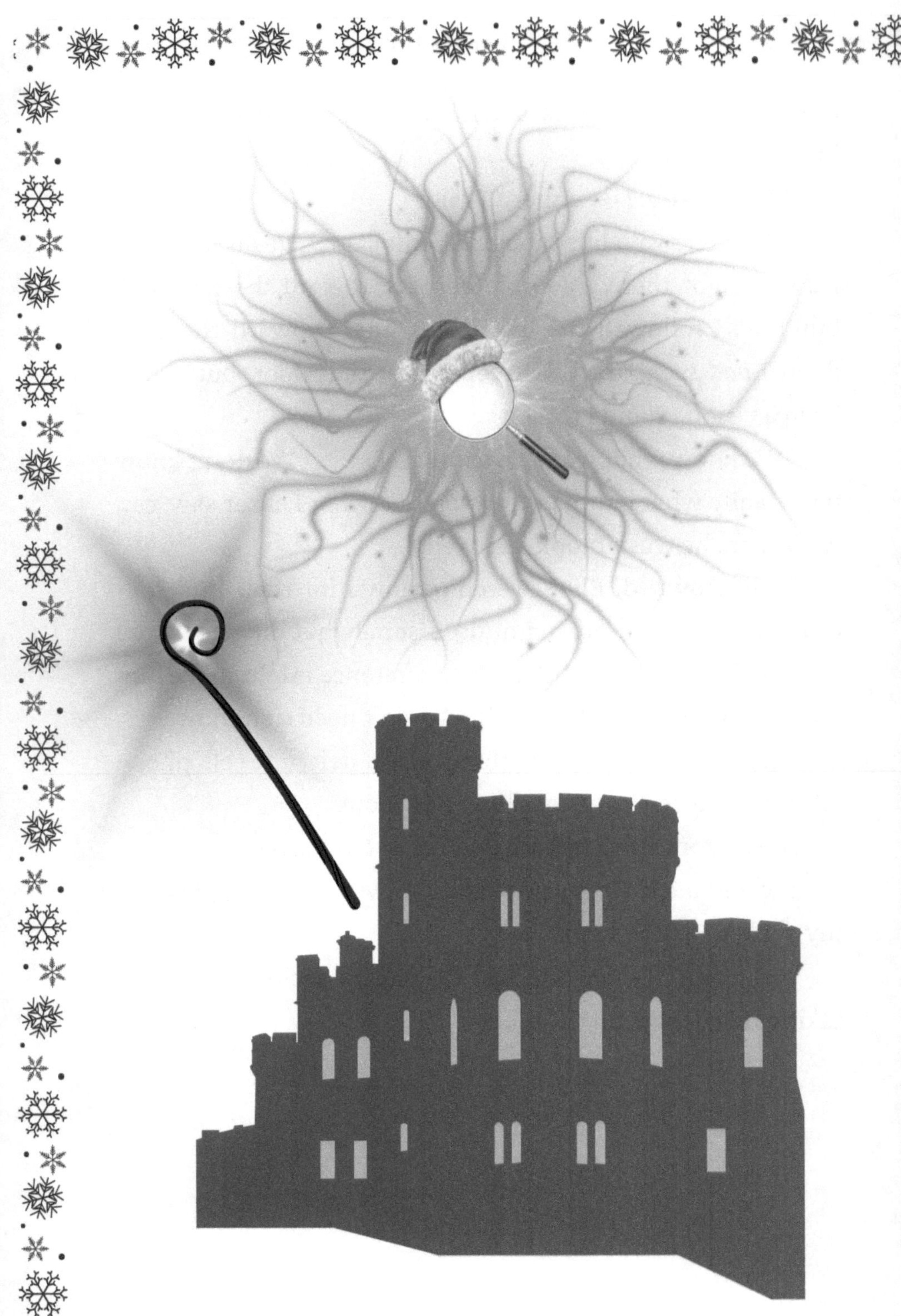

TWENTY-FOUR

One good thing about having Venir around, I could let him do the heavy lifting of *winking* us all back to Shirl's building.

We landed two blocks down, a few steps north of the subway station. The sign cast a soft white light on the pavement, illuminating the whites of the eyes of the homeless man sitting propped up against the side of the corner building. Even in this heat, he wore full length jeans and a long puffy jacket over his faded t-shirt. He clenched a fraying paper cup to his chest as he stared at us.

Darya moved toward him. Her hand reached out, moving like a pedal unfolding from a flower. The man's gaze followed her hand like he was hypnotized.

Her hand traced an intricate pattern in the air before him. After a moment, I saw pale light shimmering, sparkling, glowing. Warmth flowed through me, making me want to slowly sink into a puddle on the ground.

Venir dug his elbow into the side of my thigh. Pain jolt me. I snapped out of the spell.

"Ow." I rubbed my leg.

"You should know better than to watch a faerie work," Venir said. He was looking up at me, his head turned farther from Darya than necessary.

Right. I did know better. Watching a faerie weave a spell was as dangerous as having it cast right at you.

I stared at the cracked sidewalk until I heard the soft step of Darya's boot. When I glanced up, she was brushing her hair from her forehead. Dark shadows looked like bruises under her eyes. Her fingers trembled a little.

"We can move on now," she whispered. She nodded back toward the corner.

The homeless man had climbed to his feet. He shrugged off the puffy jacket and folded it before placing it back on the ground. Then with his shoulders squared, he headed off, walking with swift, sure steps.

"What did you do?" I said.

"I gave him the gift of seeing himself anew," she said. "That way he wouldn't pay attention to seeing us."

"No tricks?" I asked.

A wane smile crossed her face. "No tricks."

I nodded. Most faeries dealt in layers three or four deep but Darya had been straight with us all along. I had to believe she would continue.

"Let's go," I said.

We headed north.

If possible, the street was even quieter than before. The air felt heavy and thick, the coolness of earlier melting away. I checked my phone. Just after three thirty. The night was burning away faster than I wanted and still no real answers but we were getting close to something. I could feel it.

The houses had the same dark windows. The same drawn curtains but it wasn't just the deepness of the night I felt.

There was something else.

I stopped.

Venir bumped into me. "Hey!"

I held up a hand. "Do you feel it?" I said.

"Feel what?" the Elf said.

"Yes." Darya's clipped tone held as much tension as I felt.

She felt it too. At least I wasn't imagining it.

Small comfort.

"Let's hurry up," Venir said. I glanced down at him. His lips were pressed tight together.

So now he felt it as well.

Something was coming.

The air had a tense, breathless quality. The darkness seemed deeper than just a lack of light. It felt like a lack of hope.

And an abundance of menace.

"Right." I hurried forward. We reached the corner. Shirl's building was diagonal to us. The light was green to get across. Even with the street empty, I cast a glance both ways before we scurried across.

That's when I caught a glimpse of it.

Some sleek and low to the ground. Shimmering golden eyes blinked before the creature darted into the shadows of the subway station a block down.

I had a feeling it wouldn't take it long for that thing to reach us.

I kept my pace steady, let my head turn away in a smooth motion, as if I hadn't seen it.

As if my heart wasn't pounding.

"Back there," Darya whispered.

"I saw it," I said.

"Saw what?" Venir's voice lilted higher. His legs worked double hard as we hurried north again, crossing against the light. I didn't feel like waiting for it to turn green.

"Keep going," I said.

We reached the corner. The air had thickened to a deep, musky smell. I felt it like a fog pouring toward us from the south.

Pebbles skittered on the sidewalk behind us. Twenty feet. Fifteen.

My little game of pretend hadn't fooled it.

"Run!" I yelled.

We lunged forward. I grabbed Venir's arm to propel him along. My shoes pounded the sidewalk. Darya had already outraced us, flowing like water through the air.

A snarling roar sounded behind us.

I glanced back.

It came racing toward us on four legs. Black fur rippling over straining muscles. Glowing golden eyes. Mouth open to reveal four inch fangs dripping with saliva. It roared again. Its claws gouged chunks out of the pavement, flinging them back behind it.

The Jolakotturinn. The legendary Yule cat.

But this was no regular kitty. It was the size of a lion.

And it wasn't going to wait until Christmas Eve to eat us.

Halfway across the street, yellow headlights flared to my left, racing forward. A car had appeared out of nowhere and it had right of way.

I shoved Venir hard ahead of me. His boots hardly touched the pavement as he soared over the curb.

The roar of the engine almost drowned out the Yule Cat. The headlights blinded me.

I wouldn't make it to the sidewalk.

So I went up.

I managed a half crouch before I changed direction toward the car and sprang. My left toe caught the front fender. I could feel it slip on the chrome. I pumped my arms. My right foot landed smack on the hood.

Momentum carried me past the windshield. I lifted my legs higher, sailing onto the roof. Between the car's forward movement beneath and my run over top, I cleared the roof in one bound. My left foot came down solid on the back trunk, then I was leaping into the air.

I bent my knees to absorb my landing. My shoes

smashed hard on the pavement. I stumbled a few steps before regaining my footing.

I was too far down the block to head back to meet Venir and Darya. A scrape of claw on concrete told me the Yule Cat was right behind me. I put on a burst of speed and followed the road.

If I could stay ahead of the cat, I could circle the block. That would give Venir and Darya time to get to the building.

And then what?

If I didn't shake the Yule Cat, it would just attack us all together. I had no illusions that it would be stopped by a simple glass door. Not with those claws.

I was going to have to stop it on my own.

I pumped with my arms, settling into a steady rhythm in my run. But the sounds of claws was getting steadily closer. I wasn't going to make it around the block before the cat pulled me down.

I did not feel like being a chew toy for an overgrown alley mongrel.

I reached the corner and turned right. Off the main road, I passed houses shrouded in darkness. Small gardens and green lawns the size of postage stamps were encircled on all sides by chain link fences. A child's two wheeled bike lay abandoned in a driveway, half on the sidewalk.

I leapt over it. A moment later, I heard the chain jangle as the Yule Cat stormed across it.

Any moment now it was going to catch up to me.

And although my heart pounded from fear and exertion, I could feel something else burning inside.

Anger.

I was *pissed!*

Someone was killing Santas. Someone had killed a faerie who had tried to warn us, and now someone was perverting the legend of the Yule Cat.

Enough was enough!

I was the youngest son of Kris Kringle, the current Santa Claus, and I was *done* putting up with this!

I pumped my arms harder. Digging my feet in deeper, I put on a burst of speed. The next corner was coming up. I could see it a few steps ahead of me. The stop sign was a deep blood red in the darkness. The post was just to the left of the sidewalk.

I aimed for it...

As I reached the post, I grabbed it with both hands and leapt. My legs soared into the air. For a moment, I went almost horizontal, then the pull of my arms swung me around. I whipped into a circle, bringing my heels together.

And kicked hard.

I caught the cat on the side. Its roar shifted to a yowl of pain as it soared off course. It hit the pavement on its side and tumbled.

Before it could right itself, I tore after it. I jumped onto its back and wrapped my arm around its neck. The muscles strained under me like a live snake. My face was almost pressed into the black fur of its neck. I could smell the musk, thick with a slight sourness.

Wrong. It was wrong.

Something had infected the Yule Cat and was causing it to behave this way.

I had to find a way to break the spell.

Under me, the cat was regaining its feet. It gave a low growl as it gave a shake of its body. The growl rose in pitch to a full roar as it felt me on its back. The muscles under me quivered. I could feel it getting ready to pitch me off.

I had to do something.

I tightened my grip around its neck, feeling the quiver of its throat as it roared again. My nose was right next to its ear. The musk sour stench filled my nose and slithered down my throat. I could feel it making me want to cough. With effort, I stifled it and pressed my mouth to the cat's ear.

"Jolakotturinn, hear me," I said. "You know my voice. I am Santa's son. We are tied to the same celebration. We revere the same day. You must hear me."

The cat howled and writhed under me. The sourness thickened, choking me.

Whatever the spell was, it was strong.

But I was stronger.

Or at least more desperate.

"Jolakotturinn, I call to you, Yule Cat!" I yelled in the cat's ear.

The stench intensified again but this time, I felt the cat's ear flicker.

As if it was listening.

"You are the Yule Cat. You come on Christmas Eve," I said. "This is not your time, this is not your place. Hear me, Jolakotturinn."

The cat shook its head. My arm slipped on its neck. The sourness flared up, making me gag. As if sensing my shifting position, the cat twisted, bucking its back legs. I tightened my thighs but the cat twisted again. I couldn't keep my grip.

Another twist and I flew off.

I landed on my back in a sprawl just behind the cat.

Its yowl turned to a roar of triumph. The sour stench intensified.

The cat whirled to face me, jaws open, ready to devour me with five inch fangs. Golden eyes glowed as it crept toward me.

My heart hammered in my chest. I scrambled backward on my back. Gravel dug into my hands. My feet slid on the pavement.

Fear dried the saliva in my mouth. My breath came in a staccato rhythm as I fought to gain speed.

The Yule Cat snarled and crept forward, keeping pace. Hunting me.

Toying with me.

Like I was some naughty child who hadn't received any new clothes.

That was it!

A surge of adrenaline spiked through me. I stopped

backing up and pulled my legs beneath me until I was able to get up in a crouch.

The Yule Cat darted forward. Mouth open, snarling.

I shoved my right arm toward its gaping mouth.

If I was wrong, I'd be asking Venir to wrap all my presents for me in the future.

If I survived at all.

I felt the cat's hot breath on my hand. Saliva dripped from one of its fangs onto the arm of my shirt. The mouth closed down.

I winced, anticipating the slice of teeth.

But I only felt the soft velvet of lips.

Jolakotturinn pressed its mouth against my forearm, against the crisp fabric of my shirt. Its nose quivered as it sniffed.

The sourness stench intensified, wafting over the cat but it wasn't enough, I knew it wasn't enough.

Not anymore.

Whoever had cast this spell didn't understand the depth of Jolakotturinn's commitment to its duty.

"Do you like my new shirt, Jolakotturinn?" I said.

The Yule Cat gave a demure meow.

The sour stench vanished.

I took a deep breath, luxuriating in the smell of cut grass and the dust settling down to the pavement around us.

Jolakotturinn shook its head and blinked as if puzzled. Its ears flattened as it looked around. A rumble sounded in its chest.

"It's not time for you," I said. "You were enchanted to cause harm. But it's over. You're free and you can go home now."

Jolakotturinn tilted its head and gave me a plaintive meow. It gave my shirt one final sniff as if to make sure it really was as new as it expected, then turned away. It stalked away from me, tail flicking in the breeze. It passed under a street lamp and then into the shadow of a large oak tree, blending into the darkness until it disappeared.

I climbed to my feet and brushed the gravel from my pants. The darkness seemed a little less foreboding now. Even the crickets started to chirping again.

Whoever I was searching for was getting desperate. That had to mean I was getting close, I was on my way to stopping it. First the vision of Dramal and then using the Yule Cat against me. I had to be on the verge of figuring it out.

Too bad I had no idea who it was.

But maybe the deciphered papers would give me another clue.

I headed back toward the main street, kicking random pebbles on the sidewalk.

TWENTY-FIVE

As soon as I turned the corner, Venir and Darya appeared. The Elf ran forward, his white hair more frazzled than ever around his large, pointed ears.

"Boy, are you all right?" he said.

"I'm fine," I said. "The cat was enchanted. I broke the spell and it's gone."

Darya matched my pace as we moved toward the front of Shirl's building.

"I wish you had let me assist you," she said.

"You couldn't have," I said. "You don't have any new clothes."

She cocked her head and frowned. "What?"

Venir chuckled. "Jolakotturinn, the Yule Cat, stalks Christmas Eve, making sure everyone has new clothes to celebrate the season."

Darya glanced down at her uniform. The grey fabric had a fine layer of dust around her pants cuffs but no other sign of the wear and tear she'd been through, but it still wasn't new enough. I shook my head at her.

"And you have new clothes?" she said.

I plucked at my shirt. "I changed when you guys were getting coffee and donuts. I had a new shirt in my office."

"My boots are new," Venir said.

I glanced down at the worn leather on his cowboy boots. Even Darya pursed her lips.

"Well, new to me," the Elf grumbled.

"I don't think that counts," I said as I reached to press the intercom button to Shirl's apartment. The door buzzed open even before I finished pressing.

We hurried inside.

If possible, the air smelled even staler than before. I could almost feel the hush of sleeping bodies in the apartments around us as we made our way to Shirl's door. She cracked it as we approached.

She raised one quizzical eyebrow at the sight of Venir, then nodded us all to enter.

As the door clicked shut behind Darya, Shirl turned to me.

"You didn't say you was bringing your entourage," she said.

"This is Venir and Darya," I said. "They've been helping me. Darya is the cousin of the man who wrote the papers I gave you."

"Right," Shirl said. "Well, I managed to get some of it done, then everything started goin' to hell. I'll need to scan those sheets again."

Oh. Ah.

"I don't have them," I said.

"What?" Darya said. She grabbed a fistful of my shirt and yanked me to face her. "What happened to them?"

"Ah I meant to tell you," I said, "but then you were missing and the tree and the chestnut and the vision and the cat. And I, um, forgot."

Darya's fingers whitened as she clenched my shirt. Her eyes turned a deeper green. I felt static building in the air around us.

The gathering of magical forces.

Uh oh.

"That grey shadow that chased you," I said. "It swiped the papers from my office. Came right through my broken window. I thought it was reaching for me, but it grabbed the papers and retreated."

Darya released my shirt. Her shoulders sagged. The intensity faded from her eyes leaving her looking drained. The energy around us dissipated.

"What the hell was that?" Shirl said.

"Magic," Venir said. "Did you see what it was, boy?"

I shook my head. "Just a skeletal hand, like..."

"Like what?" the Elf said.

"It reminded me of the vision I had of Lekzar." I turned to

Darya. "Back at the ruins. I saw the cloaked figure. It was veiled. Remember?"

She nodded. "Yes, I recall. Was it the same creature?"

I concentrated, trying to remember, to compare the two. Both shadow shapes, man-like, the skeletal hands reaching toward me. They could have been the same thing, odds were it was, but there were a lot of other things it could be. And I couldn't be sure.

I sighed. "I don't know. I can't tell."

Shirl crossed her arms. "So no more papers, huh?"

"Sorry," I said. "Show us what you got."

"Yeah, okay." She waved us farther into her apartment, leading us to her computer set up. She slid into the leather chair and spun to face her multiple monitors.

"You said it went to hell?" I said.

"Yep," she said. "I was running a bunch of unencryption programs, some decoding bugs, even a coupla symbolism, Rosata stone type programs, seein' if anything could give me a foothold into it. The symbolism one caught something." She smirked at me. "Guess what it was?"

"Shirl, it's late," I said.

"Hell, I know it's late," she said. "I'm the one that called you and told you to come over. Think I don't know what time it is?"

I could do nothing but spread my hands, trying to get her to go on. She huffed.

"Fine, okay. Some people got no sense of humour,

Kringle," she said. She leaned forward and pointed at the middle screen. "It was a Christmas present."

I stared at the monitor. White blanked everything except for the squiggles and symbols written in lines. A few taps of the keypad magnified them.

I recognized the images from Lekzar's pages, but in the middle of the second line, one of the squiggles had morphed in a small square red box, decorated with a green bow. Tiny white snowflakes decorated the box. It was exactly what Shirl said it was.

A Christmas present.

"How? Why?" I babbled out.

She waved a hand at me. "It didn't literally say 'Christmas present' but that was the closest the program could come to deciphering it. Once I got that, there were a few other things I thought you'd wanna see."

Her hands blurred over the keypad.

The screen flashed. Another section of another page appeared and magnified. This time instead of a Christmas present, a figure on the fourth line stood out. A man in a red suit. He had a big white beard and a red hat on his head.

Santa Claus.

Dad.

My mouth went dry. I felt the prickling on the back of my neck. Everything boiled down to this: Christopher Henries dead on the fake Christmas throne, the list of dead Santas, the threat to KJ, everything came down to this little Santa icon on a computer screen.

My heart ached. Someone wanted to kill my Dad.

Then it burned.

I would never let that happen. *Never.*

My jaw throbbed from clenching. I forced myself to relax.

"Anything else?" I said to Shirl.

"Just one more before it started to crap out."

She hit the keyboard again. More squiggles and symbols flashed across the screen. Then it stopped. In the middle of screen was another icon. Stark against the white of the monitor.

A tall slender staff of black with a glowing crystal on top.

I'd seen a staff like that before. In the hand of Lord Dramal as he passed sentence on me.

Had he really been behind it after all?

"I'd like a print out," I said to Shirl. "You can send me a bill for your work."

She opened her mouth to reply, then closed it before nodding. She hit the print button and paper spit out.

I grabbed the copy and we left.

AFTER A BRIEF STOP AT MY OFFICE TO MAKE SURE I HAVE ALL THE pieces, I led Darya and Venir back to the fountain on Centre Island.

It was just after five by the time we reached the concrete

bridge. The sky was lightening above us, like a sleepy child barely opening its eyes. The darkness had shifted to a dark blue and carried a hint of moisture. It dampened the back of my shirt.

I inhaled the crisp, fresh air, smelling the grass, the dew, and the water. I didn't know when I'd be coming back to this place.

If ever.

Bird calls echoed across the concrete. I could hear them tittering in the leaves. They seemed undisturbed by our sudden appearance.

Venir sagged and grabbed hold of the bridge railing.

"Gimme a sec," he said. "I'm not a young Elf any more. I don't go travelin' like that too often."

"Wish I could help," I said. "But I haven't had time to recharge here. Do you think you'll be able to open the portal?"

"We will," Darya said.

I stood my ground as she glared at me but it was all I could do not to take a step back. Since the image of Dramal's staff in Lekzar's writing, she had changed from the helpful, duty-inspired faerie searching for her cousin's killer to a creature filled with fury. It practically crackled across her skin. Her dark hair seemed to crackle around her head with electricity. Her eyes darkened to almost black. She held her hands stiffly at her sides and I got the impressions she wanted to clench them into fists.

I did *not* want to be on the receiving end when she let go.

I gestured her forward.

"After you."

She gave me a sharp nod. Even before she began to chant, I felt the electricity tingle in the air. A moment later, the birds went silent all at once, like a conductor had cut them off. I tasted ozone in the air.

Darya spread her hands, her chant getting louder. The sky darkened above us. I could almost feel the crackle of lightning against my skin. Every hair on my body stood up, even my beard. It was the weirdest feeling to feel the tug along my jaw line.

Then a flash filled my eyes.

The air smelled wood and moist. I blinked to clear the white afterimage from my eyes.

We stood just inside the stone fence surrounding the castle.

Dawn was well on its way here. Golden light glowed off the black stone turrets of the castle before us. The sprawling building rose from the top of a gently sloping hill. I could see two wings spreading out from a main building but from the angle I knew there had to be more.

"We should get going," I said.

Before I could take a step, Darya held out her hand.

"Just wait," she said. "Look."

She nodded toward the castle.

From the main door, I spotted a squad of soldiers appear. They leapt into the air. Golden light shimmered on their wings. In a moment, they surrounded us, several landing in a circle around us, the others staying above.

Surrounding us completely.

So much for the surprise approach.

"Take us to Lord Dramal," I said. "We must speak to him."

"And call forth my Mother," Darya said. "And my cousin's Mother. They will wish to attend."

A wordless shock seemed to flow through the squad. As one the faeries all took a step back before they moved forward again to escort us to the castle.

I glanced over at Darya but she stared straight ahead, not noticing my attention.

I turned to Venir. He shrugged.

We headed across the manicured lawn with our well armed escort while I wondered, who was Darya's mother?

CHAPTER

TWENTY-SIX

In the early morning hours, the great hall glowed with sparkling sunlight. Glimmers of light twinkled above our heads as we entered. This time, the floor stretched forth in a deep, rich green, like an emerald lawn. Instead of the floating chandeliers hovering in the air above our heads, a large orb hung in the centre of the domed ceiling. From the yellowish glow across its surface, I knew it was mirroring the effect of the rising sun.

The hall was empty except for the squad escorting us. A white mist obscured the walls on either side, making it impossible for me to gauge how large the room was. Of course, even if I could figure it out it was probably a mirage. The tingling along my skin was testament to the fae magic that pulsed through this room.

By the time we'd walked halfway across the room, I

spotted the raised dais at the other end. This time, instead of a plain, black chair, a set of two elaborate thrones sat side by side on the platform. The throne on the left was sheer white and looked like it had been chiselled out of ice, the back and arms dripping with crystals that looked like shaved icicles. The throne on the left was a deep, rich brown, with vines of deep green woven around the left and curling on the arms. They ended in blossoms of blood red rubies.

Burnt coal, we were in trouble.

I glanced over at Venir. His face looked at pale as his hair. The tips of his ears quivered.

So he understood too, maybe even better than I.

We weren't just confronting Lord Flektal Dramal.

Oh no.

We were going to be confronting him before the Faerie Queens.

One of whom happened to be Darya's mother.

A little fact she'd never bothered to mention.

If ever there was a time I wished I could melt into the floor.

Darya stopped ten feet from the raised platform. Venir and I stopped as soon as she had and backed up a couple of paces.

Nope, I didn't want to be in front of her.

No way.

Darya turned to one of the guards.

"Where is Lord Dramal?" she asked.

"I am here."

Lord Dramal stepped out of the mist on our right. It swirled around his shining black boots, twinkling, before it drew back. Dramal wore his armoured breastplate over his black shirt and black pants. It was the same outfit he'd worn the other time I'd seen him. I had the feeling it was his usual garb.

All that was missing was his black, velvet cloak.

"Why have you called for a counsel of the Queens without informing me?" he said. The sternness of his voice echoed through the chamber.

"We have serious charges against you," Darya said.

We? It was 'we' now?

Darya spread her arms. The air hummed with electricity. The black wings on Darya's back vibrated and she rose an inch above the floor, hovering.

"I call to thee, my Queens!"

A blast of cold wafted from the dais, followed by a blistering wave of heat. The white mist in the room obscured the thrones, then pulled back, revealing them occupied.

My mouth went dry. I heard Venir give a slight yip.

The Winter Queen sat on the ice throne. Her gown was a glacial ice blue. Frost coated her long finger nails as they gripped the icicle armrests. Her hair of pure white curled high above her head. Drops of crystal adorned it, sparkling in the golden light. A crown of ice encircled her head, barbed with spiked edges like shards. Her skin was pale, her face oval with stark cheekbones, and her eyes were the deepest ice green. The coldness of her look could stop any heart.

Beside her, the Summer Queen perched on her throne. She wore a flowing gown of forest green, trimmed with earthen brown fur. Her nails were painted scarlet and curled together on her lap. Her black hair parted in the middle, flowed in waves past her shoulders and over the sides of the chair. Her skin was a deep, warm brown, her face rounded, her eyes a deep emerald green. She wore a crown of thistle adorned with tiny green leaves and bursting with the buds of small white flowers. As I watched, the buds opened, releasing a subtle, floral scent that drifted across the room. Her look held the threat of a summer thunderstorm whipping into a tornado.

The Winter Queen parted her lips. I heard the tinkle of shattering ice.

"Why do you summon us here to the Nether Ground, daughter?" she said.

Swirling snow, Darya was the daughter of the Winter Queen?

"Yes, daughter, why do you summon us so?" said the Summer Queen. Her voice danced high in the air like a bird.

Now that was interesting. Darya had two mothers?

Or was thie some kind of ritual?

I chanced a glance over at Venir but he stood frozen as if he had assumed that if he didn't move they wouldn't notice him.

Perhaps they wouldn't. He was certainly short enough and had managed to move almost behind me. Unfortunately, I was standing right behind Darya's right shoulder, right at eye level, an easy spot for either Queen to take notice of me.

Maybe if I imitated Venir...

"There have been crimes committed in the Human Realm," Darya said. Her right hand swept back and she rotated, hovering off to the side and revealing me to the Queens.

"A human?" said the Summer Queen. "You bring us one of the shadow people and speak of a crime in their realm? What do we care of this?"

She lifted her hand off her lap. Sparkles danced from her fingers, swirling in to blue light that began glow around her. Her image began to fade.

"Wait," I said.

The Winter Queen narrowed her eyes. It felt like a blast of frigid air.

To me it almost felt like home.

"Please, the crimes in the Human Realm link to the death of Lekzar Trayborn here in your realm."

The Summer Queen's image solidified again. Her hand dropped back to her lap but I noticed they were clenched into fists. The Winter Queen too had a look of impatience.

Fast talking, that's what I needed.

"I am Noel Kringle," I said. "My father is..."

"Kris?" the Winter Queen said. She exchanged a look with the Summer Queen. They sat back in their thrones. A smile cracked the Summer Queen's countenance.

"How is your father?" she said.

"He's fine," I said slowly. The queens nodded together.

So Dad knew the two Queens of the Fae. Funny that he'd never talked about that.

"What I mean is, he's sort of fine," I said. "There've been murders of multiple people playing the role of Santa Claus in my realm. The murder even tried to kill me. Venir contacted me to say there was threat to my dad and that he had a contact who could help us." I stepped back to reveal Venir who was doing everything he could to imitate a frozen snowbank.

"When we got here, we found Venir's contact, Lekzar dead. But Lekzar had left us some clues."

I pulled out the chestnut and the printouts from Shirl's computer.

The Winter Queen waved. "Bring them forth, boy."

My legs felt like they were wobbling so hard they would spill me to the floor. The magical force exuded by both Queens was almost overpowering. I could feel it pressing against my mind, swirling around my body. My muscles tensed and jerked as if my body was a puppet, not in my control. I pressed my lips tight together and focused on stepping across the emerald floor. With each step, the magic intensified, like sparks against my skin.

A smirk stole across the Winter Queen's face.

They were testing me, I realized. Maybe they wanted to make sure I was who I said I was.

How could I prove it? With so much magic swirling

around me, I wouldn't be able to pierce their veils to see anything beyond it.

Would I?

I was forgetting who I was. With all this energy and the force of their personalities, I was losing my own self. I forced myself to take a deep breath and let it out slowly. My pounding heart slowed a little in my chest. My legs felt less wobbly.

I was Noel Kringle, Santa Claus's youngest son, and was able to tap into any Christmas magic around.

Including the residue lingering on the map in my back pocket.

As soon as I thought of it, I felt it stir around me, rising like a shield against the onslaught from the Queens. Within a few moments, the overwhelming pressure was gone. My body felt like mine again.

I took the last few steps with ease and stopped at the base of the dais. I held the chestnut in my left hand and the pages in my right.

"Lekzar enchanted both the chestnut and the original pages. Both of the implicate Lord Dramal."

The Winter Queen reached for the chestnut as the Summer Queen reached for the pages. Cold swirled around my fingers and wrists, trickling up my forearm as the Winter Queen's fingers brushed my palm. From the Summer Queen, I caught the scent of wild flowers and a rush of warm summer wind across my cheek as she slipped the pages from my hand.

"My Queens, I protest this madness," Dramal said. "I would have no reason to cross into the Human Realm. No reason to hunt down these Santa depictions. This is a ruse perpetrated by this child to undermine the neutrality of the Nether Ground. How can we not be sure this was not the final design by his father? He established the Nether Ground and ended the Great Fae conflict but now his son brings lies and accusations to undermine our peace."

Wait a minute, what was Dramal saying? I glanced over at the fae lord who glared back at me.

"He was found with Lekzar's body," Dramal continued, "it is just as easy to believe he murdered your son."

He nodded toward the Queens but I couldn't tell which he was talking to. Both were focused on him with a serious expression.

"You say he is here to break our peace?" the Winter Queen said.

"There can be no other explanation," Dramal said.

"Wait a minute," I said. "What are you talking about?"

"You claim to be Kris Kringle's son and you know nothing about the Nether Ground?" said the Summer Queen. "Nothing about the Great Fae War and its threat to the Human Realm which your father avoided by orchestrating this peace?"

"Ahh." I looked back at Venir. Even the Elf looked dumbfounded. His mouth hung open and his ears quivered.

"Does it matter?" Darya said. "You have the proof of Lord Dramal's betrayal in your hands."

"My Queens..." Dramal said.

"Enough!" The Summer Queen stormed up in a blaze of heat. "We will uncover the truth and the guilty will be punished."

The Winter Queen rose from her throne. A swirl of frost coated the floor in front of me, turning the green tile to pale white.

"We will investigate all charges. You will all be held until we are decided."

Her hand flashed out. Cold swirled around me even as I tried to speak. I had to know more about what she was talking about. What was the Great Fae War? What had Dad done to stop it?

But before I could say anything, frost coated my eyelashes and stayed my tongue. My muscles locked as the Winter Queen froze me in place.

CHAPTER

TWENTY-SEVEN

Around me, the hall wavered under a layer of ice. The two thrones looked distorted, almost grotesque parodies of themselves. The ice throne jagged and flawed, the summer throne cracked and rippled. The air around me was cool and crisp in my nostrils, still enough that I could breathe but letting no sound or aroma in through the cold emptiness. The ice layer encasing me locked me into position so I couldn't even turn my head. From the corner of my eye, I could see a flare of flame. Lord Dramal was locked inside.

Darya had been standing too far behind me for me to tell what imprisoned her. I had to assume Venir had been imprisoned in frost like I was.

The Queens had vanished, taking my proof with them, to deliberate and make their decision.

And I couldn't say anything about it.

I'd thought it was so easy. The murders of Santas, a threat against Dad, against KJ. But there had been this whole other underlying complication. Had it all originated here in response to Dad's actions?

Although Dad's main job had been Christmas, and that intense once a year night-long flight around the world, he had other work that he did. It wasn't all running the toyshop and workshop with the Elves. I'd known that from the visits we'd had when I was younger. Other magical beings would come over and Mother would bake or invite them to stay for dinner. Dad would often take them into his study, the only room in the house were KJ and I were not allowed to bother him.

It had been adult stuff, nothing I'd really thought about when I was a kid and I'd never really considered it when I got older.

Just how much influence did Dad have?

Enough that he delivered presents to the Fae in the Magical Realm. Enough to negotiate a peace during something called the Great Fae War.

A peace I had threatened without even knowing it.

Or maybe a peace I had been manipulated into threatening.

I felt the ice shift around me, a comforting, cool sensation on my skin. It made the tip of my nose tingle and crinkled in my beard.

Had this all been an elaborate ruse, designed to make me

accuse Dramal in front of the Queens? Maybe not at first. I couldn't believe that any creature would kill so many people in Santa suits without it being directed at Dad.

But perhaps this was, for the perpetrator, a happy offshoot. Compromising Dramal and the peace as well as attacking Dad.

Layers upon layers.

Veils upon veils.

My breath caught. The cold tingled on the back of my neck. I was on to something! I knew it. Veils, it was all about veils. All about hiding, concealing, manipulating the truth.

It had all started with Christopher Henries, dead on a throne, then alive in his apartment.

A lie. A veil. An avatar to hide behind.

Then Lekzar dead and the proof he'd hidden.

Veils.

The figure in the dark cloak killing Lekzar then reaching for me in the vision. Then appearing outside my window to snatch the papers away.

Veils.

Somehow it had to tie into together. Somehow it had to make sense.

It was all about the veils.

I could almost feel something in my brain clicking into place.

It *was* all about veils. And not just the obvious veils. Maybe everything had been a veil, a mirage, to conceal the true purpose of the crimes.

Someone had been after Dad all right. Not just to kill him, but to discredit him, to smear him. To destroy what he had done.

This Nether Ground.

Halting a great war had probably left some people disgruntled. There was always someone who wanted things to go back to the 'good old days.'

I had to be close. Why else would the attacks have been more intense? The shadows at the tree. The Yule Cat. It all pointed to someone getting more desperate.

All I had to do was figure out who it was.

The tickle at the back of my neck spread down to my shoulders and then my shoulder blades. The itch was annoying. I rolled my shoulders to relieve it.

Wait. How could I roll my shoulders if I was locked in ice?

I breathed out and felt the ice before me expand like a balloon. It still tingled but wasn't as hard as before. I concentrated on my right hand, commanding it to lift up. My fingers twitched. The muscles in my forearm contracted. For a moment, all I could feel was the strain and effort.

Then my hand jerked. Only an inch.

Then another.

I shouldn't be able to move at all.

I shouldn't be able to do anything against the Fae Queen's magic, even with my own at full strength here in the Magical Realm. They were so much more powerful than I was. There was no way I should be able to move.

But I was.

Was this one of their plots?

Layers upon layers. Faeries weren't known for being straightforward. Maybe this was their way of giving me the chance to figure it out. If I could escape their imprisonment, I still had a chance to discover the culprit before their decision.

I yanked my hand up higher.

Cracks appeared in the ice before me.

My heart pounded with effort, with excitement. All I needed was a wedge and I could break out of my ice prison.

I focused on my left hand. It trembled by my hip. This took a bit more effort. I could feel trickles of moisture run down my face. The ice on my beard began to melt and drip off. Wet tendrils of hair fell into my eyes but I couldn't shake my head to dislodge them.

Not yet.

Finally I felt my left hand move an inch. My shoulders jerked as well, a little freer in their movement.

By the time I brought my left hand up to the same level as my right, I could almost move my upper body from side to side.

I brought my hands together, clasping them in front of my chest. My finger nails were frosted blue. Crystals of ice hung from the tips. My skin still felt freezing cold to the touch.

Concentrate.

Once, playing hide and seek with KJ, I'd hidden in a

frozen snow drift for what felt like hours. I had gathered the freezing air to me. I had layered the ice around me as I waited. My magic had protected me like a bubble beneath the frigid cold. I lay in wait until he came running across the ice sheet where I huddled. He had searched all through the Elf village and the reindeer stables but not found me.

I heard his boots stomping on the ice above my head. I felt the vibration through my bones. When he stopped, the ice around me had still carried the movement, humming against my skin. I'd heard him growl under his breath, "Swirling snow, where is he?" as if he was standing right next to me.

Instead he'd been standing right above me.

I'd gathered all my magic into a small ball in my hands, then in a rush, blasted it outward.

The ice had shattered. KJ had been tossed into the air then landed smack on his butt. His surprised shriek had been music to my ears.

It had been the only time I'd ever scared him.

I'd laughed at him for days even as he claimed he knew I was there, but I'd seen the startled look on his face. Wide eyes, mouth open. He'd thought I was the abominable snowman.

All I'd had to do was concentrate. Pull my magic to me in a little ball and then swirl it out.

The ice crackled around me. I could feel it almost thicken as if it knew I was going to make a break for it.

Let it harden. That cold and ice only added fuel to my own magic.

I could feel it begin to swirl in me, like a cool breeze. I had my hands up near my chest and I formed them into a circle.

Concentrating.

My left hand began to throb where I'd cut it. I squeezed my hand into a fist. The skin pulled. The cut opened. I felt warm blood on my palm as it began to flow.

Blood magic. It just added a little extra oomph to my spell.

The air rasped in my nostrils, freezing the hairs in my nose. My heart hammered in my chest. All my muscles ached from clenching.

Any minute now.

There was a crack right in front of my nose. It split off toward the left, jagged, making the image of the Winter Queen's throne look almost doubled.

I just had to hit that crack at the right moment.

I shifted my shoulders. The crack in front of my face shot another inch down.

Now!

I condensed my power into that little ball in my hands and pushed it forward.

The ice shattered. Shards of it shot into the air, soaring above my head. Within moments, it melted and fell like a pattering of rain. Other hunks of ice lay at my feet like debris, already melting onto the green tiles.

I stepped out, shaking the last of the frost from my shoes.

My wet hair flopped into my eyes. I brushed at it, trying to get the now melting ice out of it.

When I turned around, I saw that like me, Venir had been encased in ice. His lips were pressed tight together and he appeared to be glaring at me.

I glanced over at Darya. To my surprise she was also encased in ice. She stood with head bowed, as if resigned to her fate.

The crackle of flame caught my attention. From within the pillar of fire, Lord Dramal reached out toward me. He held his hand up in a questing gesture. Sweat beaded on his skin. His face was twisted in pain. His black streak hair billowed around him as if any moment it would turn to flame.

Should I help him? I still felt some residual magic tingling in my fingers, but already my shoulders slumped with fatigue. If I only had enough to get one of them out, why would it be Dramal? Was he the one behind all of this?

Or was he?

All of the proof pointed to him. The visions, his power, but something about it still bothered me.

Veils. So many layers. Could I be sure that what those visions were showing me were true? Like Christopher Henries appearing to be alive when he was really dead.

Before I could change my mind, I reached through the flame and grabbed Dramal's hand.

The heat was scorching but just for a moment as I pulled.

My hand came back out, not blackened and peeling like I expected, but intact.

Dramal followed as the flames disappeared in a final puff of grey smoke that singed my nostrils with the scent of burnt leaves.

Dramal shook himself and wiped his hand across his forehead. Behind him, his black wings fluttered out before settling. His skin looked paler and his green eyes blazed out.

"What do you play at?" he said. "First you accuse me of treachery before the Queens and now you risk their wrath by freeing me."

"I want the truth," I said, "and to stop the killing. That's all I've ever wanted. I want to know who is killing the Santas in my realm? Who is threatening my father?"

Dramal shook his head. "It is not I. I hold dominion over the Nether Ground only because of your father."

"How did that happen?" I said.

Dramal's brows drew closer together. He tilted his head. "He did not tell you?"

"No. You're going to, or I'll keep insisting it was all your fault."

The faerie lord's lips thinned.

"Very well," he said. "In the ancient times, both lands of Summer and Winter ruled equally over the world, dividing the time due both in half to share with the other. Then one became greedy, demanding more of her share, then more. War erupted between them and raged over our land. It threatened the entire Magical Realm. It even threatened the

Human Realm, spilling out as ice storms and drought. There appeared to be no end in sight but complete destruction. The Queens could not see beyond their blind rage, until your father came. He met with both, first individually, then he managed to bring them together. They sat cloistered away for weeks while the war stood at a standstill, all waiting to see what would happen. When they emerged, they had negotiated the Nether Ground, the space between Summer and Winter. Spring and Autumn dwell here, providing a buffer and a valve between the great Queens. I was chosen to rule this land and children of Summer and Winter come here to serve before returning to their homes. Your father believed this service would help keep the peace."

"Why didn't you tell me this before?" I said.

Dramal took a step forward, glaring. I stumbled back.

"You blundered in here, killing a son of Summer," he said. "As your father created the peace, how can I be sure you are not here to break it?"

"Lekzar was a son of Summer?" I said.

"Of course he was," Dramal said. "You knew that. The same way you corrupted a daughter of Winter, bending her to assist you in your crimes."

He nodded toward Darya.

I held up my hands. "I didn't know she was a daughter of Winter and I didn't kill Lekzar. Darya helped me because she realized that was true. She's been working to keep the peace just like you have." I gestured back at her. "Why did she call both the Queens 'mother'?"

"It is the way," Dramal said. "When a child of Summer or Winter comes to the Nether Ground, they swear fealty to both Queens, fealty to the promise of peace of the Nether Ground." He paused. The lines around his mouth deepened as he frowned. "Did you really not kill Lekzar?"

"I swear it," I said.

He looked startled. I knew how powerful a swearing was to the Fae. For all their manipulations and machinations, a swearing was the ultimate truth to them. When swore, no Fae would dare lie.

But would he believe me?

I held my breath.

Dramal gave me a regal nod but it did little to change the worry on his face.

"If you did not kill Lekzar, then who did?" he asked.

I let my breath out. "Good question," I said. "I think I may have the answer."

The Fae lord crossed his arms. His wings stirred on his back.

"You may have the answer?"

His voice almost dripped with doubt, enough to make me wonder if I had done the right thing letting him loose. I still only had his word that he wasn't behind this but something told me he'd been telling the truth. The same tingle on my neck told me that I was closer to unravelling this mystery than I thought. The pieces were here, I just needed to figure out how they fit.

"Yes," I said. "I may but I still need help to figure it out." I jerked a thumb back at Venir and Darya. "Their help and yours too. Can you release them?"

"The Queens may not look favourably upon that," he said.

"They might not look too favourably on us like this," I said. "But if we all figure out what really happened, that might appease them."

"And it may not," Dramal said. "It is the Queens' prerogative to decide our fate."

My mouth dried at that thought. I didn't relish the thought of dying here in the Magical Realm. But if I had at least made sure Dad and KJ were safe, it would be worth it.

"I still want to figure out what happened and stop the threat to my father," I said.

Maybe it was something in the way I lifted my chin, or squared my shoulders. Or managed not to let the squeak sound in my voice. Either way, the Fae lord nodded.

"Very well, I will assist you."

He stepped toward Darya and gestured at me to lift my hand. When I did he grabbed my wrist. His skin felt burning hot, like it was searing my arm. I expected to smell cooked flesh but the sensation must have been illusionary.

Dramal grit his teeth. Did my skin feel freezing to him? Or was it something else?

He shoved our hands toward Darya. Before I knew what was going on, he called out in a sing-song voice. It sounded more like the trill of a bird than words.

The searing heat faded to a comfortable warmth. Our

fingers were inches from the ice encasing Darya. As I watched, a melting spot appeared and spread like a ripple across the surface. A pool of water spread at her feet.

Within moments, the ice block faded, releasing Darya. She raised her head and blinked at us in confusion. She glanced around the hall.

"Where are the Queens?" she asked.

"Not back yet," I said. "We still have some investigating to finish. Are you up for it?"

She cast a leery gaze at Dramal. "Perhaps."

"We're going to work together on this," I said. I turned toward Venir before she could question me further. I knew what she was thinking, we had seen Dramal in the vision by the tree, why was I working with him?

I didn't have time to explain. We had to keep going.

With the three of us, melting the final ice block took even less time. Venir stepped away from the ice, shaking his head, sending his white, curling hair into a flying whirl and tapping his cowboy boots on the tile.

"Ah, that was refreshing," he said. "So what now, boy?"

"Now we start at the beginning," I said. "Or thereabouts. I want to know what Lekzar was doing before he contacted you and before he died. We need to retrace his steps."

"What good will that be?" Dramal said.

"Lekzar is the only non-Santa victim," I said. "He claimed to have information. If we can figure out what he was doing, we might find it."

Dramal crossed his arms over his chest. Behind him, his wings puffed out.

"You are merely casting about for nothing," he said. "You do not know what you are doing at all."

I opened my mouth to protest but Venir got there first.

"What are you talkin' about?" the Elf snapped. "This boy here's a private detective, got an office and all. He's solved cases. He knows what he's doin'."

The Elf glared up at the Fae lord until Dramal gave a curt nod.

"Very well," he said. "Where first?"

"Back to Lekzar's suite," I said. "We can then check out his post next."

"Would it not be best to investigate both at once?" Darya said.

"Agreed," Dramal said. "The Queens may return at any time. It is best we come up with answers sooner rather than later. Unless the detective thinks otherwise."

He gave me a slight bow.

Venir bristled. I waved a hand at him behind my back. It would do no good to take offense at Dramal's actions. He probably didn't appreciate us accusing him any more than his accusations riled us.

"Both it is," I said. "We'll meet back here in half an hour. If you find something out, one of you stay there and send the other to me. And we'll do the same."

"Fine." Darya made a show of brushing some fragments of ice from her arms. She moved closer to me.

"I will watch him," she whispered.

I tucked my chin down in response. Her lips curled in a slight smile before returning to impassivity. She turned to Dramal.

"Let us go," she said.

They headed off, their footsteps silent on the green tile, leaving Venir and I behind.

TWENTY-EIGHT

As they disappeared, Venir turned to me. His bushy eyebrows curved down in concern.

"You can't be trustin' him, boy," the Elf said. "That vision..."

"I know," I said. "But we still need to keep looking. Let's go."

We left the great hall, slipping off down the corridor in a different direction. Compared to the two Fae, we sounded like rampaging elephants. To my ears, our footsteps echoed off the black stone walls. Any moment I thought guards would appear at every intersection, ready to arrest us.

But the corridors stayed empty around us.

"There's something not quite right about it, about any of this," I said.

"Dramal's faerie," the Elf said. "A'course it's tricky. That's what they are."

"Do you think Darya's tricky?" I said.

"She didn't tell us she was a daughter of the Winter Queen," he said.

"She also helped us and risked herself doing it," I said.

"I suppose," Venir grumbled.

"How did you know Lekzar?" I asked, to stop him from worrying away at Darya. "I didn't know Elves and Faeries met often."

"We don't," Venir said. "Yer dad sent messages through the Realms. Sometimes I gots to deliver 'em. I bumped into Lekzar one time."

"Bumped into him?" I asked. "How did you manage that?"

He shrugged his shoulders and turned his face away from me. I got the distinct impression the circumstances embarrassed him.

The tips of his ears turning red might have clued me in.

Normally I wouldn't press but this was not normal circumstances. Every detail could be important.

"Venir," I said. "Please tell me."

The Elf huffed out a breath. "Okay, okay. I went into one of them Faerie taverns. Ain't nothing like it in the village back home. The ale tastes of shimmering sparkles." He sighed.

I raised my eyebrows. How did shimmering sparkles taste? I wanted to ask but didn't want to interrupt.

I gestured at him to continue.

"Lekzar was there and he bought me an ale. Said he'd never met an Elf before and thought it quite the sophisticated thing." Venir's chest puffed up a little. "We had a lovely conversation. "He was a bright lad. Full of zest and enthusiasm. Didn't like being so trapped in this Realm and wanted to know everything about everything. Always asking questions, he was. Every time I came to deliver something, we would meet for a drink and a chat."

A smile deepened the creases on Venir's face. He sounded genuinely happy talking about Lekzar. I wondered how many friends he had among the Elves. He wasn't like any Elf I'd met before. He was opinionated and pushy and definitely had his own way of doing things. I imagined he scandalized the Elves at the North Pole. They probably wouldn't want much to do with him. I tried to imagine him working in the toy shop or any of the other workshops or even in the barn with the reindeer but I couldn't picture it.

No wonder Dad had made him a messenger. Venir was independent enough to be able to react to unforeseen situations.

And no wonder KJ didn't like him, the Elf was just different enough that he didn't fit in to KJ's vision of how things went at the North Pole.

Kind of like me.

I knew what it was like being a little bit different, not fitting in completely, being on the outside. It made you look for somewhere else you belonged.

Or with someone else.

Had Venir felt that sense camaraderie with Lekzar? It seemed Lekzar hadn't fit in well with the Fae either. They both could have bonded over being misfits.

"Here," Venir said.

The door opened with ease. The room beyond looked the same as our first visit. Piles of clothes scattered on the floor. Papers and books piled up on the desk to the right of the doorway.

Venir stepped over a pile of shirts. "So what are we lookin' for exactly?"

"I'm not sure," I said.

The Elf snorted.

"You were the one defending me," I said.

"A'course, to that uppity faerie," he said. "But you better deliver, kid."

"We're looking for anything out of the ordinary," I said. "Anything that doesn't make sense from what you know about Lekzar. You were his friend, you should be able to tell."

The amused expression faded from the Elf's face. "Right," he said. He turned away.

Damn, I shouldn't have said that but it was true. Venir should be able to tell if anything was strange here better than me.

I just hoped he would have the sense enough to tell me.

I turned toward the desk. At least here I'd found those papers with the strange writing.

The writing that had pointed us toward Dramal.

But if it hadn't been Dramal, why had Lekzar written that it was?

Had it been a mistake in translation? Maybe. Maybe Shirl's program hadn't been able to translate it properly after all. But it had figured out the Santa symbol.

The back of my neck itched. I reached up to scratch it.

My gaze moved up along the bookshelves above the desk. Rows of thick books, bound in leather with gold stitching in Fae script. I couldn't read the titles but I recognized the images on the spines. Goblets, fire, cats.

Another stack of books was piled on the desk. I remembered grabbing the papers from top of it. The top book had a stylized engraving of a dragon.

A dragon.

Cats.

The itching on my neck deepened.

What if Shirl's program *had* successfully translated the images? What if Lekzar had written it that way?

On purpose.

And something Venir had said earlier bothered me.

Lekzar had always asked him questions.

Always.

Lekzar had pushed the boundaries, using spells to peek in on other Realms, that's what Darya had said.

Veils.

Had Lekzar been exactly what he appeared to be? A son of Summer, assigned to be a guard in the Nether Ground, to learn about the peace and how to keep it. Boring work for someone so interested in everything. Had his interest gotten him killed?

The itching in my neck almost felt like a cramp. It reminded me of the feeling at the ruins when I'd seen the vision of the figure killing Lekzar.

The vision.

Visions weren't like a camera recording. They were influenced by the person seeing them.

They could be manipulated.

They could be a lie.

But I'd found Lekzar's body. I'd fallen over it.

Like I'd found Christopher Henries' body slumped over on the peeling throne.

An avatar.

I spun around to Venir.

"He's alive," I said.

Venir startled like I'd dumped a bucket of freezing water over his head. "What?"

"Lekzar. He's alive."

The itching vanished from my neck. I was right and I knew it.

"You're crazy, boy," the Elf said. "We found his body."

"We found a body," I said. "It could have been manipulated to look like Lekzar."

Venir shook his head. "To do that, it would take a strong magic, stronger than Lekzar had."

"Are you sure?" I asked. "What if you never really knew

the real Lekzar? What if you knew only what he wanted you to know?"

Venir clenched his fists. His cheeks flamed red. The tips of his ears quivered.

"You saying I don't know when I'm being lied to?" he snapped. "You think I'm some idiot Elf, all trusting like those..." He stopped and shook his head.

"How many times did you go into that tavern before you met Lekzar?" I asked. "Was it a regular thing? Maybe someone made note of it. When Santa Claus sent a message, the Elf delivering it stopped for a drink. It wouldn't be too hard for Lekzar to figure when the next delivery would be. He could have been waiting."

Venir sucked in a breath. His nostrils flared.

"If you weren't your father's son, I'd clobber you."

"I'm sorry, Venir," I said. "I don't mean to insult you but I saw the body of a dead man dressed in a Santa suit and then it vanished. Then I found who I thought was the same man, alive. Except it wasn't him. I don't even think it was a man. It was some kind of avatar and the real man was already dead, for real. And someone wants to do that to my father." I took my own breath, steadying myself. "And I think that person may have manipulated Lekzar."

It was as far as I could go with Venir. I didn't know if he really wanted to hear what I actually thought.

That it was Lekzar all along.

But I'd underestimated the Elf's intelligence.

He shook his head, his curling hair flopping around his head.

"That ain't what you think," he said. "Why don't you say it?"

I sighed. So much for sparing his feelings.

"I think Lekzar did it," I said. "I also think he's still alive."

Venir winced as if I'd struck him. His hands stayed curled into fists but he lifted his chin.

"If that's so, where is he then?"

I glanced around the room. Everything looked the same since we'd last been here. I couldn't sense any change. I was sure even if Venir cast one of his spells we'd find nothing else out of place.

Lekzar would not have returned here. It was too obvious a place.

But I could think of another place he'd be.

I took a last glance at the books.

"I think I know where he's hiding," I said. "And I think I know how to find it."

Slipping out of the castle took us almost half an hour. I kept expecting to feel the swirling magic of the Queens at any moment, yanking us back to the great hall. But as we emerged into the early morning light, I still felt nothing.

Venir had followed in silence, his hands still clenched into fists. The age lines in his face looked deeper, like a sculptor had etched them in more permanently. They weren't laugh lines any more but lines of pain and distrust.

I had done that to him. I had cast doubt on his friendship.

If only there had been another way.

I wasn't proud of myself. He'd come to me trying to help and I'd made him look like a fool. Or rather I'd shown him that'd he'd been played for a fool. Although I hadn't done it, I had revealed it. I was really starting to understand the whole 'don't shoot the messenger' thing.

Unfortunately, Venir didn't seem to see it that way.

The sky was turning from the dark black of night to a deep indigo of early morning. The air still held the tang of morning dew. The scent of grass was slightly different, more of a mossy smell than I was used to in the Human Realm. It felt cushy under our feet as we hurried across the open courtyard.

By the time we reached the cover of the trees, the sky had begun to brighten. The first rays of golden light shimmered on the black bricks of the castle behind us. But the forest before us was still shrouded in pitch darkness.

Would I be able to find the way? I had no idea if my plan would work.

But I could only try.

I pulled Dad's old map out of my back pocket.

The paper crinkled as I unfolded it and released the

familiar old paper smell that seemed to mingle with the smell of moss and sourness of the rotting leaves. The sharp tang of fresh buds added to spice.

The mossy grass felt spongy as I knelt down and spread the paper in front of me. The faded lines still looked the same, outlining the North and South American continents on the left, then Europe, Asia, and Africa on the right. Australia and New Zealand were crunched onto the bottom on the right, split until they appeared again on the bottom left.

I felt a presence over my right shoulder. I glanced back. Venir peered at the map. When he noticed me watching, he turned away.

I was still not forgiven.

I turned back to the map.

The colours were even more faded in the dim light. I sat back on my heels, staring at the paper.

I had really thought it would work, but maybe it didn't have enough magic in it. Or maybe that wasn't how it worked at all.

I'd really expected it to show me this land.

Behind me, Venir grunted.

"What?" I said.

"His new ones just change," the Elf said. "This old one, you gotta tell it."

"Oh," I said. I touched the edge of paper. "Show us this land."

The paper began to ripple like a wind was blowing across

it. The lines seemed to shift and change. Continents moved. Lines of rivers snaked across, bisecting new marking for forests. Then to the left was the notation for the castle. And just past the centre line...

The empty clearing for the ruins.

A glowing red dot appeared at the edge of the forest.

Right where we were. It didn't seem as far as I thought.

I memorized the route and folded the map. It tingled as I stuffed it into my back pocket.

"This way," I said to Venir.

He grunted. The closest he'd come to talking to me in the last half hour.

I would take it.

We hurried through the underbrush. Spindly branches of thick, squat bushes with narrow leaves seemed to grab for me but I slipped past. I made sure I didn't touch the trunks of the trees surrounding us. I didn't want to get caught the way I had when I'd first arrived.

The ground rose under our feet. The forest thinned, the trees growing sparser and farther apart. The mossy grass gave way to dirt and gravel. I recognized the short, prickly leaved bushes that squatted on the hard-packed ground.

"Watch out for those," I said to Venir. He glared at me. Of course he knew they were like the trees, draw to our magic. As I passed one, the leaves shifted toward me but sluggish.

Perhaps the coming morning slowed them down.

We picked our way up the slope. I aimed for a large jutting rock. I grabbed the smooth surface as I reached it, hauling myself up. I turned to extend my hand to Venir but the Elf ignored me. He scurried the last few feet, using his hands to steady himself on the sharp incline.

I peered around the rock at the uneven rubble of the decimated ruins. From here, I couldn't make out the circle of smaller piles of dirt and rock that Darya and I had made. Was it still even there? Had the visions I'd had destroyed it?

We would have to head down there.

But now that we were here, I was reluctant to go.

"Is that it?" Venir said.

"Yes," I said. "Lekzar opened the portal here."

Venir grunted but it didn't sound a dismissive. I glanced over at him. His brows were still drawn together but this time he looked worried, not just angry.

Was he sensing something down there?

My mouth felt dry. I didn't really want to go down there but there wasn't much choice. I gave a nod to the Elf and then picked my way around the rock.

I was more prepared for the slope down to the ruins although my right ankle twinged to remind me to be even more careful. Dust rose around me as I moved in a controlled slide. Gravel and pebbles trickled down in accompaniment.

I managed to hold on to my sneeze until I reached the bottom. I shook my head to keep the dust from my eyes.

Venir's slide down echoed like thunder behind me. Had I been as noisy as that?

Probably.

So much for the element of surprise.

He landed with a whomp beside me, a cloud of dust billowing up around him. It tickled my nose so much that I had to fight the urge to sneeze. I spat out the taste of dirt and rubbed my nose as I stepped away from the settling dust.

"What is this place?" Venir said.

Although he spoke quietly, his voice echoed over the stillness.

"Darya just said they were ruins," I said. "She didn't tell me of what."

And I had never asked. I had only been concerned about finding the place where Lekzar had cast his spell to cross into the Between. Now it occurred to me that maybe this location had some other significance.

Too bad I hadn't bothered to find out what.

Now who was really the one that had been played for the fool?

I had been hampered right from the beginning with the oddness of the case, the half truths, the outright lies, and the misdirection. I still couldn't be sure of the Queens' motivations and I didn't know if I could trust either Darya or Dramal.

I turned to the Elf standing beside me.

"We're going to figure this out," I said. "You and me. We're going to save my Dad and stop the killing."

For a moment, Venir looked startled. The thick creases on his face thinned out and he looked younger, more vulnerable. Then his brows drew together and his lips pursed. He gave a curt nod.

"You bet, kiddo," he said.

A slight breeze came up, bringing along the sweet sour mix of the mossy grass.

And a soft chuckle.

I started.

Had I heard that right? Had it been a laugh?

It had sounded like it had come from a larger pile of rubble across the way, to the left.

Silent now.

I glanced at Venir. He looked back at me, uncertain, but when I gave a nod, he nodded back.

So he'd heard something too. It hadn't been just my imagination.

I took a breath, drawing in my magic. I felt the tingle of coolness against my skin, a hint of night still although the day was drawing closer.

I moved toward the pile of rubble, setting my feet down as quietly as I could. Venir followed, his cowboy boots making soft crunching sounds on the dirt.

Even with my awareness expanded out, I couldn't feel any magic in the place. Even before Darya and I had built the circle, I'd felt some residual energy among the ruins but now there was nothing.

Had I been wrong? Was there nothing here? Had I imagined the laugh?

I passed a pile of rubble on my left. I could still make out a few bricks in the crumbling mess. They looked almost glassy, like they had been subjected to a heat so intense it almost melted them.

What could have done that?

What exactly were these ruins?

The skin on the back of my neck began to prickle. Maybe coming here hadn't been such a good idea after all. Maybe we'd done exactly what someone had expected us to do and walked right into a trap.

And that was when the chuckle sounded again.

TWENTY-NINE

"I didn't think it would be you, Venir," said a voice off to the right.

Venir and I spun around.

A cloaked figure seemed to form out of the darkness. The hood towered over us, showing only blackness inside. The bottom edges barely touched the ground as if the creature inside was hovering.

"That's some trick," I said. "But you don't need that get-up any more. We know who you are."

The chuckle sounded from inside the hood, hollow and echoing.

But still unmoving.

"Stop it," Venir said. "Lekzar, stop it right now."

The hood wavered from side to side, almost enough to be a head shake. But it could have also been the wind.

Something about that cloak made me uneasy.

I caught a whiff of ozone. From behind us.

I grabbed Venir's arm and yanked him as I jumped aside.

A flash of energy, blazing bright blue, scorched the earth where we'd been.

Three feet behind us, Lekzar stood beside a pile of rubble. He wore the grey tunic and pants of his station with the gleaming breast plate. But instead of looking regal and over-worldly like the other Fae, his clothes were covered in dirt. His brown hair was matted and hung in strings along his forehead. His pale skin had a sheen of perspiration, as if it was taking all his effort to maintain the illusion of the cloaked figure.

But in his right hand, he held a staff of gleaming ebony. It wasn't completely straight, at several parts along the shaft, it seemed to bow or twist, but that only gave depth of its darkness. The top held a sphere of iridescent blue so cold it made my gums ache.

And felt oddly familiar.

Lekzar seemed to lean against it as much as hold it in front of himself. He glared at us, his expression twisted in fury.

I didn't know what he had to be so angry about. He was the one going around killing and threatening people.

Some people could just never be happy about anything.

"It's all over," I said.

"It is not over," he said. His voice came out as a husky

croak as if he'd been yelling for hours. "It will never be over until the abomination is dead."

"Whatda you talking about?" Venir said. "What abomination?"

"Your red lord." Lekzar spat out the words. "He broke our hold over this realm, turned us into nothing but folklore and the others all hail him as peacemaker. They are blind to how he diminished us."

"How can stopping you from killing each other diminish you?" I asked.

He focused on me, shifting the staff in my direction.

Maybe it had been a bad idea to catch his attention.

"You are his son. Another invader."

"Right," I said. "Can I ask you a question?"

He tilted his head. His green eyes gleamed with madness. I didn't want to look too closely there or I'd be trapped inside.

"What?" he said.

"Where'd you get that cool staff?"

His gaze shifted.

Just enough.

I kicked out.

My sore right ankle connected right above his. I winced but managed to hook my foot around his leg.

And yanked.

His left leg flew out. He fell backwards, landing on his rump. A cloud of dust puffed up. He yelped.

The staff slipped out of his hand.

The sky darkened. Magical energy crackled in the air. I felt it shimmer on my skin.

Damn the halls, had he been holding some dark magic back with that staff? That didn't make sense to me, that thing had the look of evil all over it, not something that held back evil.

And certainly Lekzar had seemed intent to use it as such.

But the air quivered with energy. It tasted metallic and sour on my tongue and crackled against cheeks. The darkening sky looked like some vast cloud was covering the light. My ankle throbbed. The injury on my left palm burned.

Where I'd cut myself to use blood magic.

Was the staff a focus for that? Had the deaths of the Santas not just been a statement but a gathering of magical energy as well?

If that was the case, I did not want Lekzar getting that staff again.

He was still sitting stunned on the ground, digging his fingers in the dirt. I jumped up, and almost fell over as my right ankle buckled. I hissed as pain shot up my calf.

Lekzar glanced up at me and scowled. He lifted his hands. A swirl of energy began to pulse between them, brightening at a terrifying rate.

Across the clearing, the cloaked figure began to move. Inching at first, then gathering speed toward the staff.

The staff had landed between me and the figure. I'd never make it before Lekzar blasted me with that energy ball. Or the figure reached it.

But I was gonna try.

I lunged forward. My right ankle buckled but held as I lurched. I must have looked like some ridiculous lopsided creature as I tried to run.

The smell of ozone intensified behind me.

Any moment now.

Just another two feet.

Ahead of me, the figure was swooping down, arms outstretched. Skeletal hands reaching...

"You never deserved those beers!"

Venir's shout caught my attention. I glanced back over my shoulder.

The Elf darted in from Lekzar's left. Before the Faerie could react, Venir hauled back and slugged him across the face. Lekzar's head snapped back. His hands flew apart. The swirl of energy vanished.

Ahead of me, the cloaked figure seemed to stumble. Its arms flailed as if it could no longer see.

I bounded forward the last two feet. In the gloom, the staff was a black line bisecting the ground. The air around it pulsed with energy, as if trying to repel me. I sucked in a breath that felt like it crisped my lungs and grabbed it.

The moment I touched the staff, the figure collapsed. Empty fabric fell to the ground in a heap.

I'd broken Lekzar's spell.

A force of energy tried to surge up my arm. Within it, I could feel the echo of multiple deaths. Lekzar had trapped the life energy of the people he'd killed within the staff and been manipulating it. I could feel it surging, trying for release. The smooth feel of the staff burned in my palm.

I focused, drawing the cool magic of the North Pole to me, the soothing power of my Santa Claus heritage. Deep breaths slowed my racing heart, calmed my nerves. As I relaxed, I felt my magic flow more smoothly, tracing along the surface of the staff as if calming the swirling mix of life energies trapped inside.

Slowly they began to heel, to resonate with my own magic. A steadiness flowed from the staff but beneath it, I could still feel the power residing within, ready to be unleashed if not kept under careful guard.

"That's mine," Lekzar whined. He scrambled to his feet. Blood trickled from his nostrils where Venir had landed his blow. But the Elf wouldn't get another chance. Lekzar darted away from him, staying well out of range.

When he was sure Venir couldn't reach him, he glared across at me.

"You'll pay for this," he said.

"Sure I will," I said. "Just as soon as you tell me where you got this." I waggled the staff in his direction. "This isn't something you conjured up. You got it from somewhere. Where was that?"

A smirk twisted his expression. "You'll never know and if you think you can stop me, you're wrong."

Before I could reply, a crackle of energy split the air like a thunderclap. On opposite sides of the clearing, two figures began to form out of the gloom. Shimmering entities sparkled in a brilliance I could barely make out. A thunder of sound roared around them, building to a crescendo.

Fury and indignation rippled out from them, like a building wave.

Where these the creatures behind Lekzar's rampage?

Then the gloom parted, revealing the bright blue of early morning sun.

The Faerie Queens flanked Lekzar on either side. Steam from the Winter Queen's ice blue dress drifted upward from her shoulders.

The Summer Queen waved a hand and tendrils of roots erupted from the ground. They whipped around Lekzar's legs and wrists, pinning his arms to his sides.

A moment later, the air popped and Darya and Dramal dropped from the sky, wings blurring as they landed. Darya held a woven bag almost as thick as my thigh. As she set it on the ground, Dramal held his hands out to it, as if warming them on a fire, but from the crackle in the air I knew what he was doing.

Holding back the magic contained in the bag.

"Lekzar Trayborn, son of Summer, we accuse you of using magic to usurp the peace of the Nether Ground. What say you to this charge?" the Winter Queen said.

Lekzar strained against the roots trapping him but stayed silent.

The Summer Queen tapped her foot. Tiny flower buds appeared in the ground around the toe of her shoe.

"Speak, child," she said. "Why have you acted thus?"

Lekzar shook his head. Damp hair swung in his eyes.

I tightened my grip on the staff and stepped forward.

"He believed the peace my father negotiated diminished you," I said. "He wanted revenge for you turning into folklore."

The Winter Queen pursed her lips. She raised a whitish eyebrow at the Summer Queen.

"Is this true?" The Summer Queen turned to Lekzar. "Do you believe this peace diminishes us?"

Lekzar pressed his lips together and stayed silent.

"We found these totems hidden near his post," Darya said. She held the bag out. It seemed to quiver in her hand. I could feel the energy in it pulsating and an echo of Dramal's efforts to hold it back.

It was like some kind of magical grenade.

There was no way Lekzar could have made that, just like he couldn't have made this staff.

"This is all the proof we need," the Winter Queen said. "You are guilty of trying to disrupt the peace and will face judgment."

The Summer Queen bowed her head and nodded.

"Wait a minute," I said. "He's not alone in this. There's no way he could have done all of it by himself."

The Summer Queen lifted her head and frowned in puzzlement. "What are you saying, Kringle?"

"I'm saying there's someone else behind this," I said. "Look at this staff. It's way too powerful for Lekzar to have made it." I held it out toward them. It quivered in my hand, energy pulsing even as I contained it. "And that bag." I pointed to it in Darya's hand. "Could he have made that? If he had the ability to do both of those, he should have been able to disrupt the peace long ago, but he was having to gather life energy from my realm. Someone was helping him."

"Do you know who it is?" the Winter Queen asked.

"No," I said. "But I'll find out."

"Until you do, it is not our concern," she said. "The traitor is caught and will be punished. We will dispose of the threats."

She pointed at the bag in Darya's hand. Snow swirled from her fingertips, encircling the canvas. In a moment, the bag froze into a block of ice. Darya hissed as the cold encased her fingers. She wiggled them. The bag slipped out of her grasp and fell to the ground.

It shattered into pieces. In moments, the ice melted into the ground.

Carrying the pieces with them.

The Summer Queen waved her hand over the area and buds burst out of the ground, white pedals opening to the sun.

She turned toward me and held out her hand.

"Give that to me, Kringle."

"Wait," I said. "You can't destroy this too. I won't be able to find out who was behind it without it."

She huffed out a breath. "Is that important? The traitor is caught."

"But you still don't know who helped him," I said.

"That is your concern," said the Winter Queen. "Take it if you wish. As you leave our realm."

She looked at me quite pointedly. I caught the hint.

But I couldn't believe they were just going to let it go like this.

"But..." I started.

The Winter Queen lifted her hand and placed it on Lekzar's shoulder. He sucked in a breath as ice crept across his body. He froze within seconds. The Summer Queen draped vines around him. They tingled with energy, imprisoning him. Then she too put her hand on his other shoulder and all three of them faded to nothing, vanishing in the golden light of the morning.

Dramal eyed the staff in my hand.

"You will take that with you," he said. "I do not want it here in the Nether Ground."

"Yes," I said. "I'll take it."

He nodded and gave a slight bow.

"I trust next time you wish to visit the Nether Ground you will not be stumbling over bodies and creating chaos," he said.

"I'll do my best," I said.

"I must return to the castle. Darya will open the portal here for you to return home."

Before I could reply, he turned away. He pressed something into Darya's hand and bent to speak in her ear. Then without a backward glance at us, he turned to face the castle.

His wings blurred and he lifted into the sky. A moment later, his figure shrank to a dot as he flew away.

"Hmph, didn't even say goodbye," Venir said.

I glanced over at Darya. "Will you be in trouble for helping us and for crossing in our realm?"

"I may pull night guard duty for a while," she said. "Lord Dramal does not allow family privilege to excuse breaches of duty but I suspect he will allow me some leniency. After a show of discipline." Her expression tightened. "Do you really believe there was someone else involved?"

"Did Lekzar know enough to make those things you found or this staff?" I asked.

She frowned. "I don't know. I never paid much attention to his interests, they always seemed so frivolous. But they were not."

"No, they weren't," I said.

"I am sorry I did not disclose my parentage," she said. "We denounce those allegiances when we work in the Nether Ground. And I am not in line to be queen. I am well down the line from that." She gestured around her. "I joined here to be of use."

I smiled. "I know the feeling."

She smiled back. "Will you visit some time? I will not be allowed to discuss this with anyone else." She looked from me to Venir.

"Sure we will," the Elf said. "But if it's all right with you, I'd like to find some other place than the Enchanted Glade."

"A deal," Darya said. "I'm sorry my cousin betrayed you. He wasn't worthy of your friendship."

Venir ducked his head in a nod. He cleared his throat and coughed into his fist, bending over to hide his face but through his white, curling hair, I could see the tips of his ears turning red.

"We have to get back," I said, giving cover for Venir. "But one question before we go."

Darya tilted her head. "Yes."

"Why here?" I gestured around at the piles of rubble. "Why did Lekzar choose this place? What are these ruins?"

The smile drained away from Darya's face.

"This was the location of the last battle," she said. "The final outpost before the jump between summer and winter. It was the place your father stopped the fighting. That was why the Nether Ground was established here. To guard this place and honour the truce."

I swallowed around the lump in my throat. I really had no idea of all the things my Dad had done, the difference he'd made.

It wasn't one night a year either.

"Thanks for telling me," I said.

Darya's green eyes twinkled. "Of course."

She held out her hand. A glowing purple sphere lifted off her hand. The air around it shimmered.

The staff in my hand started to tremble as if in resonance with the sphere. I tightened my grip. I didn't want to be leaving it behind or having it get lost as we moved through the portal. No telling what would happen.

A purplish glow extended from the sphere, growing as I watched. Dust swirled at the bottom as it touched the ground. The glow elongated, stretching above my head.

The staff jerked in my hand as if trying to pull free. I yanked it back.

Was I going to be able to hang on to it as we passed through the portal?

Venir must have been wondering the same thing. He glanced up at me, the creases around his mouth deepening in an uneasy look.

I had to do something about the staff, but what? Here in the Magical Realm, my North Pole magic could hold it in check but what about when we returned to the Human Realm, where my magic was low? Had I made a mistake taking charge of it?

There had to be a way to bring it to heel in a more permanent way.

I shifted my hand to get a tighter grip on the black wood and winced as it rubbed against the bandage on my palm.

That was it!

Even as the purple glow coalesced into the portal shape before us, I grabbed the bandage on my left palm with my right hand. As I tugged at it, I felt the cut tear and reopen. Fresh dribbled into my palm and onto the meaty part of my hand. I pressed it against the staff.

Burning fire lanced down my arm. Energy pulsed through my entire body down to the ground, then back and through the staff. The crystal on top glowed a fiery red then settled to a pale glow. The wood of the staff seemed to twist and straighten, before settling into a new pattern, twisting like a barber pole, from the bottom to the top. Then it began to shrink, condensing down from a tall staff until it was the perfect size of a cane.

My hand shifted to rest on the crystal which fit snugly into my palm.

Darya opened her mouth but the purple sphere sparked, outlining the portal with glowing light.

I could feel the tug of energy running through the new cane. It was pulling me toward the portal as if telling me it was time to go. I grabbed Venir's shoulder.

"Goodbye Darya," I called.

The purple glow surrounded us.

And we were gone.

CHAPTER

THIRTY

Dust tickled my nose. I coughed and blinked at the bright light.

The expanse of a gravel lot stretched before me. Heat waves made the air shimmer. A smattering of weeds poked up between cracked asphalt, spindly green leaves spreading their meagre edges up to the sun. A pair of single storey warehouses dotted the horizon several metres away.

Wait a minute.

I spun around. My office building was behind me.

Dramal's portal was a lot better than Venir's had been.

Speaking of, the Elf stepped up, brushing dirt from his jeans. His white hair swirled around his head like a cloud of snow. He wrinkled his nose.

"Hey, isn't that your building?" he said.

"Yes. I want to put this safely away." I tapped the cane.

We headed up to my office. The air felt like walking into a warm, moist sponge. Bright sunlight streamed through the hole where my window had been, highlighting the layer of dust coating the top of my desk and my office chair. I'd forgotten about my recent ventilation issue. I didn't relish taking it up with my landlord.

"You really should have a window there," Venir said.

"There was," I said. "I'll have to get my landlord to fix it." I sighed, imagining the repairs. He would probably want me to vacate while he did it.

But first, I had to check on my brother and let Mallory know the killer had been caught, even if he'd never face punishment in this realm.

I stepped toward my desk. My shoes crunched on the dirt on the tile. Everything was still pushed around from when the shadow had reached through the window and grabbed the papers.

I resisted the urge to straighten everything up. Instead I reached down to the bottom drawer. It squeaked a little as I opened it. More dust working its way through my entire office but at least I still felt the tingle of magic in my fingers.

I pulled the map from my back pocket and slipped it back safely into the drawer.

Next was the cane.

It should have been too large to fit inside the drawer but

that was the thing about magic. It allowed things that shouldn't happen to actually be.

I set the end into the centre of the drawer. A ripple of energy made the black wood thrum in my fingers. The crystal glowed under my palm. I could feel it not want to go into the drawer. The resistance made it slip against the bottom and bang against the side.

"Get in there," I said. "If you behave I'll take you out sometimes. I promise."

My words seemed to sink into the ebony wood. The resistance continued for a moment then I felt a softness as the cane relented. I pushed again and this time it telescoped down until it fit snugly against the side of the drawer. I felt the tingle of wistful regret as I slid the drawer shut.

When I stood up, Venir gestured around the room.

"Want me to sweep up while you're checkin' in with KJ?" he asked.

"I have to talk to a detective first. Don't you want to come along?" I said.

He stuck his hands into the pockets of his jeans. "Your brother doesn't much like me." His lips pressed tight together and I caught the underlying message: he didn't much like KJ.

"Okay, I should be back soon," I said.

"Sure, boss," Venir said.

Boss?

What did he mean by that?

While stopping at my apartment to change my shirt, I

called Mallory. The phone rang as I looked around at the cramped living room. I had managed to fit a loveseat and a single armchair in here with barely enough space for a coffee table between them and it still managed to attract a layer of dust.

While I wondered if I had enough magic left to whisk it away, Mallory answered the phone.

"Yeah," his gruff voice sounded in my ear.

"It's Noel," I said. "I've got word on your killer."

"Oh?" Mallory's voice perked up. I could just see him sitting straighter in his chair in his cubicle as he squinted at his computer screen.

"I found him," I said. "But you won't be able to arrest him or try him."

A growl sounded over the phone. "Why not?"

I paused a moment. With anyone else, I would have to come up with some story but Mallory deserved the truth. Fortunately, he had seen enough that he would believe it.

Probably.

"The killer was a faerie from the Magical Realm who was angry at my Dad because he brokered a peace between the Faerie lands of Winter and Summer. He was working his way up to making an attempt on my Dad but he's in the custody of the Winter Queen and the Summer Queen now."

Silence stretched on from the other end of the phone. I couldn't even hear a computer hum or if Mallory was breathing.

"Hello?" I said.

"Fairy?" he said.

"Yes," I said. "From the Magical Realm."

"Don't tell me again," Mallory said. He sighed. I could imagine him brushing his hand over his short, salt and pepper hair. "I can't put any of this in a report."

"I know," I said. "I thought you'd just want to know."

"I don't want to know *this*," he said. He sighed again. "Okay, I'll have to keep investigating for a while then it'll go into the unsolved pile."

"Sorry," I said.

"Is he gonna pay for his crimes?" Mallory said. "You said there were a pile of murders."

The look on Lekzar's face rose to my mind, his eyes widened and his mouth open in pain and fear just before he vanished.

"He's going to pay," I said. "I don't know exactly how but I'm sure he will."

"I suppose there's nothing I can do unless I want to try going to this magic place," Mallory said.

"Believe me, you don't want to go there."

He grunted an agreement and I hung up after promising him a bottle of Gellers scotch for his trouble.

I made it to the Good View Mall just before opening. Sunlight glinted off the multitude of windshields on the parked cars as I hurried to the side door. Slipping inside felt like slipping into heaven. Cool air chilled the sweat on my forehead. My shirt, newly changed, no longer felt like it was going to twist tight enough to strangle me.

Even the dimmer lighting was soothing after the harsh, vibrant glare of the sun.

I found the door to the Santa Room closed. Just to be safe, I knocked before grabbing the handle.

A loud voice called out, "Come in."

I opened the door.

KJ stood on the stage beside a golden throne. His back was to me, but he was already dressed in the red suit. His black boots were shining with polish. Fluffy white cuffs adorned the top and trimmed the length of his coat. Waves of white hair spilled out from under a red hair and curled around his shoulders.

Even during his most radical days, KJ had never worn his hair that long.

And that throne. It was a real one, not just the gilded chair draped with fabric to make it look like a throne. This one had ornately curved arms with jewels decorating the ends like lights. Huge feet that looked almost like reindeer hoofs supported the chair. The burgundy cushion looked almost six inches high. I could just imagine sinking into it.

Then I glanced around the rest of the room.

Gone were the fake trees, the cardboard backdrop, the tumbleweed-like, cotton snow.

Instead, what looked like real pine trees lined a path straight toward the stage. As I stepped closer, the sweet odour of fresh pine tickled my nose. The air felt crisper too, as if a breath of winter chilled the room.

The back wall behind the stage showed a scene of snow

along a street in a village. I recognized those black arched roofs and the cobblestone walks. The heavy stone walls and the thick drapes hanging in the windows.

That was a scene straight from the village at the North Pole!

It looked so real I felt like I could walk right down that street and feel the snow crunch under my shoes.

Then KJ turned around.

His cheeks had the same ruddy colour as Dad's got after a few hours in the cold loading parcels into the sleigh. His beard hung fluffy and curled half way down his chest. Even his eyebrows looked puffier.

If it hadn't been for the tilt of his nose, I would swear it was Dad.

"KJ?" I said.

"Noel," his voice boomed across the room. He tilted his head forward as he peered over his glasses. "You didn't find my replacement, did you?"

I hesitated and saw something flitter across his face.

Disappointment.

He was enjoying himself.

But I couldn't let him know that I knew. It would completely disrupt the trajectory of our entire relationship.

I spread my hands and shrugged. "I'm sorry, KJ, I haven't been able to find anyone."

Relief flickered through his eyes then he took a deep breath. His cheeks reddened even more.

"What do you mean you haven't found someone," he roared. "I told you one day."

I gave an exaggerated shrug. "I'm sorry, KJ, I really tried." I gestured around the room. "What happened to the décor?"

He looked at the pine trees and the throne as if noticing them for the first time.

"I thought the place needed some sprucing up. I wasn't feeling it with the fake crap that was around here." He peered back over the glasses. "Did you decorate it?"

I raised my hands. "I had nothing to do with that."

KJ snorted. "Looks better now anyway. The kids like it more." He tapped his wrist. "I've got a show in five minutes."

He tried to look stern but I could see the way his gaze slid over me toward the door. Behind me, I could hear faint giggles and whispers from the other side of the door. The mall had just opened and it already sounded like a crowd had gathered outside.

"I know I promised only one more day," I said. "But could you possibly finish the run? I don't think anyone could replace you at this point."

"Of course no one could replace me," KJ said. He jabbed a finger at me. "I'm doing this for those kids, not for you."

I nodded. "I know, I got it."

I backed away toward the door. KJ smoothed his beard and sat on the throne. From behind him, the strains of Jingle Bells started to play.

I opened the door and the squeals of children grew louder. KJ smiled and gave a mighty laugh.

Just like Dad would have done.

Just like he would continue to do.

I smiled and led the first little boy up the stairs to visit Santa in July.

JOIN MY NEWSLETTER!

If you enjoyed this story, please consider taking a moment to review it or to recommend it to your friends. Reviews help other readers decide if a book is for them.

Sign up for my New Releases mailing list and get a free copy of the *Rebecca M. Senese Sampler*, featuring stories of science fiction, urban fantasy, mystery and horror. Enjoy them all!

Click here to get started: https://rebeccasenese.com/newsletter/

Santa's son is on the case

Enjoy more Noel Kringle with The Noel Kringle Chronicles!

REBECCA M. SENESE
Santa Claus:
PRIVATE DETECTIVE
THE NOEL KRINGLE CHRONICLES

REBECCA M. SENESE
THE CLAUS CONNECTION
THE NOEL KRINGLE CHRONICLES

REBECCA M. SENESE
THE TWELVE DEATHS OF CHRISTMAS
THE NOEL KRINGLE CHRONICLES

REBECCA M. SENESE
BABY, IT'S DEADLY OUTSIDE
THE NOEL KRINGLE CHRONICLES

REBECCA M. SENESE
DO YOU FEAR WHAT I FEAR
THE NOEL KRINGLE CHRONICLES

REBECCA M. SENESE
THE MAN WHO WOULD BE SANTA
THE NOEL KRINGLE CHRONICLES

About the Author

Based in Toronto, Canada, I write horror, science fiction and mystery/crime, often all at once in the same story. I am the author of the contemporary fantasy series, the *Noel Kringle Chronicles* featuring the son of Santa Claus working as a private detective in Toronto. Garnering an Honorable Mention in "*The Year's Best Science Fiction*" and nominated for numerous Aurora Awards, my work has appeared in *Home for the Howlidays, Bitter Mountain Moonlight: A Cave Creek Anthology, Promise in the Gold: A Cave Creek Anthology, Unmasked: Tales of Risk and Revelation, Obsessions: An Anthology of Original Stories, Fiction River: Visions of the Apocalypse, Fiction River: Sparks, Fiction River: Recycled Pulp, Tesseracts 16: Parnassus Unbound, Ride the Moon, Tesseracts 15: A Case of Quite Curious Tales, TransVersions, Deadbolt Magazine, On Spec, The Vampire's Crypt, Storyteller, Reflection's Edge, Future Syndicate* and *Into the Darkness*, amongst others.

Find me online:
www.RebeccaSenese.com

www.NoelKringleChronicles.com
www.RebeccaSeneseBooks.com

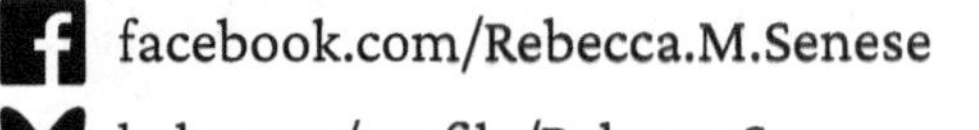 facebook.com/Rebecca.M.Senese

bsky.app/profile/RebeccaSenese.com

x.com/RebeccaSenese

bookbub.com/authors/rebecca-m-senese

instagram.com/rebeccamsenese

goodreads.com/rebecca_senese

wandering.shop/@rebeccasenese